ONDINE

ONDINE

Charles Kozloff

ST. MARTIN'S PRESS
New York

Library of Congress Cataloging in Publication Data

Kozloff, Charles.
  Ondine.

  I.Title.
PZ4.K884On [PS3561.O9] 813'.9'14 79–23065
ISBN 0–312–58502–0

PART I

Labor Day, 198–

HAROLD POWELL walked down the boardwalk with his body canted towards the ocean so that he could keep the hotels at his back. He didn't want to look at them. He wanted to put his problems out of his mind.

It was the day of the Atlantic City Pageant Swim. There was a wonderful crowd out on the beach. Usually it was all gigolos (fags beating tamborines or listening to radios turned up too loud) and old ladies. But today it was a real crowd. All ages and shapes, slick with transparent oil, they had come to watch the swimmers tackle the Atlantic.

The swimmers were already way out in the ocean, swimming downbeach. He could see their arms coming up out of the water as the distant swells lifted them high. There was a fleet of spectator boats beyond the swimmers, and the lifeguard surf boats ready to pick up anyone who might flounder.

It used to be the race was out around the Steel Pier and down to the Million Dollar Pier. But now the Steel Pier was a new hotel, and the Million Dollar Pier was a bazaar of slot-machine parlors called the Slot Dock. Down the beach he could see people sitting on the roofs of the slot-machine houses to watch the race. In their Labor Day colors they looked like puffins on a Canadian bluff.

He much preferred the boardwalk during the day. After thirty years, it was finally fun to window-shop again. There were jewelry stores, art galleries, china shops and clothing stores. There were even corporate exhibits, an idea he had dredged up himself from Atlantic City's past. It had been laughed at when he first started selling it, but now corporations were anxious to rent space on the boardwalk and improve the public understanding of their products.

When he neared the Slot Dock, Powell let his gaze drift upwards to take in one of his favorite hotels, the Terrarium. It stood where the Blenheim had once been. It was what the new Atlantic City was supposed to be. At night, the Terrarium was the only hotel that attracted the eye without a flashing sign. Nighttime he could see through the transparent shell of the buildings, all the way inside to the plants and trees, the lights glowing like fireflies, and the people weaving in and out of all the foliage like insects at

3

work. Now, during the day, its towering bronze bubbles glinted in the sun, and the copper tubing which reinforced its glass casing looked like the lattice work of a design-minded metal spider who spun his enormous web with blinding orange fibers.

Powell sat down on a boardwalk bench and watched the people go in and out for awhile. The Terrarium *was* a terrarium, its environment completely self-contained; the people had to go through a progression of three hermetically controlled chambers to get in or out. It was the only way to stop the bellicose salt sea air from invading the delicate system and starting atmospheric war.

One day the boardwalk would be all hotels of such style and conception. No more junk like Controller Jack's, a glass rectangle with a persistent huckster's pitch always turned on. *BRING YOUR SYSTEM TO US! COUNTERS WELCOME!*

It was completely untrue. As soon as a counter was spotted at Controller Jack's—despite the blazing white welcome over the door, the counters still don't introduce themselves—they broke out a special shoe that held eight decks. Few could count eight decks, and those that could got them shuffled halfway through.

Controller Jack's was owned by a syndicate from L.A. They had a hate on for the people from Tucson who owned Fortunata's.

Powell sighed.

There wasn't much pleasure left in the boardwalk for him any more. Not even on the day of the Pageant Swim. Instead of admiring what he had created, instead of seeing hotels, he saw a map of organized crime in America.

He had known some of them would come to Atlantic City, no matter how strict the laws and investigatory procedures were. These were proud and arrogant men. They would come simply because it was forbidden. What had surprised him was that *all* of them had come—every name he knew, and a hundred he didn't know. If he had thought about it, he wouldn't have been so surprised. Not only were they proud and arrogant, they were possessive, and gambling was their territory. No state legislator could regulate them out of their territory, and no corporation could buy them out of it.

Now all these territorial and arrogant men were jammed up against each other along the boardwalk, their loud signs shouting at each other. Powell could almost feel the heat emanating from the throbbing, neon egos.

At the Monopoly were the Kansas City partners. The Money Tree took its orders from Reno. The Tommy T. Flowers was named for the jazz musician but controlled by François Perrault, the power from New Orleans. The Terrarium was Boston. Viscaya was the particularly volatile and jealous organization from Miami. Sinbad's was Italian. The Pier was one of the few hotels owned by one man: Joe DePre.

Powell was delighted when DePre built the Pier, but he lamented the insatiable interest in Atlantic City that it had fostered in DePre's organization, especially on the part of Edgar Robles.

Behind the boardwalk, on the backstreets and side streets of the island, the directory of underworld men continued. But there it charted the small time. Bridgeport was at the Thunderbird, Reading was at the Seaside, and Akron had recently moved into the Xanadu on Oriental Avenue beyond the Ondine.

Powell had just returned from the Xanadu, a particularly insignificant motel filled with old people. The New Jersey state legislature had made a mistake extending slot-machine rights to anything and everything in Atlantic City. Ambitious, small men who hadn't been able to buy or force their way into the large hotels suddenly found themselves with hundreds of opportunities. They all bought motels and filled them with slot machines.

Two swimmers, tall, skinny youths with tiny lycra swim suits, were coming up the boardwalk.

"Who won?" Powell called to them.

"A girl," replied one of them happily, as if it were a pleasure to be bested by a woman. "The first girl to win since Brenda Borg back in seventy-eight."

"What was her name?" asked Powell.

"Nicky somebody," said the other one, "from Princeton."

He wasn't as happy about it as the first one. He was a little disgusted.

"He got second," said his friend, revealing the source of the displeasure.

The swimmers walked on and Powell leaned back against the bench watching them. Kids like that had started it. His mind wandered back to the war. When World War II started, the army had commandeered all the hotels to quarter troops. Nineteen- and twenty-year-old kids moved into the Traymore, the Dennis, and the Claridge and treated them like barracks. They ruined them. He had watched them out on the boardwalk marching up and down as they learned to drill. He had been proud of them. He hadn't known they were plunging Atlantic City into old age.

He wandered back even further in his thoughts, back to the twenties when he and his town had both been young. What a pleasure the boardwalk was then! People dressed in tuxedoes and formal gowns and handsome cruisewear. Some of the richest people in the world doffed top hats to him, not because they knew or cared who he was, but because he smiled at them.

The hotels then were built on a scale they didn't understand today. The Traymore had been his favorite. He'd stop in just for the fun of walking on the most beautiful staircase in the world. Who reflected that elegant history now?

He thought of Nucky. Nucky was an elegant man. He wore beautiful vicuna coats and chalkline flannel. People would come up just to shake his hand, just to make sure they said hello to the man who had made Atlantic City the playground of the world.

In 1929 Nucky invited the élite of American unstatutory powers to a three-day conference and vacation in Atlantic City. They all came: Lepke, Guzik, Jay Gatsby, Torrio, Capone, and many more. Powell had been only twenty then. He was taken with the power and show of them. They arrived in caravans of black limousines, accompanied by twenty or more senior members of their organizations. He remembered how stunned he was that Nucky's influence could produce this incredible constellation of power in one place.

Each and every one of them sent for Powell before the weekend was over. They all wanted to meet the young guy Nucky favored so much. Nucky had told everyone he was going to make something out of this ugly kid who had a talent for reasoning with people. For three days he was constantly being flattered face to face by the people who controlled the entire United States. They controlled it because they had money enough and bravado enough to have their own way with whomever they wished.

Most of them were gone now, and with them their entire style of life. The people who had taken their place were little more than unpredictable braggarts. But just as these assholes weren't Torrios or Zwillmans, Powell was no Nucky. He had to rely on persuading people, and too many of these crude and greedy bastards had no interest in being persuaded.

Ed Fingo was dealing blackjack to a full table. Donna was in the fourth seat. Ed had been a blackjack dealer at the Ondine ever since he had graduated from Glassboro State Teacher's College. He had a V-shaped face which he customized with black aviator glasses. Ed had the best hands in the Ondine. He cycled thirty percent more decisions an hour than his closest competitor, and he made half as many errors. But his skill had not gotten him promoted to floorman.

Ed knew everything that was going on in the casino. He worked hard at knowing everything, because even if it didn't get him promoted, it would help him survive the next purge. All casinos, because of their consistently poor profits, were subject to periodic purges. The Ondine itself was due for one soon.

The problem with making a profit in the casino business was the many docks along a casino's river of cash which provided employees with easy opportunities to get their hands wet. Ed noticed Gary Yates slipping an orange chip into a special pocket in his pants. Yates would pass that chip to a friend as soon as he took his break. But orange chips, a thousand dollars a piece, did not even make a wave in the great river of casino cash flow. They were strictly drinking water. The real money was drained off by casino executives.

Oscar Laboy, the manager of the Ondine casino, seemed to have his own personal spillway. Every night Laboy would step over a green velvet rope into one of the many large pits in the Ondine and sign a cashout slip for twenty thousand dollars. Ed envied Laboy. Laboy had help. The bosses always had the slips ready for him. Ed had to work on his own.

It was difficult to operate without a floorman or a boss because they watched the dealers they weren't in with like hawks. They liked to nail every cheat in the pit except their own in order to prove they weren't letting anybody get away with anything. Fortunately, Ed knew how to fix a floorman's position without making him suspicious. He used his peripheral vision to spot which way a boss was turned without looking directly at him. Nothing woke up a boss faster than a dealer constantly looking at him. Ed noted that Vasilkovsky, the boss of the E twenty-one pit, was far down the pit. He started to make his move, but suddenly he smelled Hudson behind him. Hudson was the floorman in charge of Ed's table. He put on his after shave with a firehose. Ed coughed and bent over to look between his legs for the position of Hudson's shoes. They were pointed away. Hudson had his back to him.

Vasilkovsky came by a few minutes later.

"I've got bad news for you, Fingo," he said. "Oscar wants to see you."

"Now?"

"Now."

"I'll take these, ma'am," Vasilkovsky said to Donna.

Donna fumbled the chips over to Vasilkovsky eagerly, as if he had every right to demand them. Donna was great in bed, but as an agent, she was a bumblepuppy.

Fingo made his way down the long pit. It was the largest blackjack pit in the world, and a very long walk when suspected of cheating. He passed twenty-five blackjack tables, and every dealer turned his head and looked at him with a frown of concern. It wasn't time for a dealer to be taking relief, and the direction of Ed's exit, right toward the casino offices, told a story. Fingo was in trouble. Was this the beginning of a purge?

"She bought those chips," Fingo told Laboy. "She decided it was time to charge. Why the hell would I hand some dame a stack of hundred dollar chips for nothing?"

"Because she's your girlfriend, Fingo," said Laboy. "Hector tells me you and she are living together in Absecon."

"Isn't my lady allowed to play at my table?" asked Fingo, surprised by Laboy's information but trying to stay on the offensive.

"I have it on video tape," said Laboy. "You reached into your rack and passed her a stack of chips. Nothing went into the box."

If it was on video tape, there was no point in denying it any longer. Fingo looked quietly at Laboy, waiting for the inevitable speech.

"I don't know what to do with guys like you," said Laboy, fingering the breast pocket of his mohair suit. "I try to be patient with you guys, but you all insist on fucking me until I have no choice."

Laboy was being sincere. It was his favorite tactic. The guy was something of a hypocrite.

"How stupid do you think I am?" Fingo asked him angrily.

"Oh, I get it," laughed Laboy. "You got caught stealing, so now you're mad at *me.*"

"Don't put me in the same category with the rest of them," said Fingo.

"Why the hell not?" asked Laboy. "You guys want to beat a casino, why the hell don't you come in here with your own money and put it down on the pass line like a man. Take an honest chance. You cheap little crooks never think of that. You just want to take us for as much as you can get."

"You really think I'm as dumb as the rest of them, don't you?"

"You mean you aren't?" mocked Laboy.

"Hell no, I'm not," said Fingo. "I'm not so dumb I don't know how you write yourself a phony slip for something in the neighborhood of twenty thousand every night."

"Those slips are for players," said Laboy. "You know these guys. They like to use the casino manager as their own personal messenger boy."

"Oh, bullshit," said Fingo, disgusted with the transparent lie. "Part of it goes to the ice fund—about ten thousand—but the rest goes right into your pocket. And so does another five to eight thousand that Greenhouse works off wheel four with that Puerto Rican whore. And what about the way you and the bosses in the B blackjack pit shuffle the markers every Tuesday before Perez gets them the next day—"

"Wait a minute, Fingo," interrupted Laboy. "Who's been telling you all this crap?"

"I told you I'm not like the rest of them out there," said Fingo. "I can see what's happening around me, and I know how to cover myself. So if you're trying to fire me or hang me out to dry, forget it."

"Oh, crap!" cursed Laboy.

He let out a long sigh and leaned back against the turquoise fabric of his chair.

"I would have to catch one like you," he complained.

He looked very fatigued. He drummed the buff surface of his aluminum desk with his fingers. His eyes were bloodshot. Fingo was tempted to feel sorry for him, but he was more interested in saving his job. He made good money as a dealer, even without any extras. It was a hell of a lot better than facing a bunch of whining ten-year-olds who didn't know how to read.

"If you try to fuck me," said Fingo, "I'll fuck you right back."

"All right, Fingo. All right." conceded Laboy. "Maybe I've got the wrong guy."

"I think so," said Fingo, smiling with relief.

"Look, Eddie," said Laboy, getting friendly, "I'm going to be honest with you. I've got to make examples of a few people. You're the wrong guy, but maybe we can work something out. I'm under a lot of pressure from Haaf. The people at Colony have owned this joint for a year now and gotten nothing but bad news. They're screaming for results, and we have to give them some or we'll all be out of jobs. You know what I mean?"

"Yes," agreed Fingo. "I know what you mean. You have to scare the shit out of everybody and get the place under control."

"That's right," said Laboy. "Eddie, if you know what I've been doing, you must know what a lot of the others are doing."

"Of course I do," admitted Fingo.

"You're a college man, aren't you?" said Laboy. "You're not like the rest of these guys. You can move up here. I can jump you right past being a floorman. I'll transfer you to one of the other black-jack pits and make you the number-two man there—pit boss for the day shift."

Ed Fingo saw the future. Heads would roll in this purge whether he helped or not. One way or another the Ondine would show a profit for a time, but in a few months, maybe only weeks, the same old shit would start. He wouldn't be the first dealer to become a boss for telling stories. And when the junk started again, he would be in a dramatically improved position for getting rich.

"Okay, Oscar," he said. "I think I can help you."

Laboy's phone rang. He picked it up and asked his secretary who it was. "It's Haaf calling from New York," said Laboy, putting his hand over the mouthpiece. "See the kind of pressure I'm under? They're starting to think they'll never get rich in the casino business."

Laboy arched his eyebrows and Fingo laughed. Colony wasn't going to get rich in the casino business. Getting rich in the casino business wasn't for corporate types who sat back on their asses waiting for a river of money to come flooding into their bank accounts. Those guys were all in for the same unpleasant surprise. People were busy upstream.

Laboy put his hand over the phone again, "Eddie, go tell McGray he's wanted on the phone back here."

"Sure," said Fingo, getting up.

"You can go back to your table after that," said Laboy.

"Why?" asked Fingo nervously. "What do you mean?"

"You may have to wait a little while for that promotion, Fingo," said Laboy wryly.

"What's the matter?" asked Fingo. "Don't you think I can fill you in?"

"I don't give a shit whether you can or not," said Laboy. "I've just been fired."

·2·

THE LIMOUSINE pulled away from the expressway toll station, and Tim Seagurt, ignoring the air conditioning, pressed the button to run down his window. The smell of pine trees rushed into the limousine with a warm blast. There were dense forests of pine and oak on both sides of the expressway, crisscrossed occasionally by roads which came up to the expressway and stopped.

A nighthawk fluttered out above the road beyond them, it's wings beating a pulsating brown and white oriental design across the ice blue sky.

The smell of asphalt receded. The air coming in his window turned cool.

"Slow down," Tim told the driver. "I'm not in that much of a hurry. We're almost there."

The black nose of the Cadillac pitched forward. The air got cooler and cooler as they coasted down the pines. The driver jerked, as if waking up. He turned off the air conditioning and rolled down his own window.

"That feels good," he said, turning around to Tim. "I wondered what you were doing when you put that window down at first."

"My parents used to bring us to Atlantic City when I was a little kid," said Tim. "It was a long, long trip and that was before every car had air conditioning. The best part of the trip was when the air coming in the windows started to turn cool and you knew you were almost there."

The driver nodded. "Today, they all think the best part is seeing that skyline," he said.

"What does the town look like now?" asked Tim.

"The thing has really started to take hold the past five years," said the driver. "Some really fine hotels have gone up. Used to be, the only class place was the Ondine, now you got the Money Tree, the Terrarium, and that new one, the Pier. Talk about class joints —have you heard what a cup of coffee costs in that underwater room at the Pier? Seven ninety-five. Do you believe that?"

"No."

"It's true," said the driver. "Seven ninety-five. That will keep the niggers out, won't it?"

Tim didn't answer.

"How about this guy Padgett?" asked the driver.

"What about him?"

"He's the black guy who owns the bar up in the Inlet. He's trying to get elected mayor and have gambling repealed."

"I know who he is," said Tim.

"It's all a big laugh," said the driver. "He's drumming up business for his bar. I hear it's like Hitler and the beer drinkers up there. They all sit around and dream about what they're going to do when Padgett gets elected."

"Do you think he has a chance?"

"Oh, come on," said the driver scornfully. "Where does he come off with all this holy stuff about gambling? It's like the way the Puritans were about fucking. It used to be a sin to enjoy it. The same with gambling. It's a pleasure for everybody and what's the use of hiding it. If the Morgan Guaranty approves, who is Kedar Padgett to say it's dirty?"

Tim laughed.

"If gambling isn't a real business, why does the Morgan Guaranty Trust Company lend millions of dollars to casinos?" continued the driver. "Gambling now is like selling shoes or baking pies. When the banks and insurance companies come in, you get something besides people with mob money and assholes who used to sell tit magazines. You get people from the real business world because they can finance things with banks and insurance companies."

He stopped the limousine at the tollbooth and paid for the causeway.

"I'll tell you what's going to happen in this town," he said as they started across the marsh. "It's turning into a Monte Carlo. A Nice or a Cannes—something like that."

The limousine rolled across the wetlands towards a skyline crowded with green-black towers of glass and gigantic walls of cement. Atlantic City was coming into view.

"Pull over a second," said Tim. "I want to get out and look for a minute."

The driver turned obediently to the side of the causeway and Tim got out. The sea wind washed across the wetlands and up against him with its cool bite and pungent odor.

Across the waving expanse of slick, lime-green reeds, Atlantic City gleamed like a nacreous Oz. With curious amazement, Tim stared at the hotels. The Pier, the tallest and newest in Atlantic City, rose up a giant green-black obelisk of glass. To its north, the Ondine, the great palace of the boardwalk, spread dome by dome up the beach like halves of impeccably white eggs. At the other end of the boardwalk, thirty towers to the south, right next to Convention Hall, was the Playboy, its mild exterior concealing a storm of feverish activity inside. It sat like a conservative older brother among the wild gang of hotels, glowering unhappily up the boardwalk at the unrestrained Sinbad's. Sinbad's made no pretense of respectability. It displayed its naked body of the week in a giant laser color projection against the white side of its tower. The image came up clear enough to be easily visible halfway across the wetlands, the goddess-sized tits bringing the city's campaign for tasteful toplessness up short of its goal. In the center of this fantastic skyline was the Money Tree with its giant rhinestone tree spread out high above its roof. The multicolored leaves shot bursts of light in every direction, making it look as if it were popping off flashbulbs at an incredible rate.

"Let's go," said Tim, getting quickly back into the car.

His heart was pumping faster than the flashes of light from the
rhinestone money tree. Every hotel in town was clamoring for his
attention with some kind of demanding sign. The old resurrected
hotels, like Resorts, offered *Rms $8 nitely,* barking away in their
peculiar abbreviated vocabularies, shouting for the cheapest
tourist dollar. The Monopoly marquee was more seductive, announcing *Don Novello in the Top Hat Room* in yellow and green
neon. And Controller Jack's invited in immense burning white
bulbs *BRING YOUR SYSTEM TO US! COUNTERS WELCOME!*

Beneath such colossal advertisements peeked the signs from
the hotels and motels on the side streets back from the boardwalk.
The blocks between Indiana Avenue and St. James Place were
called Junior Las Vegas because all their hotels had stolen names
from their western superiors: the Stardust, the Thunderbird, the
Riviera. Little Caesar's Palace, Tim learned from the driver, had
slot machines that were oversized busts of Edward G. Robinson
and paid off through his angry open mouth.

The limousine climbed a small bridge at the end of the causeway and Tim got a look at some of Atlantic City's ruin. He could
see block after block of old buildings and urban shacks. Many of
the ruined buildings had fallen over to make mounds of bricks
and trash. In one block every single house was down, as if the
whole block had erupted like a pustule, spewing debris all up and
down Baltic Avenue. Tim watched an old Dodge weave its way
through the mess like a drunk.

When the limousine descended the bridge, the ruin disappeared behind the bus station. They crossed Atlantic Avenue
slowly. When they finally took the left bend onto Pacific Avenue,
traffic was jammed up as far as Tim could see. It took them ten
minutes to make the first two blocks. Tim was excited by all the
hotels and motels now that they were so close. He wanted to dash
out of the crawling limousine and run inside every one of them.
Every hotel, motel, restaurant or store had its own demented thrill
to offer him.

The limousine finally made it to the Ondine. Tim walked
through the busy lobby to the front desk. The clerk had a reservation for him, and watched with mild curiosity as Tim filled out the
registration card.

"Will you be staying with us long, Mr. Seagurt?" he asked, reading Tim's name off the card.

"I hope so," said Tim.

"Very good," said the clerk in a measured, gracious tone. "Is it business or pleasure that brings you to Atlantic City?"

"I'll be managing the casino here for awhile," said Tim, not believing in keeping little secrets from the curious.

"The casino," said the clerk, coming to attention. "Very good. I'd heard they'd be replacing Mr. Laboy. Congratulations, Mr. Seagurt."

"Thank you," said Tim.

The clerk shuffled among some slips below the desk. "Let's change something here," he said smiling. "They've put you in the wrong suite."

It took the clerk a minute or so to make sure one of the grander suites was available. While they waited, he told Tim several times to ask him first whenever a room was needed for a player or for Tim's family or friends. He was very anxious to please the new casino manager.

Tim had been in many hotel rooms traveling for Colony, but this one was the first he'd seen worth spending more than one night in. It had a large livingroom with overstuffed chairs, and a long sofa that was almost five feet tall. He walked through to a kitchen bigger than his and Caro's back in Manhattan. Beyond that was a dining alcove with beautiful Danish chairs. He found two bedrooms, and a den with a lot of Danish wood and natural leather.

He went back into the larger bedroom to unpack. The bellman had left his suitcase on the luggage stand across from a big bed. He unpacked slowly. Thinking about the desk clerk and his big reception began to taint his good mood.

The clerk's enthusiasm notwithstanding, Tim's position at the Ondine wasn't all that glorious. Tim might have acted eager with Alfred Oakes, the chairman of the Colony Companies, and he might have made something of a clever deal, but the fact was, Tim had been sent to preside over a de-acquisition. It was the kind of job Colony executives got a few months before they were asked to resign. Caro, in her careful, diplomatic way, had been trying for months to warn him that he was going in that direction, but he hadn't been able to listen.

He found Caro's traveling picture in his suitcase. It was leather-framed, and she'd given it to him when they first met. He wasn't taking her along on business trips then, so she made him take this picture with him whenever he went away. It was supposed to induce fidelity. He'd never gotten out of the habit of leaving it in his suitcase ready to travel.

Tim loved Caro's face in the picture. She had full brown eyebrows. Her eyes and cheekbones were so prominent they seemed isolated from the rest of her face. Her nose was fat at the end, but straight and handsome. She had a large mouth.

Though she liked this particular picture, Caro didn't think much of her arresting face. She worried about her fat nose and big mouth. She was more confident about her body and always dressed to show it off. It was a strategy of some merit. The small curve of her boyish hips turned down into long legs with the same creamy texture as her cheeks. She was even more vain about her legs than her rich, womanly bosom, and she was meticulous about keeping them like satin. With her large breasts and her tapering legs, she looked feminine and coltish at the same time, making it very difficult to study her nose and mouth too closely when she was wearing shorts and had a few buttons undone on her blouse.

Tim put her picture back in the suitcase pocket and went over to gaze out the window. Down below, the boardwalk was busy with post-Labor Day traffic. An oversized gold and red golf cart poked its way slowly through the crowd. A Hispanic youth in some kind of uniform was chauffeuring several women down-beach in it. He watched the cart crawl all the way down to Fortunatas, while a green and white one very much like it passed it coming up towards the Ondine. He remembered from the report he'd read on the Ondine that each hotel on the boardwalk was allowed to send out one cart for every hundred rooms they had in operation. The carts drove up and down the boardwalk looking to ferry people to their home hotels. The Ondine, with twenty-eight green and white carts, had the largest fleet on the boardwalk. Looking further down towards the Money Tree and the Monopoly, Tim could see all the different colored carts crawling through the crowd like different kinds of lady bugs.

Looking down on the boardwalk made him want to go out and scout it for an hour or two before he met with Dean Haaf. He wanted to see most of it before Caro arrived so he could give her the grand tour himself. He tore himself away from the window, put on his suitcoat, and headed downstairs to the hotel and casino offices. It would have to wait; he was going to get his wheels turning first. Like most people newly arrived in Atlantic City, Tim had a plan for getting rich.

A bellman took Tim to the hotel offices. They walked around the edge of the casino, and the bellman kept Tim so busy with talk about what he could do for Tim anytime he wanted it, that Tim could only glance over at a few twenty-one games before he found himself going down the corridor which divided the hotel and casino business offices.

He had to wait a few minutes in Haaf's empty office. Once a famous financial figure, Dean Haaf was now the executive hotel manager of the Ondine. He had come out of nowhere a year ago to sell Alfred Oakes on the idea of buying the Ondine Hotel and Casino. To pay him for the idea, Oakes had given Haaf responsibility for overseeing the hotel operations. Across the hall, Oscar Laboy had run the casino; Oakes had insisted that running the casino called for specific experience in the gambling business which Haaf lacked.

Yesterday Dean Haaf had convinced Alfred Oakes that Laboy had been looting the casino for the past year. Very angry, Oakes had ordered Haaf to fire Laboy, and then called Tim around to his office. Tim had learned he was taking Laboy's place the following day, whether he had any expertise in the casino business or not.

Dean Haaf was an incredible slob. Stacked up everywhere in his office, on tables, cabinets, and the floor itself, were pillars of brokerage reports, prospectuses, 10-Ks, and brittle yellow back issues of *The Journal of Commerce.* Most of it had been with Haaf long before he came to take over the Ondine. His desk itself held an amazing collection of clerical junk. Only the mind which had invented the conglomerate could think in the midst of such a mess. He had two pencil sharpeners, both of them electric, and both drooling yellow shavings. There was also an automatic stapler, and a desktop shredder with shredded paper caught between its wire teeth. In the corner of this incredible debris stood a large photograph of Haaf as a wrestler. *Utah State Champion, Flyweight, 1958,* it said on the silver picture frame. Dressed in black tights and red ear-protectors, the gangling young Haaf looked more like a large fly than a wrestling champion.

A door opened and Haaf came hurrying in.

"I just finished with the vault people," he said perfunctorily. "It's a matter of policy to change the vault numbers when the casino manager is changed. Come on, I'll show you how it all works."

Now past fifty (he had been only twenty-six when he started expanding NTS), Haaf was still as tall and thin as he was in his wrestling picture, except for a little ball of a pot stomach which he patted nervously when he seemed especially anxious to be understood.

"All right," agreed Tim. "Thank you."

Haaf took Tim on a tour of the casino offices, then showed him through the video room (which doubled as the counting room; there was a long table with a honeycomb of wooden pigeonholes to hold the bills), and down the elevator to the underground vault. The elevator door opened into a dark room walled with what looked like safety deposit boxes. They were the lockboxes which held cash that gamblers were hiding from the IRS. As he showed Tim how to work the vault, Haaf kept up a stream of comments about the casino and how to handle it.

He rankled Tim. Because of the man's financial acumen, Dean Haaf had always been a hero of Tim's. He did appreciate Haaf's mind, but there was something about the way Haaf talked that eroded Tim's admiration. Haaf didn't talk so much as he lectured, and hero or not, Tim didn't like lectures. When they returned to Haaf's office, where they had to wait a few minutes for Don McGray, Haaf's tone got even more didactic. Finally McGray, the assistant casino manager, came into Haaf's office to meet Tim, and Haaf had to stop.

McGray was an old Irishman with frayed brown hair. His face burned with red hairline veins. He wore a baggy, almost threadbare suit.

"Sorry I made you wait, Dean," he said to Haaf. "I don't care what these young wise guys say, the only way to make sure you have a counter is to stand there and count right along with them."

McGray smiled at Tim while he spoke to Haaf. He had several roulette chips in his hand which he shuffled unconsciously.

"Don, say hello to Tim Seagurt," said Haaf.

"Hi, Don," said Tim.

"Hi, Tim," said McGray, flipping the chips into his left hand and mixing them just as expertly there while they shook hands.

"I guess you guys in New York are sore about Laboy," he said.

"Alfred Oakes is ready to shut us down," said Haaf. "He's so mad about Laboy, he's got the idea in his head that the first night the casino has a loss is the night to close it down and put it up for sale."

"That fucking prick Laboy," said McGray. "I knew it was coming. It had to come. This casino had been a free-for-all for months."

"And still is," added Tim.

"No sir! It is not!" said McGray loudly.

The chips mixing in McGray's hand sped up. The veins in his cheeks glowed like fibers of red neon. Tim had kicked him where it hurt.

"Vasilkovsky and I have them walking the straight and narrow now," he continued, "all of them! We might not know who they are, but they know who I am. I am no Oscar Laboy. They know I'll send them on their way. I don't care if it's comping their cousin a free dinner, I don't care what it is. If they fuck with me, they're out!"

"That's interesting news," said Tim. "You've cleaned up everything in twenty-four hours?"

McGray went through an astonishing change, turning suddenly winning and friendly, as if Tim's sarcasm had charmed him out of his shoes.

"It's true, it's true," he said, grinning mischievously, all his anger gone. "Of course I shouldn't say we have it all, because there's always going to be a little something going on no matter how tough you get."

Tim grinned back at him, wondering if there was some truth in McGray's claim. In his baggy old suit, McGray didn't look like a man who had been getting rich off the casino.

"Don, we're going to start doing things differently now that Laboy is gone," said Haaf.

"Anything you say," agreed McGray.

Haaf began going through a long list of responsibilities he would be taking over. It was getting more and more obvious to Tim that Haaf had no intention of just running the hotel and leaving the casino to Tim. Haaf kept giving instructions to McGray until Tim was left with little more to do than sit at Laboy's desk across the hall and wonder why there were no drawers in it.

"I'm sorry, Dean," said Tim, suddenly standing up, "but we can't work things that way."

The two of them looked at him, McGray curious, Haaf irritated.

"What do you mean?" asked Haaf impatiently.

"We're not going to do things that way," said Tim flatly. "You run the hotel and I'll handle the casino. And the first thing I want, Don, is for you to send the chief of security to my office."

Tim walked out of Haaf's office before either of them could say another word. Hector Knute, the chief of Ondine security, appeared in his office two minutes later.

·3·

WHEN HE walked out into the middle of the casino with Hector
Knute, Tim was astonished by its size. Studying the material on
the Ondine in the Colony files hadn't prepared him for the enor-
mity of the casino itself; neither had his quick walk around the
edge to the offices. Fascinated, he stared at the dice tables in the
center. There were twenty-five of them drawn up together in the
middle of the casino in a protective hexagon. The rest of the
casino floor spread out so far from them, it made the tables and
the people playing at them seem three-quarter size. There were
countless formations of blackjack tables, roulette games, and slot
machines, all grouped in different shapes and sizes. The blackjack games alone required eleven pits.

There was something religious about this incredible vastness.
Above the casino was a planetarium dome which vaulted up as
high as an Italian church, creating an artificial night so much
like outer space that everything below seemed insignificant. Soft
lights hung down by invisible lines close to the moss green felt
of each table. There was no overhead lighting, only the white
glitterings in the black dome reproducing the Milky Way and
the major constellations of the summer sky. Glowing among
them were large balls of color representing the planets and their
moods: Mercury, a penetrating silver beacon; red Mars; and Ju-
piter, a massive, tranquil blue. Looking up, Tim felt like an as-
tronaut spilling out of his capsule to whirl about space in a plat-
inum suit.

He began a circuit of the casino with the chief of security.
Hector Knute was plump and well past sixty. He walked alongside
Tim with anxious shoulders hunching and unhunching like an
accordian. They passed a thousand gamblers making a deafening
storm of noise, but the ringing bells, the shouts, the coinfalls, the
frantic shuffling of chips and silver were all absorbed into the
great dome overhead. The noise disappeared as fast as it was
made. Tim began to feel as if he were walking outside. He felt as
if he were circling a quiet country lake beneath a perfect summer
night. A waitress in a green bodice hurried by, the freshly poured
glass of ginger ale passing so close to him it coated his nose with
tiny cool bubbles. He shivered with pleasure. He had fallen into

something far more than an exotic business problem; he had inherited his own principality.

Hector pointed out who was who in the casino hierarchy. They went up in order from dealers to floormen to pit bosses to shift bosses to the assistant manager McGray to Tim himself. They were all dandies. The dealers liked ruffled shirts and tight black satin pants. The bosses wore bow ties as big and brilliant as bluebirds. They smoothed their black velvet evening jackets like grooming hounds as they watched Tim pass.

Doug Vasilkovsky, whom McGray had praised so highly, wore cufflinks of rough gold nuggets as big as macaroons. Hector said Vasilkovsky had started wearing them six months ago, and the fashion had caught on in the Ondine pits. Now every boss and most of the dealers had them. They hadn't stopped at cufflinks, though, but had gone on to rings, pins, bracelets, watches, necklaces and studs. All of them gold.

"It's not hard to see why the profits here are so low," said Tim.

"What do you mean?" asked Hector.

"I can read payroll figures, Hector," said Tim. "These guys are all wearing more than a year's salary—including tips."

Hector gave him a look of surprise, his mouth twitching nervously.

"I want to take a look at those cameras," said Tim.

They went upstairs and Hector showed Tim a gangway leading to a great wooden porcupine of protruding studs and beams. There were cameras mounted everywhere. Tim picked his way around the cameras and through the wooden elbows until he had climbed high up onto the framework. The Ondine dome was tightly stretched canvas. The planets were bulbs in holes the same size the cameras looked through. The Milky Way was a runner of klieg lights shining through tiny holes in the canvas. Tim rotated one of the cameras aside and looked down at the casino. He saw the gigantic dream engine spread out below in a faraway sea green. He gazed down on his kingdom with a mixture of suspicion and awe.

"Alfred Oakes made Colony by buying companies past the peak of their fashion," Tim explained to Hector as they returned to the casino offices. "There's a ballooning effect in a company when its industry gets hot. The men who run it get amazed at all the money they're making, and they get all loaded up with plant, equipment, marketing, advertising, right at the top of their cycle, and the next thing they know they're spending more and more money to make less and less."

Tim paused and Hector looked at him apprehensively. Hector's mouth was wiggling. Tim had noticed it was always moving whether Hector was talking or not. It made him look like a feeding goldfish.

"That's exactly what happened in Atlantic City," continued Tim. "Resorts started out making incomprehensible amounts of money. Eight years later the boardwalk was jammed with casinos, but only the newest ones were making good bucks. The rest were struggling. Dean Haaf picked the perfect time to sell Oakes on buying the Ondine. 'Six million for comps?' Haaf scoffs to Oakes. It's an expense dying to be cut by seventy percent. Four hundred thousand for stationery? These gamblers must be letter-writing fools.' "

Hector laughed and Tim laughed with him. He liked the round little man.

"It was an Oakes expense balloon if he ever saw one, so he bought the Ondine and sent Haaf down here to put a needle in it," said Tim. "But it didn't work, did it?"

"No," agreed Hector, his nervousness returning. "You're not going after the expenses?"

"Sure you can go after the expenses," said Tim. "But they aren't a significant variable."

"That's right," said Hector, surprised. "That's right."

As the new manager of the Ondine casino, who had been in the business less than an hour, Tim was saying more than Hector expected to hear.

They came back through the casino to the suite of offices. Tim went through the outer offices to his own new office. It was a long rectangular room with white walls and an orange carpet. A telex sat in one corner beneath a print of poker-playing dogs. At the other end was Tim's new desk, a buff slab of aluminum with no drawers, and a turquoise chair. Laboy, who had equipped the office, had seen small function in drawers.

The door to the video monitoring room was open. Tim went in and Hector followed him. Tim stood and stared at the galaxy of television monitors stretching the length of the twenty-foot wall.

"How many monitors are there, Jimmy?" he asked the technician at the console whom Haaf had introduced earlier.

"A hundred, Tim." said Jimmy. "One for every two tables. But we can turn them any way we want to. We can have twenty-five cameras on a single table if we want."

Jimmy could swivel the cameras up in the dome in any direction. He could adjust the zoom and focus for each lens from his console. His job was to sit there and stare at this incredible wall of eyes and try to find a dealer stealing in one of them.

"All these electronics are useless the way they are," said Tim. "We have to give this monster a brain."

"Give it a brain?" asked Hector.

"The weak point in the chain of money is right there where the dealers and customers meet," said Tim. "That's where it all has to happen. We've got to know which eye of that monster to be looking at. Maybe the cameras don't even matter. What matters is knowing who and what to watch for."

Hector looked morose. Tim had stopped surprising him and now was only making him unhappy. The telex in the corner of Tim's office started to chatter. Hector hurried out of the video room to the machine.

"It's from World Casino Credit," he told Tim, pushing a couple of keys. The machine began typing rapidly.

"Who is World Casino Credit?" asked Tim.

"It's a credit service in Vegas," said Hector. "They rate the credit and monitor the gambling activity of every well-known gambler in the world."

"How can they monitor gamblers?" asked Tim.

"If some guy comes in here and loses a hundred grand, we put it on the wire to them," said Hector. "So does every other joint in the world. That way their credit figures are up to the minute."

"How do the players feel about that?" asked Tim.

"They don't even know it exists," said Hector, "unless they go on a binge. Then they find out the hard way."

"What do you mean?"

"Some of these guys get so they can't stop playing," said Hector. "They'll gamble their whole credit line in one town, and then, when they can't get any more action, they'll fly to another gambling town and try to play against the credit they've already exhausted."

The telex stopped printing. Hector tore the yellow sheet of paper off the top.

"This one's for you personally," he said, handing the sheet to Tim. "Henry must have found out we have a new manager."

#138710, Ondine.
#245891, Casino credit.

Attn Tim Seagurt:

I understand you are the new manager of the Ondine casino.
I have designed a computerized system for controlling casino

pilferage which may be of interest to you. It is based on the tracking of each gaming table by computer. The theory of retained percentages suggests that over the long term every game should hold a specific percentage of its drop. When it doesn't and the per fluctuates radically instead, the casino manager should suspect trouble. Every casino manager should consider having the pers of each individual table tabulated daily by my computer system. The computer can then automatically notify the casino manager of any sustained aberrations which would indicate theft. Would you like to see such a system installed at the Ondine?

> Yours,
> Henry Moore
> Director of Computer Programming
> World Casino Credit
> BS, Computer Sciences, UCLA
> BA, Casino Management, UN-LV

"Do you know this guy?" Tim asked Hector.

"Sure," said Hector, laughing. "I used to talk to him a lot over this thing when I was working in credit. He's a bright guy."

"Then why are you laughing?" asked Tim.

"He sends out the same message every time a casino changes hands or gets a new manager," said Hector. "There isn't a joint in the business that hasn't gotten Henry's sales spiel a few times."

"Does any one take him up on it?" asked Tim.

"No," said Hector. "Henry sort of rubs the people in this business the wrong way."

"Ask him what kind of computer he'd use," said Tim.

"Graphic Terminals 300," replied the telex.

"Tell him to get on the first plane out here from Vegas, and I'll have the computer here before him," said Tim. "We've found a brain for the monster."

Hector typed out the message, and Henry Moore responded by ringing the telex bell seven times.

"You seem awfully pleased about the computer he picked," said Hector.

"Graphic Terminals is a Colony Company," said Tim. "I know their hardware inside out. I helped buy them into the company."

"You really think you can fit computers into the surveillance end of the business?" asked Hector. "Nobody's ever used them for that before."

"That's no reason not to have them," said Tim, getting excited.

"If Watson had thought that way, IBM would still be a third-rate tabulating company. You probably think IBM is a brilliant technological company, don't you?"

"They aren't?" asked Hector.

"Their hardware was never worth a shit until the late sixties," said Tim. "Sperry was way ahead of them, and IBM was scared to death when GE announced they were getting into the market. But neither Sperry nor GE ever mounted much of a threat to IBM's business. They missed the whole concept. They thought the whole market was with engineers who could understand their wonderful machines, and they all ended up talking to each other while Watson went after the American businessman. Watson got his salesmen all dressed up in fresh white shirts, and not only did these IBM guys look like businessmen, they talked like businessmen. They didn't run on about ergs and memory circuits. They talked about inventory and cost of goods sold. That's how computers got sold to American business. That's how IBM beat Sperry and GE all to hell. It certainly wasn't because they had wonderful machines. They got their great reputation for brilliance because they explained their shitty low-grade technology in terms a businessman could understand."

"No offense, Tim," said Hector, looking very curious, "but I'm beginning to wonder what a guy like you is doing here."

"What do you mean?" asked Tim.

"You're not the run-of-the-mill casino manager," said Hector. "When they bring someone in from outside the business, he's usually an ex-player who used to manufacture dresses or lay sewer pipe or something like that."

"And they think because they've learned one business, they know them all," said Tim.

"Yeah," said Hector.

"And they convince themselves they can get away with anything in a casino, no matter how dumb it is," said Tim. "Like Laboy."

Hector's head wobbled up and down. "Like Laboy. Sometimes even dumber. At least Laboy came up through the business."

"No more Laboys for Alfred Oakes," said Tim. "Laboy convinced Oakes that Haaf couldn't control casino expenses working from the hotel offices. That's why I'm here. But then, I'm not really worried about expenses, no matter what Haaf and Oakes say."

"You're not going after expenses at all then?" asked Hector brightly.

"I'm working on the per," said Tim. "As soon as we get the

computer hardware set up, I want you to work with this Henry Moore and McGray. We're going to stop all this dealer stealing."

"And you're not going to worry about expenses?" asked Hector again.

Tim sat up straight. He'd seen Hector's ninety thousand dollar salary on the casino payroll and he'd been surprised; but, since it fit with his perception of what was important in a casino, namely catching crooked dealers, he had figured a guy good at it was worth ninety thousand. Now he began to see something more in Hector's anxiety than worry about the arrival of a new boss. He began to wonder if Hector's feeding goldfish mouth was the outward sign of some secret nibbling.

"Hector, your big job here is keeping dealers from stealing the casino's money, isn't it?" asked Tim.

"That's right," said Hector.

"How many dealers have you had to fire in the past six months, Hector?" asked Tim.

"Two."

"Two?" said Tim. "That doesn't say much for you."

"I know."

"It makes me wonder what you get ninety thousand for." said Tim.

Hector looked at Tim apprehensively. His mouth moved nervously and his shoulders curled in little spasms.

"You're going to see it as soon as you start going through Laboy's books," he said. "You're too smart."

"See what?"

"My job for Laboy, my real job, was to get him bills and receipts," he said. "He'd give me a list of markers and I'd go out and offer players to cut their markers in half if they'd supply me with phony bills to the casino—like that four hundred thousand for stationery you mentioned. Half the money would go to Laboy and half would go against their IOUs. Some months I'd handle several hundred thousand in phony bills. That's why he paid me so much."

"I knew it!" Tim jumped up off Laboy's turquoise chair. "Everything comes down to the stealing! Beginning, middle, and end, it's the stealing! It never was an expenses balloon. You can't puncture this one and make it go away."

Tim walked up and back across the orange carpet, punctuating his shouts with cracks of his fist into his palm. Hector's shoulders had stopped hunching and begun to sag. His constantly moving mouth was slowing to a halt. He looked like a defeated old man.

Tim stopped and looked at him, realizing why Hector had gotten
more and more morose since they'd met.

"I guess you'll want to let me go," said Hector, hunching up to
protect himself from the answer.

Tim hesitated.

"Look, Tim," he said, begging a little, "I'm getting to the age
where I can't get new work in this business. Put me back in credit.
That's where Laboy found me. I know all the big players and their
credit lines. All the time I was Laboy's detective, I still had to
make all the big credit decisions for the cashier."

"How come?" asked Tim. "What about World Casino Credit?"

"It takes experience to know how far to let a guy go," said Hector. "No matter what the telex says, you have to have a feel for a
guy. Andy Map is always too nervous to decide himself. He likes
taking charge of the cage, but he's no good at credit."

"Okay, you go back to credit," said Tim, "But no more of this
ninety thousand a year."

"You're a sport, Tim," said Hector, suddenly animated and
happy. "Goddammit, you're a sport."

"I'm going to put Moore in charge of credit over you," added
Tim. "So every decision you make has to go through him."

"Thanks, Tim," said Hector, limp with gratitude. "Just when I
get to thinking this business is full of bricks of shit, and I mean
twenty-four carat, ingot-grade shit, a guy like you comes along.
You're a goddam sport. I mean it. I really mean it. You're a sport."

Obviously Haaf had been getting angrier and angrier as Tim
walked around the casino with Hector. Hector had been gone only
a minute when Haaf came in to pick up what Tim had broken off
an hour earlier. He got right to the meat of it. He threatened to call
Oakes if Tim didn't do things his way.

"I let Alfred press you on me because I thought I could guide
you, Seagurt," he said, his hand inside his coat, squeezing the
hard little ball of his pot stomach. "I thought you might be a good
thing because you don't have the bad habits of a Laboy. But you
don't listen to anything. I've never met anyone as sensitive as you.
You can't even stand for me to explain how to open the vault. How
the hell do you ever learn anything?"

"Dean," said Tim calmly, anxious to handle Haaf in a way that
couldn't be used against him, "I understand that you're worried
about my not having any background in the gambling business,
but I'm used to figuring out industries I haven't seen before. I've

spent eight years looking at all kinds of companies for Colony."

He smiled at Haaf, trying to reassure him, understanding his anxiety, but knowing he wasn't going to be Haaf's flunky.

"Why do all you assholes on Wall Street think you can see right to the heart of a business in ten minutes?" Haaf demanded, shaking his head. "You people, you go out to lunch, get drunk, and tell each other what geniuses you are until you all believe it. You blow so much air into each other's balloons you get dizzy, and you lose all conception of what reality is. You don't learn a business looking at reports—"

He stopped and his head went *no, no, no,* with frustration.

"I'm trying to get back up with this thing," he said urgently. "I've got what's left of my life invested in this idea, and no matter how smart you think you are, we're going to do things my way."

Tim had only an instant to reflect that something was out of control inside him before his eye began to blink and he started shouting. He told Haaf that if he thought Tim had come down here to be his clerk, he was full of shit. If there was any question about who had the authority in the casino in Haaf's mind, he could call Oakes; but for the time being, since Oakes had given Tim the job of casino manager, Tim was going to exercise the authority. And if Haaf didn't like it, he could go fuck himself.

PART II

March, 1979

· 4 ·

WHEN BUDDY turned into the Bridgewater pool parking lot, Caro began to feel silly. It had been six years since she had swum in a meet. She had started swimming again only for exercise. She wished she hadn't let Buddy talk her into this.

"Isn't this some pool?" Buddy asked her when they went inside.

The pool had a high arching ceiling of beams supported on curving rafters which peaked in gigantic cupid's bows. Buddy had sold her on the idea largely on the merits of the pool. In his mind, it was worth the trip just to see the pool.

In the locker room she felt sillier and sillier. She put her green tennis duffel on a bench, next to an older woman. The woman said she was swimming in the hundred fly. She looked a little saggy in the muscles a swimmer needs for the butterfly, but Caro concealed her skepticism. Her doubt was later justified when the older swimmers flapped down the pool looking more like moths caught in a glass of water than Mark Spitz.

Caro stretched her suit up over her breasts. She had bought a new one for the meet, and had chosen one a size too small so that it wouldn't get too loose around her hips. She had slim hips, and suits which fit her through the breasts tended to wrinkle up like old panty hose around her ass. She sacrificed modesty for fit and bought a suit which blatantly showcased her sizable bosom.

The pool was crowded with swimmers. They ranged from her age group (she was twenty-six) up to some who were in their seventies. One old man, Buddy told her, was eighty-one. There was nobody else alive in his category. Everytime he swam it was a national age-group record.

The water was too cold and very high in chlorine. Her eyes burned as she warmed up. After a slow three-hundred, she stood up in the shallow end rubbing her eyes. The odor of the chlorine was so strong it came right up off the water and stung her nose. When she finally got her eyes open, she found herself standing beside a tall swimmer. He had broad shoulders, a big, square face, and light eyes. He was standing up on his toes trying to prevent the water-line from climbing up over the edge of his suit.

"Jesus, it's cold," he said.

He had curly auburn hair and a big, muscular swimmer's chest.

31

"Getting wet is the hardest part," he said to her. His eyes were copper colored, shining like polished pennies. Throughout his auburn hair were little wirelets of the same copper color.

She smiled at him. He looked familiar, but she couldn't place him.

"What are you swimming?" he asked her.

"Fifty free," she said. "What are you swimming?"

"Two-hundred fly."

"Two-hundred fly and you can't stand to get wet?" she gently mocked him. The two-hundred fly was the most demanding race in swimming.

"I'm okay after I'm wet," he said.

He was looking at her tits. The cold water was swelling her nipples against her suit. The tight lycra made her look almost naked and he made no secret of his interest.

"You'd better get started," she said, pointing at the clock, high on the wall. "The meet starts in ten minutes."

"Yeah."

He took a couple of hops forward and dove into the water. He swam down the lane with an elegant, leisurely freestyle. Caro realized why he looked so familiar. She recognized the stroke. It was Tim Seagurt. She remembered seeing him swim for Penn. He had been one of their stars. He had almost made the '72 Olympic team in the two-hundred-meter freestyle.

She got out and sat down in the deck stands next to Buddy. Buddy was nervous. He talked incessantly about the splits he planned for his hundred free. Caro watched Tim as he finished his warmup doing long, slow lines of fly. He made the difficult stroke seem effortless. Buddy said he had seen him at meets before. He always went through the two-hundred fly like it was nothing. It was always that same fluid style, never missing a beat.

The starter announced the five-hundred free. Tim got out of the pool and dried off. He stretched out on a bed of kickboards he had laid out on the deck. The five-hundred free was a popular event and it took forever.

Caro studied Tim stretched out on his kickboards. Unconsciously she visualized him in postures that accentuated the swell of his chest. For an instant she thought about using him somehow at work. But she decided she didn't want to transform him up into something an idiot from Proctor and Gamble would find acceptable.

Caro wandered over in his direction. If she were going to draw him, it wouldn't hurt to get a little of his personality into it.

His eyes were closed when she went by him the first time.

"Hi," she said, returning and standing over him.

One light eye opened. "Hi."

The starting beeper went off behind her for another heat of the five-hundred free. They didn't use guns any more. The starter had a microphone with a red button on it which made a high pitched beep when pressed.

"I think I saw you swim for Penn," she said.

"You probably did," he said, sitting up.

"It was up in Hanover," she said. "You're Tim Seagurt?"

"Right."

He held out his hand. She gave him hers and he took it in long, powerful fingers and squeezed it gently.

"Caroline Laux," she said.

"Have a seat," he invited, patting the kickboard next to him. "Did you go to Dartmouth?"

"Yes."

They talked about swimming. She had grown up admiring swimmers, and she liked their muscular bodies. She had been in pools working out with them since she was thirteen, and suddenly she realized that she missed it. Buddy and his other swimming friends, whom she had met only recently, weren't quite the same as Tim. She hadn't seen anyone like him since Hanover.

Her admiration for him was not diminished when he swam his two-hundred fly. He was incredibly gifted, with the flexibility and strength to be able to swim the fly effortlessly. He broke two minutes, beating his closest competitor by half the pool.

"Nice swim," she said when he returned.

He laughed. He was breathing hard. His shoulders and back were red hot from the race.

"Beautiful swim," agreed Buddy, who had joined him. "How far are you going a week?"

"A few grand," he said, still huffing as he started to dry himself off.

"Don't give me that," said Buddy. "You have to be going at least fifteen thousand yards a week to go under two minutes."

Tim laughed again, a charming, silly smile curling his wide mouth.

"Not some people, Buddy," said Caro enviously. "Some people have so much talent, they don't have to practice much of anything. They can get in and go. Right, Tim?"

"Right," said Tim.

Buddy shook his head. "Amazing."

"Why don't you and Buddy meet me at the Y where I work out some night," said Tim. "We'll go a few lines together."

"Okay," said Caro. "But you don't do a lot of speed work, do you? I'm the no-talent, no-exertion kind of swimmer. I don't like to give myself headaches when I work out."

"Like you say," he said, grinning his friendly grin. "I have so much talent, why should I turn purple in practice?"

He started naming nights to meet. He lived at Eighty-seventh and Lexington and worked out at a Y a couple of blocks uptown. She waited until he named Wednesday, because she knew Buddy was always busy on Wednesday nights.

She met him at his Y at seven that Wednesday. It was nine-thirty before he was finished swimming, and by then Caro had found out what Tim had thought was so terrifically funny in her little speech about how easily things come to the talented.

There is a way of measuring a swimmer's exertion during a workout by the color of his back. When his back turns pink, he is coasting along at the lowest level of effort. Pink was always Caro's style of swimming practice. Rarely, if ever, did she go beyond pink to the brilliant red which signifies serious sweat. There were colors beyond red which Caro never even got close to. With more than an hour of really strenuous effort, the brilliant red on the swimmer's back gets deeper and deeper until it becomes purple. Caro's high school coach loved to run up and down the deck of the pool yelling "Turn it purple! Turn it purple!" And if someone actually did get it all the way to purple, the coach would get him up out of the pool, turn him around, and praise his back to the team as the color of a winner.

Caro had stopped swimming an hour before, but Tim had gone on. He had just finished his eighth one-thousand free. He was turning them out every ten minutes. Caro couldn't do a thousand free in fifteen minutes, let alone eight of them under ten minutes with less than twenty seconds rest between each one. He was standing in the shallow end, hunched over and gripping his knees to keep himself from toppling over in exhaustion. He had his back to her. She had been watching it get deeper and deeper purple as he spun up and down the pool at top speed. On his fifth one-thousand, the purple color had started to brighten. She had walked up and back alongside the pool as he swam, looking at his back to make sure she was seeing what she thought she was seeing. He was turning orange. As he'd swum on, his skin had brightened and brightened until it was a sickly yellow ochre. It was a color and a level of exertion so rare, she hadn't even known it existed.

The pace clock swept by the zero and Tim made no move to swim again. "Are you finished?" she asked.

He grunted. He couldn't even talk. He was coughing as if he were drowning, and she could hear water vaulting up out of his lungs. His back now looked as if he had an ugly case of jaundice.

He didn't straighten up for several minutes. Fascinated, she watched his back come down through a Hansa orange and slowly deepen to violet. The muscles seemed to tighten as he rested. With the return of their purple color, they knotted up and stood out. The way he was standing, bent over holding onto his knees, he looked like a weight-lifter straining to get a tremendous barbell off the floor.

They walked down Lexington Avenue to his apartment house, and she got on the elevator with him without their negotiating whether she was going to come up or not. She wanted to and he knew she wanted to.

He had a handsome, two-bedroom apartment. She went into the kitchen with him and fixed herself a gin and tonic while he poured himself a beer. He drank it before she finished mixing her gin and tonic, and took a second one out of the refrigerator.

"Do you drink like you swim?" she asked.

"I have to get in my carbos," he said.

"Carbos?"

"Beer is liquid carbohydrates," he said, holding up his glass. "Beer is the fuel of athletes, not Wheaties."

"That's a myth," she said.

"Tell it to Wheaties," he said.

"I'm not talking about Wheaties," said Caro. "It's a myth that beer has a lot of carbohydrates. Orange juice has far more carbohydrates than beer."

"Really?" he asked, intrigued.

"You ought to try what the East German swimmers are drinking this year," she said.

"What's that?"

"Malted mashed potatoes," she said.

"You're making that up," he said, going out into the living room.

"What?" she demanded, following him out. "You think I'd make something like that up? You don't believe the entire East German Olympic team is swilling down enormous steins of liquid potatoes?"

"No," he said, sitting down in an imitation Eames chair. "I think you're making that up."

She sat down on the sofa across from him. She asked him about his job and he told her the story of his career. After college he'd taken a job with Canada Dry as a marketing flunky. He had been a psychology major and had been considering getting a Ph.D., but since he'd have to pay most of the cost of more schooling himself, he'd decided he was finished with it. Then Canada Dry convinced him to go back to school. It wasn't their paternal policy of encouraging employees to continue their educations that convinced him; it was their dullness. The more people he met in positions of corporate authority, the more he was sure he had to make business a serious career.

He went back to Penn and got a degree in business administration from Wharton. From there he became a securities analyst at the Bank of New York. After three years at the bank, one of his bosses with a social connection to Alfred Oakes got him a job in the acquisitions department at Colony. Tim was twenty-four then. His boss predicted Tim would be a vice president at Colony before he was thirty, and he was right. Now twenty-seven, Tim was the Colony Companies' youngest vice president.

In between the dry data about himself, Tim made sexy cracks and Caro tossed them right back. She got cuter and cuter, which meant she was getting drunk. Sex did not work too well for her when she was drunk. If he kept talking and she had one more gin and tonic, neither one of them was going to have an especially remarkable time making love.

"Why do you keep looking at me like that?" she asked, interrupting him.

"Like what?" he asked. "Why are you laughing?"

She was trying to smile innocently but it had turned into a laugh. "You keep looking at my bosom."

"I do?"

"You do," she said. "It's making me laugh."

"It's a very lovely bosom," he said.

"Thank you," she said.

"Since you've raised the issue," he said, "how is one not supposed to look when you leave four buttons unbuttoned?"

"That's for fashion purposes only," she argued.

"Bullshit."

"You think I like to show them off," she said.

"I think you do," he said," and I think it's a fine idea."

"You want to see what they look like without clothes," she said.

"I want to see that very much."

She unbuttoned her blouse and took it off. Her problem with the laughing disappeared. Her throat was too tight to laugh. She unfastened her light bra and laid it on top of her blouse on the sofa. She faced him, sitting up straight.

"Here they are."

He leaned back and looked at her. His chair creaked as he took a long drink of his beer, studying her through his glass. She looked down at herself. She thought they looked good, but he didn't seem impressed. Except that his hand trembled when he put his beer down on the coffee table.

"Do you like them?" she asked.

His left eye quivered a little but he just kept on looking at her. She had never acted this way with anyone before. She wondered what she was going to do if he persisted in sitting there and looking at her like he was at a nightclub.

"What do you think?" she asked.

"I think," he said, his voice strained. "You are the sexiest looking, sexiest acting woman I have ever met."

He stood up, leaned over and pulled her up off the sofa by her hands so he could kiss her across the coffee table. He liked to kiss. They stopped several times on their way to his bedroom to kiss.

"I want to undress you," she said when they got inside the bedroom.

He was wearing a loose, floppy dress shirt. Looking around later, she found a closet full of beautiful suits, but all his shirts were the same oversized tents which fit him only across his broad chest. She pulled this one out of his pants and unbuttoned it from the bottom. When she reached his chest, her fingers touched his skin through the button hole. He was hot to the touch. She got his shirt open and found his chest still bright red from his swimming. She turned him around to look at his back as she pulled off the shirt.

"What's wrong?" he asked.

"It's still purple in spots across your back," she said.

"I know," he said. "The colors come back one by one. It usually takes me an hour to get back to Caucasian."

She wrapped her arms around him from behind and hugged as hard as she could. He pressed his head back and rubbed fondly against her forehead.

"You're something," he said.

She slid her hand down his flat stomach past the elastic of his boxer shorts. She fumbled around, his belt pinching her wrist, until she got a hold of his cock. His chest and back were hot, but his cock was hotter.

"You're something, too," she said.

Once she'd touched his prick, he was as eager as all other men. He got her undressed and the rest of his own clothes off in a hurry and they got right into bed. He manipulated her clit while she held onto his dick. He was a perceptive and considerate lover. When she stroked his cock faster, he sped up on her clit, and she led him that way to making her come. She kissed him as he got over her and slid inside. He screwed without breathing hard. It seemed as effortless as his butterfly. She caught his rhythm and moved with him, kissing him and sucking on his tongue as if she could get sperm out of it too. Suddenly he slid his hands under her ass and took hold of her cheeks to keep her still. He was coming. He bucked into her violently, making a lot of noise. She held still until he was finished. His hands relaxed their hold on her and he lay down on top of her, crooking his chin over her shoulder. He was breathing hard now. His cock was still inside her, though she could feel it shrinking. He lifted his head up from her neck and kissed her again. She kissed him back.

They propped themselves up to watch TV without bothering to clean up. Both her pussy and his cock gave off the faintly acrid result of sperm mixing with vaginal juices. She knew it wasn't exactly ladylike, but she had always liked this pungent after-odor of sex.

It was an hour before his back lost all its color. She made him turn over beneath the night light at every commercial so she could check the changes. As he promised, the rest of his colors returned one by one.

"It's so beautiful that you can turn colors like that," she told him when he had finally come all the way back to a pinkish white.

His big, square face broke out in a silly grin.

"I'm serious," she said. "It makes you look like some kind of molting bird. It's strange and really beautiful at the same time."

"Thank you," he said, trying to sound gracious, but she could tell he was uncomfortable with the compliment.

"I saw a Schielle watercolor once in a Madison Avenue gallery," she said, trying to explain why she was so much in love with his back. "It was a self-portrait. Schielle had done himself from the back, and most of it was all accurate flesh tones, but he'd colored his backbone as a column of rainbow spikes. His back was all this realistic flesh, but the ridge of his spine was done with startling, jagged particles of color."

He knew Schielle's work. She took hold of his cock and started caressing it again. She wanted him in her. He got hard in a hurry, and before he had it halfway up on the first push, she felt the familiar rush of anxiety and pleasure which signalled she would soon be thinking about whether or not to let herself fall in love. She shivered as he slid up and down her. This time the feelings were much stronger than usual, both the pleasure and the anxiety.

PART III

September, 198–

·5·

WHEN CARO came home from work, she was still shocked by her lunch with Tim. Then Konnie Odo called to invite them out to dinner. Tim had told him that Oakes wanted Tim to go to Atlantic City the following day.

"Will Marly be there?" asked Caro suspiciously. "Is this some sort of farewell dinner?"

At lunch Tim had said his mind wasn't made up yet. If Konnie and Marly were going to give them a farewell dinner tonight, maybe Konnie knew more than Caro did.

"No, Marly's not coming," said Konnie. "It's a business dinner of sorts."

"A business dinner?" She was anything but anxious to listen to Tim recite the list of his financial heroes again. Warren Buffet. A.W. Jones. Jimmy Ling. Twenty million. Thirty million. A hundred million. She knew all their names and numbers the same way a woman married to a sportscaster knows all the Knicks.

"I'd rather not tonight, Konnie," she said gently. "Tim and I have to talk tonight."

"But Caro," said Konnie grandly, "King Cerkez, the man who is going to do for Atlantic City what Guy MacAfee did for Las Vegas, has invited you and your husband out to dinner."

"Konnie, Tim and I have to talk."

"You can refuse an invitation from a man who named himself 'king'?"

"Yes."

"Don't," said Konnie. "He'll help you make up your minds."

Konnie Odo had been Tim's best friend long before Caro had met him. He was a lot like Tim in some ways, but very unlike him in others. He wasn't particularly good looking; he was big and a little heavy. He had a scraggly moustache and a snaggle-toothed salesman's grin which he always kept turned on. His grin could be annoying, but behind it was a bright charm he had carried out of growing up in Las Vegas. His humor was earnest and ironic. He could be very funny when she least expected it, and Caro and Konnie had evolved a friendship that was mainly based on laughing at each other's jokes.

She and Tim met Konnie at the Palace that night, and he introduced them to Cerkez. Cerkez had known Konnie as a kid. He was a former Las Vegas hotel operator, and had come to New York to sell Konnie's brokerage firm on a bond deal to build a hotel in Atlantic City. He was short and old. He had a round pink face, and during dinner he talked on and on with an energetic, babyish charm about the gambling business. Tim didn't like him. Konnie kept egging Cerkez on, then turning to Caro and raising his eyebrows. She began to realize that this dinner was Konnie's way of telling them both to avoid Atlantic City. Konnie was constantly raising his eyebrows because he wanted Caro to do what she could in order to discourage Tim.

"What brings a Westerner like you East to go into the casino business, King?" she asked. "How come you left Las Vegas?"

"I'm bored," he said. "I've been retired twenty years and I'm sick of it. I never wanted to get out in the first place."

"Why did you leave?" asked Caro. "Did the mob force you out?"

"The mob, the mob," said Cerkez in a mock groan. "Everybody outside the business is positively in love with the idea of the mob."

"So why did you quit?"

"I made a mistake, that's why," said Cerkez. "The Bobby Kennedy thing fooled me."

"What Bobby Kennedy thing?"

"You don't know about that?" asked Cerkez, looking slyly at Konnie.

"No," said Caro. "Should I?"

"He's going to get into the gambling business, and you don't know about that yet?" asked Cerkez. He turned to Tim. "Don't you know anything about the business?"

"Nothing," said Tim pleasantly.

Caro knew that wasn't true. She had heard him discuss it with Konnie. She knew he had read books on it. It had been a natural function of his friendship with Konnie to become well versed in the gambling business. He was setting his favorite little trap for King Cerkez.

"Really?" asked Cerkez, brightly, pleased at the prospect of initiating Tim. "This is something you ought to know, then. It happened when Kennedy was out at Tahoe taking a vacation from the presidential primary in California. I guess they were afraid of him because of the way he'd gone after Hoffa, and they wanted to get something on him."

"Get something on Bobby Kennedy?" asked Caro dubiously.

"They got something all right," said Cerkez. "They busted into his room and took pictures of him in bed with a couple of broads."

"Bobby Kennedy?"

Cerkez laughed. "Yeah. Bobby Kennedy. Those Kennedy boys always did like to screw."

"I don't believe it," said Caro. "What about his security?"

"I don't know about his security," said Cerkez. "But I saw the pictures. It was Bobby Kennedy and he wasn't playing doctor."

"Really?"

"I saw the pictures."

"Incredible," said Caro. "That's kind of funny."

"The funny thing was it didn't work," said Cerkez. "They couldn't blackmail Bobby over screwing broads. Those Kennedy's are proud of all the dames they lay."

Tim and Konnie laughed.

"It's not all that funny," said Cerkez. "It made him mad as hell, and he swore he was going to close gambling down in Nevada the first week he was president. He was just the guy to do it, too. It seemed to me that the only thing standing between Kennedy and the White House was Nixon. So, gambling houses in Nevada had just turned into very poor investments. The minute I saw those pictures and heard what Bobby said, I put my joint up for sale."

Caro tried to stop grinning. She wanted to give a loud cheer for Bobby Kennedy, but she was afraid Cerkez wouldn't appreciate it.

"It was the right move," said Cerkez, more to himself than anyone else, as if he were rehashing something in his mind for the thousandth time. "There was no way Kennedy wasn't going to get elected, and once that guy made a promise, he kept it. Hell, I had no idea he was going to get shot."

King Cerkez slammed the dinner table over his bad luck.

"I wish I'd never seen those pictures," he complained. "I've been trying to get back in the business ever since. Once you've been in it, you don't like being out."

"What's been keeping you out?" asked Caro.

"Every joint you look at is so expensive," he said. "And I'm not crazy about Atlantic City, to tell the truth. Down there you have this crazy boogie trying to get elected and outlaw gambling. He'll be dead by the end of the year. But even so, the honeymoon is over in Atlantic City. Only three or four casinos are making the big bucks. The rest are marginal."

"That was the mob that took those pictures of Kennedy, wasn't it?" asked Caro. "I guess they're involved in all the casinos in Nevada."

"The mob isn't as powerful as you people want to believe it is," said Cerkez.

"No?"

"They sent a guy over to see me when I was getting started in Texas," said Cerkez. "This guy told me I was going to pay him a hundred a week for the little back room flat shop I was running, so I—this is off the record now, okay? Konnie, she understands what off the record is, doesn't she?"

"Of course," said Konnie. Konnie looked bored. Evidently he had heard this story many times.

"You do, don't you, Caroline?" persisted Cerkez.

"I do," promised Caro.

"I killed him," said Cerkez. "And that was the last I heard from the mob while I was in Texas. So much for the all powerful mob."

"You killed him?" asked Caro, shocked. She looked at Konnie. Konnie didn't believe him.

"It's the only way to handle the Italians," said Cerkez, as if he were a tout letting her in on a good horse. "You've got to return their own message. It really spooks them when you kill one of their gophers. They stop calling on you right away. The only thing is, you got to make sure you kill a little one and not a big one. They get too worried about themselves when you kill a big one."

"You mean they never tried to get back at you?" asked Caro.

"What for?" asked Cerkez. "They were happy to cut their losses and leave me alone. Most of these guys are just pretending because they have Italian names, anyway. They aren't the mob. As a matter of fact, I sometimes wonder if there is such a thing."

"What is it then, if it isn't the mob?" asked Tim. He sounded as if he were exploring a very mild personal curiosity. Caro knew what he was starting.

"I don't know," said Cerkez. "But if they're tough, you can't prove it by me. I never had any trouble with them in forty years in Las Vegas."

"Did you pay any of them money in Las Vegas?" asked Tim innocuously.

"Hell, no!" responded Cerkez, insulted, but delighted to have the opportunity to say again that he was tougher than they were.

"A lot of people say you can't manage a casino without the Mafia," said Tim, "They say you'll get ripped off too much and you'll go broke."

Cerkez chuckled as if Tim had just told a joke.

"Some people say you're in organized crime yourself," said Tim mildly.

"I know what goes on," said Cerkez. He smiled his babyish grin at Konnie. He looked like a little kid trying to keep a secret about the dirty work going on inside the cookie jar, as if it wasn't really his hand that was doing it.

"Is that all?" asked Tim.

"Why is it that everyone thinks everybody in this country who has touched a pair of dice is mixed up with the mob?" he lamented.

Tim laughed and his light eyes flared. "I can see that you are different."

"Very, partner," said Cerkez.

"How would we define a mobster?" asked Tim.

Cerkez shrugged.

"A man wouldn't qualify just because he ran an illegal gambling room," said Tim.

"Hell, no."

"And just because he knows everything that's going on in the criminal world," said Tim blandly, "that wouldn't mean anything."

"No," said Cerkez, looking at Tim as if he were waking up to something."

"And just because he killed a man to protect his own interests . . ." Tim let it dangle without finishing, but there wasn't anyone at the table who didn't know he had just called Cerkez a mobster.

"Okay, Tim, okay," said Cerkez. Suddenly the braggart was gone from his manner; Tim had punctured him. "There are some things you have to do in this business that you don't have to do in other businesses."

Tim looked away. He had played his game with Cerkez and had no interest in taking it any further. But Konnie had something to say.

"That's not true for everybody, King," said Konnie.

"I know, I know." said Cerkez quickly. "Not everybody has to do them. Your father was different."

"What was different about his father?" asked Caro.

"His father was the smartest man who ever walked in a casino," said Cerkez proudly, as if it was to his own personal glory to have known him. "Bar none."

Cerkez went off on a long story about Vegas in the forties. It was supposed to be all about Laddy Odo, but it was all about King Cerkez. Tim was staring off in one of his dazes. Caro watched him. She knew his mind was already made up about Atlantic City. He didn't really have any choice. He was a low-level vice president with a reputation for being a pain in the ass. He wasn't in a position to refuse anything Alfred Oakes wanted him to do.

Though only thirty-two, he had already ruined himself at Colony.

It had been agony to watch. There was no question that Tim was good at figuring out what made various companies tick; his success in the stock market had proved that. In the five years of their marriage, they had accumulated seventy thousand dollars, having invested less than fifteen thousand to start with. But something was working against him at Colony.

He didn't get along with the business mind. Caro had the feeling Tim didn't really like business at all. He was pursuing his career at Colony only because it was difficult for him and he couldn't stand to give up on anything that challenged him, whether he was suited to do it or not. Konnie had begged him many times to quit and be a stockbroker, saying he was too good to let himself get stuck at Colony, but Tim insisted that he had no reason to believe he could make it anywhere else if he couldn't make it at Colony. Unfortunately, the mediocrity so common in businessmen, which he had been so certain would work to his advantage, defeated him. Few of the people he worked with understood what he was talking about. He couldn't get his perceptions across to them. When he turned out to be right about something, no one appreciated how or why he'd known. His analytical ability was often dismissed as luck.

It was very frustrating, and Tim's reaction was to wait for the opportunity to make them look stupid. There was no hope of restraining him. He was so sensitive and so aggressive at the same time that his frustration had to come out. He could be as subtle about it as making the two-hundred fly look easy. Just as there were thousands and thousands of yards of stomach-wrenching swimming behind those two hundred easy-looking yards, there was the same effort behind his business perceptions; and when they didn't, or couldn't appreciate it, he had to have his revenge. He always made it seem innocuous and bland, but somehow he never left them in any doubt about how he felt. He could be subtle about it, and they *were* stupid; but, just like Cerkez, no matter how dumb they were it was never too hard for them to figure out when Tim was kicking them in their professional nuts.

"He's not in the mob?" Tim cracked as soon as the dinner was over and they were out of King Cerkez's earshot. "If we gave him the Minnesota Multiphasic Personality Inventory, he'd score somewhere in between Carlo Gambino and Johnny Rocco."

Caro laughed. Tim was, if nothing else, unfailingly funny about these people. The only trouble was he couldn't walk away from all the presidents of textile companies, computer companies and shoe companies he had helped buy into Colony the way he'd just walked away from Cerkez. After Colony bought their companies, Alfred Oakes put these men on his executive committee, where they decided who would be the next senior vice presidents and executive vice presidents. Tim's was a name which never got the required support.

·6·

THEIR DOORMAN Manny helped Caro pack the bags in the car. Tim had left hours ago while she was still packing. He had to see Oakes before he took the train to Philadelphia and a limousine to Atlantic City. He wouldn't tell her what he was seeing Oakes about until something was signed.

When she finally started driving, she felt harried and angry. They had not been happy at Twomey when she asked them for a leave of absence. They were always irritated when she went on a business trip with Tim in the middle of the week, so her request for an unspecified leave of absence was like asking to be fired. Eventually they had agreed she could take a vacation; but if it lasted too long, they would replace her.

She didn't really want to go to Atlantic City and had told Tim so after their dinner with Cerkez.

"You don't have to," he'd said quickly. "I'll go alone."

He had said it so fast that cold sweat leaked out of her temples, and she'd sat in the cab watching her hands curl up in her lap like bugs turned over on their backs.

"I didn't mean it that way," she'd replied after a long silence. "I want to be with you. I was just complaining."

She drove across the Verrazano Bridge heading for the Outerbridge Crossing. It was dusk and the lights on the bridge were already on. It would be dark when she reached Atlantic City.

She regretted having told Tim she didn't want to come. He was a strange mixture of vulnerability and toughness. Her being in love with him gave her no license to criticize him. If anything, it reduced her right to be critical.

He was an ardent feminist, more so than she. He used her feminism to trap her over and over again, making sure he kept a distance between them. "We agreed," he repeated time and time again. "You're on your own. I'm on my own.'"

He carried this independent, self-reliant theme much too far. He refused to buy her meaningful presents. Christmas, birthdays, anniversaries, St. Valentine's Day all came and went unnoticed or marked with token presents. He had given her a ring this last Christmas. It was an antique, an old silver fork twisted into a ring. It was ten years out of style and cost fifteen dollars, an amount which must have equaled the number of minutes he spent looking for it on Fulton Street.

He had even refused to buy her the ruby band she'd wanted for the wedding ceremony. His entire participation in their wedding had been limited to making an appearance in it. She had found the superior court judge to marry them. She had reserved a suite at the St. Regis for a party afterwards. She had called all his friends to make sure they were coming. He wouldn't even call to invite his parents, and then he wouldn't let her call them either. He didn't want any of his family at his wedding. It seemed like he didn't want himself there, either. When they left the apartment on their wedding day, she felt like she was kidnapping him.

Her mother and father wondered where his parents were, but she didn't get into it with them. She didn't get along too famously with them anyway, so she understood how Tim felt. She did, however, talk to him about her parents. As a result of three years of psychoanalysis, she talked about them all the time. Growing up in Miami Beach as a spoiled wasp princess caught in the middle of an ongoing contentious divorce had put ideas in her which called for continual self-analysis. (Tim paid willing attention to her speeches about her parents, enjoying the opportunities to talk about psychology.)

Caro was the younger of two sisters. Though they both lived with their mother after their father moved out, Patti's loyalty remained with her father. Her mother surrendered Patti to him and gave all her time and attention to Caro. It was this obsessive interest in Caro that finally put Caro in a psychiatrist's office: her mother, going through her drawers, found a bottle of speed beneath Caro's blouses.

Both the psychiatrist and Caro agreed that the real problem was her mother and the divorce, but they found some incidental value in figuring out what made Caro tick. She liked him. The analysis calmed her down, and her grades shot up. Her mother was so pleased (both with Caro's change and the large bills her father had to pay) that she kept it going until Caro departed for college in New Hampshire.

Caro found it puzzling that Tim, the psychology major, never found it necessary to talk about his own parents in any detail. He made ironic cracks about his father, a doctor in Connecticut; but whenever she tried to pursue anything about him or Tim's mother, Tim was evasive. Her curiosity, piqued by his iron refusal to invite them to his wedding, led her to try again and again, but she couldn't begin to penetrate the curtain he drew around them.

He was always playing his little game to establish his omniscience. It reminded her of the least likeable quality she'd found in her psychiatrist. Her shrink had always pretended that he had some kind of mysterious doctor's power working for him. He refused to answer any questions, especially personal ones, which would threaten his doctor's mystique. Tim was the same, and he added his own little twist to this doctor's game. He never said a word about anything he didn't know well. He scrupulously avoided saying anything that could be taken as foolish. And then, when some unsuspecting cluck wandered into an area of Tim's expertise, Tim let the guy have it with his practiced nonchalance. It gave one the impression that beneath his silence, Tim knew everything. He was so quiet about it, letting only little granules of knowledge out one at a time, that it gave one the feeling he was hoarding the rest of it, as if he couldn't bear to part with it, as if he needed it for some magical, unknowable godlike scheme.

It had become a burden for Caro to play this game with him. It had been fine for Tim to appear potent and omniscient when he was rising at Colony, but he wasn't rising anymore. The lack of deeds to support his image had made him into something more hostile and secretive than powerful and all-apprehending. She worried that he might be slipping into something uncontrollable.

It was getting difficult to be alone with him. He couldn't sit still. She had the feeling he was approaching a painful metamorphosis, and the energy of the change wouldn't let him rest. He seemed to be cracking. She could almost feel vibrations beneath his skin when they made love, as if he were going to turn a dark, bottle-green, crack like glass, and some new Tim would come out like a reptile shedding its cool armor.

He had been training at swimming with an unmatched intensity. She couldn't believe that he could actually train more than he had when they'd first met, but he did. He wanted a fatigue so pervasive he wouldn't have to think about anything.

But he thought anyway, and it was all about business. She had grown tired of business and his obsessive interest in it. She didn't like spending all her nights going out with him and Konnie and the people from Wall Street they thought were smart enough to share their company. They had a fight about it.

"You don't like business because you won't see its complexity," he snapped at her. "If you can't get a hold of something right away, you won't take the time to understand it. Business is like anything else worth doing. It's no less complex than being a doctor or anything else that's supposed to be hard. It's as subtle and difficult as your own capacities can make it. Of course if you're dumb, it seems simple."

He had called her stupid, but she still believed it was his stubbornness, his need to tackle things simply because they were difficult, which led him on at Colony. It wasn't because business was truly interesting. There was so much of Tim that loved paintings and plays and music, so much more than the part of him that worried over business formulas. She couldn't believe he would let that small, dull part of him take him over. That was exactly what he was doing, though, and that was exactly why she had to drive down the Garden State Parkway to some weird gambling town at the risk of her job.

Atlantic City came rolling up the darkened causeway like a planet of sparking colors reeling out of control. Unconsciously she pressed down on the gas with excitement. She looked to find the Ondine's sign among all the shooting colors. She found it to the north, a two-story mermaid with emerald scales splashing pink wavelets of water above the casino dome. Down at the other end of the boardwalk, Sinbad's had a sailor with luminous yellow boots. He was far more than the usual line representation of most neon art. He was a mass of twisting tubes of light. Between his shirt, his chest and belly glowed purple. As she sped closer, she saw another sign exploding upwards from street level like an oil fire in an Arabian desert. She couldn't make out what it was because the source of the red and gold light was obscured by other hotels. When she got several blocks down Pacific Avenue, she saw it was a hotel called Fortunatas. The creators of this domesticated comet clearly favored red and gold, but the light had no recognizable design. It was magnified neon interplaying with polished chrome mirrors, which resulted in the candle power of klieg lights but with the circulating effects of neon. It was light for the sake of light, so bright her pupils shrank when she looked directly at it. When she got close she had to look away, and she felt as if she were colliding with it rather than driving past it.

By the time she reached the Ondine, her sense of reality was badly battered. She felt drained and excited at the same time.

These were the feelings of which paintings were made. Her pulse quickened. Here were colors and events that had never been put through the mill of art and turned back out as paintings. Oh, yes, here was something which had been ridiculed by every cartoonist and wiseacre on the East Coast; but who had really taken it all in, chewed it up and played it back out with love and respect to see what they'd get? Who had been willing to take a chance on something so eminently foolhardy as this incredibly pretentious firestorm of color?

Two bellmen rushed over to the car to help her with the suitcases, saying Mrs. Seagurt this and Mrs. Seagurt that over and over again. Inside the busy hotel she felt dizzy and anxious. Atlantic City was supposed to be fantastic and eerie, but this was too powerful. It wasn't like fantasy or dreaming so much as like having too many drinks. She had difficulty walking straight and she had to concentrate just to follow the bellman through the lobby towards the casino. She felt stranger and stranger as he led her through an enormous green casino into an office with an orange carpet and a turquoise chair. She went through an open door into a large bare room where she was confronted by something which startled her more than anything she had yet seen in Atlantic City. It was a giant metal Argus with a hundred large opaline irises.

Argus was a monster from Greek mythology. She had drawn him once for a classics paper at Dartmouth. He had a hundred eyes and he never slept with more than two of them closed at a time. He was charged by Helen with guarding the beautiful Io. With his hundred eyes he could see everything all the time, so there was no hope for Io to escape. Pining for her, Zeus sent Hermes to rescue her from the monster. Argus, whose interests matched the number of his eyes, was fascinated with Hermes' urbanity, music, and stories.

Now here was Tim, staring at this new electronic version of Argus, engrossed. He was studying it like Hermes trying to figure out how to put all the eyes to sleep so he could jump up and cut its head off. He hadn't even realized that Caro had come in, and this incredible monster was suddenly staring at *her* with all hundred iridescent eyes.

When Tim went upstairs to join Caro in their new suite, he found her in the bathroom. She had just finished showering. The bathroom had a sun lamp and she was standing underneath it while she was still wet. She picked up her towel and dried her back, turning her shoulders to make her luxurious breasts sway. She was purposely teasing him.

"You want it?" he asked her.

"I've got to get dressed," she laughed. "We're going to tour the boardwalk, remember?"

She closed her eyes and turned her face up to the sun lamp. The yellow light made her caramel nipples turn lemon. Her whole body looked like yellow candy. She began to breathe a little hard from holding her head back. The small indentation in the middle of her slightly muscular stomach became deeper and deeper as her muscles stretched. The neat depression of flesh descended right to her naval where it turned into a faded line down her flat stomach. Her swimming kept her stomach taut, all the way down to the fluff of her bush. There were a few beads of water standing out above the hair.

She turned her head away from the sun lamp and caught him looking at her.

"Are you still ogling my body?" she asked.

"Yes."

"My tits are starting to sink," she said, taking them in her palms and raising them a little, then bouncing them around for his benefit.

He took her by her head, his hands pressing her ears against her soaking hair, and he wiggled his tongue all around the inside of her mouth. She had a large, arched mouth, the upper half of it cut in the middle with a deep *V.* It was a pleasure simply to kiss her. While they kissed, she looked at him with eyes which said she didn't care about getting dressed any more; and when they broke, she lay down on the bathroom rug underneath the hot yellow light. Her breasts spread. He took off his coat and pants, got over her quickly, and dropped his hard-on into her mouth. They enjoyed a long sixty-nine on the bathroom rug without Tim ever getting his shirt off. After she came, Tim got into her pussy and tried to fuck her slowly, wanting to make it last, but she reached up under his shirt and scratched his back with long gentle strokes. The affection in her gesture made him come right away.

7.

THE SLOT Dock, the former Million Dollar Pier, was a long pier of slot-machine emporiums. Tim and Caro found one slot machine as large as a tool shed. It looked like an oversized tank tipped over on its side. It was at least twenty feet across. Tim said there was supposed to be a bigger slot machine at the Money Tree but Caro found that hard to believe. She had to hang from this one's six-foot handle with all her weight to get its reels to spin. It took five dollar bills (Tim explained how optical bill scanning had freed slot machines from coins) and paid off anything from fifteen dollars up to the grand jackpot, a fifty-foot cabin cruiser parked right on the pier in front of the parlor. If a player lined up ten boats on the machine's reels, he got to take the big boat home. There were snapshots of previous winners standing beside their prize with various expressions of ecstasy. Caro put fifteen dollars in it but failed to win a thing.

They moved along the Slot Dock a few parlors where Tim showed her a race horse slot machine. It was the size of a jukebox and had a little oval track with eight plastic horses lined up ready to run. They each deposited a quarter and picked a horse. Tim pressed a red button, a race track trumpet sounded, and a nasal electronic voice called, "It is now post time!" The eight little horses all took off around the grooves of the little oval track. They moved in spurts and jerks as if a drunk were inside turning the gears. The lead changed hands many times. Flag Boy, Caro's horse, won with exciting spasms of speed down the last eight inches of the track, and the machine paid her seven quarters.

"It's not a very big payoff," she complained.

"It's not a high-risk, large-reward concept machine," said Tim. "The attraction is the jerking horses."

Caro went into a parlor specializing in machines which required skill. Caro tried electronic ping pong. The machine picked on her backhand and beat her 21–6. The change girl assured her it wasn't a bad score for a first effort. Subsequent tries got her score up to eleven, for which she won back her quarter. The rest of the parlor had electronic versions of chess, football, hockey, and the like. In the corner at the back they found a young guy driving the Indianapolis 500 against Parnelli Jones, Jimmy Clark, and Tom Sneva. He drove with bare feet, he explained, for a better feel. He finished first and won fifty dollars. He said it was his third time tonight, and the manager was now coming by every fifteen minutes to hassle him over I.D.

"He looks like he's been training on that machine for months," said Caro as they left.

"He has," said Tim. "That's why this game playing stuff will never fly. You have to concentrate. The fun in playing a slot machine is in pulling the lever and letting the machine do all the whirling. Who the hell wants to work for the money?"

They went out to Pacific Avenue to visit some of the motels. There they found single-minded machines which paid off nothing but jackpots, lenient machines which paid off with jackpots even when they didn't get the watermelons in the center of the window, and lemonless machines which didn't seem to pay off at all.

They made a point of visiting Little Caesar's Palace. With quiet delight they walked up and down row after row of left-handed Edward G. Robinson's with mouths full of silver dollars.

"Hector says we have to visit the Money Tree," said Tim when they were back out on the street. "We have to see the biggest slot machine in the world."

"All right," agreed Caro. "I'm dying to see something bigger than that tank you play to win the boat."

The Money Tree's casino was almost as big as the Ondine's and every bit as impressive. A multitude of dice and card games were spread out beneath an enormous tree made entirely of silver. In the center of the casino was the tree's large trunk, at least six feet in diameter, a mass of knotted, twisting silver. Great argentine branches arched up to the ceiling and back down, tapering into turned silver sheets that spread out all above the busy casino. Many of the branches hung down to the eye level of the gamblers, bowed by their own weight and that of their exquisite black-veined silver leaves.

"I'm tired of pulling handles," said Tim. "Let's shoot a little dice."

"What about the world's largest slot machine?" asked Caro.

"We'll get to it," said Tim.

They went down the steps into the sunken casino. When they got into the crowd, Caro saw that it was tarnish that made the leaves' veins black. The fashioned knots on the silver branches were partly tarnished too, and when she looked at them from the right angle, they made fascinating whorls of tar and white light. The crowd was thicker than it looked from the entrance; once they got into it, they had trouble moving. A girl in a sexy gray lamé evening gown, waving a handful of hundred dollar bills over her head, rushed by them as if she were on an urgent errand. Caro watched her get into a plastic booth beside the trunk of the silver tree. The booth turned out to be an elevator which lifted her high into the crown of the tree. She stepped off onto a small platform, but it was too dark up there to see what she was doing.

The noise in the casino was deafening. People were shouting, chips were clacking, and coins were showering out of slot machines that rang little sirens with every jackpot. Tim explained, shouting to make himself heard, that the Money Tree was crowded because of its new promotion. They had been getting it ready for months. It had originally been scheduled to start with the opening of the hotel in May, but they hadn't been able to get it going until last night. They were hoping it would recapture some of the momentum they had lost from the Pier opening just two weeks after they did.

"You'd think they'd learn their lesson after the chuckwagon breakfast," said Tim, "but they don't."

They had found their way to some free space along a wall behind one of the crap tables where they could crowd together to hear each other.

"The chuckwagon breakfast?" asked Caro.

"It was the first really big promotion in Las Vegas," said Tim. "Konnie told me about it. His father started it when he bought the Last Frontier. Every night at midnight, Laddy set up a tremendous buffet of food that reached all the way across the Ramona Room. It was table after table of eggs, sausages, hams, steaks, pancakes, croissants, pig's ears, coffee, juice, and everything else you can think of that had anything to do with breakfast. You could eat as much as you wanted of it for ninety-nine cents."

"Wow," said Caro. "Why was it so cheap?"

"To get people into the Frontier," said Tim. "Every night around eleven-thirty, which is the hour they let most gamblers out of their cages, the Frontier hopped like no other hotel on the Strip had ever hopped before. Everyone was coming to the Frontier for this fabulous breakfast."

"How could they afford to feed everyone in Las Vegas for ninety-nine cents?" asked Caro.

"Arrival in the Ramona Room required passage through the casino first," said Tim.

"I see," said Caro.

"But then something happened," said Tim.

"What happened?" asked Caro.

"The Potlech at the Thunderbird," said Tim. "The Grubstake at the El Rancho. And so on. Gambling houses are like comedians; they have no respect for originality."

"As soon as every hotel on the strip had a midnight breakfast, it was no longer an attraction," said Caro.

"That's right," said Tim. "It was only another expense. Six months after it started, it was gone. But Laddy Odo started the wheels turning, and the promotions have been coming and going ever since. This one here at the Money Tree, however, is supposed to be the ultimate. The promotion to end them all."

"Really?" asked Caro. "What is it?"

"You'll see."

"Well, let's at least find the largest slot machine in the world," said Caro. "It's getting a little close along this wall."

"You'll see that too," said Tim. "But why don't you give me a chance to shoot some craps first."

"You keep saying you want to shoot craps, but you can't even get close to a crap table," complained Caro. "Why don't you show me the machine?"

"I'll get a place at the crap table when you see the machine, which also happens to be the promotion," he said, his voice rising because a loud piercing shriek was suddenly ringing out above the casino, "and I think it will be very soon."

Tim pointed to the platform at the top of the silver tree. The girl in the gray lamé dress was jumping up and down in front of something that looked like a computer console. Caro could see it now because it was throbbing with silver light. Suddenly a siren went off, and the girl was bleached white by brilliant spotlights. She lifted her arms and shook them back and forth in a silent victory signal. The casino erupted with cheers.

"What the hell is going on?" shouted Caro.

"She hit the jackpot," shouted Tim. "Look!"

There was money coming out of the silver tree. It was whirling down between the silver branches. The bills got thicker and thicker until they were falling into the casino in a torrent of green paper. Caro reached out and grabbed one. It was a dollar bill.

"I don't believe it!" she shouted over the din. "They are giving away real money!"

"Come on!" shouted Tim. He grabbed Caro by the arm and dragged her to the crap table where several vacant spaces had suddenly appeared. Caro found herself wedged in next to the stickman. The stickman was holding the dice in the center of the table, absentmindedly moving them back and forth with his stick as he waited for the excitement to pass.

"See?" shouted Tim. "The whole tree is a slot machine. It's the worlds biggest slot machine and the ultimate promotion at the same time."

"But they're giving away real money," said Caro. "Why would anyone gamble when they can get real money for free."

"They do, honey," volunteered the stickman without looking up. "They do."

"But how long can a casino keep something like this up," Caro asked him. "You must be losing a lot of money everytime somebody hits that jackpot."

"It's only frogs," explained the stickman. "All singles."

"Aren't one dollar bills money?" asked Caro.

"The joint doesn't lose anything on the deal," said the stickman. "It takes a hundred dollar bill to play that thing."

"A hundred dollars a pull?" asked Caro in astonishment.

"That's right."

"And you don't even get the payoff when you win," marveled Caro. "It goes to a mob of hysterical strangers. Look at them!"

People were standing on their toes shouting and pushing as they reached for the money. A few were popping up and down like jack-in-the-boxes, snatching the money out of the air before a waiting hand could grab it.

"What kind of idiot would play a machine like that?" asked Caro.

"Lots of them," said the stickman. "I've seen them fight to get on that elevator."

The falling money had begun to thin out. A single bill fluttered onto the baize dice layout before them. It lay there undisturbed. The players standing around the crap table stared at it with blank faces.

"What an incredible idea," said Caro.

"I don't think so," said the stickman. When no one picked up the dollar bill, he flipped it up with his stick, like a trashman in the park, and tossed it over the wall of the table in the direction of an old woman who was crawling about the floor snapping dollar bills up off the carpet like a beetle. "It's just another promotion. Most players like to make fools of themselves over real money, not frogs."

Tim and Caro stayed up all night, seeing two shows and stopping at the Ondine casino in between so Tim could talk to Haaf and then glare at the electronic Argus for awhile. After Tim closed the casino, they were too excited to go to bed, so they went to the Diving Belle, the underwater cafe at the Pier, where they watched the sun come up through their underwater window. The ocean had gone from a thick black to charcoal gray, then taupe, and now was a smoky, light sepia with silver splinters of sunlight.

Caro took a long drink of brandy. The maitre d' of the Diving Belle already knew Tim was the new casino manager at the Ondine, and he'd sent over a bottle of brandy that was eighty years old. It was smooth and subtle, stinging her throat with a faded electric tingle.

"I don't care if we only last a day here," she said. "I'm glad I came."

"We're going to last longer than that," said Tim.

"What about when Haaf calls Oakes and tells him you told him to go fuck himself?" asked Caro.

"He isn't going to," said Tim.

"How do you know?" asked Caro.

"He told me," said Tim. "He's decided he tried to go too far. He was very apologetic. He was nice about it, in fact."

"Rah, rah. The management team?" asked Caro.

"Something like that," said Tim. "With me as captain of the casino."

"Good for him," said Caro, immensely relieved. She had been worrying about it ever since she'd decided she liked Atlantic City.

"Dean Haaf," Tim explained to Caro, "was the first guy to put all kinds of companies which had nothing to do with each other all together in one firm."

"You mean he invented the conglomerate," said Caro.

"That's right," said Tim. "But the conglomerate itself was an accident. What he really invented was a way to buy companies for nothing."

"How did he do that?"

"He went after cash-bloated companies and used their money to buy them," explained Tim. "Wall Street was really hot for paper in the sixties, especially high yield convertible bonds, so Haaf would sell convertibles with big fat coupons and use the money to buy XYZ Company, which always happened to have thirty or forty million in the bank. Once he had control of them, he'd use that money to pay off the bonds he'd issued. The effect was that XYZ paid for Haaf to buy them."

"How did that lead to the conglomerate?" asked Caro.

"Haaf didn't care what kind of business a company was in," said Tim. "All he cared about was how much cash they had. He bought retailing, electronics, aluminum, he bought everything. NTS became a patchwork quilt of industries. *Voila*—the first conglomerate."

"He was NTS?" asked Caro, surprised.

"Yes, that's him," said Tim. "He invented the invisible indenture that made NTS."

"But they went bankrupt," said Caro.

"Only after some very sophisticated kicking and screaming," said Tim. "Some of the tricks he dreamed up to save it were masterpieces of byzantine finance. Convertible preferred with warrants attached to buy more of the same convertible preferred, for one. It all collapsed in a heap of paper in the bear market of the seventies, and the SEC closed him down. They said he was trying to get something for nothing, which was a polite way of calling him a crook. All the stuff he dreamed up is illegal now, but the concept of the corporate patchwork survived. People like Alfred Oakes proved it could work as long as you bought companies with real money instead of funny bonds."

"You'd think a man like Haaf would have trouble getting Alfred Oakes to buy the Ondine," said Caro. "Oakes is so conservative."

"Something happened to Haaf when NTS busted," said Tim. "You only have to talk business with him for thirty seconds to see it. The guy is terrified of debt now. He thinks the only way to buy companies is with cash. And that's exactly how he got Oakes interested in the casino business. A casino is all cash. A casino produces the stuff clean acquisitions are made of."

"There's still one thing I'm not clear on," said Caro. "What made Oakes think of you for this?"

"I don't know," said Tim. "One minute I was talking to Tony by my desk, and the next minute I was in Oakes's office with Haaf. Haaf had a copy of Laboy's tax return which showed a million dollar profit in foreign real estate, an obvious maneuver for laundering money stolen from the casino, and that was the last straw for Oakes. He wants to get rid of the Ondine, and I'm here to keep the casino open until he can find a buyer. He's not closing it right away, because it's a secret he's looking for a buyer. If everyone knew he was looking, it would weaken his negotiating position, and you know how Alfred Oakes feels about a weak negotiating position."

"It doesn't sound too good for you," said Caro quietly.

"I know," said Tim.

"It is a de-acquisition then," she said. She knew what it meant to be assigned a deacquisition at Colony.

"Yes."

"Why didn't you tell me?" she asked. "I shouldn't have complained."

"I wanted you to make up your own mind," he said. "I didn't want you to come just because I wanted you to."

"Oh, Tim, don't say that," she said. "Of course I'd go anywhere you need me to go. Besides, I was wrong." She paused and laughed. "This town is so exciting. These people are all so crazy and they all know it . . ."

"I'm glad you like it here," he said.

"It's so weird," she laughed. "I didn't realize how bored I'd gotten with New York. I love it. You really like it too, don't you?"

"Yes, but it's not the place so much," he said, looking down into his brandy. "It's the change. I was starting to feel like I was in a cage."

"I know," she said, then testing carefully to see if the door was open, "I was beginning to wonder if I shouldn't say something."

His head snapped up from his brandy snifter. "What do you mean?"

"You've been so unhappy at Colony," she said. "I thought maybe you should try a new job where you could start fresh with no enemies to worry about."

"If I can't make it at Colony, why should I think I can make it anywhere else," he asked, irritated.

"You're so good at analyzing companies," she whispered, trying to keep him from talking too loudly. "A new firm might be more impressed with that than—"

"No, that's exactly what's wrong," he interrupted quickly, whispering too now, his speech filled with sharp whistles and hisses of emotion. "I couldn't analyze one more company if you put a forty-five to my head. I can't listen to any more dumb shits brag to me about how they made their company great. They don't know, Caro. I swear to God, you know more than they do. Most of them don't have the first fucking idea of how their company really works. That's why they end up in Oakes's office in the first place, because their earnings have dropped through the floor and I've figured out how to blow them back up. And then Colony gives them all kinds of cash, and the guy grins at me like we both understand how smart he is. I know I'm better than ninety-nine percent of these guys. No, not ninety-nine. A hundred percent. If I had been forced to make pals with one more stupid shit company president that Colony was going to make rich and put on the executive committee, I would have jumped across the guy's desk, got him by the hair and asked him how he could justify paying anyone as stupid as himself so much money."

"I know," she said. "I know."

"And if he couldn't have given me the right answer, I'd have bashed his brains out right on his blotter," he added angrily.

"No wonder you have so many friends on the executive committee," she said.

He laughed. "You mean I've let one too many idiots know he's an idiot?"

"That's what I mean."

"Fuck them," he said. "We don't have to worry about it anymore, anyway."

"Why not?"

"Because he had the employment contract ready for me to sign when I went down there this afternoon," he said grinning. "And I signed it."

"What employment contract?" she asked nervously.

"How would you like to have all the time in the world to work on whatever you wanted to?" he asked her. "No more deadlines and the sloppy work they lead to. No more jerks from Proctor and Gamble asking, telling you to make their deodorant look something like a hard-on, but not exactly like a hard-on. How would you like to follow your own talent wherever it led you?"

He had summed up her initial rationalizations for agreeing to come to Atlantic City. Though she should have been used to it, it was still unnerving to hear Tim recite her own thoughts to her.

"Of course I'd like it," she said.

"Then you're going to have it," he said. "Because we're going to make enough money here in the next year to last us the rest of our lives."

"Really?" she asked. "In one year? How can we?"

"Because I got a percentage from Oakes," said Tim.

"You did not!" she said excitedly.

"A percentage of the casino profits," he said.

"That cheapskate never gave a percentage of anything to anybody," said Caro.

"He gave it to me because I dropped one on him right where it counts," laughed Tim. "Right in his greed basket."

"What are you talking about?" asked Caro.

"The Ondine had been such a miserable failure, I told him that if he gave me ten percent of last year's profits, my pay for that year would be seven hundred dollars."

"You got ten percent?" asked Caro, her heart thumping. "That could mean millions."

"Hell no, I didn't get ten percent," said Tim. "Oakes isn't that stupid."

"So what did you get?"

"I gave up my salary to get it," he said, teasing her. "We have to live, eat, and sleep at the Ondine everyday because I don't get a salary."

"What a punishment," she said.

"The deal is, I get my tiny little percentage at the end of each month for a year or until its sold, whichever comes first," he said.

"How much is your tiny little percentage?" asked Caro warily.

"Point seven percent," said Tim.

"Seven-tenths of a percent?" cried Caro in amazement. "Tim, you moron. That's infinitesimal."

"Now you're talking like Haaf," laughed Tim, his eyes glowing with triumph. "He warned Oakes I wasn't being fair to myself with that kind of suggestion. I had to take a salary. The casino would have to make an awful lot of money for point seven percent to be a significant percentage."

"Isn't he right?" demanded Caro.

"It sounds something like the size of Ishmael's share of the Pequod's profits, doesn't it?" he said. "But Oakes, the championship miser, he was all for it. 'Tim is a complete novice in the casino business,' says Oakes. 'Tim can't expect to make a fortune overnight in a new business,' he says."

"And he's probably right, too," said Caro.

"No, Caro," said Tim. "He was wrong and Haaf was wrong too. The numbers are so big, a small swing in the *per* will be plenty. That seven-tenths of one percent Oakes is so sure he's cheating me with will do it all in one year. And one year is all we'll have, because once Oakes sees how much money I make, he'll want that percentage back. We'll give it back, too, because we'll have had our year, and we'll have made all we need."

"What if he sells it?" she asked.

"He won't sell it," snapped Tim. "Once Oakes sees something turn around, he can't bear to let it go."

His eyes were fired with the almost luminous electricity that went through them every time he knew he was right about something. The incredible frustration and anger which had tormented him the past few months were gone. She leaned over and grabbed him by the leg underneath the table and slid her hand along his pants.

"I know what you've got down there when you talk like that," she said, her hand finding the big lump and pressing it.

She wasn't sure whether he was a satyr or she was a nymphomaniac, but whoever was what, they kept each other busy. When they got back to their new bedroom, she undressed quickly. She lay back against the big headboard of their new king-sized bed and played with herself while he watched her. Her pussy was hot and wet and her clit quickly got fat. Finally he got his shirt off. He had the ultimate swimmer's body. His enormous chest narrowed into a small tight waist and long legs. His erection was nodding up and down while he watched her.

He waited until she made herself come before he got onto the bed and got into her. She shivered, almost cold, drifting down from her orgasm, when he started sliding his cock in and out. Three strokes of it made her hot again. The heat radiated from her pussy up her abdomen. It strung hot wires to her nipples, climbed the back of her neck and made her ears glow. He kissed her. His tongue was an icicle.

"You're hot," he said.

"I'm coming again," she whispered.

The heat drained back down her spine through her anus to her pussy and her clit. She stiffened and she lost everything for a long moment. Then reality came back. She tried to make it go away again, focusing on his dick sliding up and down between the lips of her cunt. But the orgasm waned and the mouth of her cunt melted around his cock like softening wax.

How DID they steal so much? Tim couldn't figure it out. They had to be doing it, but if there was so much of it, how could it be so invisible? Tim watched the suspicious tables for hours at a time and saw nothing.

He had gotten Henry Moore's computer system installed and working within a week. Henry turned out to be a serious young man in his middle twenties. He had a mild disposition and was very polite. He was tow-headed and wore big, round tortoiseshell glasses on top of a large nose. Except for the nose, he looked young and callow. It was hard to believe he lived in Las Vegas where his father had been a waiter at an Italian restaurant out on the Strip past the Sands.

When he was talking about casinos, Henry was intense and serious. The callowness would turn penetrating, and he would stare at Tim as if he could see through his oversized glasses right into Tim's brain. He had an annoying habit of always asking Tim what he was thinking. At first Tim thought it was Henry's way of being friendly, but it turned out to be something different. Henry never commented on what Tim thought. He would ask, and, getting the answer, would fall silent, withdrawing into himself to ruminate on the machinery of Tim's mind.

"Your per in May was ten," Henry told Tim.

"What's per?" asked Caro. She had stopped in to try to get Tim to go out to lunch.

"Example of per," said Henry. "One night you have a drop of $100,000. The winning players cash out $90,000. Your win in what's left, $10,000. $10,000 is what percent of $100,000?

"Ten percent," said Caro.

"Right," said Henry. "So your per would be ten."

"Is ten a good per, then?" asked Caro.

"It's horrible," said Henry. "And some of these individual tables have pers down below five. They should have McGray breathing right down the dealers' necks."

"You don't like McGray, do you, Henry?" asked Tim.

"No," said Henry quickly, "I don't."

"Why not?" asked Tim.

"Because he thinks I'm full of shit," said Henry.

"He says he watches the tables you tell him to very closely," said Tim.

"He's lying!" exploded Henry. "He doesn't watch those tables. He doesn't even look at the readouts I give them. He throws them away as if I'd blown my nose in them."

"Henry, do you know how sensitive you are about your system?" asked Tim.

"Yes, I'm sensitive," returned Henry. "So sensitive I've spent hours up on top of that dome watching McGray through the peeks. I'm telling you he avoids the worst tables deliberately."

There was a moment of quiet as Henry looked at Tim angrily. Henry was so mild ordinarily, Tim was amazed at his explosion.

"All right, so I'm pissed off," said Henry. "There's something about people like McGray that get to me. He knows what's going on and he doesn't care. Why does McGray, and everybody else in this business, take all the stealing and dishonesty so calmly? Doesn't it piss you off, Tim?"

"It's just part of the business, isn't it?" asked Tim.

"Is it?" demanded Henry. "All these guys take money off whenever they want to? Who do they think they are? How different is it from holding up a gas station because you need money for a trip to Florida? Not too much, as far as I can see."

"Inventory control is a big part of most businesses, Henry, not just gambling," said Tim, liking Henry more and more. "You're taking it awfully personally."

"I should take it personally," said Henry. "I sat with my system doing two-bit programming work at Casino Credit for three years before you hired me. In those three years I sent out fifty or more telexes and letters to casino managers. They all ended up in the hands of people like McGray. Not one of them hired me. Everything has computers now. Even cars have them right in the dashboards. Why does everything have computers but casinos?"

Henry paused only for an instant, his hands dismissing his own question.

"Because the people in this business don't want the stealing stopped, that's why," he said. "Oh, they pretend they're taking precautions. They buy elaborate TV rigs and then ignore them. They hire private eyes like Hector and send them out to bag markers. They don't want to catch anybody. They're part of all the stealing themselves. They're up to their lips in it, so they're not going to do anything to somebody else doing the same thing."

"Henry, just because they didn't buy your system, it doesn't mean they're all crooked," said Caro.

"No?" asked Henry sarcastically. "I say there never has been a casino run honestly. Not one. Whether the money is skimmed, or thieving dealers and bosses are going wild, or there is some naive slob in charge insisting on trusting everyone, there never has been a casino that returned anything near what it could."

"Am I the naive slob who trusts everyone?" said Tim.

"Oh, no!" returned Henry apologetically. "I didn't mean you. You come from outside the business, but you're not naive. You're suspicious of everyone."

"Is that good?" asked Caro.

"It's more than good," said Henry. "It's essential. The thing about your husband is that he's not dirty like the rest of them. He's suspicious, but he didn't get that way because he's a crook. That's why he's the only guy in this business who has any kind of a chance to find the answer to the big question."

"What's the big question?" asked Caro.

"The big question is," answered Henry, annoyed that Caro hadn't perceived the obvious, "how much money can you make in a casino that is totally honest?"

Henry's persistent distrust of McGray persuaded Tim to hire Clarence Oxman, a freelance casino expert Henry knew from Vegas. Clarence was a bitter man. He had a slack jaw and the skin of his face was creased over it like folded sandpaper dense with abrasive. He didn't like shaving. He wore half-lenses, saying whole glasses were too heavy, so he was always tilting his head back when he wanted to look someone carefully in the eye.

He got quite a reaction when he first entered the casino. The floormen in the *E* Blackjack pit saw him first, and they came together to talk right away. As Clarence passed one pit after another, the pit bosses all came together in knots of two or three, heads nodding in his direction. Then the dealers caught on. Cards stopped coming out of shoes, and dice lay undisturbed on the layouts. Everyone was watching Clarence work his way back to the casino offices.

There was something very wrong about Clarence's walk. One of his legs was badly bowed. It was twisted at the knee in a curve so pronounced that it was six inches shorter than the normal leg. He wore a built up heel to compensate for the difference. The weight of the bulky heel made him labor to drag the twisted leg along at the same speed as the good one. His face was always contorted from the effort of his walking, making him look as if he were spoiling for a fight. He looked like he had sprung full grown from Henry Moore's head, a malevolent, Venus-like incarnation of Henry's hatred for dishonesty.

The story was that his leg had been broken in Oklahoma by some hoods. They had dumped him out on the prairie and run over him. Then they left him there, thirty miles from the nearest town.

One brave floorman called out a greeting to him. Clarence reared back and looked at the boss through his half-glasses. He smiled and waved. He delighted in how nervous he was making everyone.

Clarence liked the video monitoring room. Tim spent a lot of time watching Clarence watch the monitors. Clarence, at Henry's request, was zeroing in on *BJ 67.* Jimmy had the first five monitors of Argus's hundred eyes showing *BJ 67.* Each was a different angle with its own telephoto focus. Nothing the dealer could do would go undetected. Tonight *BJ 67* was a middle-aged woman, a black guy, and a young whore (or "Hustlin' woman," as Clarence called her), and a big beefy guy playing three hands at a time. He considered himself an expert at blackjack and insisted on giving the hooker lessons.

Tim watched them with Clarence for two hours.

Nothing happened. The black guy, who remarked "I'm gambling, I'm really gambling," everytime he lost a hand, eventually went broke and quit.

Clarence had Jimmy turn the sound off because he got fed up with the beefy loudmouth's stupid instructions for winning at blackjack.

Hector came in. He knew the loud mouth. His name was Ron Roskoe. He owed the Ondine over fifty thousand in markers.

"Maybe the cheating isn't there," said Tim to Clarence in frustration. "If it were there, we'd have seen it by now."

It was getting late, almost four. The casino closed at six.

"Henry says the per here is four," said Clarence.

"Maybe Henry's system is wrong," said Tim. "You say they like to operate when the casino is crowded. This table isn't even full."

"One empty chair," said Clarence. He had dealt with such na iveté before and it made him weary. "One empty chair in the biggest casino in the world, and he thinks all the cheaters have gone home."

Clarence was hard to talk to, quite a different kind of man than Hector Knute. Hector was amenable and flattering, easy to like; but Clarence preferred confrontations to flattery. He was spoiling for opportunities to prove he would be accommodating to no one.

"What about bad luck," said Tim.

"What about it?" returned Clarence.

"It does operate against the house once in awhile, doesn't it?" asked Tim. "That table could have a bad *per* because of prolonged bad luck, couldn't it?"

"Bad luck," snickered Clarence.

"Yes," insisted Tim, annoyed. "Bad luck."

"You know who these guys are?" asked Clarence, suddenly looking away from the monitors and tilting his head back to study Tim through his half-glasses. "Have you read Knute's file on this guy Fingo for example?"

Fingo was the dealer at *BJ 67.*

"Let me tell you about the kind of people that work in casinos," said Clarence. "These are the guys who have all flopped at real jobs. Either they're too lazy or too dumb or too crazy to work like real people. Like Fingo here. He was a checkout clerk in a supermarket and he paid his way through college short-changing old ladies. You've even got an embezzler in here that almost went to jail for taking off a bank. They've all got clean records all right, but that's because they didn't get convicted, not because they didn't do it. Look, Tim, it's just the nature of these guys to steal.

Who did you expect to find in these joints anyway? Guys with engineering degrees?"

Tim sighed. He didn't like lectures.

"Just don't start thinking that all the money is disappearing because you're having bad luck," continued Clarence. "That's a gambler's rationale and it's pure—"

He was suddenly quiet.

"What's wrong?"

"Now he's got all orange checks," said Clarence, quickly. "You made me miss it. Roll it back Jimmy. Take it back a couple of minutes. It happened while I was shooting my mouth off."

Jimmy pressed some buttons and rolled the video tape back. The three of them watched in silence.

"There it is!" shouted Clarence angrily.

In an instant he was off his stool and hurrying out the door, dragging his bad leg along behind him much faster than usual.

"I didn't even see it," said Tim. "Did you see it?"

"I'll show you again," said Jimmy.

He rewound the tape and Tim looked again. This time he saw it. Fingo was very quick. He was changing stacks to pay the hooker's dollar bet. Red checks. The stack came out in his hand, dropped a red check next to the girl's dollar, then suddenly Fingo's hand was empty and an all orange stack was standing right in front of Roskoe.

Orange chips were a thousand dollars a piece. The beefy loud-mouth quickly drew back to him other checks as if he won a bet.

Fingo went on to pay the other hands. No one at the table even noticed what had happened.

Tim suddenly understood how cheating could be widespread and serious enough to affect the Ondine's results without being readily visible. With one move, which had required only an instant to perform, Fingo and Roskoe had stolen thirty thousand dollars.

"LISTEN, TIM, I was only trying to get back to even," said Roskoe in a loud, grating voice.

He was sitting across from Tim's desk. He was bigger than he looked on the monitor. He was as tall as Tim, though he weighed forty pounds more. His stomach swelled out between the lapels of his polished cotton suit. From the moment the security man had brought him in, he had been talking to Tim as if they were brothers.

On Roskoe's heels had come Fingo with Clarence. Fingo was insisting he hadn't done anything. He wasn't going to be fooled with any video tape story. He wanted to see it. Clarence had shoved him in the video room and quickly slammed the door.

"I wouldn't cheat," continued Roskoe in his grating voice. "I'm not that kind of guy. I'm so far down to you guys, and I've got such business problems, I had to try to get even. I wouldn't have actually taken any money from you guys."

Roskoe looked to Hector Knute and then to the guard for some encouragement. He even looked all the way around to Henry who was busy at the telex.

Getting no encouragement, he turned back to Tim. His face was puffy. Even from across the desk he smelled of too many cigarettes. His fingers, between his first two nails, were amber with nicotine.

"You understand, don't you, Tim?" he asked.

He was affecting sincerity. He had the air of someone who was used to being believed, no matter how obvious his lies might be.

"I mean I owe you a lot of money," he added.

"How much does he owe us, Hector?" asked Tim.

"Fifty-two thousand," answered Hector. "If you want to give him the benefit of the doubt on the eight thousand he had in chips before Fingo passed him the stack of thirty. You probably don't want to give him the benefit of the doubt, because it's a safe bet he and Fingo took that off, too. If not tonight, last night."

"Did you steal the eight thousand?" Tim asked Roskoe.

"Steal is a strong word for it, isn't it?" asked Roskoe.

"Answer the question," snapped Hector.

"No, I didn't steal it," said Roskoe, "I won it. Come on, Tim. I'll cooperate with you guys. I admit Eddie passed me a stack. But, listen, I wasn't going to walk out of here with any of that money. I was going to have it taken off my marker. I was trying to get even. That's all."

"Mr. Roskoe, will you please stop bullshitting us," said Hector, moving his round little body quickly in front of the big man. "You were going to cash out as much as you dared and split it with Fingo. He hasn't been passing you checks every night because he's worried about your markers, has he? He does require a little cash for *his* cooperation, doesn't he?"

Hector stood before Roskoe, his mouth puckering animatedly.

"You look at my record, Tim," said Roskoe, trying to ignore Hector. "You'll see I've been paying my markers down. I haven't taken cash out of here in months."

"How high has his debt been?" asked Tim.

"A hundred and twenty thousand," said Hector.

"See," said Roskoe confidently. "I only got into this because I'm having trouble with my business."

Roskoe talked on about how tough things were for him, his obnoxious voice mixing with Henry's work at the telex to make an irritating combination. He looked up at the ceiling as he spoke, as if he were pretending he weren't there. His tone accused them all of stupidity. Any fool could see they had no right to put him in this unpleasant situation. His cheating the Ondine out of thousands of dollars was eminently forgivable as far as he could see.

It got to Hector again.

"We have the whole thing on tape, Mr. Roskoe," Hector interrupted. "You talk like a martyred saint, but we have pictures of you committing grand theft."

"What do you mean?" Roskoe's face grew even puffier, like a blowfish inflating when it's threatened.

"You're a thief, Mr. Roskoe," said Hector angrily. "When you steal those chips, you steal money. Fingo didn't explain that to you, did he?"

"Hey, Tim, I'm sorry about this," he said, his swollen face now full of genuine fear. "They'll put me out of business if this gets out."

"Who'll put you out of business?" asked Tim.

"I'm in the liquor business," he said. "I can't be accused of a felony. I'll lose my license, and so will my brother-in-law. I've already taken several hundred thousand out of the business to pay for some of this gambling I've been doing. If I go out of business, my sister will sneak into my house and put a bread knife in me. She's already found out about all the money I borrowed against the business—"

"Please, Mr. Roskoe," interrupted Hector with disdain. "No more bullshitting."

"It's true!" he said. "It's true. You guys got your share of it, I swear. If you don't believe me—"

"All right, Roskoe, that's enough," said Tim. "You don't have to whine. We're not going to put you out of business."

As obnoxious as Roskoe was, the mention of his business problems touched a nerve in Tim.

"I'll pay back the fifty-two thousand," said Roskoe, as if he hadn't heard Tim. "You don't—"

"Sixty thousand," corrected Hector.

"All right, sixty thousand," conceded Roskoe. "I'll pay you back a thousand a week. We'll fatten the whiskey bills each month, and I'll refund a thousand every week. That way I can make it. Believe me, I don't have a cent of my own."

"We do business with him?" asked Tim.

"Sure," said Hector. "He supplies every hotel in Atlantic City with booze. He's the local wholesaler. He's rolling in dough."

"No, I'm not!" protested Roskoe. "I was. Sure I was. When all these hotels came in, I was making plenty of money. But now my expenses are impossible."

"Expenses?" asked Tim. "What expenses? Liquor sells itself."

"He's talking about his gambling debts," said Hector. "Guys like this have a way of calling them expenses."

"I owe everybody," said Roskoe. "I owe Playboy. I owe the Pier. I owe Sinbad's. I owe you guys. I'm on the edge and another thousand a week will probably do it, but I have no choice. Right? I never did. Do you think I got involved with this creep Fingo shoving chips across the table at me because I enjoy it?"

"No, Mr. Roskoe," said Hector. "We think you got involved with Fingo because you're a thief."

"Yeah, right," said Roskoe bitterly. "Flush Roskoe down the tubes like every other shit heel that can't pay. That's what all you guys say, isn't it?"

"No," said Tim.

"Then what?" demanded Roskoe. "You think a thousand a week isn't going to do it? With this thousand, I'm up to five thousand a week. Plus what I play in cash. Show me a business that can support that kind of load, and I'll get right into it."

"Is he telling the truth?" Tim asked Hector. "Does he owe money all over Atlantic City?"

"Who knows," said Hector.

"He does," said Henry from the telex. It was chattering away. "He owes ninety thousand at Playboy, twenty at the Pier, forty at Flowers, and a hundred and fifty at Sinbad's. They're all being paid off by arrangement."

"How much cash have you lost to us?" Tim asked Roskoe.

"Thirty, forty grand at least," said Roskoe. "Maybe fifty. Who counts?"

"Okay, that's enough then," said Tim. "But don't ever come back in here."

"What?" asked Roskoe.

"I'm going to tear up your markers," said Tim. "But don't ever come back in here. We won't let you play."

"You're letting him off?" asked Hector, shocked.

"That's right," said Tim.

"Thanks a lot, Tim," said Roskoe, flashing a giant smile. "You're a gentleman. A real gentleman. Thanks a lot. And don't worry. I'll never bother you guys again."

He was gone quickly, grinning in triumph at Hector as he left.

"That fucking son of a bitch," said Hector as the door closed. "I have never heard such bullshit in my entire life. Shit! Why the hell did you let him go?"

"We don't have to put people out of business to make money, Hector," said Tim.

"He isn't going out of business!" spit Hector in exasperation. "That's player's bullshit. And shit! Even if he is going broke, he'll be down at the Terrarium ten minutes from now, playing on credit and making some kind of arrangement with them. You got to make these people pay or you're going to fill up the casino with deadbeats."

"Hector's right, Tim," said Henry quietly. "Credit in casinos is a funny thing because of the people who lie all the time."

"Damn right!" said Hector. "Roskoe will have to pay at Sinbad's. He'll have to pay at Playboy. He'll have to pay everywhere but here. What's going to happen to us when he starts telling everyone how he sold you sixty thousand dollars worth of bullshit."

"We'll get more business?" mocked Tim.

"All the wrong kind," said Hector. "And don't think he's going to call you a nice guy when he brags about how he got out of paying. He's going to call you a stupid asshole."

"He can call me an asshole if he wants," responded Tim angrily. "But he's the asshole. And so are the people at Sinbad's. And Playboy. And whoever else who thinks they owe it to themselves and their honor and their business to nail idiots like Roskoe. They're the assholes. Not me."

Hector threw up his arms in despair. "In the next week we're going to get at least two hundred bad checks. You watch."

The door to the video room opened. Ed Fingo came walking sullenly into the office, followed by Clarence.

"Sit down," ordered Clarence.

Fingo sat down in the same chair Roskoe had just occupied.

"Tell him," Clarence ordered Fingo. "Only the swindles you've seen yourself or the guys who have bragged to you personally. No rumors. Just the ones you know for sure."

Fingo looked at Clarence with impatience. He had worked hard at making an impression on Tim. He was one of the few dealers Tim called by name. He didn't like Oxman making him out to be some kind of a hand job.

"Hey, look, Tim, I'm sorry," said Fingo, tossing his thick black hair up off his forehead. "I know you must be pissed off at me. Hell, I didn't like doing it to you. I don't mind sticking somebody like Laboy or McGray. They're pricks, but I know you like me, not that I'm a favorite or anything—"

"Kissing ass isn't going to help," interrupted Clarence.

"I know," said Fingo, irritated. "But Donna really needed the money because she has to put her younger brother through Duke . . ."

Everyone involved with gambling seemed to have a nozzle and hose connected to the same incredible reservoir of bullshit, and Tim was suddenly tired of being sprayed with it.

"Eddie," he said curtly, "just tell me if you know any other dealers and bosses who have been stealing regularly."

"I've seen Ferguson working with a black guy," said Fingo. "It's the old one with the green felt vest. Johnson is working with a retired hooker at BJ 64. I think she's in it just for the thrill, because Jonnie says she doesn't need the money. She never had a pimp and she saved it all. Then at number 57 right behind me, Elaine works with the young marrieds. She has a new pair of them in there every night. Lord knows where she gets them all. Next to her, the Jewish guy, what's his name, Firestein?"

"What are all the floormen doing while this is going on?" asked Tim.

"It depends," answered Fingo. "Nothing happens when Teddy Long is around because everybody knows that domino will nail you in a second, white or black. But Hernandez and Whitcas, they don't do anything even if they're right on top of it."

"They see you and do nothing?" asked Tim, very irritated.

"They have their reasons," said Fingo. "Hernandez is just plain chickenshit. And Whitcas, he cheers me on because he gets twenty percent of everything. That's why his name is on most of my fill slips."

"Whitcas takes twenty percent of everything you steal?" asked Tim.

"Well, yes," granted Fingo, then looking up at the ceiling like a bad boy. "At least he thinks it's twenty percent anyway."

Henry Moore moved quickly to the door and went out into the outer offices where his computer was.

"Those are the ones he's seen himself," said Clarence. "Now

let's hear about the ones that bragged to you."

"I'd say your crap pit is your worst problem," said Fingo knowl-edgeably, his voice taking on a professional tone. "I hear they are taking out some real money over there. They get whole teams of guys to come in and fill up a table. If a legitimate dollar tries to crowd in, they get nasty with the guy until he goes away. Once they have things set, they slip in the bustouts. Man, when they get cooking with those funny dice, they really make the check racks rattle."

Fingo had several more similar stories. He bragged that he knew far more than most about what was going on in the casino. He compared himself favorably to McGray several times. Tim listened quietly, now too amazed to be angry.

"Look, I've been stealing and I admit it," said Fingo. "But I'm telling you right now you've seen the end of it. When I give my word, I mean it. Now, I think I've proved myself valuable to you."

He let this last assertion hang. He looked at Tim, waiting for him to agree.

"What are you getting at, Fingo?" asked Clarence suspiciously.

"I deserve a chance, Tim," said Fingo, ignoring Clarence. "Laboy was going to make me second man in the B twenty-one pit. I think I can do a good job there."

"You mean you want to be a pit boss?" asked Tim.

"Sure," said Fingo nervously. "I've just proved how valuable I can be. I know what's going on. I can stop these guys for you."

"You're not going to be a pit boss, Fingo," said Clarence, his disgust twisting his sandpaper jaw at an ugly angle. "You're going to jail. We've got you on tape, and you're going to jail."

"You want to put him in jail?" asked Tim.

"Of course," said Clarence, turning on Tim. "You can't make this guy a pit boss. Don't you know that's how half of them got to be bosses. They're snitches. Cowards. They never forget how to steal, either. That's what's wrong with the whole rotten mess out there."

"Wait a minute, Clarence," said Hector. "You can't ask Tim to start putting guys in jail. He doesn't know what that means in this business."

"What does it mean?" asked Tim.

"It's just not done, Tim," said Hector. "And if you started, you'd get a mutiny on your hands out there. I don't know how or what they'd use to get back at you, but they would, and like Clarence keeps saying, these are not nice people."

"Hey, listen, Tim," said Fingo. "I may be a little bit of a snitch, but I'm no coward. I can handle these guys, I swear."

Tim thought about it. He didn't like the idea of putting someone in jail for doing something that was almost a custom in the business. And he also didn't like the way Clarence kept talking to him like an idiot. It pained him that now, with Fingo's revelations, he needed Clarence more than ever.

"You're thinking about making him a pit boss, aren't you?" demanded Clarence.

"He's not going to be a pit boss," said Tim. "Eddie, you're finished here. You'll have to find a job somewhere else."

"Damn!" said Fingo, looking away from Tim in disappointment.

"Get out of here, Fingo," said Clarence.

Fingo got up and went for the door.

"You're lucky you aren't on your way to jail," said Clarence. "Make sure you tell your buddies that the next one I get on tape is going."

Fingo stopped in the middle of the door.

"You cocksucker," he said to Tim. "I tell you every story in the casino and you fuck me."

He slammed the door hard.

"You've got to put them in jail, Tim," said Clarence, shaking his head in disgust.

"You and I are going to do some hard work together, Clarence," said Tim. "We're going to watch these guys Fingo was talking about, and I want you to teach me how to spot this stuff myself."

"Fine," said Clarence. "I'm happy to do it. But we're wasting our time unless we start putting them in jail. What do they have to lose if we don't? Fingo will go to the next gambling town and get a new job now. Any of them can do the same. So what's to discourage them from stealing you blind?"

"Where's Henry?" Tim asked Hector. "I want the *pers* on every table Fingo mentioned."

"He slipped out in the middle of Fingo's speech," said Hector. "I'll get him."

Before he got to the door, Henry came rushing into the office.

"I've got it!" he crowed.

He was grinning and his eyes were shining through his oversized glasses.

"I told you there was no such thing as an honest casino manager," he proclaimed.

"What are you talking about?" asked Tim.

Henry laid a sheet of gray repstripe paper on Tim's desk. It was a readout from the computer. It had a long column of numbers on it, some of them circled in red.

"We've got McGray and a group of ten of them," said Henry. "It goes back to the day Laboy was fired. The information was in there, but I hadn't asked the computer the right question. It finally came to me when Fingo was talking about fill slips. This fill slip recap proves they're stealing more than twenty thousand a night."

Tim looked at the column of figures. The ones circled in red were all within a few dollars of twenty thousand. Every night since Tim had arrived at the Ondine, McGray had signed for twenty thousand at different pits around the casino. The bosses who countersigned in each pit were always the same.

"Twenty thousand a night," said Henry. "Think of what that's doing to the per. That's six million in a year."

When Tim stepped into the dice pit the next night, McGray came running up to him waving Tim's memo at him.

"I'm not going to do any of this!" he called from across the casino.

His cheeks were glowing with bright red crosshatching. He had been drinking before he came to work. He favored martinis, and at Sinbad's they came in large beakers.

"What are you trying to prove?" he demanded of Tim. "You think you are ready to take over everything here, don't you?"

Everyone looked around to see who McGray was shouting at. He was always blustering about the casino after someone or other. When they all saw it was Tim, several dealers and bosses began to crowd around.

"I simply want to sign every fill slip for ten thousand or over," said Tim, making an intense effort to stop himself from doing anything stupid.

"I'll bet it's this little creep's idea," said McGray, pointing at Henry.

Henry grinned at McGray. "I helped."

"You'd better keep this little prick away from me, Seagurt," warned McGray. "And Oxman, too. I don't want to have anything to do with either one of them. And just forget about anyone bringing you any slips to sign."

McGray's booze sweet breath was washing all over Tim's face in warm disgusting pulses.

"I want to see those slips before the chips are paid out," ordered Tim, anger creeping into his voice.

"What the fuck are you talking about?" McGray asked. "You Wall Street guys are incredible. You think you can come in here and treat a casino like it's an insurance company. You just write a memo and everything changes, huh?"

McGray turned to the crowd of dealers and bosses.

"Did you see his memo about comps? He thinks he's going to cut comps in half."

There were muffled laughs across the pit. A host shook his head in disapproval.

"You cut comps in half and there won't be a hotel on the boardwalk that will give our players a show reservation. You didn't think of that, did you? You're just jerking off, Seagurt. This signing slips is the same kind of crap. I'm not going to salute this kind of bullshit. What do you want to sign slips for? You couldn't tell a real one from a phony if they came in different colors. I could take a million dollars a week out of this joint, and you'd never see it. A million dollars a week and you'd never see it. Signing slips won't stop a damn thing."

Tim was so furious he couldn't stand to look at McGray. He averted his eyes and his gaze was caught by McGray's hand unconsciously shuffling a stack of dollar checks.

"Go back to your offices and leave the casino to me," ordered McGray.

"Get out of here, McGray," said Tim, staring at the chips, anger cracking his voice as if he had a cold.

"What?"

"Go home," said Tim. "Somebody will bring you a check for what we owe you."

"You can't fire me," grinned McGray. "You wouldn't have a prayer here without me."

"You're out of here now. That memo was your last chance to survive."

Tim looked up at him and the message began to register.

"You want to play rough?" asked McGray in disbelief. Executive types, in McGray's experience, seldom required more than one loud bluff to quiet.

"I don't give a shit if they all pick up their tables and follow you out of here, Don," said Tim, his voice cracking again. "You get out of here now or I'll have somebody lead you out."

McGray looked at him in shock, suddenly dull and stupid, his hand manipulating the red checks even faster.

"It's not that easy," bristled McGray, recovering from his shock. "Don't think this is all there is to it."

"What can he do?" Tim asked Hector later, after McGray had made his angry exit from the crap pit.

Hector didn't answer. It was Hector's policy not to be the bearer of bad news. His silence worried Tim, despite Henry's enthusiasm for the way he'd humiliated McGray in front of an entire pit.

HAROLD POWELL sat down on his favorite bench in front of the Terrarium. His meal was weighing heavily in his stomach, making him drowsy. He had just come from Fortunatas where he'd had lunch with Jeff Crolich. Crolich was the latest in a long line of people who wondered what the hell this guy Seagurt was up to at the Ondine.

Powell had been trying to handle Seagurt carefully. Seagurt was not the usual kind of man who came to Atlantic City to manage casinos. He had an Ivy League education. Powell was an enthusiastic reader and he liked smart people. He wanted more people like Tim Seagurt to come and run casinos in Atlantic City. But Seagurt, for all his Ivy League, Wall Street background, was turning out to be the same kind of wild and belligerent imbecile as all the rest. Partners and owners from all up and down the boardwalk had been filing into the Ondine to play courtesy money at Seagurt's tables and meet him, but Seagurt didn't even come out. He sent Oxman out, full of pep.

Seagurt's firing of McGray was bound to make things worse. It meant trouble with Kedar Padgett, the black candidate for mayor. Padgett had been unhappy with Seagurt from the beginning because Seagurt hadn't called him and invited him over. Padgett liked to be paid off in person at least once. It was a different but clever twist. Padgett knew he was protected as long as he made the casino manager pay him personally. He was fond of saying it would cost a casino its license to try to put him in jail.

Powell had delayed explaining Padgett to Seagurt. Seagurt was too new to Atlantic City. Powell himself had kept Padgett happy with five thousand of each week's income from the Ondine. (There was considerably more coming out, but McGray and his crew and Powell himself had to have their shares because they were taking the risks.) But now Seagurt had fired McGray in front of the whole casino, and everyone knew it was over the money that was going to Padgett. Except Seagurt, of course. His was the mixture of ignorance and arrogance that trouble is made of. Especially now, because Padgett wanted a visit from Seagurt with some money, and he wanted it right away.

Powell leaned back against the boardwalk bench and fell into a light sleep. He began to dream. The Blenheim materialized before him in black, yellow, and white Moorish grandeur. He could see people up on its mezzanine patio. The women were wearing white satin evening gowns and their escorts wore black swallow tails and high hats. They promenaded back and forth across the patio. They were stiff and terribly erect. They seemed to be gliding on tracks, reminding him of white pipes moving across a shooting gallery. (Shooting galleries had been very popular on the boardwalk when the Blenheim was built.) Suddenly shots spit through his dream, making funny noises like sandpaper against metal, and flaring like sparks from a welder's work. The bullets showered on the figures on the Blenheim patio. They weren't real people; they were porcelain. Many of them collapsed in white shards from the shower of bullets. Powell twitched uncomfortably. A few of the hollow figures continued moving back and forth on their tracks. One had half his face shot off. Another was broken at the shoulder, leaving a jagged hole where her arm and gown had been.

"Cut that out!" Abe hissed at the kid.

The kid turned the rifle away from the old man and cranked a shower of sparks in Abe's direction. Abe started for him.

"Buzz off, nigger," said the kid, then turned away and fled down the boardwalk at full tilt.

Abe turned back to the old man. The noise of the gun and the shower of sparks hadn't disturbed him. He was still snoring. Here was an easy mark if Abe had ever seen one. The luxurious blue blazer issued a compelling invitation to explore inside for the cash that had to be in one of the pockets.

The loose folds of Powell's raspberry cheeks quivered as he snored. His nose, long but square on the end, made him look a little like a dog with a blunted snout. He took in air with a loud sucking noise. Abe had to grin as he watched him sleep. Powell's ears looked as if someone had taken a small cookie, cut it in half, and then stuck the halves to either side of his head. And they weren't level with his eyes where they belonged. They were much lower, as if the person cutting the cookie had been new at building faces and thought the ears belonged in the middle.

"Wake up, Mr. Powell," said Abe, touching Powell gently on the shoulder. "Wake up. You have a call."

Powell came up out of his dream with a start. He was surprised to find himself looking at Abe, and behind Abe the Terrarium, where the Blenheim had just recently turned into a shooting gallery.

"Sorry to wake you," said Abe, "but Mr. DePre wants you to call him right away."

Abe looked at him apprehensively. He was concerned about Powell's falling asleep all the time. Abe's twisted face was all the stranger when it was contorted with worry. Abe called himself Powell's butler. Powell thought it was ridiculous for a black man who didn't know the first thing about manners to call himself a butler, but he understood: Abe didn't want to be mistaken for a bodyguard or a fighter. It was a realistic fear because he was big enough, six-four, and more than ugly enough. His scar, from a burning he had gotten as a kid, was getting whiter and whiter as he got closer to fifty. The scar went all the way down his black cheek to his big lips. His lips had been burned in the fire, too, and they looked as if they had melted uphill right into his scar. The white, striated mark went all the way up into his hair, where the bordering curly bush had turned white too. The rest of his head was glistening black, so that the patch of scarred scalp and white hair looked even uglier. But Abe never acted ashamed of it. In fact, he presented the scar rather proudly, except that he always talked out of the good side of his mouth.

"You know what I like about you, Abe?" said Powell, finally getting up off the bench.

"No, sir."

"I like you because you're so ugly," said Powell.

"Yes, sir, I am," said Abe. "But you ain't no beauty yourself, Mr. Powell."

Powell laughed. "That's another thing I like about you," he said. "You don't take any shit off anybody. Not even the most powerful criminal in Atlantic City."

Now it was Abe's turn to laugh. He knew all Powell's secrets. "You aren't the most powerful criminal in Atlantic City," he said. "You're just the *oldest.*"

They walked down the boardwalk towards the Tommy T. Flowers and Missouri Avenue. Powell still lived in the House on Missouri and Pacific that Nucky had given him fifty years ago. It was a two-story frame house, with his real estate office in the basement. He had made enough money in the past fifty years to buy half of Avalon, but he had refused to move out. He remained loyal to Nucky, which meant loyal to Atlantic City. He had lived through the ruin of the fifties and sixties when almost everyone moved out because they couldn't stand the ugliness. He had lived through the rebuilding of the seventies and early eighties when the rest of them had moved out because they got rich or went busted. Now there weren't twenty faces left on Pacific Avenue he recognized. All the people who had made Atlantic City's glorious past were gone. What the hell was he being loyal to?

"You fell asleep again, Mr. Powell," said Abe.

"I know," said Powell, then whispering because he didn't want the people walking on either side of them to hear. "Did you talk to DePre, or to one of his men?"

"Ernesto Polo," said Abe.

"Was he mad?" asked Powell, knowing the underlings usually reflected their leader's attitudes.

"Impatient," said Abe. "Like all the rest, he seems to think you wait by the phone for his calls. What do you think he's calling about?"

"The same thing everyone is calling about, Abe," said Powell, "Kedar Padgett."

"DePre is the owner of the newest hotel in Atlantic City," added Powell. "He's got a right to be nervous."

"Sure," said Abe sharply.

According to public record, the Pier was owned by a French oil company. Organized crime favored the corporate veil, preferably foreign, as a means for keeping their ownership of hotels secret. It was often suggested in the media that the real owners of Atlantic City hotels were unknown. But the truth was, almost everyone knew. The Casino Control Board knew because it heard rumors. The FBI knew because it monitored the right phones and heard the bragging. And the people who worked at the hotels knew because they were told whom to bow to.

Powell and Abe passed the Shelbourne. A great, dusty blockhouse, it was the last remaining ruin of the old boardwalk. Somebody named King Cerkez from Los Vegas was thinking about buying it and putting up something new.

"Mr. Powell, any fool could have come along and stuck his hand into your jacket while you were snoring there," said Abe. "Don't you think you ought to see a doctor about the way you're falling asleep all the time."

"No," said Powell firmly, precluding any more suggestions.

He knew why he was falling asleep all the time. It was all the traveling. It used to be he could keep these people happy, waiting for them to come to town and visiting them at their hotels. Now he was constantly being summoned to this city or that on a moment's notice to explain about Padgett. And one trip was seldom enough. Their capacity for paranoia was astonishing. They all had wild stories about how such and such a bastard from somewhere had done so and so to them for whatever. They all seemed to be certain that their own personal enemies were behind Padgett, and they wouldn't mind getting to the root of the problems by killing both Padgett and whomever it was they loved to hate. The range and complexity of their delusions was startling. It took hours to unravel even the simplest fabric of their hatreds and to explain that they, their territory, and their lordly honor were not in danger. It was draining to argue with them. He had to bear the brunt of their hostility.

The frequency of these sessions was getting intolerable. The thought of going up to New York that night to face DePre again made him tired. DePre, perhaps with some justification, thought he was the cleverest extra-legal power figure in America. The trouble was, so did all the rest of them. Each and everyone of them, no matter where they ranked in reality, thought they were the cleverest, the bravest, and the most ruthless of all, right down to the guy from Akron who just bought Xanadu. Yesterday this man, who owned a thirty-room motel, a tiny little bush beneath a forest of hotels with five hundred rooms or more, had passed Powell all of a thousand dollars and leaned over to whisper, in confidence, that he expected to figure in Atlantic City. And figure big. They were all like that.

"Maybe I should just let DePre make Padgett disappear," said Powell. "Then I could get some sleep."

"If Padgett gets hurt, those kids will run into Sinbad's or some place like it and start a war. Then where will Atlantic City be?"

"Of course they will," agreed Powell with obvious irritation. "You try explaining that to some of these guys. It only makes them grin."

They had reached his house and they walked down the outside steps to his basement office. Abe unlocked the door and Powell followed him in. It was an unpretentious office that actually looked like its occupant might be in the business of finding rooms for boarders, which Powell had done, in fact, for twenty-five years. Of course there were no boarding houses left now. He missed having people come to his office begging for the first opening at Sally Levitt's table. Sally, long since dead, knew how to bake a pie.

"Why doesn't Padgett shut up?" demanded Powell. "How much does he want? Doesn't he know he's making himself a target? One of these small town guys might kill him just to get it all started. Doesn't he worry about that?"

"I don't think so," said Abe.

"These guys are all so tight up against each other on the board-walk—"

Powell didn't finish. Abe had heard it before.

"Why is he so stuck on the Ondine?" asked Powell.

"The Ondine is right on the border of the Inlet," said Abe. "Its the one they all see everytime they step outside. Of course they've got a case on about it."

Powell dialed the number Abe had jotted down on his blotter. "I'll probably have to go up there again tonight. If I don't, he'll insist on sending Robles down here."

"You don't want that man here working on your problems," said Abe quickly.

"You don't have to tell me that," sighed Powell. He felt a morbid wave of affection for Nucky. Nucky could handle people like Robles. Yes, even people like Robles. He had handled Joey Adonis when he went after Lansky's new wife, hadn't he? He could handle people like Robles, all right. Powell couldn't. With Edgar Robles in town, the thin tissue of reason he had wrapped around all the hate incubating up and down the boardwalk would be nothing more than flashpaper in a shower of sparks.

The stealing in the Ondine was uncontainable. Everywhere Tim and Clarence looked, they found theft. Patience was no longer needed; no table required more than five minutes to find the bad move. It was an education for Tim. He and Clarence replayed the video tapes of every move they caught until Tim had the idea and pattern behind everything wrong that could happen at a gambling table. After three hours of it, he began to find the bad moves almost as quickly as Clarence.

They called the dealers in and fired them as they caught them. It was a simple ceremony. None of the dealers argued. Tim and Clarence waited for the word to spread through the casino and stop the reprisal. Tim was certain it was all a reprisal for his firing McGray. It was their way of making good on McGray's promise to take millions without him seeing any of it. But he was seeing it, and it was costing them their jobs, and he didn't think these dealers had the kind of psyches to be martyrs. He imagined they wouldn't care much about evening anything up for McGray if it meant their jobs. He imagined it would stop soon.

They fired eighteen dealers in three hours, but it wasn't enough. The cheating continued, and the payout sheet told an ugly story. Money was flooding out of the Ondine. For every dealer they caught, ten went on taking what they wanted undetected. And every dealer Tim fired grinned at him as if he knew something Tim didn't.

"You won't put them in jail," said Clarence, "so they laugh at you."

"Let's just catch them and keep cleaning out the bad ones," insisted Tim.

"This place is too big," said Clarence. "They are going at it all the time and the place is too big. We might have to live with some losses until we get this mess cleaned up."

"Losses?"

"Didn't they tell you every once in awhile a casino loses money?" asked Clarence sarcastically.

"This one had better not," snapped Tim. "Or Alfred Oakes will close it."

"He'll close it?" asked Clarence, looking at Tim through his half-glasses as if he were insulted. "He'll close it for one night's loss?"

"That's right."

"All right," said Clarence, clenching his unshaven jaw. "I'll stop these guys for you, and I'll stop them tonight."

"How are you going to do that?"

"You watch," he said, turning back to the monitors.

The door from his office opened and Caro came in. She and Tim had a date to meet Butch Crolich, Jeff Crolich's son, for the show at Fortunatas. She was wearing a pink blouse and skirt with a matching pink sport coat. The silk blouse was unbuttoned for the first four buttons showing the round tops of her tan breasts. He went over to kiss her cheek.

"Jesus, you look beautiful," he whispered in her ear.

She smiled. "Are you ready?"

"I can't go."

He took her to the casino bar, and they had a drink while he explained. He told her to go alone if she wanted and she readily agreed. When they had first come to the Ondine three weeks ago, she had spent several nights sitting in the casino with him for long hours, but she didn't like it any more. There was something about it that made her nervous now.

Tim was returning to his office when he heard a shout from inside the video room. He opened the door and found Clarence with a dealer named Johnson.

"Look at that, man," Johnson was moaning. "Look what you did to me. Look what he did to me, Tim."

He showed Tim a knob on his shin just below his knee. It was swelling up right through the tight fabric of his pants making an ugly satin egg.

"Let me alone, Clarence," said Johnson. "Let me get back to work."

"I'm going to take your knee right off," said Clarence.

He swung his bad leg at Johnson again. He whipped it around with a violent twist of his hip, and it was surprising how quick he was. The big club of his built-up heel swung towards Johnson's knee like a black baseball bat.

But this time Johnson was ready for it and he hopped back out of the way.

"Fuck you guys," said Johnson. "I'm getting out of here. I quit."

He hobbled by Tim and out the door.

"What the hell are you doing, Clarence?" asked Tim.

"If you don't want a loss in this casino tonight, we've got to start beating the shit out of some of these guys," said Clarence. "That's the only way to stop a stampede like this one."

"We're not going to beat people up," said Tim, annoyed.

"It's the only way to stop them," repeated Clarence.

"If that's the price, I'm not going to pay it," said Tim. "I doubt if it would help anyway."

"So what?" asked Clarence angrily turning back to the wall of monitors. "At least we can get some licks in on these sons of bitches."

Tim stared at Clarence. Clarence was scanning the monitors eagerly. Clarence wasn't unhappy about the situation at all. He was delighted to be presented with an excuse for beating the hell out of a few dealers.

"Oh, no," said Clarence suddenly, "Oh, shit!"

Tim looked quickly at the bank of monitors. "Which one? What's happening?"

"*BJ 43,*" said Clarence.

Two men were sitting down at *BJ 43*. One of them was an old man; the other was a giant.

The old man had raspberry stained cheeks which hung down below his opaque eyes in loose folds. He had a swollen nose which came to a blunt end. His hair, brown and short, was fluffy and thick like animal fur.

"No wonder all these guys are going wild," said Clarence. "No wonder the place is out of control."

"Who are they?" asked Tim.

"It's Harold Powell," said Clarence. "He's got Edgar Robles with him. I can't believe it. What are they letting Robles loose for?"

"So that's Powell," marvelled Tim. He had heard much about this criminal figure and he found it fascinating to see him.

"Yeah, and the big one is Robles," said Clarence. "He doesn't look sixty, does he?"

The big one was six-nine or more and weighed at least two hundred and eighty pounds. He had the classic symptoms of a thyroid disorder. His jaw jutted out and his hands were quite large. But while most thyroid monsters are made ugly by over-sized hands and jaws, this one had long, graceful fingers and his jaw came out on a straight line. His nose, equally straight and well formed, was large enough to make the jaw proportionate. He had hooded dark eyes. He was handsome. He looked closer to forty-five than sixty. He reached into the pocket of his leather sport coat and produced a packet of thousand dollar bills to buy chips.

"You're a quick study, Tim," said Clarence. "You know it all already. You don't need me any more."

"What are you talking about?" asked Tim.

"I've got to get back to Vegas," said Clarence. "There's no future in screwing around with Edgar Robles."

"What's so bad about Robles?" asked Tim, amazed at Clarence. "We've had mob people in here before. You usually run out into the pits to taunt them."

"Robles isn't like the assholes that have been coming around here," said Clarence derisively. "I'm going back to Vegas."

"You don't even know what he wants," said Tim. "You're leaving simply because he sits down to play blackjack?"

"He wants more than a game of cards," said Clarence, starting by Tim. "That's why you've had all this stealing tonight."

Tim caught his arm as Clarence started to leave. "Wait a minute. What do they have to do with all this stealing?"

"Every dealer in here must have been promised their protection," said Clarence. "Now I've kicked around somebody who was under Robles' protection, and I'm getting out of here before he finds out."

Clarence shook himself loose from Tim's grip and walked away with the peculiar rocking motion that meant he was in a hurry. His twisted leg curled rapidly up and down as he rocked himself through the door and disappeared.

"Put *BJ 43* on the first five screens," said Tim.

"Right," said Jimmy.

Robles was taking out another packet of thousand dollar bills. He must have lost the first buy already. He bought twenty-five thousand more.

Powell didn't play. He sat and watched Robles. Robles was playing like an idiot. He was playing five hands at a time, leaving a spot open for a Vietnamese man. He waved off hitting eight. He hit nineteen. He was deliberately losing.

"Put the sound on," said Tim.

In an instant, the din of the casino came rushing into the quiet monitoring room. Tim heard Robles talking to Powell with a deep Cuban accent.

"How about this one, Harold?" he asked Powell. "Shall we hit this one?"

The hand was an ace and a king, a natural blackjack. Powell smiled an indifferent feline smile. Robles was playing a little game he didn't wholly approve of.

"Is it illegal to hit this one?" he asked the dealer.

"Not for you, Mr. Robles," said the dealer.

"Then give me a card."

"The man hits soft twenty-one," called the dealer theatrically.

He drew a card out of the shoe. It was a ten.

"He makes hard twenty-one!" announced the dealer.

"Give me another card," said Robles.

The dealer drew out a jack.

"Chinga!" sniggered Robles in mock despair. "Now I'm really busted."

"True," said the dealer. "But you have the distinction of having scored the first soft forty-one in the history of blackjack."

Robles laughed appreciatively.

"This is fun," he said.

At five thousand a hand, he was losing twenty-five thousand a deal. He withdrew a fresh bundle of thousands from his leather jacket. Tim could hear the paper crackle as the dealer counted them right on top of the mike. The Vietnamese watched with interest.

"Fifty thousand," said the dealer.

"Where's Seagurt?" Robles asked.

Tim felt a tremor of discomfort.

"Get the boss out here," said Robles. "Tell him I want to play ten grand a hand."

·11·

POWELL SURPRISED Tim with his charm. He gave off a personal
warmth that was very pleasant. It was a strange quality to find in
such an ugly man.

Robles was the opposite. He was quiet and hostile. Now finished
gambling, he sprawled across the couch in Tim's office watching
impatiently while Powell talked about the gambling commission.

"Do you think they do much to keep this town orderly?" Powell
asked Tim.

"No," said Tim.

Tim had met the commission in the process of getting approval
as casino manager of the Ondine. If something was keeping Atlantic City orderly, it wasn't them. Powell was making it clear
that it was Powell himself.

"Tim, I can protect you from your dealers," he said.

"Thank you, Harold," said Tim, being polite and respectful.
(What was the point in making somebody with Powell's reputa-
tion angry?) "But I'd rather do it myself. That's why I came to
Atlantic City."

"You're not doing too well right now," said Powell.

"I know."

"Tim, I'd like you to take Don McGray back on," he said, the
warmth in his manner glowing suddenly brighter. "He got a little
drunk and tried to make a fool of you. So what? He's a good man.
I've known him ever since he was a dealer at the 500 Club forty
years ago. I'll vouch for him."

"I'm sorry, Harold," said Tim, getting ready for a difficult argument. Powell interrupted him.

"I'd also like you to hire back all the dealers you fired here
tonight," he said. "Who you fire after I walk out of here tonight
doesn't matter, even if it's the same guys, but for now, I want you
to take them all back."

"I wouldn't have any control over anybody in the Ondine if I did
that," said Tim.

"I'll keep control for you," said Powell quietly. "I also want you
to pay Kedar Padgett with the hundred and twenty-five thousand
Edgar gave you."

"Padgett?"

"Not all of it, of course," said Powell. "He's not that expensive.

What he doesn't need, you keep for yourself."

"I don't understand," said Tim. "Are you so worried about Padgett that you'd give me money to pay him off?"

"Yes."

"You think he's a real threat to legalized gambling?" asked Tim.

"Yes," said Powell. "Just because the state legalized gambling, it doesn't mean Atlantic City has to have it. Atlantic City is a municipality with its own rights. Gambling can be voted out of a town the same way liquor can. Just like one of these Quaker towns voting themselves dry."

"Okay, but who would vote for it?" asked Tim.

"Fifty-eight percent of the registered voters on this island are black," said Powell.

Suddenly Tim got the idea. No wonder they were all paying Padgett what he wanted.

"I haven't heard anything from Padgett," said Tim. "He hasn't even asked me for anything."

"That's not the way it works, Tim," said Powell. "You have to call him."

Tim was silent.

"He has the position," said Powell. "He's entitled to be paid by everyone. That's the way he wants it, and we have to cooperate with him."

One of the most troublesome things about the black candidate was his insistence on receiving his money personally. He was almost proud of his willingness to be corrupt, and he didn't care who knew it. He seemed to think it would get him more votes.

"What about how everyone else would feel if you didn't," said Powell. "You would make yourself unpopular with some ugly people."

Robles stirred on the couch.

Powell stared at Tim expectantly.

"That was the Ondine's money he was gambling with," said Tim, nodding at Robles.

Robles laughed. "You call that gambling?"

"No, it wasn't," said Powell. "What they all took tonight, they keep. I'm not getting anything back from anybody."

"A hundred and twenty-five thousand dollars is a lot of money to risk on the chance I'll do what you want," said Tim.

"I have a lot of such money," said Powell philosophically. "I won't miss it. The attitude of the IRS makes my money good only for the things in life which come without receipts. One of the most satisfying is buying men like Padgett."

"Either you pay Padgett," said Robles from the couch. "Or you take his place as the man everyone hates."

"Listen, Tim," added Powell, "when you pay a guy like Padgett, don't expect to lose all your dignity as a man. It works the other way around. He's the one who turns to shit. You'll be surprised how good it feels to own this nigger tuba to toot as you like."

"I'm sorry, Harold," said Tim, smiling apologetically. "I can't do it."

"You mean you *won't* do it," said Powell wearily.

"I mean I can't," insisted Tim. "I have no way of getting that money out. As soon as it goes into the box, it's in the casino machinery, and from that moment there's nothing I can do to get it out."

Powell looked at Robles, clearly irritated with him. He turned back to Tim.

"Come on, Tim," said the ugly man. "I know you're a newcomer, but you didn't get into this business because you don't know how to cover the exit of some money from an operation this size. I've heard you're a real pro at bookkeeping."

"Yes," said Tim happily. "I've been working on bookkeeping controls ever since I got here. Now nobody, not even me, can sneak money out of the Ondine without several clerical alarms going off."

Powell glared at Robles. It had been Robles' idea of fun to gamble money instead of giving it to Tim directly. Powell had been against it because of all the attention it would attract, but Robles had refused to be persuaded.

"Now he has an excuse," Powell said to the giant.

Robles got up off the couch and walked around behind Tim's desk. Tim instinctively stood up. Tim wasn't used to looking up at people; few were that much taller than he. It made him uncomfortable to have Robles so close and to have to look up into his dark eyes.

Tim had taken a perverse delight in telling Powell he couldn't take the money out of the Ondine stream of bookkeeping. Tim wouldn't have agreed to pay Padgett even if Powell had given him the money directly (since he was certain it was the Ondine's money one way or another), but he was delighted to get the best of Powell without a confrontation. He imagined his delight had shown, because Robles was furious now.

"You go out into one of your pits and write a few payout slips," ordered Robles. "You can take all the money you need for Padgett with a few signatures."

"I'm not going to do that," said Tim. "If I do that, I'm no different than Laboy or McGray. If they see me doing that out there, I'm giving them all a license to steal. I didn't come to Atlantic City to loot this casino or to watch anyone else do it either."

Robles turned his head and spat on Tim's desk, as if trying to get the taste of Tim out of his mouth. He turned back, looking down at Tim with hooded eyes.

"You are a fool," Robles said to Tim. "You think you can run a dirty business and act clean. I think you ought to get out of this business if you want to be so clean. Leave gambling houses to people like Mr. Powell who understands them. You believe this is like trading bonds on Wall Street, and hope everyone else will go their own way. No!"

Tim's left eye began to tremble, a signal since childhood that he was frightened. To his amazement, he realized that Robles scared him. He wasn't ready for this. He had never even thought of people like Powell and Robles coming into his office to threaten him.

"You have come into our world," continued Robles, talking to Tim as if he were a child, "now you will respect our business. You are a *puta maricon* like every other casino boss. Now it is time for you to get fucked, so you take off your clothes and bend down like all the rest. Don't answer me 'no' like you've been doing to Mr. Powell. You take his money and do what he wants."

Tim's eye was blinking in spasmodic rushes. His fear was gone. It had been obliterated by his anger. He wanted to start it himself now. He wanted to snap his fist right into the Cuban's face.

How could he be so stupid? Simple surrender would take care of Robles. It was suicidal to think of hitting him. Suddenly Tim realized that as menacing as Robles was, he wasn't the real danger. Tim himself was the danger. Robles was only an iceberg, the same iceberg he had been throwing himself up against again and again at Colony because he couldn't control himself. It was his own emotion that had been screwing him, and it was more powerful than ever now. He didn't want to tell Robles to go fuck himself like he'd wanted to tell half the executives at Colony. He wanted to hit him. He wanted to get him down, and then kick him in the head or balls or wherever he had to to keep him down.

"I'm making you angry?" mocked Robles, suddenly delighted.

Tim had to make himself turn around. He had to turn and walk away. The reality of it was that Robles would crush him, but he hated himself for walking away. He stood there staring at the wall, almost begging himself for permission to turn back and smash Robles as hard as he could. There was a noise, and for an

instant he thought Robles was going to hit him from behind. He
flinched, but Robles was walking towards the door. He heard him
speak to Powell.

"He'll figure something out now," Robles said in triumph.

He felt a rush of shame. The office door closed as he turned
around. The danger passed, he exhaled with relief. Powell
watched him. Tim began to wonder if he hadn't imagined the
desire to hit Robles. It was so stupid that he couldn't believe it had
been a real emotion.

"The stealing is going to stop when I walk back through your
casino," said Powell. "Between what Edgar put into your blackjack game and what you win for the rest of the night, you should
avoid a loss."

Tim looked quickly into the opaque eyes, trying to see if Powell
knew what a loss would mean.

"Yes, I know," said Powell, "All corporate owners are the same.
They get very nervous when their casinos lose money."

Powell stopped at the door Robles had just closed. "Please make
an arrangement with Kedar Padgett, Tim, or you *will* have a loss
tomorrow night. I don't expect you to make a thief of yourself in
front of all your employees as Edgar says, but you do have to find
some way to work things out with Padgett."

Unlike Robles, Powell issued his threats without menace. He
gave Tim a warm smile and went out. Tim sat back down at his
desk. His eye was still trembling. It was several minutes before
he stirred from his chair. He walked into the long video room.
BJ 43 was still on the first five monitors. He flinched again, seeing
Robles's ghost unfolding thousand-dollar bills. But there was no
trace of him or Powell now. The table had all new faces. Even the
Vietnamese was gone.

Tam Van Tram had sensed something different happening at
the Ondine. There was a smell to the way the guards were acting.
Like Saigon *cahn-sat,* they paid attention to nothing suspicious.

Tam, a former colonel in the Army of the Vietnamese Republic,
knew bad security when he saw it. He had been special liason to
MP's in Saigon. They had given him a nickname: Tommy Van.
Americans still called him Tommy Van, though now he was only
a clerk living in a Seven-Eleven store.

At five feet, four inches tall, Tommy was small by his adopted
country's standards. He had a large forehead because his hairline
had retreated back up to the top of his head. Many men in Vietnam looked the same.

For years he had wondered why Americans stared at him so intensely, more than at other Vietnamese. Then he found out it was because they thought he was stupid. He resembled the American idiot children. They were all short with large foreheads and oriental eyes. He found it a laughable mistake. It was enjoyable when they talked to him with the same kind of affection they would show a pet.

Tommy divided his time between his Seven-Eleven store and Washington D.C. He liked to go to D.C. because his friends were there. His wife and Thitch took care of the store while he was away. He and his friends had gone to the capital because they had believed it would be like Saigon. He often tried to persuade them that Atlantic City was better, that the boardwalk was the *cho den* of America. But there was a limit to what a Vietnamese could do in Atlantic City. The work was manual, and Tommy's friends were accustomed to owning stores or commanding batallions. There was no such private enterprise or status in America for Vietnamese, not even in Atlantic City. There was work in hotels as waiters and busboys, and some even found jobs as deckhands on pleasure boats. But Tommy's friends were bitter about such work. They wanted more. It shamed them to learn that Marshall Ky ran a liquor store in California and General Van Ba sold tires in Maryland. And they barely concealed their contempt for Tommy's selling milk and soda in Atlantic City.

Was this what they had clawed their way out of Saigon for in the last days of the republic, they asked him. Unlike simple farmers and fishermen who were fleeing the *bo doi* in blind panic, they hadn't been running away from anything. They had been following something, a way of life they knew the Americans were taking with them. They had assumed they would share a life of money and ease with the Americans as readily as they had in Saigon, only it would be better because the Americans would be the hosts. They had been very much disappointed. The Americans made good guests, but they were cruel hosts, and lately the money had begun to run out.

They had made little new money since leaving Vietnam. The vices they had thrived on in Saigon were difficult to market in the States. Tommy sold chicken, some pills (mighty max became "speed"), *com sa,* and even girls. But the trade was small and the profit smaller. New Jersey wasn't like Saigon where GIs were everywhere eager to buy. Tommy had found out GIs were a special kind of American. They had more appetite. Not all Americans had such desires, and everything was secret in America. Chicken was secret. Pills secret. Even *com sa* was secret. As an officer in the ARVN, he had dealt openly with GIs. Here people were suspicious and afraid. Secret things need trust to market, and Americans didn't trust him. And some police couldn't be bought. Two of his cousins were in jail.

The only vice that Americans pursued in the open was gambling. They gambled incredible sums, the kind of money Tommy was used to handling in Saigon. Tommy wanted to get into the gambling business. As soon as he had seen it, he had moved to Atlantic City from Washington and taken over the Seven-Eleven. Since then he had invested a lot of money in casinos, trying to make friends with the bosses behind the ropes. He was pursuing the same simple plan that had made him rich in Saigon: Find the important Americans and make friends with them. That was how he had gone from a sidewalk cowboy to colonel in the army in less than ten years. He had found the powerful Americans and given them what they wanted. But the men behind casino ropes, though they smiled at him and said hello, were indifferent. It was a long and expensive process of ingratiation.

Tommy had been startled when the old man sat down at the blackjack table with the giant. He had never seen a person look so much like an animal. The old man looked exactly like a banana cat. He had the small ears, the snoutlike nose, and his hair looked like fur because it was so light and fine. The *bac-si chos* called them *kinkajous.* The GIs called them banana cats because they loved bananas. They were from South America. They were half-dog, half-cat. They came to Vietnam on boats that went through the Panama Canal, where they were bought and then sold to GIs for pets. At first they were valuable, worth ten thousand *dong.* But those that escaped multiplied quickly. They were funny to look at. He had heard they climbed trees and hung from their tails. They always had a serious, worried look on their faces which made them look nervous. The old man looked exactly like one, right down to the worried look.

Everyone moved away from the blackjack table because of the giant. The giant took all the betting spaces except Tommy's. At first Tommy had been very puzzled, but it wasn't long until he understood what was happening. Tommy recognized a pay off when he saw one. He knew he was right when the new boss of the Ondine came out and took the two men back to his office. When they came back out, Tommy followed them. They stopped in one casino after another. They didn't gamble any more money, but they talked with all the big bosses. People feared the giant and respected the old man. Perhaps the giant was the banana cat's weapon. As they went from hotel to hotel, Tommy felt himself getting more and more excited. It was clear he had found what he had been seeking for months. He had found the most important man in Atlantic City. He followed them to an old house on Pacific Avenue. At first he thought it was another visit, but the giant came out and left. It was the banana cat's home.

Tommy returned to his apartment behind the Seven-Eleven, very much excited. He took Hanh while she slept. She woke up as he finished.

He told her she and Thitch would have to take care of the store alone now; he would be spending most of his time at the Ondine. Something was going to happen. When it did, he would be the first to bring the news to the old man who looked like a banana cat. The banana cat obviously ruled Atlantic City.

·12·

CARO HAD to resist the temptation to go into Viscaya when she passed by on her way to meet Butch Crolich at Fortunatas. She had had a big night there last night.

She had started playing blackjack a week ago. Bored with her work, she'd come downstairs and found Hector in Tim's office complaining about some chips from the Tommy T. Flowers. He had cashed five hundred dollars' worth of them for a big player. It was a throwaway favor because the Ondine and the Tommy T. Flowers were mad at each other. There was no way they'd give Hector the money for the chips.

When Hector saw Caro, he got an idea. He asked her to take the chips down to the Flowers, sit at one of the five-dollar tables with them for a while, play and have some fun for an hour, then cash out and bring him the change. Whatever she had left, it would be an improvement over zero.

Tim seconded the idea and Caro accepted the offer gladly. She was bored and secretly thrilled with the prospect of performing this quasi-criminal act of deception. But she wasted no time with the five-dollar tables. There were lines there. She sat down in the company of the twenty-five-dollar-minimum players.

She went back and forth with Tommy T. Flowers all afternoon and finally cashed out seven hundred and fifty dollars, five hundred of which she returned to a pleased Hector. For the rest of the week, she delighted in gambling all up and down the boardwalk with Tommy T. Flowers' money. She had her peaks and valleys, at one point getting within a card of going busted; but then, last night, she caught a hot shoe at Viscaya.

The experience would live in her memory forever. She had blackjacks simply for the wishing. It seemed like she won hands by willing the right cards in her direction. "Why don't you give me an ace ten?" she had asked the dealer once, doubling her bet, and it had come out exactly that way. In order: ace, ten. She would have asked for another one on the next hand, but she didn't want to get too greedy and spoil it. But no matter what she did or said, and no matter how drunk she got (and she did get drunk; the hands began to look like they were twirling through windows in a slot machine), she won one hand after another. It got so bad that the dealer offered to pay her bets without going through the formality of playing out the cards. She made so much money that night she was afraid to carry it home. She was also afraid Tim would give her a lecture about it as soon as he saw it. She left it in one of Viscaya's lock boxes.

Now on the way past the scene of so many thrills, she was tempted to go inside and visit for awhile, but she hurried on. She had to meet Butch before the show.

Butch was sorry Tim didn't come, but it didn't stop him from being very amusing company. Caro liked Butch. He had rich black hair and white skin. What a contrast Butch was to Tim. Butch was happy to bask in the glory of his father's position. He talked about his father constantly. Jeff Crolich was one of the major partners in Fortunatas, and Butch had a lot of time to tell stories because his main responsibility in life, as he explained it, was spending a few hours in their casino every day so that his father had a reasonable excuse to pay him his very large salary.

After the show, a rousing succession of country and western hits by a very famous singer, Butch stopped in the casino by an empty hundred-dollar-limit table to talk with one of the bosses. To keep Caro busy while she waited, he snatched a handful of hundred dollar checks out of the table's rack and gave them to Caro to play with. The pit boss pretended to make out a marker for Caro. Caro had assumed she was shilling for fun, but when Butch finished his business, he insisted she cash out.

"I never saw anyone play so lucky," he mocked as they drove down towards Avalon in Fortunatas's courtesy Rolls. They were on their way to a party. The country and western singer in the show they'd just seen liked parties, so she had to have one every night.

She was staying with a friend of Butch's named Larry.

"That exercise had nothing to do with luck," said Caro. "Luck was what happened to me last night at Viscaya."

"Didn't have anything to do with luck?" he asked. "You have a thousand dollars now you didn't have before. Isn't that luck?"

"I have it only because I happened to be with you," she laughed.

"Of course," he said. "That's exactly where the luck comes in."

The party was in a big beach house on top of one of Avalon's dunes. Butch and Caro separated after they arrived, and Caro ended up drinking with a couple from Dallas up on the deck. The house had a long cedar deck overlooking the pool out back. Beyond the pool were the dunes and the long dune grass, a combination of black and green beneath the searchlights on top of the house. Like everyone else, the Texans were talking about the singing star who was staying with Larry.

She was packing them in at Fortunatas. She was getting a half-million dollars for two weeks' work. Even the Texans thought that was a lot of money for someone who hadn't sung on stage for twenty years. They got excited when they looked over the railing and saw her sitting down by the pool. She was dangling her heavy legs over a light in the glowing water. Caro was surprised to see Butch in a bathing suit sitting next to her. There was a little bit of a crowd around them. Caro crept away from the Texans and went downstairs.

"I can't believe you're almost thirty," she was saying to Butch and everyone in the crowd around her. "You've got too young a body."

He did look cute in a bathing suit. He was slender, and the only hair on his body was two black tufts beneath his arms. He was pleased with the singer's attention.

"Want to take a bath?" the singer asked him. She had begun to play footsie with him underwater. She winked at the crowd around her.

"It wouldn't have to be anything sexual," she said slyly. "I'll take you upstairs and give you a good soaping. Come on. We'll go upstairs and use Larry's big tub."

The crowd giggled. A woman urged Butch to take his opportunity. Butch told the singing sex goddess to send someone for the soap and they'd take a bath right there in the pool, and she could soap anything and everything she could get her hands on. That brought a loud laugh from the group, and the singer's husband came rushing over and pushed Butch into the pool from behind.

Her husband was a small man with an Italianate beard. He had been strutting around the patio taking Polaroids and showing off his flat stomach. His vanity was a symptom of his business. He was a cosmetics millionaire.

Butch came to the surface wondering who had pushed him in. He found the husband standing at the edge of the pool shouting at him and thrusting his hips forward aggressively.

"Who do you think you are, señor?" he shrieked with an affected Spanish accent. "Do you think I don't know how you have been talking to my wife. You're trying to seduce my *wife,* señor. Nobody seduces my wife. Only I seduce my wife. You want to fight? Come out of the water, señor, and we will see who takes her home!"

The millionaire and the singing sex goddess were famous for this. Butch was now supposed to jump out of the pool and send the millionaire to the hospital, where the singer would spend hours at his bedside telling him how brave he was. Larry, the owner of the house, waved at Butch. He wanted Butch to get out of the pool, beat up the millionaire, and make the party. Butch laughed at the hairy rooster and backstroked down to the other end of the pool. The crowd, indifferent to this unsatisfactory ending, followed the singing star who had retreated inside to the living room. It was her custom to disappear while her husband brawled.

Butch got out of the far end of the pool and struck up a conversation with Les Convery. Caro knew Les from the Ondine. She had met him while spending an afternoon with Tim in the casino. Les was one of Tim's day-shift blackjack bosses. She had learned from Tim that Les would sometimes get out his dick and wave it around at parties. In Atlantic City everyone had a parlor trick, and Les's was his prick. It was supposed to be the biggest cock in New Jersey.

The cosmetics millionaire suddenly spotted Caro and came over to insist on taking her picture. He flashed his Polaroid in her eyes several times and then ran to fetch her a drink as payment for her cooperation. He put his arm around her as he showed her the pictures. She squirmed with discomfort and looked for Butch to rescue her, but he was too busy drinking at the poolside bar with Les.

Her discomfort encouraged the millionaire to become puppyishly affectionate with her. He asked her what she did; and, when she said she was in advertising, it set him off about his good friend Mary Wells. It required all her patience not to be rude to him. She had met too many like him as the casino manager's wife. They bragged about themselves and flattered Tim mercilessly. She had met them as a blackjack player too, when they sat down next to her and grinned at her for hours as if they knew a lascivious secret. This one was going to call up Mary Wells and persuade her to hire Caro at an incredible salary.

She would have laughed at him, but she had heard so much of this talk lately that it was beginning to take on an aura of realism. She was beginning to wonder if there weren't something wrong with *her.* Maybe she should make up a story to tell about her millions and how she could do the biggest favors with the shortest phone calls. This had to be what Tim had been complaining about in the people at Colony. They were all so transparently dumb and so full of posture, it was a strain to talk to them. But it couldn't have been this bad at Colony. Atlantic City, she suddenly realized, was a collection basin for the worst of them.

As the millionaire talked on, somebody dimmed the outside lights. Caro was startled to see Les Convery, now inside walking about the living room, which was as bright as a stage, showing his cock to all the women. He was obviously quite drunk. While Caro watched over the millionaire's shoulder, the singer stared at the long soft tube with interest.

A few minutes later, Butch came out onto the dim patio to make up his fight with the millionaire. The millionaire had given up on Caro and gone on to a showgirl, but he wasn't too busy to accept Butch's graceful apology. He granted Butch's request for the camera to take a picture. Butch was saying something as he focused when suddenly the millionaire hurried inside. Butch, still holding the camera, came rushing over to Caro.

"Come on," he grabbed her by the hand. "You've got to see this."

Inside, Butch stopped at the first door in a long hallway of bedrooms. The millionaire had run down the hall and around the corner.

"The stupe," Butch said. "He missed it."

He cracked the door slowly open. Caro could make out a couple on the bed. The woman was squatting carefully over the man. It was Les and the singer. She had a hand on his enormous cock, trying to fit it all the way up into her. It looked like she'd fallen on a baseball bat.

Caro felt someone breathing on her shoulder. She assumed it was someone from the living room who'd seen them come rushing inside. She stepped aside to give him room and was surprised to find it was the millionaire, immobile with shock. Butch was looking at him with a half smile which said more than a thundering laugh of triumph.

The cuckold, overcoming his shock, let out a howl of outrage.

The lovers looked up in surprise at the noise. The singer, seeing her furious husband, jumped off Les's cock. She scrambled off the bed, anxious to get away from the scene of her husband's fury. But their family badger game had come apart. The millionaire wasted no time on Les. He went right for his wife.

He slugged her in the stomach. She lost her breath from the blow, but it didn't satisfy him to see her gasping for air. He had to slap her face back and forth while she tried to breathe. His hands were studded with jewelry. Cuts and welts appeared all over her face. Butch was taking pictures with the millionaire's Polaroid. The singer began to fight back. She didn't scratch or claw. She made a good fist, thumb on the outside, and cracked him right in the cheek. They had an appetite for it. Caro thought they would get tired of hurting and stop, but they kept hitting away. They weren't going to let pain interfere with the pleasure they took in beating the shit out of each other.

The next day Caro didn't get out of bed until noon. Tim had already gone downstairs for the count which began every morning at eleven. She ordered breakfast and a paper from room service. While she waited, she went into the second bedroom which the hotel had made into a studio for her, compliments of Dean Haaf.

A sketch she had been working on three days ago was still on her drafting table. Since then she'd been out taking pictures, collecting ideas with the camera.

Her breakfast arrived, and she put down the photos, deciding to go out and take some more shots after she ate. She wasn't interested in anything she had. Nothing seemed worth working on.

When she sat down to eat, the newspaper startled her. Bruce had sold one of the Polaroids he'd snapped to the Atlantic City *Press.* It was on the front page. The singer was snarling at her husband, her face swollen with welts from his rings. The millionaire's right cheek looked like a plum.

Butch called to brag about how much AP had paid him to put the picture on the national newswire. She cut the phone call and their friendship short.

AFTER THE count, Tim went out for a walk. They had won eight hundred dollars. It was a tiny win, but it was enough to keep the casino open. He walked up Oriental Avenue all the way to the heart of the Inlet. It was a little past noon and the sun was hot. His feet swelled up inside his loafers from the hot asphalt. There were no sidewalks.

He wandered around for an hour looking for Padgett's bar. All the houses he passed were either ruined or badly neglected. He could see signs that people were living inside. Chairs and bikes on porches. Televisions blaring out cracked windows. He passed one house whose porch was propped up by a rusty steel girder. There was a rummy looking young black sleeping on a broken sofa beneath it. His shirt was wet with sweat from the heat. If that girder slipped, and it was already heeling over at an impossible angle, the whole porch would come down on him.

He passed over a hundred houses, some of them partially collapsed but being lived in just the same, and he didn't see one that was genuinely habitable. Eventually he found the bar on Lexington Avenue. It had an old painted sign: *Armstrong's Double Saw House.* It was right next to something called the Church of the God of Mt. Sinai Training School.

"Hey, Tim!"

Tim looked up the stairs in front of him. It was Teddy Long coming out of the bar. Teddy was the pit boss Fingo had been so afraid of.

"How did we make out this morning?" he asked.

"We won a couple of dollars," said Tim.

Teddy broke out into a big grin, showing a set of meaty red gums. He was one of the blackest guys Tim had ever seen. His skin was the color of printer's ink. Tim would have thought he was Moorish if he hadn't had a wide African nose.

"What are you doing up here?" he asked. "Padgett?"

"Yes," said Tim. "Who is Armstrong?"

"That was his old man," said Teddy. "He never replaced the sign after his father died."

"Teddy, tell me something," said Tim. "Is he really so pissed off he'd bring the whole thing down on top of everyone else?"

"Padgett is," said Teddy. "The rest of them I'm not so sure about."

"What do you mean?" asked Tim.

"Padgett is a little suicidal," said Teddy. "But the rest of them are only moaning middle-class jarheads waiting to get a crack at the tip box. That's all they talk about in there, how much was in MGM's tip box last night, or the Pier's, or Sinbad's."

"Why do you call them middle-class jarheads?" asked Tim.

"Because they aren't militant," said Teddy. "Militants are niggers with knives who want whitey's wallet for free. Militants are guys who grew up on the streets in gangs. These guys don't know anything about that. Half of them went to college. These are the boys who stayed in school and got their grades because they were mama's good little boys."

"Is that what you did, Teddy?" asked Tim, knowing it was, because he'd looked at Teddy's file after he'd fired Fingo.

Teddy grinned. "I was the valedictorian of my class at Woodrow Wilson in Camden. Followed by four years of honors at Cheyney State."

"Last night you were the only pit boss who brought anyone back to the office for stealing," said Tim. "There were thirty floormen out there, and you were the only one who caught anyone."

"I'm glad you noticed," he laughed.

"Why were you doing your job when no one else was?" asked Tim.

"Because I'm chicken shit," he said, smiling.

"What do you mean?" asked Tim.

"If you fuck around, sooner or later you get fired," he said. "I don't want to get fired. I like my job."

He talked a little longer with Teddy before climbing the stairs to the door. He stepped into the bar cautiously. It was cold from too much air conditioning for late September. He walked past a guy playing an electronic game. He was sinking ships with torpedoes. Tim approached the bar. It was one thirty and the place was already crowded. He looked around for Padgett, hoping to recognize him from the pictures on the election posters. He didn't see him. He didn't see any of the fire-breathing revolutionaries the press had described either. They were young but very familiar looking. He groped to recollect where he had seen a crowd like this before. Then it came to him: the IRS. They looked like they had just come from a day's work of filing. People like that had been all over the IRS building when he had gone there to be interrogated for clearance by the commission. They were also the same as the guys that worked in the offices of the SEC in New York. They were like the black guys he had gone to college with, except these were the guys who didn't get the jobs after they graduated. It showed in their appearance. They looked down.

"Hi," said one of them. He was about twenty-five, and his shirt had a big beer stain on the pocket. "Looking for somebody?" he asked politely.

"Padgett," said Tim, "Is he here? I'm Tim Seagurt."

He knew who Tim was. They all did. In a minute, Padgett came through a door to the kitchen. The warm smell of food rushed out into the cool air with him.

He didn't show the vitality Tim had expected. He was only forty-two, but he looked as if he were many years past the best time of his life. He was overweight, carrying two hundred pounds on a broad frame less than six feet tall. He wore a plaid cap, the kind Ben Hogan had made famous.

"I'll give you one thing, Seagurt," he said, shifting a cheap cigar to the other side of his mouth, "You're the first guy to come up here. What's the matter? Don't you get spook fever?"

The nearby drinkers laughed at that. Tim smiled and took Padgett's hand goodnaturedly. The cigar went back to the other side of his mouth. Padgett had a scruffy beard which crawled along his jaw like black bramble, shaped in nineteenth-century style.

"Come on," he said, scratching his beard. "Let's sit down."

As he followed him away from the bar, Tim noticed a back-brace pressing up against Padgett's shirt. He asked him about it as they sat down in a booth.

"I'm all screwed up back there," Padgett acknowledged. "I just got out of the hospital last week."

"Did they fuse it?" asked Tim.

"Oh, no!" said Padgett, "That ain't the way. I don't let them cut me."

"Did they want to?"

"I didn't let them start talking about it," he said. "There was this guy down the hall from me with the same problem that let them cut him. He was in for the fourth time. Now they've cut him four times, and he says there ain't nothing about it that's getting better. He just lays there and cries about not being able to get out for a hand of blackjack because he's in a cast that goes from his knees to his neck."

Tim laughed. Padgett had charisma. He could see why he'd captured everyone's attention.

"You ought to try swimming," said Tim. "A thousand yards a

day would loosen up your back all you need. You'd never see traction again."

"Exercise?" he asked. "I'd rather let them cut me."

"Forget I mentioned it," grinned Tim.

Padgett's cigar rolled from side to side in his mouth as he looked Tim over. The cigar was half-green and half-khaki, it's spit line having advanced halfway out the wrapper towards the burning end.

"You know why I'm here," said Tim.

"Abe mentioned you'd be coming," said Padgett.

"Abe?" asked Tim. "Who is he?"

"He's Powell's maid," said Padgett. "I guess he's also the special liaison for nigger relations. I don't hear much from Powell himself."

"I see," said Tim.

"Nobody does," said Padgett. "You should feel honored by his visit last night."

"He didn't honor me," said Tim. "He just scared the hell out of me."

"I know," said Padgett. "So how much did he scare you?"

"I can't pay you very much money," said Tim.

Padgett frowned. Tim explained that the Ondine was set up so he couldn't take any money out. He could get a couple of thousand out as a campaign donation, but nothing like what Powell had talked about. The Ondine simply wasn't geared to be stolen from like every other casino in town.

"Hey, come on, Seagurt," said Padgett, pretending to get mad. "Don't you know what's happening in this town? You don't have to pretend anymore. I'm leading a movement here. I'm bringing back the good old days when you didn't have to be ashamed to be a crook. We're all going back to the days of Nucky Johnson when all this shit and corruption was out in the open. Honest corruption, that's my motto. Isn't that what they wanted for this town? Legalized crime."

Tim had to laugh at this approach. There was something enjoyably funny about Padgett. He wondered if Padgett really had any plan other than making a lot of noise.

"Okay, so I'm a crook," continued Padgett. "I'm only angling to get paid off. But Tim, I want to be paid off, not mouthed off. Two thousand stinks."

"You're contradicting yourself," said Tim. "You're going to vote gambling out because Atlantic City is too good for it, which makes you as clean as the God of Mt. Sinai next door, but you want to be paid off because you're corrupt. You can't have it both ways."

"Don't talk to me like a lawyer," said Padgett. "I hate lawyers."

"Don't you realize this referendum could pass?" asked Tim. "You'd win the battle and lose the war. You'd be mayor of a ghost town."

"What do you think it is now," said Padgett, getting genuinely angry. "You take a look at how some of these guys live and tell them to worry about turning Atlantic City into a ghost town."

Tim remembered his walk through the Inlet. He saw what was behind Padgett's anger.

"The guys that hang out around here come here hoping to make a living," said Padgett. There was nothing funny about his delivery any more. "They have plans. You talk to them night after night and you'll hear the same story. They want to save enough money to go back home and buy something of their own like this bar—maybe not a bar, maybe a laundromat, who knows, but something they can call their own. They blow all their money on dealer's schools, they get their clearance and working cards, and then what happens? Nothing. There are supposed to be thousands of dealing jobs coming open every month. So why have some of them been waiting two years for jobs?"

"I've been here thirty-one months," called a voice from the next booth.

"Why don't you go back home?" Padgett called back.

"There ain't nothing at home."

"Are you getting it?" Padgett asked Tim.

"I'm getting it," admitted Tim.

"They had a big campaign for bringing minorities in back when the first couple of hotels opened," said Padgett. "They made so much noise people came from all over the country. But now that they have what they need to satisfy the Casino Control Commission, it's 'to the back of the bus, nigger.' "

Every casino in Atlantic City had a quota of black employees and they kept strictly to that quota. They never hired any blacks they didn't have to. Hector had mentioned it to him once. The people who ran gambling houses tended to hate blacks.

"I don't spend any of the money I get from all these bastards," said Padgett. "We buy houses. These guys have families and they need a place to live. The only trouble is, there isn't much money left over to fix any of the houses up after we buy them. The people that own them want to get rich. Houses which used to go for back taxes cost fifty thousand dollars now."

"Why do they have to live in Atlantic City?" asked Tim. "They don't have to live right on the island."

"Yeah," snickered Padgett, "you'd love to get us all out of here.

Then you wouldn't have to worry about having gambling voted out."

"What the hell is this crusade you have on about gambling?" asked Tim.

"Let me tell you something about that," said Padgett. "My old man was a crap shooter. When he grew up in this town, there must have been forty places he could go to shoot dice whenever he wanted to, so he got pretty smart about it. Now for example: If I come into your casino and play smart I can get your advantage down to point seven percent. That means every time I bet a dollar, the house takes seven-tenths of a penny. Not even a whole penny. Only seven-tenths."

"You mean over the long run," said Tim.

"Right, over the long run," he agreed. "How many decisions can a crap table hand out in an hour? A hundred maybe. So that means it should take me about an hour or more to lose my dollar, right?"

"Right," agreed Tim.

"But it doesn't take an hour to lose my dollar," said Padgett. "It takes a minute. So what's going on?"

"You're not going to say we cheat," said Tim. Casinos rarely cheated their customers, if ever. It simply wasn't necessary.

"No, you're not cheating," said Padgett. "You don't have to cheat, because there's something going on inside of me that has nothing to do with the numbers of the house advantage. I'm finding ways to shove money across the table at your guys. I'm taking hardways. I'm doubling up, trippling up, and flinging chips at snake eyes. I'm reaching after something I can't get hugging the line on that seven-tenths of a percent. I can't stand having only seven-tenths at stake. I want to win my dream. How can I win my dream risking less than a penny a dollar? Is that what my dream is worth? Hell, no. My dream is worth everything, and the next thing I know I'm pushing money at you, trying to crush that dream out of you, and that's what you guys are waiting for. That's when you go to work. Soon I'm drunker than Topper's dog and about as smart, because I'm giving you ten cents of every dollar. And its not frogs anymore; it's yards."

Tim started to say something but Padgett wasn't finished.

"A lot of people come to Atlantic City because they're having some kind of crisis. Something is crashing in their lives so they're all caught up in this big dream stampede. That's why this town is always so intense. They all have some bullshit to get out of their system so they come to Atlantic City where they can shit it out.

That's what you're cashing in on. You're sucking off human weakness, Tim, and it's no fucking good."

Finished, Padgett stared at him, waiting for an answer.

"I've got a suggestion, Padgett," said Tim. "I won't talk to you like I'm a lawyer if you don't talk to me like you're a preacher."

Padgett laughed. He had a very big laugh. It was so loud it filled the bar and a hundred faces turned around to see what had made their man so happy. Suddenly Tim knew he wasn't going to have much more trouble with Kedar Padgett. Padgett didn't really care about how moral or immoral gambling might be. He was using it to get something. He wanted something that went far beyond money, and it wasn't only the housing and feeding of Atlantic City's neglected minorities. Tim knew exactly what it was, and in the same instant that he understood it, he saw how to give it to him and solve his own problems at the same time.

·14·

ANDY MAP, the Ondine casino cashier, picked up the next box. It had *C-27* painted on its metal side with white enamel.

"Craps twenty-seven," he said.

"Craps twenty-seven," repeated Franco Perez as Andy put the large box down next to him. The Ondine had very large boxes, the largest in Atlantic City, because they counted only once a day.

Perez, the hotel cashier, was seated at the counting table in the video room, his daily count sheet before him. He picked up his key ring and opened one of the locks next to the little door at the end of the box. He passed the box to the state inspector. The inspector opened the other lock and then the little door to the money.

"Craps twenty-seven," said the inspector, checking his sheet. He sat beside Perez at the counting table, keeping the same records for the state as Perez kept for the hotel.

"Craps twenty-seven," said George Coursey, picking up the opened box and turning it over above the counting table.

George was the boss of the counting team. He was the assistant vice president in charge of the Guarantee Bank's branch on North Carolina and Atlantic. He counted for the Ondine as a sideline. He had two of his tellers with him.

"Remember the guy in the linen suit?" asked Teddy Long as the money spilled out. "He put a lot of fresh money into this one."

Tim had invited Teddy to the count because he had worked so hard the night before. Teddy had taken over as the new assistant manager of the casino. It had been hell getting all those dealers organized in time to start them all on the night shift.

George reached into the box to get the last of the bills and slips out. When it was empty, he showed it to Perez and the inspector to verify it was empty. They nodded and it went on the cart with the other empty boxes which had already been counted. The cart would go down the private elevator to the vault when it was full. The boxes were kept in the vault until the casino closed, when they changed places with the full ones beneath all the tables. The full ones were brought up every morning at eleven for the count.

George returned to the table to help separate the red fill slips from the bills.

"There shouldn't be too much red in this one," said Teddy.

When the fill slips were separated from the bills, George gave them to Perez. Perez totalled the payouts as the counting team began to sort the bills by denomination.

"Eight thousand, three hundred and twenty-six paid out," announced Perez, entering the total under the column labeled *C-27.*

He gave the slips to the inspector who began to check the total on his own machine.

Craps twenty-seven was going to make money. There was much more than eight thousand in cash on the table. It was taking the three men a long time to get the denominations separate.

Tim watched them handling the bills. He never tired of watching the count. There was something hypnotic about all that money. He had read hundreds of earnings statements with amounts in the millions, the tens of millions, and even hundreds of millions, but those totals had never seemed like anything related to the money he kept in his wallet. This stuff was. This was the same stuff that wiggled out of his wallet faster than he could load it in. Here, spread out on the table before him, was enough cash to fill his wallet until it was unfoldable, with enough left over to fill every pocket in his suit. Enough to fill every pocket in a magician's suit, one of those tuxedoes that came with thirty pockets big enough to hold thirty rabbits. This pile of real live twisting dollars that George and his crew were now sorting had to be worth far more than all the totals he had ever read in any financial report.

It was taking them an uncommonly long time to sort craps twenty-seven.

"Let me help, George," said Tim, moving excitedly to the table.

"You concentrate on the fifties. I'll take the hundreds."

"Thanks," said George gratefully. "You must have had a crowd at this one last night, Teddy."

"We did," said Teddy. "And the dice were on our side all night."

"Look at this!"

Tim had uncovered a large packet of hundreds. There were forty or fifty of them together, as clean and neat as a new bankroll from the bank.

"That's the guy in the linen suit," said Teddy with relish.

When the table was finally clear, Tim counted out all the hundreds he'd collected. He fanned them out in series of five across the table. When he finished, they covered the entire table. There were four hundred and twenty of them.

"That makes the night, Teddy," said Tim with more than a little exaltation. "There's no doubt about it now. It worked."

"It sure as hell did," agreed Teddy with a grin.

"All those guys did a great job, considering it was their first night handling live money," said Tim. "And it will get better every night."

Tim watched George count the fifties. The table was going to win at least sixty thousand. Something was purring inside him, and he felt like he wanted to let out a long hoot of pleasure.

The buzzer rang and the guard outside said that Mr. Haaf wanted to come in. Tim buzzed the door open.

"Hi, Tim," said Haaf. "How is it working out?"

"Great," said Tim, his voice loud with his excitement. "Look for yourself."

Haaf read the count sheet over Franco Perez's shoulder.

"Check craps twenty-seven, Dean," said Perez. "The one we're counting now."

"Look at the hundreds," said Andy, tapping a section of wooden pigeonholes along the back of the table. All the hundreds from the previously counted boxes were wrapped and stacked in an entire section of the pigeonhole squares.

"It's a whole section," said Haaf in amazement.

"I told you to trust me," grinned Tim.

"Yes, you did," laughed Haaf happily. "And you were right."

"You're damn right, I was right!" said Tim.

He heard himself shouting but he didn't care. His elation had been building inside him from the moment they'd opened the first box, and there was no controlling it now.

"I was sitting up there with Padgett in his bar yesterday, and I began to see it," he said. "Of course Laboy and McGray were rotten. They had started as dealers and come up through the whole rotten system. There's a moral infection that runs through this business, and everybody we had working for us had it. Here were all these black guys hanging around Padgett's bar with work cards and no work. They'd never worked in a casino. They had never learned how to steal, or all the bullshit rationalizations that go with it. They hadn't been infected with the disease because they couldn't get jobs. Let's face it, Dean, the people in this business hate blacks, quota or no quota."

"True," agreed Haaf.

"Amen," cracked Teddy.

"That's what was bugging Padgett," said Tim. "It wasn't the gambling. It was the hate. He was getting even, that's all."

"You think so?" asked Haaf dubiously.

"I know so," said Tim. "He said so when I made him the offer. You should have seen his face. It was like I was giving him candy. He doesn't give a shit about outlawing gambling."

Haaf had been worried sick the night before when he'd come into the casino and found nothing but black dealers behind the tables. To make matters worse, he found fifty of the fired dealers and bosses waiting for him in his office screaming for Tim's head. Haaf had come running into the video room demanding to know what Tim had done. Tim explained he'd promised Padgett he'd make the Ondine casino all black, excepting only the security police, credit, and Henry Moore. He'd promoted all the black dealers he already had to bosses, put the new ones at the tables, and put Teddy in charge of the whole thing. Haaf was so nervous he barely heard a word Tim said. He didn't say a thing about calling Oakes, but Tim could see it in his eyes. Tim begged him to trust him. It was the only chance they had, because Tim was not about to pay off Padgett with cash and risk going to jail. Haaf said he couldn't watch. He hoped it worked but he couldn't watch. He ducked upstairs to his suite, leaving his office full of angry ex-dealers and bosses. He didn't come down all night.

"I told you to trust me, didn't I?" said Tim.

"Yes, you did," said Haaf. "And don't think it was easy, but as long as it worked, it's all right with me. Even if I can't figure out why."

"I'll tell you why it works," said Teddy. "All these guys come from black families that made it one way or another. They're smart kids, not cheap hoods bouncing from job to job, and they've found out that as long as they're going to be stuck with asshole labor all their lives because they're black, they might as well be paid for it. They want to work and earn the money, not steal it."

"Dean, they're an entirely different breed than the thieves we had working for us," said Tim. "They've had decent educations and reasonable family lives. They're solid middle-class people with middle-class values. They aren't infected with that rip off cynicism that runs through the whole gambling business. I've eradicated that infection, I've changed the whole mentality of this casino."

Tim's excitement made Haaf laugh with pleasure. He reached out and grabbed Tim by the neck, like a wrestler working for a takedown, but instead of wrestling Tim over, he shook his shoulders affectionately.

"I think you have, Tim," he said, warmly. "Damn. What an idea."

"Thanks, Dean," said Tim. Envy from Dean Haaf was more than welcome.

"I can't tell you how this makes me feel," said Haaf.

"You don't have to," said Tim. "I know how you feel. It's how you must have felt when you started expanding NTS. This is different than looking at reports and bullshitting people. Making it work yourself is something very different. It makes you feel like Einstein."

When Caro came downstairs after finishing her breakfast in bed, she found an elated Tim. He had just gotten off the phone with Padgett. He grabbed her by the hand and led her out through the casino. They were going up to the Vermont House to visit Padgett's campaign suite.

Caro had been out most of the previous day and night taking pictures and she hadn't come into the casino. Passing by, she had noticed it was fuller than usual, but she hadn't gone in. Tim hadn't disturbed her when he'd come to bed after closing, so she had no idea of what had happened. Tim told her on the way up through the Inlet. She was amazed at the story of the success. She had been feeling small tremors of emotion for him ever since they'd come to the Ondine, and now a powerful feeling of affection was heating her up inside. It was the same thing she'd felt when they made love for the first time that night after they swam. But then he'd started struggling at Colony, and her excitement faded. They had continued fucking constantly, but her sexy adulation of him had waned, and with it went the heat in their mating. She needed his success as much as he did. Nothing could have made that clearer to her than its long absence and sudden return. She was tingling with sexual excitement.

"Caro, what are you doing?" he asked, looking down at her hand unzipping his fly and trying to keep his attention on the road at the same time.

"It's not hard," she said. "Don't you know what I've been thinking about?"

"I do now," he said, growing quickly.

She bent over before the steering wheel and began moving her mouth up and down on him. She could feel the car take several turns and then climb a bridge. His dick was getting harder and harder in her mouth, the way it did just before he climaxed, and he began to make his coming noises.

"Wait a minute," he said, twisting his cock away from her mouth with his hips. "I'll hit something if you make me come while I'm driving."

She sat up and saw they were in Brigantine. They were driving down a wide street between modern beach houses. It was a contrast to the Inlet.

"Where are you going?" she asked.

"I'll find a place," he said, turning towards the beach.

She bent over and got him back in her mouth before the car came to a halt. He turned to lean against the car door while she sucked it, lifting his hips for her to get his pants down.

"Oooo, the seat is cold," he said.

His cock had softened, so she stuck her tongue in its little hole, straightening it quickly.

"What about you?" he asked her.

"Don't worry about me," she said, holding onto it with her hand.

"I worry. I worry," he said, as she started sucking again. "But, damn, that feels good."

She held onto it as she alternated between licking the underside and sucking on the head. When he started to come, she hooded her lips over the head and pressed up and down on the shaft with her lips while he squirted.

She slowed down to long smooth movements as he relaxed. When she sat up, he had his eyes closed. She opened her bag and spit what she hadn't been forced to swallow into a tissue. She put it in the litter bucket and took out another tissue to clean the wetness off his shrinking cock.

He shivered. "That felt good."

She laughed and tucked him back in. "Congratulations on getting rich."

The campaign suite told the story of Padgett's constituency. There were several of the young black men there, but even more in evidence were older black women, the mothers of black families. There must have been fifty of them in the suite. They were by far the largest group. After them came the Hispanics, in all ages, sizes, and sexes. There were even a few Orientals walking around. The fact that Padgett had united such a diversified population in opposition to gambling graphically demonstrated how little casinos had done for people who populated Atlantic City.

It was a welcome irony to Kedar Padgett that the growth in casinos had led to a white voting minority. Atlantic City had been split down the middle between whites and scattered minorities when gambling came in. The casinos had then bought up all the better neighborhoods close to the boardwalk, and the white population moved off the island with their profits. A construction boom was followed by massive unemployment of black construction workers. The building boom stopped after the boardwalk got crowded. Nobody wanted to build in the Inlet. There were the MGM and the Hilton on the other side of it down past Gardner's Basin, but the Inlet remained undisturbed. Many of the construction workers stayed on, waiting for the magical bubble to keep expanding, but they ended up broke and, like the dealer hopefuls, getting more and more bitter.

They and their families lived in intolerable old hovels ignored by absentee owners waiting to get rich. The landlords refused to make any improvements or repairs. In fact, they wanted the black families out. They couldn't evict them, so they were all waiting for the buildings to fall down and force them out. The landlords were all certain that they were only a jump away from the rebirth of the building boom. But gambling was becoming legalized all over the country and there was no more rush to build in Atlantic City. It was never going to happen.

Nobody had noticed what was happening until Padgett started a voter registration drive in the Inlet. The drive was getting so hot it seemed like black and other minority groups would make up almost seventy percent of the ballot. The only reason they were all registering was to turn gambling out, and everyone knew it. Everyone had assumed Atlantic City would be all new buildings one day, and none of them had realized there would be a point in the middle where the blacks and the Hispanics and the Orientals who lived in the hovels would suddenly become a threat.

Padgett came over as soon as he saw Tim and Caro and led them to a corner of the suite to talk. Caro, not really included in the conversation, stood there politely. Padgett was a little hostile, but funny. He looked older than Tim said he was. He wasn't very attractive. His beard was a mess. But he was as elated as Tim. He said every hotel on the boardwalk would soon be copying the Ondine.

"Of course they will," agreed Tim. "It works."

"If there's one thing these bastards understand," said Padgett, "it's a lot of money dropping into their boxes. It will sweep Atlantic City."

A big older black man with a burn-scarred face came over to meet Tim, and Padgett took Caro aside with the obvious intention of charming the casino manager's wife. She had been a target of it for a month now, and she was weary of the two major symptoms: a big smile, and a lot of praise for Tim.

"Next to me," said Padgett, "your husband could be the best thing ever to happen to Atlantic City."

"I agree," said Caro. "Although I might reverse the order."

Padgett laughed. He had a loud, boisterous laugh. Caro loved loud laughs and she immediately began to like Padgett, even if he was kissing up to the casino manager's wife.

Tim was telling a story to Abe, the older man with the scar, and a group of younger blacks about how the fired dealers had messed up Haaf's office.

"That couldn't have been much work," said Caro, nodding at Tim. "Have you ever seen Haaf's office?"

"No," said Padgett.

"It always looks like he's doing his taxes," said Caro.

Padgett laughed again. "You're a funny lady."

They got into a conversation about Atlantic City. He said that Tim had made him a sure thing to be the next mayor, but talking about it seemed to depress him. He sounded as if he were losing something by winning. He led her to a window overlooking the Inlet. The Vermont House, the only black hotel of any significance in Atlantic City, was surrounded by the worst part of the Inlet. Caro stared out trying to imagine how this slum had once been the richest neighborhood in Atlantic City.

"What was it like before?" she asked.

"It was always old," said Padgett sadly. "That's the way I remember it as a kid, anyway. But it wasn't dead. It wasn't anything like this. It was still beautiful. It was worth rebuilding. We were going to rebuild it, but ten years of gambling trashed those plans."

"How did gambling trash it?" asked Caro.

"Prices got too high and buildings started falling down." He said it like it was a formula he had repeated so many times that it didn't have any meaning any more.

"How were you going to rebuild it?" asked Caro.

"With black money."

"I don't get it," said Caro. "Blacks in Atlantic City didn't have any money before gambling."

"That's a white chamber of commerce lie, honey," said Padgett, and suddenly he was an excited salesman, taking deep drags off his joint as he talked and looking straight into Caro's face for her reactions. "This could have been our town. This is a beautiful seaside island with an incredibly beautiful beach. Nothing could change that, not all the garbage in the world. We always had the natural beauty to look forward to. We could have made this *the* black resort."

He stopped looking at her, off and running on a stoned rap.

"Middle-class blacks were getting more and more money," he said. "We could have rebuilt this town with the money black businessmen make. Niggers would love to come to a city of their own by the sea. They would come from all up and down the East Coast, from all the way out to the Mississippi. Let the chucks have Ocean City, Avalon, Stone Harbor and all the rest. We would take the original jewel after they'd left it for garbage and polish it for our own pleasure."

"What a beautiful idea!" said Caro.

"But they wouldn't let us have it!" he protested, and his speech slowed down. "After they ruined it—and they used it up, emptied it of its beauty as if it were a whiskey bottle—we started cleaning up the mess. We were buying houses and rebuilding them. But they wanted it back. They had to let this whore gambling loose and turn all our plans to shit."

"But you're still working at it," said Caro.

"It's too late," said Padgett. "We thought we'd scare the real estate values down with the election threat against gambling, but all these assholes are raising their prices even higher. They figure they have the hotels in a squeeze. They figure the hotels will have to buy them out to get us out. Gambling makes things worse and worse."

Padgett stopped. He had to take a phone call from someone downtown. He handed his joint to Caro as a woman gave him the phone. She puffed on it while he talked. It was very good dope. She looked down from the window and saw pimp Cadillacs pulled up to the canopy below, one after another. They were brilliantly colored scarabs with nigger exercise boys. She giggled. She was high.

An idea bubbled up into her head. It was a good one and she knew it.

"I've got it!" she shrieked with glee. "I've got the answer!"

"What?" grinned Padgett as he hung up the phone. "What's the answer?"

"Repeal gambling!" she said. "Go ahead and really do it. Then watch what happens to all the property values in the Inlet."

Padgett looked puzzled. "Your husband runs a casino," he reminded her.

"And better yet—" she said, "oh, I'm really stoned because this is the idea of the century—"

She paused, losing it for a second.

"What's the idea of the century?"

"The hotels all go down in value, too," said Caro with delight as it came back. "They'll all close down because gambling is what keeps them open. They'll all go bankrupt. Do you see it?"

Padgett didn't seem to be getting it.

"You'll buy them for pennies," explained Caro. "Black businessmen, the ones with the money, can buy them for nothing at bankruptcy sales. The Ondine, The Pier, The Money Tree, all of them. You'll operate them and make money because you bought them so cheap. You'll have black people coming from all over the country to stay at these fabulous hotels. They'll be coming just for the sea and the beach and the air because there'll be no gambling. You'll have your dream."

Padgett took out another joint and lit it.

"It's right, isn't it?" asked Caro excitedly. She hadn't spent five years listening to Tim talk business without learning anything. "It will work, won't it."

"Maybe."

"Then you'll try it?"

Padgett inhaled deeply. "This is all stoned bullshit. You know that, don't you?"

"It doesn't have to be," protested Caro. "Just because we're stoned, that doesn't mean it won't work."

"It would work all right," he said, and his speech started to slow down again, "except for one thing . . . I just can't . . . the thing you keep forgetting . . ."

They gazed out the window together, staring at the brilliant metal insects below.

"What?" asked Caro, trying hard to concentrate. "What am I forgetting?"

"The day that gambling actually gets repealed," he blew out a heavy stream of gray smoke, "is the day Powell and the rest of them punch my ticket."

He was a sham. Somehow he had meant to keep it from happening all along. But why had he pushed it so hard? He had been all over the newspaper for weeks. He'd even been on network national news. It was only an accident that Tim had come up with something to get him elected without having gambling repealed. Padgett hadn't planned on it. There was something out of control about Padgett.

"Wait a minute," she said, getting another idea. "I've got it again. You've got to find a way to make it happen without it being your fault. You don't have to be bought off with a few more blacks getting jobs in casinos. You can have the whole town."

"I don't believe this," laughed Padgett. "Here you are yelling at me to have gambling repealed, when it will cost your husband his job."

"Come on," she said angrily, "that's not the point."

"I don't think he'd appreciate the advice you're giving me," grinned Padgett.

Caro had to stop and think again. The grass was really working on her now. It slowed her down, turned her away from the grinning Padgett and down a long, introspective corridor. Why the hell was she so interested in the repeal of gambling all of a sudden? She was crusading against it with something very close to hatred.

HENRY CAME into Tim's office almost dancing. He had returned from his expedition to New York. His serious-minded, penetrating glare was gone, and a smile of pleasure was in its place.

"You look happy," said Tim.

"I am," conceded Henry, waving a book in the air. "I'm a cinch to make it."

"Congratulations," said Tim, deliberately not asking what it was Henry was so happy to make.

"Aren't you curious about why I went to New York?" asked Henry.

"As long as it has lifted the vapor of gloom from your brow, I'm satisfied," said Tim. "Tim is happy that Henry's happy."

"You're a superior person, Tim," said Henry. "You pretend to be a nice guy, but deep down you think you're pretty smart."

"I do?"

"You care about things like this," he said, waving the book at Tim. "I've found you out."

"Things like what?" asked Tim.

"Things like being smart and superior," said Henry. "I found out you graduated third in your class from Penn. You never said anything about going to an Ivy League School."

"I didn't know people from the West knew there was an Ivy League," said Tim.

"We've heard of it," said Henry wryly. "And we've all got an inferiority complex about it."

"Try not to hold your inferiority complex against me," said Tim. "I didn't like it in the Ivy League."

"Why not?"

"Because too many people are there to give themselves superiority complexes," said Tim.

"You hated it so much," said Henry, "that you went back and graduated fourth in your class at Wharton."

"I know I should be ashamed of myself for that, Henry," said Tim, "but I just can't bring myself to be."

Henry laughed.

"How did you find me out in such detail?" asked Tim.

"I'm not telling."

"Oh, yeah, I forgot," taunted Tim. "It's pointless to ask anyone in this town how they found anything out. No one tells. They all pretend they know everything magically."

"I plugged into the great American data bank," confessed Henry. "You know computers gossip like women. One of them even told me you almost flunked third grade."

"It's true," laughed Tim. "But why do you care?"

Henry smiled and rubbed his big nose sheepishly.

"You've declared perpetual open season on casino managers," cracked Tim, "and you're looking for my fatal flaw. Is that it?"

"No, no, that's not it," protested Henry quickly. "I wanted to play a little game with you, so I had to find out what the odds of my winning were."

"Oh?"

"I was so scared when I saw how smart you were, I decided against it," said Henry. "But then I scored so high today, I don't think you can catch me."

"Catch you how?" asked Tim.

"For smarts," said Henry. "I took an IQ test today."

He handed the book he'd been waving about to Tim. It was an instruction manual on how to take IQ tests, and it had several sample exams in it. Henry had been practicing to get into Mensa. He had a friend in New York who had urged him to join, and one had to score high on an IQ test to get in. Henry had scored so high in New York, he now wanted Tim to take one of the practice tests to see if he could do better.

"I always wondered what you were doing in your spare time," said Tim. "I'd built up this image of your taking hookers up to your room to play hide the broom."

"Very funny," said Henry. "But I don't like hookers."

"I can see that," said Tim, leafing through Henry's book.

"I like slot players," said Henry. "Tall ones."

Tim laughed. Henry did have a reputation for leading tall girls out of the casino by the hand.

"Come on," said Henry. "It only takes a half-hour. I'll score it for you."

"I'm out of shape for this," said Tim. "You've been practicing."

"If you're smart, you're smart," said Henry. "Let's see if you can beat one eighty-five."

"One eighty-five?" asked Tim, impressed. "Your IQ is one eighty-five?"

"It was today," said Henry proudly. "Let's see if the Ivy League can top that."

Curious, Tim opened the book to where Henry had it marked. The first question instructed one to insert the missing word: measure (. . .) king.

"I can't do this," chuckled Tim. "I can't even figure out the first question."

Henry looked over his shoulder. "Ruler. I'll give you that one for free. Go ahead."

"How the hell do they get ruler out of that?" asked Tim.

"A ruler is a measure and a king," said Henry.

"Look, Henry, being smart was always work for me. I'd have to go at this book and ten others like it for two weeks before I could hit one eighty-five."

"Excuses, excuses," said Henry merrily. "You're conceding without a fight. UCLA hammers the Ivy League to the canvas in ten seconds of the first round."

Tim laughed. "Okay, I'll finish, but only because of my deep and powerful loyalty to the red and blue."

Which is the odd item out: Telephone, blotter, newspaper, ap-

pointments, coffee, drawer? asked the test. Followed by: *Which of the following is not a fiber: loow, octont, rhyshtg, onlyn?* And many more.

"Time's up," said Henry after a half-hour.

Henry took the book and began to add up Tim's score, grinning as he went. The grin gradually evaporated. It was replaced by a look of confusion and disappointment.

"What'd I get?" asked Tim when Henry finished, now anxious to know the result.

"Eighty-three," said Henry.

"I lost by two points?" asked Tim, disappointed.

"You got eighty-three," said Henry, shaking his head. "Not a hundred and eighty-three. I beat you by a hundred and two points."

"What?" asked Tim stunned.

"The fact of the matter is," said Henry, brightening a little, "you are within two answers of being a moron."

"I told you I was out of shape," said Tim. "Eighty-three? Christ!"

"And I gave you one of them." marvelled Henry.

PART IV

November, 198–

·16·

CARO TREMBLED as the heavy sea air rushed in through her bulky sweater. It was cold out. She hurried along Oriental Avenue away from the Ondine. This was the southernmost reach of the Inlet, where hotels and motels mixed into slum. Oriental Avenue was a flurry of red and white *Padgett for Mayor* posters. There were still a few days left until the election, but the fall winds had already reduced the posters to tattered patches of paper and color.

She turned into the Xanadu beneath its small sign: *Xanadu, The Stately Pleasure Dome, Kitchenettes.* Xanadu's lobby was many-tiered. All about its walls, climbing from tier to tier on one side and descending on the other, curled a river of sparkling slot machines glowing with windows of oranges, limes, plums and apricots. Their flickering progress girdled the entire lobby, broken only in the highest corner where Kubla Khan himself, dressed in orange and black pajamas, stood to observe the flowering of his royal decree.

"Hector told me you'd be here," she heard a voice behind her. "I didn't know whether to believe him or not."

It took her a moment to come up out of her playing trance. The machine had become the torso of one of the muscle-bound gigolos from the September beach. She was seeing polished dimes tumbling through his lucite arteries like star showers.

"Tim, what are you doing here?"

"I thought you'd like to have lunch," he said. "how long have you been here?"

"About a half-hour," she lied.

She set her crinkled wax cup of dimes next to the bottle of alcohol by the machine. Instantly she regretted attracting his attention to the alcohol.

His eyes darted to her hands. He took her hand by the wrist to look at her fingers.

They were covered with the dirt that comes from handling coins hour after hour. It was a black and sticky film which only alcohol could remove.

"A half-hour?" he asked.

"It's only dimes," said Caro.

He stared at her, adding things up.

"Where do you get the money for this?" he asked.

She told him about her gambling. He listened with interest. He didn't seem upset about her losing the thirty thousand she'd won. She told him she had taken to playing slot machines as a defense against playing blackjack.

"What kind of defense do you need when you don't have any more money?" he cracked.

She laughed.

"Where do you get the dimes to play the slots?"

She shrugged. She wasn't about to tell him that she had borrowed a hundred dollars from Trudy, a hooker Caro suspected was trying to turn her out, and paid it back by taking Trudy out to lunch a few times where the bill was certain to be comped because she was Tim's wife.

"Maybe I'd better call Konnie," he said.

"What for?" asked Caro, puzzled.

"Our stocks are all in joint name," he said. "I was going to sell everything anyway because I don't have time to watch them. I'll tell him not to send you any money no matter what, okay?"

"Why would you do that?" asked Caro, irritated. He was treating her like she was a thief.

"Because if you can't get money," he said, "you can't gamble."

"Tim, I'm so bored here," she said. "You can't believe how bored I am. At least the slots give me something to do."

"What's going on with you, Caro?" Tim asked pensively. "This doesn't sound like you."

"I don't know what's going on," she said. "I can't work. I get ideas, but the excitement of everything here works down to nothing so quickly that I quit. All I'm left with is an incredible itch for something really exciting, and the only thing that's remotely exciting is playing, even if its only for dimes."

"You have to make yourself work," said Tim.

"Oh, screw that," said Caro.

"Why do you say that?" asked Tim unhappily. "You had some great ideas a few weeks ago."

"I can't work here," she said.

"Do you want to go back to New York?" he asked.

"It's too late," she said. "They've replaced me by now."

"Caro, you've got to get off of this passive tune," he said, looking very unhappy. "You've got to fight it out. You've got to get a hold of some idea and work it."

"I get plenty of ideas, Tim," she said. "I get so many they all fight around inside me and nothing comes out right."

"Then you've got to take the time to sort them out," he said.

"I can't," she said. "I stand there and I try, but anything I do comes out so wrong that I can't bear to look at it. And it hurts, Tim. It physically hurts."

"Keep after it no matter how much it hurts," he said, still upset and looking at her as if he wished he could give her a transplant of some of his legendary grit. It reminded her of arguments they had when they swam together, Tim always urging her to make it hurt, and she always laughing at him.

"All right," she said. "You're right. You're right. I'll try."

"You'll work at it no matter how much it shits?" he asked.

"I will," she promised. "I'll try anything."

"Good," he said, breaking out his big happy grin.

The pain of not working had been hard, but the pain of working was even harder. She drank three cups of dark espresso over the course of every morning's work. Her strokes darted around the canvas like water bugs on a stagnant pond. Every half-hour she had to run to the bathroom to let loose little squibbs of diarrhea. When she returned she found, instead of the beautiful idea she thought she had been working on, wild and revolting collages of unrelated images. She often felt the urge to shortcut the tubes of color and a lot of work by simply turning her backside to the easel when the next cup of espresso rumbled through her bowels.

Tim walked down the deck behind the bar chairs with Hector Knute, Henry Moore, and Dean Haaf following him. He had gotten in the habit of having lunch brought into him at Neptune's Barge after the count. Set in a large artificial pond next to the baccarat tables, Neptune's Barge was the casino bar and lounge. It was a beautiful, hand-fashioned teak boat with longlegged chairs standing in the water around it like wooden storks. The bar itself was above the boat and fixed with cedar posts. The bartenders walked up and back in the rocking boat, their heads level with the bar, handing up drinks like cabin boys not allowed on deck. The long indoor tub that the boat and stage floated in was bulwarked with tall round pilings and lined with crosshatched stainless steel.

Hector and Henry always joined him for lunch, and today, so had Haaf.

"Did you vote?" Hector asked Haaf. It was election day.

"Not yet," said Haaf.

"You better," said Hector.

Haaf nodded agreeably.

Hector had been campaigning for the past week. Anyone who had lived in the Ondine long enough to vote got at least one passionate speech about turning out to vote against Padgett's referendum to outlaw gambling.

"How do you think it's going to come out?" Hector asked Tim.

"You mean Padgett, or the referendum?" asked Tim.

"Oh, shit, we're stuck with him no matter what," said Hector. "I mean the referendum."

Tim shrugged. He'd lost track of Atlantic City politics. He was weary from having spent the previous night staring at thousands of pairs of hands. He had been staring at the monitors all night because the per was on its way down. Money was bleeding out of the casino.

The per had started down the very next night after he'd hired all the black dealers. (Hector kept calling it the Night of the Niggers, provoking several ugly looks from Teddy Long.) That first night had been an extremely lucky one. The dice and cards had played in favor of the Ondine and made the per artificially high. The next few nights showed a much lower level of winnings. The results were still a big improvement over Laboy's regime—enough of an improvement to renew Oakes' interest in keeping the Ondine—but it was nothing like what the first night had led Tim to believe it could be. Tim had accepted and understood the luck part of it without complaint, but the past few weeks had proven there was more at work than luck. This morning's count had shown another downtick in the per. Across the casino, from table to table, the pers were going down in unison. It meant only one thing. The black dealers were learning how to steal.

As they waited for the coffee shop to bring their lunch into the bar, Hector and Henry were silent. Haaf, however, was eager for analysis.

"How far has it spread, do you think?" he asked. "How many did you catch last night?"

"I only caught three," said Tim. "It's not like the night Powell came in. The cheating is much harder to spot. It's subtle now, not blatant. They aren't trying to teach me a lesson anymore. Now they're trying to get away with it, and they're getting pretty good at it."

"One of them was an old boy," said Hector. "He was a dealer we made a boss. He's been with us for years."

"Maybe it's just a small rash," said Haaf. "Maybe it's just the old boys acting up and you can clear it up by cleaning them out."

"That's it!" said Henry excitedly. "He's got the answer, Tim."

"It's not that simple," said Tim.

"Fire all the old dealers you made bosses," said Henry. "Make the sharpest new dealers bosses. Hire more black women. Maybe we should make the place all female. How come this casino has always been so down on women dealers anyway?"

"That was Laboy's policy," said Hector. "He said women were no good as dealers because their boyfriends could beat them up and make them steal for them."

"That's an interesting perception," said Tim wryly. "Hasn't he ever heard of women corrupting men?"

"Let's do it then," pressed Henry eagerly. "You didn't cut deep enough the first time. You can hire more women. It won't hurt you with Padgett as long as they're black."

"After the election we'll hire more women," said Tim. "We'll hire anything that moves, regardless of race, sex or the number of arms they have coming out the middle of their backs. If they can count to twenty-one, they'll get a chance."

"You sound bitter, Tim," said Haaf.

"I am."

"Why?" asked Henry, quickly. "We're making good money. We may not have all the answers, but we're making good money."

"It's not working, Henry," said Tim. "And it won't work. Changing the color or sex of the dealers is as futile as changing the dice on a crap shooter with a hot hand."

"Why do you say that?" asked Haaf.

"You can't change human nature," said Tim. "It's in the nature of people working in a casino and handling the money other people are throwing away to want to steal it. It's even in the nature of people wanting to be dealers in a casino. It's there before they ever get a job. The job itself only brings out the inevitable."

Henry stared at Tim carefully, his big magnified eyes flicking back and forth across Tim's face as he deposited that little item in the inward bank where he kept all his data on honesty in casinos.

"We had a good couple of weeks, but not because these black guys are honest and untainted by the casino tradition of stealing," said Tim. "We had a good couple of weeks because they were inexperienced at dealing. They were too busy getting their work down to steal. They'd only handled dummy money in dealer's school, and so it was all they could do to get their live cards and checks straight. Now it's automatic to them, and they're getting plenty of time to figure out their funny moves. They're also getting over their paranoia about being caught and they're getting into their greed. That's why the per has been going down in a straight line and why it's going to keep going down."

"But we can control it," said Henry earnestly. "It will never get back to where it was with Laboy. You're catching them."

"Not fast enough," said Hector.

"How fast you catch them doesn't matter," said Henry, annoyed with Hector.

Tim turned around in his barstool and looked out at the casino. The Ondine was always nighttime when the games were open, but in the hours before one o'clock, when the slot players had it to themselves, five large mercury vapor lights were turned on and the casino was brilliant with five white-blue suns.

"Of course it matters," Tim said to Henry. "It's too big for it not to matter."

Fivefold daylight did not shrink the Ondine casino. It was acres and acres of green tables and machines. The cleaning crews were busy in the pits getting the games ready to open. The white-blue light glaring down on them showed dense swarms of ashes and dust at work in the turbulent casino air.

"It doesn't get any bigger than your own honesty," said Henry. "No joint is any bigger than the example the casino manager sets. If they perceive your honesty, eventually they'll respect it."

"Honesty?" laughed Tim. "It's too big, Henry. It's madness to try to control something so big, and they all know it."

When Tim returned to the casino offices after his nap, Haaf came in to talk to him. Tim's initial success had turned their uneasy relationship into friendship. Haaf now religiously cleared with Tim anything which might faintly infringe on Tim's authority as the casino manager. And instead of trying to lecture Tim, Haaf sought his praise. Day after day he came into Tim's office to trot out the good ideas he'd had with NTS and illustrate his results with a crumbled yellow *Journal of Commerce.*

He loved hearing Tim tell him how smart he had been. Tim liked doing it. He found in Haaf something which had been missing in every other older man with whom he'd ever been friendly. Haaf was interested in Tim because he wanted to learn from Tim. Tim had always thought that his problems with his father would disturb his relationships with older men as long as he lived. It hadn't occurred to him that *he* could become the hero, and the father figure the pet. That was what Haaf had turned into, a domesticated, affectionate version of the angry oedipal monster.

Even though the per had started back down again, Haaf's respect for Tim remained high. He was keen on Tim's analysis of everything and anything, and today he had something personal to talk about. He had been having trouble with his wife. She was leaving town in a couple of days. He felt very guilty.

"It's those screwing rooms," he said. "You ought to bar me from using them."

Tim laughed. Every casino kept hotel rooms aside for high rollers who weren't staying at their hotel, so that if a player wanted to knock off a whore, he wouldn't have to cash out and go back to his own hotel to do it. But gamblers seldom used the screwing rooms. They were always too busy playing. The rooms were used mostly by high-level casino employees to boff girls who came in looking to get laid by somebody behind the ropes. With a casino suddenly full of black bosses, Tim was now beseiged with such offers, all of which, at Haaf's request, he referred to Haaf. Haaf said it was a fact of female physiology to get all engorged in the genitals whenever they looked at men working in casinos, so Haaf often stood out in the pits, with Tim's permission, and pretended he knew what he was doing there while he waited for Tim's referals.

"You ought to at least bar me from posing in the casino," said Haaf.

"Fine," said Tim. "Tell Teddy I said you're barred."

"She knows what I'm up to," he said. "That's why she's leaving."

"She's definitely going then?" asked Tim.

Haaf nodded.

"She doesn't want any money," he added. "She knows I don't have any. She's talking about a no-fault divorce."

"I see," said Tim. Haaf had once told Tim he hated divorces.

"She's right," he said. "I don't pay any attention to her anymore."

"If she wants to go, Dean, let her go," said Tim.

Haaf smiled at him affectionately. "I guess you're right."

"Why are you sad?" asked Tim. "From what I've seen, you'll both be happier."

"I feel like something less than a man," said Haaf, patting his sport coat over his belly. "It's a disgrace to get a divorce. My parents taught me it was a failure before God and your family to get a divorce, because it's as much the man's fault as the woman's."

"Dean, you don't even believe in God," said Tim.

"I know," granted Haaf. "But I still feel like a failure."

"Religion and parents are ghosts from childhood," said Tim lightly. "They are the witch doctors of modern superstitions. Root them out and do what's best for you."

"Tim, listen," said Haaf, suddenly grave. "Don't get so wrapped up in this casino that you forget your wife. It's not Linda's fault I started in with the screwing rooms. She's a fine-looking woman. It's my fault."

Tim scowled. The return of the bossy Haaf was something he could live without.

"Maybe you should think about getting out of Atlantic City," said Haaf. He was up and squeezing his little pot belly. "Maybe you should think about whether this town is worth your marriage."

Obviously he knew about Caro's gambling, and he had it all mixed up with his own remorse.

"Dean, please don't project your problems onto me," said Tim cooly. "Caro has her work to keep her busy, and it's her responsibility to work. It's not my business to make her, and it's not my problem to solve by moving her somewhere else."

·17·

HE WAS exuberant over the work he and Henry had done on his inspired new idea. They were both certain it was going to succeed. (Tim was a genius, Henry kept saying, promising to get him into Mensa without an IQ test). All they had to do now was wait for the hardware. He walked into Caro's studio. He found yet another new pile of canvases stacked up next to the window. He looked through them. The results weren't too good, but she had been spreading a lot of paint across canvas.

She was still depressed. She didn't argue about anything with him anymore. She seemed to have no emotions. She shrank from anything intense, including sex. She hadn't been interested in fucking for a week.

He found her downstairs in the coffee shop. She was pleased with his invitation to go shopping. She wanted to know what for, but he insisted on keeping it a mystery, and she liked that even more. They walked out onto a sunny boardwalk. One of the Ondine cart drivers called to Tim, wanting to know if he wanted a ride anywhere. He refused. It was too nice a day not to walk. They set out downbeach arm in arm.

"Hi, Tim!"

"Say, Tim!"

"How ya doin, Tim!"

"Hi," returned Tim automatically to each strange face. It was a reflex action now. A thousand people a day said hello to him, and he had learned to return every greeting like an automaton, though he had no idea who they were, whether they were players, tourists, hotel people, or even his own employees.

Some had to talk to him. They had to congratulate him on saving gambling in Atlantic City. Padgett had been elected handily, but the referendum to repeal gambling had been defeated. It was a narrow defeat, and everyone gave Tim credit for it because he'd hired all the black dealers. They tended to ignore the fact that Padgett had campaigned vigorously in the Inlet against his own referendum.

It took him and Caro an hour to make three blocks. The bright sun took the temperature all the way up into the seventies. Not really paying any attention to the people talking at him, Tim watched flock after flock of Canada geese fly in over Convention Hall and land in the waterways behind the island. Dressed in black, white and gray morning suits, the geese looked like early morning wedding parties, the grooms out in front with the best men, and the ushers gliding along behind in disorderly v's.

Eventually they reached the Terrarium. It was a proud tower of natural greens refusing to conform to November's faded browns. Caro's heart raced as they waited in the Terrarium's entryway chambers. Harris's was in the Terrarium. Harris's was famous for its rubies.

The smell of the Terrarium's indoor rain forest permeated Harris's, making Caro feel as if she just stepped off a plane in Nicaragua. Her skin was coated with a film of humidity. It was hot inside Harris's, or maybe she was hot with her excitement over the ruby channel bands. The salesman had presented her with a selection of twenty. He was a handsome young Englishman in a morning suit. Harris's was very formal.

She narrowed the selection down to three, then closed her eyes and reached out blindly. She found herself holding the silver one with all square little rubies.

"A lucky selection, Mrs. Seagurt," smiled the salesman. "The small, square rubies are rare."

"Can we really afford it?" she asked Tim. She had wanted it so

long, it was hard to believe she was really getting it just by the
pointing of a finger.

"September was good to us," said Tim. "October wasn't so hot,
but September was great, even at point zero zero seven."

The salesman put the ring in a new satin box.

"How much is it?" asked Tim.

"Three thousand, two hundred dollars, Mr. Seagurt."

Tim took out a large handfull of bills. He counted out thirty-two
hundreds. He counted them out like a dealer. The bills spread out
across the glass case almost of their own volition. She realized he
had to be counting money every day at the Ondine to handle
money that way.

Finished, he pointed to a solitary ruby in the showcase below.
"How much is that one? Let's try it on for fun."

The salesman got it out and slipped it on Caro's finger. It went
on too easily. The ring was too large.

"I have some other stones in the vault, Mrs. Seagurt," he said,
withdrawing it gently from her finger. "We could mount one for
you this afternoon if you'd like to choose one."

"Bring them out," said Tim.

The salesman disappeared into the back of the store and returned with a cloth folded up to make a bag. He opened it and
dumped several stones out onto his long gray pad. The rubies
splashed across the gray felt like a stream of translucent blood.

"Look at this one!" said Caro excitedly, picking up one of the
larger ones. It was a glittering spike with a perfectly round head.
She imagined Tim driving it into her ring finger with a diamond
hammer. No ring to hold it on, just a brilliant red tack nailed into
her bone to feed on the marrow inside.

"That one is forty-three thousand dollars," said the salesman
proudly.

Caro trembled. She looked at Tim.

"We'll take it," he said. His beautiful sienna eyes were glowing.

When they were alone on the Ondine elevator, he took her by
her shoulders and kissed her. She sucked on his tongue and
rubbed her breasts against him.

Tim breathed heavily as he let her mouth go. "There's something about spending that kind of money that's exciting."

"I know," she said.

"You want it?"

"I want it."

The elevator door opened on their floor and their flirting was interrupted by a noise from down their end of the hall. The door to one of the nearby rooms was open. As they came down the hall, they realized the noise was a man sobbing.

They could see him inside. His wife was trying to comfort him.

"It will be all right," she was repeating over and over again. "It will be all right."

She had her arm around his shoulder. They were both in their sixties.

"It's not going to be all right!" He broke away from her and faced her angrily. "I lost eighty thousand."

"Eighty thousand?" She couldn't comprehend it.

"I'm sorry, Tina. I'm sorry." He broke into sobs again. "What was I thinking? I didn't know what I was doing."

His wife turned away from him. She held onto her temples with both hands. Her fingers quivered uncontrollably.

"Russ, Russ, Russ."

"We'll have to sell the house," he said. "We'll have to move into an apartment. . . ."

"They'll see us," whispered Tim, taking Caro by the arm and leading her away.

Inside their suite, they got undressed and got into bed together. The curtains were open. Tim played fondly with her breasts. He began to kiss them. She held onto his erection, staring out into the beautiful cloudless sky. Tears came spilling down along her cheeks onto her neck, making her quiver from the chill of them. At first Tim thought it was passion, and his hand moved down across her abdomen towards her pussy. In an instant, he realized something was wrong, and he sat up quickly, looking at her in surprise.

"You're crying."

"I'm sorry," she cried, reaching for the night table. She snatched a tissue out of the box and tried to stop her tears with it. "It's not a nice time to start crying, is it?"

"What's wrong, Caro?" he asked anxiously.

It was a few minutes before she could answer, because the crying got worse. He always got very upset when she cried. She could see him studying her through her tears. He was worried and nervous. His erection was gone. All the eroticism between them was gone. There was no longer any way of hiding it.

"Caro, what's wrong?" he asked again.

"That man has to sell his house," she said, "and here we are buying rubies."

"I know, I know," he said. "It's too bad things like that have to happen."

"Why do you let them go on until they're ruined?" she asked.

"That kind of thing is an accident," he said. "It happens because it's so hard to tell when they are lying about how much money they have."

"Can't you give him some of his money back?" asked Caro.

"If he's that kind of gambler, he'll just go down the boardwalk and play somewhere else with it," answered Tim.

"Why do we have to stay here?" she asked. "Let's pack up and get out of here."

"We're trying to make a bundle of money," he said hollowly. "Enough to last us the rest of our lives."

"I don't want to make it this way," said Caro.

"What do you mean?" he asked

"Didn't that man mean anything to you?" she asked. "You walked right in here and got undressed without saying a word. Didn't you feel anything about him?"

"Yes, I felt something," he said. "I hate that as much as you do."

"I don't think you do," she said.

He turned away from her and looked out the window. His silence hung between them like a poisonous gas. She couldn't see or guess what he was thinking, but she couldn't let it pass now, no matter how dangerous it was to throw it up at him.

"Do you know what you're like in the casino?" she asked. "Do you know why I stopped coming in there to see you?"

"No."

He had asked her night after night to come down to the casino with him, and she had continually refused, making up phony excuses. He'd known she was avoiding it on purpose. Now he looked back to her, puzzled, and hurt that she'd been keeping the reason from him to use as a weapon when she needed it.

"What am I like in the casino?" he asked in his hollow, disinterested voice.

"You're always watching one big player or another like you are in some kind of war with him." she said. "You grind your jaw and sometimes your eye blinks and you call whoever it is all kinds of names. The same guys you give big smiles and handshakes when they come in, you call bastards and pricks all night long. I remember one night when one poor man was losing forty thousand at craps. Every five minutes you'd jump up off your bar stool and run down the deck out into the casino to see how he was doing. When he cracked, when he got to the point they all get to, where he was pushing money across the table at you thousands at a time, you came hurrying back to me in the barge with a big shit-eating grin on your face. 'We got the fucking son of a bitch now,' you said to me, like it was the best news in the world. I'd never seen you so delighted."

"I was worried he was going to beat us," said Tim, remembering the incident well. Caro had looked at him like she wanted to hit him.

"The poor guy thinks he's coming to the casino to have a good time," said Caro, getting angry. "How can you be so delighted he's ruining himself?"

"That poor guy beat us for twenty thousand the night before," he said. "He could afford to lose some."

"How do you know he could afford it?" she said. "You just said you can't always tell."

"That one I was sure of."

"I don't believe you," she said. "I think that's what you say to rationalize it. Nobody can afford to throw away that kind of money."

"Most of them can," said Tim. "I don't take pleasure in ruining people, Caro."

"Really?" she asked. "Not even when it's going to make you enough money to last you the rest of your life?"

He got out of the bed and started dressing. She watched him slowly button up his shirt. It fit snugly. She had made an impression on him about his shirts. It was the only thing she could think of he'd allowed her to contribute to their marriage: tailor-made shirts. He stopped at the door, unwilling to leave her angry.

"Let's not fight any more like this," he said. "It's not worth it. Atlantic City is only temporary for us."

"I can't stand it here for another ten months," she said.

"It won't be that long," he said. "I took you out shopping today to get you the ring because we won't be here that much longer."

His eyes had the boiling, excited look they'd had when he told her at the Pier they were going to get rich on his point seven percent; and after that first lucky night when he'd hired all the black dealers. Now he had something new to glow about, and she would have demanded to know how he was so fucking certain it was going to work, but she couldn't stand to be convinced again. He could see she was still upset, and he sat down on the bed beside her. He reached up underneath her hair and tenderly scratched her scalp. She started crying again.

"Tim, what's happening to us," she asked through her new tears.

"I don't know."

"Something is so wrong," she said. "Things are really wrong when we're not fucking each other all the time. You know that, don't you?"

"I know," he said.

"I feel helpless," she said. "I feel like I'm at the mercy of everything and everybody."

"We'll be out of here in two weeks," he promised urgently. "We'll take a trip somewhere. We'll forget this town and all the shit that's happened here."

Even though Tim was very busy wiring some new kind of hardware into the casino computer, he came up to the suite every morning after the count to wake her by noon. Some mornings he fucked her like he was doing his duty. Then they went out to lunch together. They went out to lunch every day, duty done or not. Their fight had disturbed him, and now he wanted to keep her as happy as he could. He spent lunch with her like a divorced father taking his daughter to the zoo on weekends.

Today they were eating at the Water Company, the bar and restaurant on top of the Monopoly. They had one of the big windows with a view of the beach and ocean. The beach was crowded with seagulls bombing the sand with clams. The ocean was rough, a thick, spitting cream of asparagus soup. Far out on its rim, a pillar of gray was climbing the sky.

Caro played with a pack of Water Company matches. They had a cute inkline water tap on the cover. It was a nice logo. She'd done one like it for a hi-fi company two years ago.

They ate their appetizers without conversation. She didn't enjoy these lunches. The main course came but she didn't look at her plate. She had a slight sickness and it didn't leave her much of an appetite.

The pillar of gray was traveling towards them surprisingly fast. It had grown into a huge column of smokey charcoal. It glimmered with flickers of lightning.

"Look at the thunderstorm," she told Tim.

"Yes," he said, looking at it for a moment, then glancing at her plate. "You're not eating your bass."

"I'm not hungry."

"You're losing weight," he said.

"Let's go back to the hotel," she said. "It's going to rain soon."

He shrugged and motioned for the check. It quickly appeared and he signed on the line of the comp stamp and left a big tip in cash.

As they waited for the elevator, she watched the thunderstorm arch up into the sky in a black hook. There was a puff of brilliant white at the bottom. The high winds of the storm drew it upwards, sucking long white streamers into the roiled black clouds above it. Suddenly the thunderhead, which had been climbing the sky ever since she had noticed it on the horizon, stopped its ascent. It turned downwards towards Atlantic City, descending like liquid lead spilling down a chute. The tendrils of white clouds were obliterated with black.

Everyone in the dining room was watching apprehensively as the storm rolled right in on top of the Monopoly. Lightning was crackling all around them, and the towering hotel shook like an airplane caught in the overwhelming winds. The lights flickered and went out.

A hush fell over the dining room. The only noise was the creaking of the big plate-glass windows, which sounded as if they were going to pop out of their frames. People sitting next to the windows started leaving their seats.

The lights came back on with a surprising flash, and the elevator door opened.

The first passenger off was Kedar Padgett.

He had a large entourage which got off behind him. They were different than his preelection crowd. They were much younger and more stylish. The Hispanic and Oriental elements were gone. They were all black.

He was surprised to see Tim. It had been some time since they'd met.

"They told us not to come up," he said to Tim, the thunder distracting his attention for a second. "Do you think it's going to blow the building down?"

"No," said Tim.

They spoke as if they were the best of friends, as if they'd only just left each other's company minutes earlier, but Caro could sense the hostility between them. They both wished they'd passed each other in different elevators.

"I've got to talk to you," said Padgett.

"Okay," said Tim. "I'll be right back, Caro."

Tim walked back out into the empty dining room with Padgett following. Padgett's group filtered slowly and cautiously behind into the darkened room, and Caro followed along. Tim went right to the big table by the window which had obviously been reserved for Padgett's large party. He sat down and looked out the window at the angry weather, as if it were a novel and enjoyable treat to lunch during a thunderstorm. Padgett kept looking back and forth between the storm and Tim. A bolt of thunder cracked especially loud, and everyone jumped, including Tim.

"Noisy, isn't it?" said Tim. "Sit down, Padgett. How many times in your life will you have a chance to eat ringside to a thunderstorm?"

"Are you crazy, Seagurt?" asked Padgett. "Is this your mad Thomas act?"

"I don't get it, Padgett," said Tim. "I hear you're mad at me. What are you mad at me for? I gave you everything you wanted."

Padgett looked around to see if anyone was listening to them over the noise. His entourage had retreated several yards, and the rest of the dining room was empty. Frightened by the violence of the wind against the creaking windows, everyone in the dining room had retreated to the bar.

"The election is over and suddenly you're not hiring my friends anymore," he said over the noise, moving close to where Tim was sitting. "I send people down to the Ondine and they don't get jobs. Other guys come around telling me they've been fired."

"I caught them stealing," said Tim.

"You said all the other hotels would copy the Ondine," said Padgett.

"You said that," said Tim. "I agreed with you because I thought it was going to work. But it doesn't work."

"What do you mean, it doesn't work," said Padgett. "You're getting rich on it."

"Most of your boys are stealing now," said Tim. "So much for the concept of racial, educational and sociological purity, huh?"

"And now that the election is over, you think you're off the hook," said Padgett, looking at Tim with angry wonder.

"Now that the election is over, and the pure-race theory has been thoroughly discredited by both black and white, I'll hire anyone who can do the job," said Tim.

"Fooled again brothers," Padgett turned to shout back to his crowd of supporters. Turned out in cashmere and leather, they'd come to have lunch with their disheveled hero. They all seemed to know Tim and hate him. "We sold out for a few rotten jobs in one lousy casino!" he called to them.

He turned back to Tim. "Fool me once, that's okay. That's your bite for being toad enough to do it. But fool me twice and that's my bite for coming back for more. I never come back for more, Tim. I don't get fooled again. You've got to come up with some money now."

"Why should I?" asked Tim.

"Hey, what's wrong with you?" asked one of Padgett's crowd. He was younger than Padgett. He wore a handsome russet tweed suit. Tim recognized him. His name was Terdell something, and he was one of Padgett's new commissioners. He was a machine democrat.

"We're not asking for anything unusual," he said. "We have some campaign debts to pay, that's all."

"Campaign debts?" mocked Tim.

Padgett laughed his rich, ingratiating laugh. The storm had quieted down and suddenly they could hear each other talk without shouting. The hiatus seemed to suck some emotion out of them, and suddenly they were friendly again.

"What happened to the honest corruption platform?" Tim asked Padgett.

"I'm still going with it," said Padgett. "Don't pay any attention to him. What happened to the honest casino?"

"It's a little harder to accomplish than I figured," said Tim. "But I'll get it."

"Oh, come on, Tim," said Padgett. "You gave up on that bullshit already. You were just waiting for the election to pass so we couldn't do anything to you."

"What makes you think so?" asked Tim.

"You're getting rich and you don't want anyone to know about it, but you can't keep a secret in this town," said Padgett. "Everyone in Atlantic City knows you spent a million dollars on the boardwalk a couple of days ago."

"A million dollars," laughed Tim. "Where the hell did you hear that?"

"You were up and down the boardwalk buying out every store in sight," said Padgett, annoyed. "You don't think you can walk into Harris's and buy a two hundred thousand dollar ruby and nobody's going to talk about it, do you?"

Tim chortled to himself, taking a twisted pleasure in this incredible rumor. In general, Atlantic City's enthusiasm for exaggeration was great; but when it came to money, its powers of distortion were astonishing.

"What are you chuckling about?" asked Padgett, getting mad again.

"It's funny," said Tim.

"What's funny?"

"I didn't spend anything near that kind of money," said Tim. "And I only went in one store."

"You're a liar," said Padgett. "You either help us with some

money, or gambling's ugly friends are going to rub your face
where you don't want it."

"You want to get rid of gambling?" mocked Tim. "Go ahead. Put
it back on the ballot for next November and vote it out."

"You don't believe I will?" shouted Padgett.

"I don't care what you do, you greedy son of a bitch," said Tim,
standing up and glaring at Padgett.

"Hey, wait a minute," shouted Terdell in the tweed suit. "Don't
you know who you're talking to, Seagurt?"

"Yes, I know who I'm talking to," answered Tim quickly. "Lester
Maddox in blackface."

Padgett snatched his cigar out of his mouth and stared at Tim
with hatred. "All right," he said, his rich voice barely audible, "I
hear you."

He threw his cigar down on the table. The ash rolled across the
spotless linen tablecloth leaving a trail of orange embers and
black burning pock marks. He turned around and pushed his way
out among his court.

"You asshole," Terdell said to Tim. "Don't you know this guy is
every bit as crazy as you are?"

He hurried away to join Padgett and the rest of them, leaving
Caro standing alone where the entourage had been.

"Did you hear that?" he asked her.

"Most of it."

"That silly bastard thinks I'm going to put the Ondine's license
in jeopardy and my head in a noose so he can tighten it whenever
he likes," he said. "Fuck him. I'll be out of here with my money
long before he can put gambling on the ballot again."

The storm had picked up again. Black roiled clouds were washing right in against the window. She couldn't see more than a few
feet out. The nearly liquid mist slammed against the thick glass
in waves, making the window creak and groan like a bulkhead
trying to hold back inky seas. Spokes of lightning whirled about
so close outside she could feel static electricity in the air inside the
dining room. The lightning began to hit the building. Somehow
it reached into the wiring of the hotel, and blue sparks several
inches long came flaring out of a nearby outlet with a terrifyingly
loud *SNAP!*

THE MONEY Tree was crowded. There were long lines at the low-limit tables. She'd gotten ten thousand for the ruby, so she had enough to go right to a hundred-dollar-minimum table. She bought in for two thousand.

It disappeared quickly. She might have wanted to show a little patience and cut back to smaller bets, but it was a hundred-dollar minimum so she couldn't. She didn't feel like waiting in line for a five-dollar seat either. She bought another two thousand.

Hector's lecture haunted her. He had stopped her a couple of days ago and talked at her. He'd spit it out quickly, as if he were afraid she was going to slap him. "Can't you find something else to think about besides how lucky you are?"

Something different was happening to her now. She wasn't concentrating on the cards. She couldn't pay attention. She was so afraid of losing that she couldn't watch. Something was wrong. The cards' entire function was to absorb her, but they were frightening her.

Hector was right. She should go back to the Ondine and make herself work again. But work had become something she couldn't do while there were casinos open. The thought of working and working and working on something that might completely fizzle out led directly to the idea of playing blackjack, where at least she had a chance of luck intervening and making something great out of shit.

The big siren went off, and the searchlights came on overhead in the silver money tree. Money started coming down. It made no impression on any of the players at the hundred-dollar table. Caro sat there looking back and forth at the other players, envying them their absorption and telling herself again to cash out because she couldn't lose herself in it anymore, but she sat there, playing blackjack and feeling sick.

There was a big heavy man sitting next to her. He had three squares staked out with hundred-dollar chips. He stared at his cards intently. He was playing unlucky like everyone else at the table, but he didn't say a word besides *hit* or *stand.* The only hint that there was any emotion going on inside him was the way he smoked cigarette after cigarette down to the filter. His fingers were yellow with nicotine stains.

Suddenly he took all the money he had left, near nine thousand, and asked the floorman's permission to bet it all on one hand. The floorman accepted his bet.

He saw Caro looking at him.

"It's about time I got a blackjack," he said. "I was here all last night, and I didn't get a blackjack after two-thirty. Not one. And I haven't seen one today since they opened. I'm about due, don't you think?"

"Yes," agreed Caro.

He drew fifteen, hit it, and went busted.

"That's a shame," said Caro.

He sighed and lit another cigarette. The shift boss appeared at the table as if he had been called by some signal. He had a white card in his hand.

"Where do I stand, Felix?" asked the man.

"Ten so far today, Mr. Roskoe," said Felix.

"I'll take another ten," said Roskoe.

"Another ten thousand, Helen," said Felix.

Helen measured out nine orange chips and ten black ones. She passed them over to Roskoe. He went back to playing three hands at a time.

Now he bet two hundred dollars a hand instead of one. He was silent again. He didn't say hit or stand anymore, but signaled with his hand. The cards ran a little better for Caro, but they continued to punish Roskoe. His play got more and more reckless, his bets higher and higher. He stared at his cards with intense concentration, but Caro wondered if he really saw them. The way he was playing the hands had no relation to reality. The hands simply provided the pauses in between his pressing more and more money on the Money Tree.

She lost her sympathy for him. He revolted her. Her neck started to hurt. Now it was cutting through the blackjack, and as she watched this Roskoe behave like an idiot, she felt like she was more like him and all the rest of them than she'd let herself believe.

It wasn't only that she played cards with the same masturbatory greed as Roskoe and all the rest of them. It wasn't only that she ruined money like they did. It was that she was every bit as disgusting inside as they were. They would do anything or say anything, no matter how stupid, to get to the heart of that giddy, all-powerful feeling that came with winning. She had to have it too, and at the same incredible cost. Maybe they were more blatant about it because they also chased it with their mouths, pumping themselves up with fantasies of their own greatness, while Caro at least omitted that part. Goody for her; her pursuit of blackjack, squinting over the cards trying to find *luck*—the word suddenly had the power to make her nauseous—was just as sick as any mouthings of any cosmetics millionaire. She was as disgusting inside as any of them, except she preferred to keep the poison secret, pretending—God, she didn't know what she was pretending. Suddenly she felt herself throwing up.

She had downed a couple of drinks to quiet the espresso from the morning's work. It all gushed up onto the layout in a dark brown stream. She didn't even have time to get her hand up or turn her head. Helen jumped back. The other players started shouting at her, but it was impossible to stop. She retched uncontrollably. They were all out of their chairs and retreating.

The Money Tree started to spin, and then somebody had a hold of her. He was helping her to her feet. It had to be a security man. She reached for her chips as he started to help her away from the table. He stopped and let her get them. She fumbled them into her purse as he helped her out of the casino. The side entrance of the Money Tree opened out on Park Place, and she thought he was going to dump her out there and let her throw up in the gutter, but he kept hold of her and started up the street towards the boardwalk. This was a lot farther than most security men went, and when she looked up to see why, she discovered he wasn't a security man at all. He was Konnie Odo.

He helped her into one of the Ondine boardwalk carts. The ride back made her nauseous again, so he bought her a bottle of kaopectate in the drugstore and took her up to the suite. After a couple of spoonfulls of kaopectate, her nausea retreated. She thanked him for helping her, saying it was lucky he was passing by when he did.

"That wasn't luck," he said, grinning. Konnie was always grinning.

"What do you mean?"

"I'd been watching you for awhile," he said.

Caro suddenly felt sick again. She rushed into the bathroom, fell over the toilet and gagged. Her stomach tightened up into a hard ball and she kept gagging and gagging, but the most she could bring up was a little bit of the kaopectate.

When she came back out, Konnie was waiting by the bedroom window.

She walked over and stood beside him.

"What are you looking at?" she asked him.

"I look at this place, and I see Vegas," he said. "The colors, the people. It's hard not to see it."

He looked up from the boardwalk and out at the late November surf. It was taupe, flecked with white to the horizon.

"Except for the ocean," he said. "We had mountains, instead. And desert. We used to come across that desert at night coming into town from military school, and when we saw Vegas glowing in the night, this incredible thing painting a navy sky with colors . . . I've stayed out of this town until now, because . . ."

He was lost in a reverie, looking out on the ocean as if it were a gray and white desert.

"It's almost Thanksgiving," he said. "Thanksgiving was always the first vacation of the year. It was only four days, but, man, were we glad to see Vegas."

He smiled at her with his big grin and she smiled back. Military school had a way of creeping into much of his conversation, and she was never left with any doubt as to how much he hated it.

"I called Tim while you were in the bathroom," he said. "He's coming up."

"Oh, Jesus, Konnie, you're not going to tell Tim," she said.

"I'm going to tell him, Caro," he said. "He's going to find out anyway. Hector can only cover you so far. He's been using up all his favors on your comp slips because he got you started, but there comes a time when a friend stops throwing things down a gambler's well. When you start picking thousand-dollar chips up off dressers, nobody can cover for you."

"Hector knows about that?" asked Caro. She was surprised. Except for his one little lecture, Hector always smiled at her and talked to her like she was a princess. "I thought Bruce never even realized it was gone."

"They always know how many checks they have," grinned Konnie. "Caro, what has Tim been doing while all of this is going on?"

She laughed. "He's busy in the casino with Hector and Henry. They're down there all day and most of the nights wiring all the tables for something."

"Wiring the tables?" asked Konnie, puzzled.

"The three of them are like Hoppy, Gabby, and Lucky after a gang of bank robbers," she said. "I see Tim once a day for lunch. Did you ever notice that Hoppy never had any girlfriends? He couldn't let go of his pals Lucky and Gabby long enough."

Konnie laughed. She smiled weakly at his appreciation of her jokes. She realized how much she had missed seeing him.

"Are you going to throw up again?" Konnie asked.

She did feel woozy. "Maybe I should have a little more kaopectate. I threw it up before."

He got the bottle and fed her two more tablespoons of it. "Yuck!" she said. "That's bitter."

They heard the door open out in the living room, and they went out to meet Tim. Tim was so pleased to see Konnie that it took Konnie ten minutes to start making his way toward the point. Caro waited, dreading Tim's reaction, wanting to run out of the room, but making herself stay because she had to tell him why she had done what she'd done.

"I knew exactly what was wrong when you called me about not giving money to Caro," said Konnie. "But I've found out how much good unsolicited advice does for people. About as much as solicited advice—zero. But then Hector called me, and so here I am, trying the impossible."

"Is this the same kind of advice you gave me when I first told you I was coming here?" asked Tim.

"The same," said Konnie.

"Hector never said anything to me about knowing you," said Tim, obviously trying to change the subject.

"Of course Hector knows me," said Konnie, flashing his big snaggle-tooth grin beneath the moustache. "You'll find that people in the gambling business fall into two large categories: either they know Hector, or they used to work for my old man."

Tim laughed, and for an instant Caro believed Konnie was going to make it all better.

Then they were quiet.

Konnie had a rare, serious look on his face. His features were disturbing when he wasn't smiling. Caro could see he knew what he was risking. He was Tim's best friend, but Tim could still cut him right out of his life for something like this. She'd seen him do it to other people for less.

Tim started to say something but stopped. He resigned himself to listen to it. Only Konnie could make him sit still for something like this.

"Caro has been playing, Tim," said Konnie. "Playing quite a bit. I have a feeling you're going to start hearing about her markers from other hotels soon."

"Only one," said Caro. "I was afraid Tim would find out."

"It's not as bad as it could be then," said Konnie. "But she has a problem, Tim."

Caro was staring at Tim. She'd been staring at him since he'd come in, but he hadn't looked at her once.

"Why do I get the feeling Tim knows all about this?" asked Konnie. "Am I spitting into the wind here?"

"Of course I know about it," said Tim angrily. "When the wife of the manager of the largest casino in Atlantic City goes out and plays at every joint in town, there are plenty of volunteers to bring the story back home."

"You've known about it all along?" asked Caro in astonishment. "All the blackjack after you caught me at the slots?"

"Yes."

"And you didn't say anything about it?"

"Why should I?"

"God, Tim," she shouted. "Didn't you care?"

"You're damn right I care," he said. "But what you do is up to you."

"I can't believe it," she said, almost shrieking. "You knew all along. I'm going crazy worrying that something's going to get back to you, that you're going to get hurt, and I'm feeling so guilty, and, and—and you don't do a thing to help me. Even though you know what's happening, you don't do or say anything."

"I bought you a ruby," he said. "I took you out to lunch. I tried to get you to work."

She was amazed at how calm he was about it. He had already had this argument with her in his mind, and, as usual, he knew what she was going to say before she said it.

"Tim, I've been trashing myself and everything between us," she said. "How can you not say anything about it?"

"Why should I?"

"Why should you?" she screamed. "Why should you? We're married. You're supposed to take care of me, you son of a bitch!"

"Oh, am I?" he was shouting too, even louder than she. *"You* wanted to marry *me!* I didn't want to marry you. I never promised to take care of anybody. You might have thought you were going to get that out of me, but you didn't!"

He had been saying it for years, but she hadn't heard it. She remembered his first little speech, before they got married, about her being on her own. He had posted her on it weekly from the day after they returned from the honeymoon. But it was always about separate bank accounts and who was going to buy the groceries which week. It was a parlor game to get his way on which movie to see. It was his way of making sure she didn't spend too much of her money. What the hell did it have to do with getting in trouble? It couldn't possibly go this deep. It couldn't possibly be one of his traps.

But it was. It was a trap five years in the making. Only Tim could work that long on fooling somebody. She had been going along thinking somehow this mess would end because he would see how helpless she'd become and he would have to rescue her. He wouldn't be able to stand it when he finally saw it. She had dreaded the moment all along, but she had hoped for it too, because it was the only way she was going to make it out. But he could stand it. He was determined to stand it. She was so stunned she couldn't quite grasp it. She had to sit down. She looked up at Konnie inquisitively, as if he could interpret this new data for her.

Tim was still angry.

"Why the hell should I take care of you?" he demanded. "Are you going to take care of me?"

"Why should I take care of you?" she asked stupidly.

"Exactly," he said bitterly.

"But nobody needs to take care of you," she said, looking at Konnie again, waiting for him to say something.

"Don't look at Konnie," said Tim. "Let me give you the bad news. You're on your own. Beginning, middle and end. When you fuck up, it's your fault. When I fuck up, it's my fault. Nobody wants to take care of me and nobody wants to take care of you!"

Now she had no answer to this ugly motto of his. She *had* agreed they were on their own.

The familar, ugly, poisonous silence that had punctuated all their recent dialogues closed this one as well. It was more than a minute before Konnie spoke.

"Tim, you've got to get out of Atlantic City."

"Fuck, Konnie, I know I've got to get out of here!" said Tim. "I've been going crazy here. I can't tell you how much fun it is to have people come up to you and try to score points off your wife's vice. He looked at Caro with hatred. "I can't tell you how much fun it is to go into that casino every night knowing everybody on both sides of those ropes is trying to steal your money. I can't tell you how much fun it is to have some ignorant bastard walk off a fifty-thousand winner. I can't tell you how much fun I'm having here in the Playground of the World. Is that what you mean when you say I've got to get out of here?"

"That's what I mean."

"I can't go now," he said.

"Why not?" said Konnie, "No. Don't tell me the reason. Whatever it is, it's not good enough. You and Caro belong together, Tim. I don't care how you settle this crap about who's supposed to take care of whom, you still belong together. Okay, Caro's been out fucking herself up on the sly, but Tim, you put her in a bad position. You yanked her away from her job and stuck her in a gambling town where the only thing she could do was gamble."

"What do you mean?" said Tim. "It's not my fault she gambles."

"The hell it isn't your fault," he said. "If you lived down in Avalon, maybe, just maybe, she'd have a chance. But holy shit, you've got her stuck right in the middle of the biggest hotel in the Atlantic City, and the town is all around her. There's no way anybody can work in this kind of atmosphere. Nobody, Tim. How the hell can you work when everybody around you is having a good time, and telling you you have to have a good time; and man, this whole town is shouting as loud as it can twenty-four hours a day: Have a good time!"

Caro sat passively in the oversized sofa. She felt like a baby in a big leather crib. If Konnie couldn't convince Tim to leave Atlantic City, she didn't know what she was going to do. Maybe she'd jump out the window and make a splash on the boardwalk. It would turn up some vivid colors.

"I'm working," said Tim. "Why shouldn't she?"

"What a load of shit," said Konnie. "You aren't working. You're having a good time. Or maybe you're past that. Maybe you're on the hook now like Caro's been. But don't say you've been working, because you haven't been. You've been trying to get high just like everybody else in this town. You've been trying so hard you refuse to see what's happening to Caro, and what will soon be happening to you."

Tim shook his head. "You don't understand, Konnie. I'll be out of here in a week."

"Make it an hour," said Konnie. "Okay, so you're both pissed off. You'll get over that. Take what you have left while you still can. Go somewhere else and do something else, but leave this alone."

"All right, Konnie, maybe I will," said Tim. "But you let me explain something first."

"Nothing can explain staying here," said Konnie.

"Konnie, you grew up in Vegas and you're convinced that everyone has to learn that all gambling towns are hell, so you can't even listen to me," said Tim.

"That's right," agreed Konnie.

"I'll make a deal with you," said Tim. "If you listen to me, I'll listen to you."

"What do you mean?"

"I'll explain why I can't leave," said Tim. "I'll explain it right into your blind prejudice; and, if you can still say that I don't have a chance, Caro and I will pack our bags the instant you say it."

"That's a deal," said Konnie.

"One thing more," said Tim.

"What?"

"Don't lie."

"Me?"

"Give me your word you won't lie just to get me out of here," demanded Tim.

"All right."

"I came to Atlantic City a little innocent about what casinos were like," said Tim. "I'd figured out that the per was the most important thing, and that the big problem was stealing. But I was wrong when I thought I could change it simply by hiring naive, uncorrupted dealers."

"Of course you were wrong!" said Konnie. "The job itself is corrupting. Anybody with a reasonably decent mentality quits it in less than a week."

"Right," said Tim. "So my per keeps going down and down as they get better and better at cheating."

"So what's the new system?" asked Konnie.

"Henry Moore sold me on the idea of tracking the *per* on each table day by day using a Graphic Terminals mainframe in the office," said Tim, "but we lost interest in that when I hired all the new dealers. We thought we had all the dishonesty whipped."

Konnie laughed.

"You remember when I helped buy Graphic Terminals into Colony?" asked Tim.

"Sure."

"Do you remember its story and why it's done so well?"

"Aside from a routine mainframe business," answered Konnie, "they developed a small computing pack that could compute at the terminal instead of going all the way to the mainframe."

"Right," said Tim. "The biggest cost in computer technology had become the cost of interfacing with the core computer, and Graphic Terminals reduced the need for interfacing by ninety percent."

"What does this have to do with casinos?" asked Konnie.

"Well, we were using only the Graphic mainframe and getting nowhere because the Ondine is so big," said Tim. "Sure, we know which table has the lowest per and we watch it, but we don't even know which of the dealers at the table is involved. We have to watch for hours to catch somebody, and meanwhile things are getting worse every night because while we're watching one table, fourteen others are going crazy."

"So what's new in the casino business?" cracked Konnie.

"The optical scanner," said Tim excitedly, his light eyes glowing. "That's what's new in the casino business."

Caro began to see something in Tim she had been missing ever since they'd come to Atlantic City. As he talked about the computer and the casino, he walked up and back in front of Konnie like a big cat. She had read something in the newspaper about lions during one of her many solitary afternoons. The article had stuck in her mind for days and now she knew why. The lions were like Tim. The paper said lions don't feel angry or murderous when they're chasing something they want to kill. They don't even have any idea they're inflicting pain on their prey when they catch them. They're like kids running down long fly balls in "Three Flies and You're Up." They're having fun, and that's all they feel. A magnified, pure, bestial fun. That was exactly what the casino business was to Tim. It was something to solve for the fun of it. He had no idea how much he was hurting people. The per was something to catch, and the harder the chase, the more powerful the fun.

"You mean the scanners they use for paper bills in slot machines?" asked Konnie.

"That's right," said Tim. "With optical scanning, we can count the drop as it drops, and I've finally got them installed at every table in the Ondine."

"What good are they going to do you?" asked Konnie. The stealing is done with chips."

"I've got see-through chip trays so the computing pack can count the chips going out with a light annunciator," said Tim.

"But you still won't know if the dealer is paying off a dollar bet with thousand dollar chips," said Konnie.

"I know," said Tim. "I'm going to use the optical scanning and the small pack computer to compute the per of each table from instant to instant."

Konnie's big craggy brow furrowed. Caro could see Tim had him going in his direction.

"Do you see it?" asked Tim eagerly. "The Ondine is so big, it's so fucking big, it's a whole universe unto itself. That's its biggest weakness, right?"

"Right," said Konnie, still puzzled but starting to see where Tim was leading.

"I think I can make that weakness into a strength," said Tim. "Probability theory says that the larger your sample of numbers is, the closer their average will have to be to the norm, okay?"

"Yes."

"So when you have a lot of games in a casino," continued Tim swiftly, "they should be coming out very close to the law of averages. The Ondine, the biggest casino in the world, is a whole universe of numbers. You can't get a bigger sample. It's so big the numbers must conform to the law of averages from second to second."

"Holy shit," said Konnie.

"You see it, don't you?" asked Tim. "With optical scanning, I can predict when a dealer is most likely to steal. Profound deviations from the law of averages will be like a big finger pointing right at the guy."

"Wait a minute," argued Konnie. "You have to correlate the pers, and each of the computer packs is doing only the per at its own table."

"The packs are wired to the mainframe," explained Tim. "They send in the pers and the correlation is done by the mainframe. It predicts where the cheating will be."

"I see," said Konnie. "It prints out the number of the table."

"Better than that," said Tim. "It selects the table from what's coming in from all the cameras and displays it on it's own monitor. I'm telling you, I've given that hundred-eyed monster a brain, an incredible brain. I've made it the Einstein of casino surveillance."

"I should have known you'd come up with something like this," said Konnie.

"It will revolutionize the gambling business," said Tim, starting to sail. "We can nail these creeps right in the act. They say twenty is a good per in this business? I'll make it forty. I'm going to catch every little bad move a dealer, a boss, or even a slot machine attendant can make. It will be adaptable to everything. I'm going to—"

"Tim! Tim!" Caro heard herself shouting. "Stop it!"

Konnie and Tim had gotten so busy with each other, they'd forgotten Caro was there, and they both stared at her in surprise.

"What's wrong?" asked Tim.

"You sound exactly like the rest of the idiots in this town," she said. "All these people are going on and on about how smart they are, but none of it makes any sense, because they're all airheads. They're nothing but obnoxious, posturing clucks. The same kind of people you have been telling me for years how much you despise. They're all trying to get people to believe in a stupid, ruinous, obvious, fucking *lie* because they're all *morons!*"

"You think I'm one of them?" asked Tim angrily. "Just another moron?"

"You sound like one!" she insisted.

"I'm on the other side of the table," he said coldly. "Ask Konnie. It will work."

She looked quickly to Konnie.

"Now tell the truth, you son of a bitch," said Tim.

"It might work, Caro," said Konnie. "But," he added turning back to Tim, "whether it works or not is irrelevant. You should still get out of here."

"Why?" asked Tim. "Christ, I've got to at least try it."

"But it doesn't matter," argued Konnie. "Being in the gambling business is a mistake, no matter how much money you make."

"But I won't have to be in it that long," said Tim. "If it works, I'll simply sell it to Colony. It's worth a few million at least."

"It's worth a hundred million if it works," said Konnie. "But this business isn't so easy to revolutionize."

"We'll see," said Tim.

"You know, Tim, I knew somebody who actually did revolutionize the gambling business once," said Konnie. "This fellow got the idea that as long as there was such a thing as a law of averages, there had to be a specific longterm hold for every kind of gambling game. He figured them out and started using them at the Nugget and, to the amazement of the gambling world, it worked. Within three months everybody on Fremont Street had copied him, and now every gambling hall in the world in one way or another keeps 'the figgers,' as he used to call them. You know what 'the figgers' are, don't you?"

"Per," said Tim.

"That's right," said Konnie. "And the fellow who figured it all out was Laddy Odo."

"I never knew that," said Tim, amazed at Konnie's keeping that secret.

"I never told you," said Konnie. "But I'm telling you now because I want you to see that it didn't revolutionize gambling at all. It's still full of all the same predators and thieves it's always had. All my father did was revolutionize the record-keeping."

"At least your father was smart," said Tim. "Mine doesn't even believe in the theory of evolution. Can you imagine that? A doctor who doesn't believe in the theory of evolution?"

"Don't change the subject," said Konnie.

"Look, Konnie, I'm not planning to spend the rest of my life in the casino business," said Tim. "I won't be more than another week here."

"And if it doesn't prove what you want it to prove in a week, you'll leave?" asked Konnie.

"Yes."

"And money grows on trees, too," said Konnie.

Tim stared at him in annoyance. "You can't say it won't work, can you?"

"No, I can't," admitted Konnie.

Caro struggled up out of the deep sofa. "Is that it Konnie? You're giving up?"

"What can I say, Caro?" he asked her, shrugging. "I made a mistake. I promised not to lie."

"We're going to stay?" she asked Tim.

"For a week."

She turned away from them and walked out of the room, quietly closing the hall doorway.

"You were damn cruel, Tim," said Konnie.

"She's been cruel to me," said Tim.

"I've heard about Margarite Boehm," said Konnie.

"Good for you," said Tim. He had enough advice.

"Man, if you want to trade Caro for her, you're crazy," said Konnie. He could see Tim had had enough instructions, but he wasn't going to stop. "And there's something else you should know about the gambling business. In addition to the personal corruption, you have to worry about the gangsters. It's hard to get by without an alliance with one. It's the nature of the game. I imagine some of them have been around."

"I don't have anything to do with them," said Tim.

"Fine," said Konnie. "But that means you're risking becoming one yourself."

Tim laughed. "You have an answer for everything."

"They won't leave you alone," continued Konnie. "You'll have to protect yourself."

"I've completely neutralized them, Konnie," said Tim. "When I defeated the anti-gambling resolution, I made myself so popular that they don't dare do anything to me."

"They'll be back, Tim," said Konnie. "Popularity irritates them."

"In the next week?" asked Tim.

"Sooner or later you'll have to protect yourself," said Konnie,

ignoring the reference to one week because he didn't believe it.
"You might be interested to know you have most of the qualities
a first-rate gangster has."

"Really?" asked Tim. "What are they?"

"Anger and outrage, mostly," said Konnie. "The feeling of being
something so special that laws were made for people lesser then
you. Sort of like Hitler. It all mixes together and violence comes
out. The only question I have for you is, do you have the heart for
it?"

"Thanks, it's not every day I'm compared to Hitler,"said Tim.

"Okay," said Konnie. "Make it Carlo Gambino."

"That's much better."

"Tim, don't laugh about this," said Konnie. "If you hang around
too long after things get started, and you don't have the heart for
it, you'll get killed."

·19·

TIM DROVE slowly through the geometric streets of Margate. It was
relaxing to let the BMW creep about the regular blocks. Margate
was very quiet; even the houses themselves seemed calm and
sedate.

He passed beach houses of many eras. The biggest were aging
piles of stucco with tile roofs. They were salted across Margate in
a pattern which had more to do with survival than planning. He
stopped the BMW in front of one of the larger ones for a closer
look. It was the same stucco box with the same tile roof as the rest,
standing on one of the bigger lots of geriatric brown winter grass,
but it had a grand, arching entrance. The arch was ten feet long
and speckled with rainbow tile. The different-colored small chips
of tile decorated the underside of the deep arch in irregular
swirls, like technicolor snow frozen into a curved sky. On the front
of the archway, the same colors were arranged in perfect squares
with Arabic precision. He wondered who owned it and who built
it. Margarite would know. He reminded himself to ask her.

He pulled away slowly, puzzlingly sad about something. He
continued driving around the square blocks of Margate, taking
turns wherever he felt like it. He saw several art-deco houses.
They all had a nautical look to them, their second-storey porches
looking like ships' bridges. There were also many modern houses

with clean lines and stained cedar siding. There were brick houses of all sizes and shapes which outnumbered all the stucco, stone and frame houses combined.

When he reached Lucy the wooden elephant, he turned around. He drove all the way back up Atlantic Avenue, through Margate again and Ventor, finally reaching the border of Atlantic City. Just past the small billboard—*Welcome to Atlantic City, The World's Playground*—were four old mansions left over from the turn of the century. They were neat and well kept. People with minor money didn't buy these houses. They were too expensive, and there was no way to justify them in any economic sense. They were only for people who didn't need them for anything in particular, people with so much money to spend that they'd given up testing the limits of their fortunes and bought whatever appealed to them without thought.

The biggest of them occupied half a full block. It was a giant red-brick Victorian mansion with a porch circling its entire swollen girth. It was too big, and its roof rose into several peaks of different sizes without any sense of proportion or design. From the street, it was anything but pleasing.

Inside it was remarkably beautiful. The chestnut stairway at the entrance led up onto a wide, long hallway with a substantial beehive fireplace kept loaded with flaming logs and orange coals from dawn till midnight in the winter. As big as the fireplace was, it was barely enough to keep the hallway warm because the ceiling was at least fourteen feet high.

There were several open doorways down the long hallway. One led to an outsized dining room behind which was a kitchen still larger. Other doorways led to a salon, a rumpus room, and a small library directly across from the fireplace, it's doorway nearly as long as the library itself. Despite it's large open door, the library was intimate and comfortable. It was paneled with the same rich chestnut which framed every doorway on the first floor. The entire fireplace was blocked with a gigantic, flickering double-T of chestnut. The wood, nearly a century old, had been polished and rubbed weekly since the first of the house's three generations had moved in ninety years earlier.

It was Margarite's house. She was expecting him, but he didn't feel like going in yet. She would need to get excited about something—she liked to keep manic—and he felt like shit. He turned the BMW around and started down Atlantic Avenue.

He estimated an asking price in the back of his mind for every house which appealed to him. He realized he was indulging himself in a futile exercise. He would need a real-estate agent.

"A real-estate agent?" he asked himself. "What the hell am I thinking of?"

He didn't have any money to buy a house, or any reason to. But he wanted one anyway. It came to him why he was riding around and looking at houses instead of keeping his date with Margarite. He missed Caro already. She had been gone three hours, and already he was trying to figure out some way to lure her back. His plan was a little grandiose, but it was the idea that was important, not the execution.

He brushed his realization aside. She had left him. He had tolerated everything, and she had left him. There was no chance he was going to do anything to bring her back. Fuck her. He didn't need her. She needed him.

Margarite didn't say anything about his being late when he came in. She greeted him in a navy-blue silk shirt and pale slacks.

"I have a surprise for you," she said, waiting patiently as he took off his coat in front of the fire.

She handed him a glass of champagne and he threw his coat across one of the hallway chairs. She went into the small library and he followed her, watching her pick up an official-looking piece of paper from the blotter on the built-in chestnut desk. She handed it to him. It was the title to the BMW.

"I'm giving the car to you," she said, eagerly.

He studied the title. It had his name on it. She had sent someone down to get it done that morning while he had been fighting with Caro.

"You don't seem very excited," she said in her cool, mature tone.

He looked up at her. Her changeability between maturity and youth had begun to preoccupy him. She could act and talk like the forty-six she was, but just as easily as she could become young and petulant. Beneath her need to be in a good mood, she was sad. When she was up, she was intelligent and urbane, with a surprisingly keen mind for business; but down, she had the appetites and emotions of a thirteen-year-old girl.

Her mouth was pretty. Her upper lip was always raised slightly in the middle, giving her a happy-looking smile. He kissed her.

"Is that better?"

She arched her thin eyebrows indifferently, and sat down in the chocolate-felt sofa.

"I'm sorry," he said, genuinely apologetic.

He should have been able to muster some real excitement for the car. No one who wasn't an expert on foreign cars would have taken this one for anything more than a curious German immitation of an old Nash, but he had loved it from the first time he'd driven it. It was a short coupe with a round nose and a flat back which descended from the roofline between two small fins. The only thing impressive about its exterior appearance was its rich purple paint. Margarite had been unsatisfied with the original BMW color and had it redone with several coats of Rolls Royce paint. The cool purple result was subtle and beautiful, luxurious and deep, like the car itself; beneath its unimposing exterior was an iceberg of German technology. It could change directions very quickly, reminding him of the purple martins he used to chase in his back yard when he was ten. They played a game with him. They would willingly give up their pursuit of the twilight's last few mosquitoes to tantalize him. One or two would wing down in front of him, gliding slowly like jumbo jets coming in for a landing. He would put on a burst of speed (he had a sprinter's acceleration which commanded respect in touch football) and reach up to swat one of them out of the air. No matter how fast he accelerated or how quickly he reacted, the martin tacked away, suddenly flying at full speed in a turn he would have thought should tear its wings off; but zip, it was gone, leaving another waiting its turn to show its speed. He'd sprint up and back after them until his legs hurt. He responded to his father's ridicule by saying he was training for his football career. He never did play football; he had to work in the afternoons after school. Still, he chased the swallows until his family moved into Hartford where there weren't any more birds.

He'd forgotten all about them until he got inside the BMW and made it go through a few right-angle turns at forty. Driving the BMW was like being one of the martins himself. It reduced the rest of traffic to lumbering ten-year-old kids.

"I've never seen anyone so *underwhelmed* by such an extravagant present," she said.

"I'm sorry," he repeated. "I enjoy driving it. I enjoy it very much, but I never expected you to give it to me. I get the feeling you think I was angling for it by taking it back to the Ondine with me every night."

"You don't know me." she laughed. "If I thought you were expecting it, I never would have given it to you."

She sat in the sofa, waiting for him to sit down. She was pretty. She had a short, straight nose and round eyes. She had been pretty all her life, and she was beginning to wear it with a kind of boredom. The navy-blue silk of her blouse was dark but sheer, spotted with fleur-de-lis. He could see through it to her breasts and their small nipples. She would put on another, darker blouse before they went out. Her breasts were on display for him, not the general public.

She had been disappointed when he'd first asked her if they were sculptured. They were packed with a new synthetic jelly that Boehm Drugs had invented. They were normally resilient. Nobody was supposed to be able to tell they weren't the breasts she'd been born with. They weren't big. It was the shape she'd been after. They were perfectly symmetrical, both of them. Their perfection had led him to figuring it out.

Those perfect breasts were the center of her eroticism. She liked having her pussy touched only at the end of lovemaking, after a long period of playing with and suckling her breasts. It made him curious about her pussy, and he began to touch her there when they weren't making love, teasing her. It was always lubricated, even if she wasn't aroused, and he wondered if that wasn't the source of some embarrassment to her. He wondered if it wasn't the reason she didn't like him to go down on her and only wanted his cock inside her when he actually had to come.

Eventually he found out that she *was* embarrassed about her vagina; but the lubrication was more the result than the reason. When she had turned forty, the walls of her vagina had started to get dry, and she now kept it lightly oiled with something she'd brought back from her clinic in Brazil.

"You have to keep it that way all the time?" he had asked her childishly, curious about an aspect of feminine facts of life he'd never been exposed to.

"Not all the time," she said. "Only when I know I'm going to see you."

He'd felt so flattered that he'd flushed with embarrassment.

He'd been fascinated with and attracted to her from the first night they'd met. She had come into the Ondine with some of her friends, and Hector had pointed her out because of her money. Her family had founded a drug company in the late 1870s. The company had prospered, and now it was the fourth largest ethical drug company in the world. It was still privately held. He knew the firm by reputation and managed to get someone to introduce him to her. He was very curious about what it was like to be the major stockholder in such a large, closely-held company. She had been pleased to answer his questions, even encouraging. She enjoyed talking about business.

Her looks, exceptional by most standards but remarkable in a woman her age, would have been enough to attract him, but she had something more. Something he found positively engrossing. She had natural business acumen. He had asked for her impression of casinos that first night, trying to see how smart she was outside of the field she'd grown up in. Her answer startled him. She understood casinos so well that he was sure she was a player. But she played craps with dollar chips if she bothered to play at all. She confessed she seldom came to casinos. She liked Atlantic City for its shows and its mood. Gambling, she said, was for people who had little more than a rudimentary understanding of money.

When she said that, he knew he wasn't going to take her up to one of the screwing rooms. It would have been easy. She had been breathing desire all over him. But he didn't want to insult her. He went home with her and her friends instead. They had seen each other every night since.

"What's wrong?" she asked him. He still hadn't sat down. "You've been morose ever since you got here."

He sat down beside her and put his arm around her. She was wearing a sharp perfume, and it almost made him dizzy.

"You're wearing a lot of perfume tonight."

"I spilled some on me," she said. "Is it still too strong?" I tried to wash most of it off."

"It's all right."

"I could take a bath," she said. "It's no trouble."

It was an invitation for him to watch her in her hot tub.

"I don't mind it that much," he said. "I was a little surprised you'd wear so much, that's all."

"What is wrong with you tonight?" she asked.

"Why are you such a compulsive giver?" he asked her.

"Why don't I just take the car back," she said.

"You gave me a Rolex," he said, "I was surprised and happy. You gave me diamond studs. I was pleased. Now you give me this car, which, to tell the truth, I like better than all the rest, but I'm running out of gratitude."

She got up from under his arm and went quickly over to the library bar. She poured herself another glass of Dom Perignon. In their young affair, they had had one quick fight. She hadn't become angry. She had drunk champagne in quick sips, talking in an icy, matter-of-fact voice, throwing arguments at him like darts. She would allow him an instant to retort as she took another sip of champagne. Whether he said anything or not she went right ahead with the next point. As he watched her arming herself for their second fight, he tried to figure out if there was some way to short-circuit it. He wasn't ready for another argument, no matter how markedly it might contrast with his earlier battle with Caro.

"I didn't mean to offend you," he said. "I'm sorry if I did."

"You're worse than sorry," she said, "You're a mess tonight."

"Oh, fuck you," he said.

"Has something happened between you and your wife?" she asked suspiciously.

She'd met Caro once when he was taking Caro out to lunch at Viscaya. Tim had watched her looking at Caro from across the dining room all during lunch, staring at her with cool jealousy. She had liked talking about Caro, but seeing the flesh itself had gotten under her skin.

"Yes, something happened," admitted Tim.

"You expected it all along," she said. "Why are you so depressed?"

"It was pretty fucking embarrassing," said Tim.

"Tell me," she said, sitting down beside him again.

"I was talking to Konnie in the living room and I had no idea what she was doing," said Tim wryly, "until there was a knock at the door. I opened it and found the boardwalk police. They were all apologetic. They hated to bother me, Mr. Seagurt, and all of that, but it looks like somebody is tossing things out of one of my windows. I run down the hallway to the bedroom, denying it all the way, and I find Caro in her studio. She's been painting prices on her paintings in big sloppy red numerals. Thirty-eight cents, she has on one, and just as the cops and I come in, she wings it out the window like a Frisbee. She'd been doing it for ten minutes. There was a big crowd on the boardwalk below, and two of the Atlantic City police cars were right up on the boardwalk with their bubble gum machines turned on, announcing to anyone within eyesight that there was another extemporaneous freak show going on. But this time the star maniac was Caro Seagurt."

Margarite was laughing.

"Konnie thought it was funny as hell, too," said Tim sarcastically.

"It is funny," she said.

"After the cops went," he added, "she packed up her things and left. She must be back in the apartment by now."

"Didn't she say anything?" asked Margarite.

"She said a lot," said Tim. "And I said a lot too, but I couldn't stop her."

"And you miss her," said Margarite solicitously.

"Yes," he said, "I miss her."

Margarite liked to talk about Caro. She had been curious about his marriage from the first night he'd come back to her house. He had refused to discuss Caro with her for a week, but eventually his guard dropped. Caro's mindless gambling had dropped it. Caro had panicked him and he didn't know what to do. Margarite understood his tortured, passive reaction to what Caro was doing; and at the same time, she defended Caro. She admired Caro. She kept saying that Caro had a lot of intestinal fortitude. It was a strange posture from someone he was sleeping with, someone he was sleeping with in a clearly romantic way, but he hadn't questioned it. He'd needed it too much to question it.

"I know why you miss her," she said.

She put her white arm around his neck. Her skin touched just beneath his hair and he felt a cool shock on his neck. She was always cool to the touch. He had mentioned it once and gotten an ugly reaction. Later, he'd figured out her cool body was a function of her age. That cool body was what kept a fire roaring in the hallway from dawn to midnight.

"Why do I miss her?" he asked.

"Her body," she said.

Tim laughed. "I can get all I want of bodies."

"Whores can be very cold fucking," she said. "You had something different with Caro and you've been missing it ever since she stopped being interested in sex with you."

Tim didn't answer. He began to regret talking to her about Caro.

"You married her for that body," she persisted. "Admit it. Those big young tits. Mary, madre, any man would go crazy over a set like that."

She was laughing at him, trying to jolly him out of his mood. For better or for worse, she was always working on his mood.

"You're jealous of her," he said, working on hers.

"I'm joking, but there's some truth in what I say," she said, ignoring his insult.

"Some," he said.

"Men like younger women," she said. "They can't help it."

"Especially young women with bodies like Caro's," he said, still trying to reverse the onus of the exchange. Let her try to give him therapy over Caro. For every smug little bit of maternal wisdom she had to offer, he would return equal understanding of her favorite problem. "You're feeling sensitive about your age now, aren't you?"

"But that's not what I'm talking about," she said plaintively. "I'm trying to figure out a way to cheer you up tonight. I should give it up as impossible, especially since the BMW didn't do anything for you. But I do have one little piece of magic left."

"What's that?" asked Tim, curious as to what could be more impressive than the BMW.

She went over to her desk. She opened one of the drawers and took out a small bottle. It was very small. The four capsules inside filled it.

"There are some interesting perks to being on the board of directors of one of the world's largest pharmaceutical companies," she said.

"I don't want to get high," said Tim, quickly. "I have had *enough* of getting high and watching other people get high."

"No, no," she said. "This isn't a high. It's something very new. The best part about it is the fact that its not a high or low."

"Oh, swell," mocked Tim, "the flash drug discovery of the century. Take it and nothing happens. It will be the biggest thing in consciousness alteration since water."

"It's an aphrodisiac," she said, ignoring him. "A pure one. It gets into the brain and stirs up the serotonin with some kind of sexual excitement."

"Really?" asked Tim, intrigued.

"Most aphrodisiacs are either based on the itch principle," explained Margarite, "or the breakdown-of-consciousness principle. The itch principle creates drugs like the Spanish fly. They make the genitals itch and give the illusion of sexual desire, but in fact, you could scratch and get every bit as much satisfaction as fucking would give you. The consciousness-breakdown principle uses psychoactive ingredients to remove inhibitions so that you are very suggestible to sex, but the problem with that is that you are suggestible to a lot of other things too."

"I love it when you talk like a pharmacist," said Tim.

"These are supposed to work on the brain without breaking down consciousness," she said, still ignoring his wisecracks. "Neurologists have always thought that high sexual appetite was a function of the limbic system, glandular in nature; but if these work the way they're supposed to, that theory is going to be secondary to one involving a chemical solution of the brain."

"Have you ever used them?" he asked, getting interested.

"No."

"You want to try it now?" he said.

"Oh, no," she said quickly. "I'm not going to use an untested product on myself."

"It's not tested?"

"Not unless you count monkeys and salesmen," she said.

"Salesmen?" asked Tim.

"If you know anything about drug salesmen," she laughed, "you know they're willing to try anything. Especially something like this."

"What do they say about it?"

"They love it."

"An aphrodisiac that works," marvelled Tim. "You're going to make a fortune with it."

"You want to try it?" she asked.

"Not if you're not going to," he said.

"I have an idea," she said. "Let's go out and pick somebody up. We'll bring her back and give her one. We'll see how it works. It's supposed to be harmless. If she wants to screw, you can screw her. If nothing happens, then nothing happens."

Tim laughed.

"It would be fun," she said.

"It's not dangerous?" said Tim.

"No," she said.

"Okay, let's try it."

THEY WENT to the Slot Dock first. The teenage visitors to Atlantic City tended to congregate near the arcade with all the game-playing machines.

"You were right, I am a compulsive giver," Margarite whispered mischievously as they approached the arcade. "Now I'm going to give you something nobody else can."

"What?"

"A teenage body."

"I'm not sure my super-ego is ready for the teenage part," said Tim.

"It is wicked," she said. "But I can't wait to see you make it with one of these young ones."

But everything they saw on the Slot Dock was too cheap-looking. They had youth, but no style; and Margarite wasn't going to let him screw somebody with no style.

They walked through several different hotels. They inspected cocktail waitresses, dealers, change girls, and keno girls for signs of youth, beauty, and style. Margarite could find nothing that suited her in the hotels. They started going into the shops and looking at salesgirls. They went from one shop to another until they found the girl they wanted in a dress shop next to the new Ritz.

She was a tall blonde with a familiar, friendly manner. Margarite tried on several outfits and drew her into polite conversation. Her name was Gwen. She was only working in the shop for a weekend diversion. She was wearing a cashmere skirt and sweater she confessed she bought there. She liked working there because she could buy clothes at a discount.

"She's gorgeous," whispered Margarite, after sending her to look for some sweaters so she could talk to Tim. "Have you noticed her skin? I think she's lying about her age."

"I don't think so."

"Tim!" she said, annoyed. "She can't be a day over seventeen. You think she's older because she's tall. She says she's twenty-one so she can gamble. You look at her skin."

When she came back with the sweaters, Tim looked at her skin. It was smooth and lustrous. She wore no makeup except for a light gloss on her pastel orange lips. She looked exceedingly fresh. Margarite nodded at him knowingly. She was under twenty.

"Do you think I should invite her back?" she asked Tim when Gwen had gone back to write up her bill. "How do you pick someone up like this? Maybe you should do it."

"I'll try if you want," said Tim. "But my guess is that the first word I said would kill it."

"You're right," she laughed. "You've been staring at her for the past half hour as if she were naked."

"Given the circumstances, it's hard not to," said Tim.

"And the body," she said. "It's not just the circumstances."

Her height was mostly legs. She was wearing the pleated skirt to show them off. Her bosom wasn't the biggest they'd seen that night, but it was big. Her cashmere sweater was tight enough to make it easy to infer the shape and size of her breasts. They had one thing in common with every other girl Margarite had shown an interest in: they were rounded and big like Caro's.

Despite her talk about Gwen's skin, Tim knew Margarite was interested far more in her bosom than anything else. Margarite's idea of perfect tits had been changing. Her own were no longer completely satisfactory. She had shown him pictures of herself nude, beautifully-done color photographs. They were recent pictures taken in Brazil. After Margarite had seen Caro, she had begun to wonder if she wouldn't look better as something in between Caro and herself. Gwen seemed to fit right into that category. Tim wondered if there were other, earlier photographs of Margarite hidden away, pictures of her with several different kinds of bosoms. Did she change them like shirts?

Gwen had finished filling out the credit slip. She handed Margarite her card, and showed her where to sign. "Are you the Margarite Boehm from Boehm Drugs?"

"Yes, I am."

"You live in the big brick Victorian house on Atlantic Avenue, don't you?" asked Gwen.

"When I'm in Atlantic City."

"It's a beautiful house," said Gwen.

"Not really, Gwen," said Margarite. "It's a monster from the outside, don't you think?"

"Oh, no, I don't think so," said Gwen. "I love Victorian houses."

"It's much prettier inside," said Margarite. "Would you like to see it some time?"

She agreed to stop by after work. She was off at seven and had a party to go to at eight, but she'd love to stop in at seven-thirty. Margarite assured her seven-thirty was perfect.

She arrived on time and they both took her on a tour of the house. In the upstairs kitchen, Margarite suggested they all have some champagne, and Gwen readily agreed. She was fascinated with the house and she walked about listening to Margarite's stories of its history, drinking her champagne, unaware that it was laced with the aphrodisiac.

Gwen's favorite part of the house was the grand ballroom with its own bandstand.

"My parents used to have dances here in the summer," said Margarite.

"Would a lot of people come?" asked Gwen.

"They'd fill up the floor," said Margarite. "I keep meaning to have a dance myself sometime, but I don't. I imagine I'm too private a person. My parents were so social, I'm afraid they made me into a recluse."

Gwen stared at her with frank admiration. It was clear she'd give anything to be Margarite Boehm, with millions of dollars in the bank and her own dance floor.

"My mother loved surprise parties," said Margarite, responding to Gwen's heroine worship. "If it was eleven o'clock at night, it wasn't too late to have a party starting at midnight."

"That's what I'd like," said Gwen, walking dreamily across the ballroom. "Imagine having your own band in a room like this."

"One night mother and father came back from a play," said Margarite, joining Gwen on the far side of the ballroom. Her voice bounced back across the wooden floor with a spectral quality. "My room was on the third floor and I could hear them talking as they climbed the stairs. It was a horrible play, they said. It was called *The Vegetable* and it had been written by somebody named F. Scott Fitzgerald. They went on about it being so bad, and the writer's name stuck in my mind; I grew up thinking that this F. Scott Fitzgerald person was a malicious criminal. They were still going on about it when people started to come up the stairs behind them for a dance. This whole ballroom filled up. There were at least a hundred couples, and there wasn't a face among them I recognized. I remember this all very vividly because I was only five years old and I was just beginning to understand what a dance was. All these people were milling around up here, and the servants were working frantically in the kitchen, running up and down the service stairway to get the punches and snacks up to the ballroom. Then everyone started buzzing louder and I saw the whole orchestra from the Traymore coming up the service stairs. My mother had the stairs painted lavender then—I don't know why anyone would paint a staircase lavender—and I still remember all those solemn-looking men with their instrument cases coming up that lavender stairway dressed in formal black and white. The next day I found out my father had hired them to play on the spur of the moment, and all this crowd of people I'd never seen before was the audience from *The Vegetable.* My father had invited everyone in the theatre home to a dance. It was his way of getting even with this criminal F. Scott Fitzgerald for boring them all to tears."

An hour later they were sitting in the small library sipping champagne. Tim had been trying not to look at Gwen the way he had in the dress shop, because it occurred to him that such looks might frighten her off. Then, if the aphrodisiac did work, the first thing she might do would be to leave and find a boyfriend.

"Could I use the powder room?" Gwen asked Margarite.

Margarite showed her the way and returned quickly.

"She's so agreeable," said Margarite. "I'm almost glad it's not working. I'm starting to feel very guilty about the whole thing."

"I feel guilty too," said Tim. "Let's get her on her way to her party and go upstairs. I'm getting a case of blue balls."

Gwen did not take the hint about her party when she returned. "Oh, I don't care about that. They won't miss me."

She wanted to hear more about Margarite's childhood. She encouraged Margarite to try to find her baby pictures, but they were all in Boston. She asked Tim for more champagne. When he bent over to pour her a glass, he almost reeled away in shock. She had sprayed herself with an incredible amount of toilet water when she had gone to the bathroom. It was far worse than what Margarite had on from spilling it on herself. He laughed, thinking she'd done it because she noticed how pungent Margarite was.

She was restless as she talked with Margarite. She wanted a fourth glass of champagne and Tim poured it for her. He was getting used to the reeking perfume, so he sat down on the sofa next to her. He intended to wedge his way into the conversation and maneuver her out of the house. As he waited his chance, he began to smell something else beneath the powerful toilet water. He almost jumped off the sofa when he realized what it was. It was her pussy. It was the odor of a very excited pussy. No wonder she had gone into the bathroom and doused herself with toilet water.

"Excuse me, Gwen," said Tim, interrupting Margarite. "But would you mind if I asked you a personal question?"

"No," she said, looking at him with nervous eyes. "I wouldn't mind."

"Have you been thinking a lot about sex?" he asked.

She looked at him in surprise. "What do you mean?"

"I mean, have you been thinking about sex the past few minutes?" asked Tim. "Or longer."

She looked at Margarite and then back to Tim. "How do you know?"

Tim laughed.

"Have I ever been thinking about sex," she said with a big sigh. "How did he know that?" she asked Margarite. "I keep drinking champagne to make it go away because I can't go to this party feeling like this. I'll end up screwing Ned and I don't want to screw Ned." She turned back to Tim. "How did you know?"

"He's very smart that way," said Margarite.

"There's something about him," she said to Margarite. "I keep getting pictures in my head of him and me, and that's another reason I can't leave. This is really weird. I've never felt this way about anybody, no matter what kind of hunk he is."

"Don't be embarrassed," teased Margarite. "He affects me the same way."

"You don't care?" asked Gwen. "You're not jealous?"

"Why should I be?"

"That's funny," said Gwen, "I've been trying to figure out a way to get rid of you."

"What for?" asked Margarite.

"So I could get Tim to take me somewhere," said Gwen.

"Where?" continued Margarite, leading her on.

"Anywhere," said Gwen rolling her eyes, and laughing nervously. "Anywhere where I could convince him to make love."

"Well, I'm sure you can convince him," laughed Margarite in return. "But you're going to do it right here, because I'm going to watch."

"Holy Joe," said Gwen.

When they got up to the bedroom, Gwen took her panties and skirt off. Tim stood awkwardly and tried to kiss her while Margarite undid his pants and took them down.

"Get him onto the bed," Margarite told Gwen, "so I can get his pants all the way off."

Gwen pulled him on top of her on the bed. He tried to guide his cock into her with his hips.

"Wait till I get your shoes off," laughed Margarite.

While Margarite worked on his shoes, he helped Gwen off with her sweater. He played with her nipples and began getting over her again when he felt Margarite's cool hand on his prick.

"What are you doing?" he said.

"I'm putting it in," she said.

He raised up and locked down to watch.

"I've always wanted to do this," said Margarite.

She spread Gwen's vaginal lips with two fingers and placed the head of his cock inside.

"Come on, fuck me," said Gwen.

He fucked her half on the bed and half off. He had trouble keeping his balance because his thighs were right on the edge of the mattress. He couldn't really get on top of her and push, and he couldn't put his feet on the carpet either.

"Why don't you two get in the middle of the bed," suggested Margarite.

"Good idea," said Tim, pulling out.

"Oh, no!" said Gwen. "Don't take him out. We could have moved without taking him out."

She slid rapidly back across the thick comforter and got in the middle of the bed. She lifted her long legs up and flashed at him. It was supposed to be obscene, but her legs were too pretty to be obscene. Tim felt like he was staring at a new kind of fashion ad from *Seventeen.* It occurred to him that his super-ego was now more than ready for this. As a matter of fact, at that particular moment, he couldn't think of anything he wanted to do more than get back into Gwen's cunt and stay there for the rest of his life.

He climbed her, got his cock in, and started kissing her. She turned her head away. He followed her mouth and kissed her again. She struggled away.

"Don't kiss me," she said breathlessly. "Just fuck me."

"Why don't you like kissing?" he asked, stopping.

"Don't stop."

"You don't like kissing?" he asked again, making his dick slide up and down her as he spoke.

"I like fucking," she said. "I'm no good at kissing. That feels so good. What's she doing?"

Margarite had gotten on the bed next to them, and suddenly Tim felt her cool hand on his cock again. He stopped. "What are you doing?"

"Come on," insisted Gwen. "You're stopping again."

He resumed his rhythm, acutely conscious of Margarite's fingers.

"I'm just feeling it," said Margarite. "I want to feel you two fucking."

Something about her saying that along with her cool hand feeling up and down his cock as he drove in and out of Gwen made him come. It was an incredibly intense orgasm.

"Wow," he sighed, gradually slowing down to a halt. "That felt awfully good."

"I haven't come yet," said Gwen, "Can you keep going?"

Tim laughed. "Not just now."

"Holy Joe," she said. "Can you play with me then? I have to come."

Tim raised off her and reached down to masturbate her gently. Her cunt was wet and viscous.

"That's good." she said. "Keep doing it that way."

"That is good," said Margarite. She had gotten up and was standing at the end of the bed watching.

"Why are you watching?" asked Gwen, breathing very hard. "You're crazy, aren't you?"

"Yes, I'm crazy," conceded Margarite. "He's rubbing his come all over your button. Can you feel that?"

"Yes, I can feel it," she said.

"You're getting a rash," said Margarite, walking around the side of the bed to inspect Gwen's chest more closely. "You're going to come, aren't you?"

"Why are you watching?" asked Gwen.

"Because you're pretty," said Margarite. "And because he's going to make you come."

"Yes, he is," said Gwen, her voice becoming loud. "I'm coming."

Tim could almost feel the orgasm course through her clit. She shouted several times. He felt like he was rubbing the shouts out of her.

After he finished her, she lay on the bed quietly for several moments.

"I'm exhausted," she finally said.

Now that he'd come and so had his partner, Tim's heat had drained out of him. He felt his sexual super-ego returning. He had taken this pretty, though perhaps not so innocent, young girl and tricked her into bed with chemicals. He felt embarrassed and guilty.

"That felt good," said Gwen, suddenly sitting up, her pretty tits swaying gently, "but I'm still horny."

They had gotten the optical scanning system on line and working the day after Caro left. It worked perfectly. They caught dealer after dealer stealing. They also caught customers putting things over on lazy floormen. It seemed like they were catching it all. Then suddenly things stopped happening. After the first two nights, they went for several days without one dealer making a single bad move. The only conclusion was that they had stopped it all. Henry was ecstatic. At last he would find out what real *per* in a completely honest casino should be.

Hector had the dealer's locker room and lounge wired. What he picked up supported Henry's belief they had stopped it all. There were a few braggarts (Wayne Brady, to name the loudest), but most of the dealers had been scared to death by Tim's walking out those first two nights and collaring dealer after dealer within a minute of their move and then showing them themselves on tape. Suddenly they were all terrified of the computer, and all they talked about in the locker room was how they weren't going to try any bullshit, not the smallest little bit, as long as the computer was watching them. By all counts, Tim had revolutionized the casino business.

Except for one count. The only count that mattered. The one that took place every morning at eleven. That one showed smaller and smaller wins and a shrinking per.

As the per went down, Tim watched the large computer screen

idly. His glance wandered aimlessly back and forth between the wall of monitors and the computer's large single screen. Nothing of interest happened no matter where he looked. He was back to where he started. The single screen showed the same routine play as the wall of eyes. The Cyclops had become as gullible as Argus. Every night, Tim had left earlier and earlier for Margarite's house.

He closed and locked the door to the casino offices. Wednesday night's boxes were in the vault. It was four thirty. He made his way with Hector and Henry through the debris of another night's work. The carpet was littered with coin wrappers and paper cups, the milder expressions of the Ondine's customers' indifference to her luxury. There was something relentlessly oral about gamblers. Those that didn't smoke chewed gum. The gum, dropped on the carpet as soon as the sugar was gone, was ground into the Ondine's luxurious pile just like the burning cigarettes. The players also spilled drinks, discarded lipsticks, and tossed enigmatic torn-up scribblings over their shoulders like salt.

"When I first came here, I couldn't believe you had to replace the carpet once a month," said Tim, pausing at the outer casino door before he locked it. "Look at this place. It looks like one of those trucks that eats garbage backed in here suffering from intestinal flu and spit up a load from the Inlet."

"Gamblers are animals," agreed Hector. "I was walking through Viscaya the other night and I saw a guy pissing all over himself. He was sitting at a blackjack table, drunk, and I saw something yellow on the top of his pants next to his fly. It looked like a button. I took a closer look and it was pee. It was bubbling up right through his pants. His whole pant leg was soaked. He was just sitting there peeing."

Henry made an ugly face. Hector was full of such stories and Henry didn't appreciate them. Besides, something had been on Henry's mind for several days, and from what Tim could tell, he was getting near the time when it would bubble up to the surface. Henry was secretive and self-contained, but every once in a while his secrets became too much for him, and they boiled off the top of his head with surprising energy.

Tonight the secret was his frustration over Tim's growing indifference to the casino. It came out as Tim bent over to get his key into the lock on the metal bottom of the glass door. He fit the key into the metal cylinder.

"You don't care any more, Tim," said Henry behind him, his voice immediately raised to an emotional pitch. He required no warm up to get angry. "You're getting just like him."

Tim turned around, still squatting, looking up at Henry while he withdrew the key. The "him" Henry was referring to was Hector. Hector wiggled his mouth innocently at the insult. It might be an insult, but it was true. Compared to Henry, Hector was enormously indifferent to corruption. Hector never responded to insults that were true.

"You're right, Henry," said Tim, standing up. "I guess I have gotten to the point where I don't pay much attention to anything."

"Why?" he asked plaintively. "What's wrong with you?"

"I don't know," said Tim.

"Let's go to the coffee shop," said Henry. "Hector, can I talk to Tim alone?"

"Sure," said Hector, looking at Tim jealously. "Why not?"

Hector hated being excluded from anything Tim said or did. When Tim joked, Hector laughed raucously. When Tim was sad, Hector looked as if he had a headache. When Tim was angry, Hector was furious. Henry, whose loyalty was every bit as strong, but more of a silent and brooding character, regarded Hector's histrionics with suspicion.

"Let's all go into the coffee shop, Henry," said Tim. "If you can't trust Hector, who the hell can you trust?"

Henry didn't answer, though it was clear he had an answer in mind: no one.

"Yes, we're missing something," said Tim in the coffee shop. "Somehow there's something we don't understand that they're capitalizing on."

"I know one thing," said Hector. "Whatever is going on has nothing to do with Teddy Long."

"Why do you say that?" asked Henry skeptically.

Teddy Long had come to occupy the place in Henry's heart vacated by McGray.

"I've followed him for a week, every hour he was off," said Hector. "He never met Padgett or any of his current pals. I tell you something else, too. That guy busts his chops out there for you, Tim. He's going crazy trying to find out what's wrong."

"I know," said Tim.

"Why were you following Teddy?" persisted Henry.

"Because I think Padgett is mixed up in this," said Hector. "I wanted to make sure Teddy wasn't seeing him regularly."

"Padgett?" said Tim,

"You got to consider it, Tim," said Hector carefully. Padgett was a subject that touched Tim off quite easily.

"Why Padgett?" asked Henry.

"Didn't Padgett say he was going to start a campaign against gambling again?" asked Hector.

Tim had come back from the Monopoly raving after his thundering exchange with Padgett. He had raved about it in detail for two days afterwards. Hector and Henry knew every word that had passed between him and Padgett.

"He hasn't done anything about voting gambling out," said Henry.

"That's right," said Hector. "And I'll tell you why. He and Powell have worked out some scheme to get into us. They're getting even now just like they did the night Tim fired McGray."

"Whatever it is, it has to be incredibly precise," said Henry. "It's unbelievable that they could be precise enough to beat the computer."

"They're all smart, remember?" said Hector. "Most of them college graduates. They're too smart. Used to be you could break down something big like this by picking away at the stupid links, but none of them are dumb. Look at the beautiful charade they're putting on moaning in the locker room."

"Maybe," said Henry, thoughtfully. "Maybe there is some kind of coordinated effort. It would screw up the relationship of the pers from table to table."

"Look at something else," said Hector. "He promised Tim somebody would be by to rub his face in it."

"Nobody has been by," said Henry.

"His thing is he has to get a pay off from the casino manager personally, but we hear nothing," said Hector.

"And none of Powell's ugly friends come to see me either," said Tim, beginning to wonder. "What the hell is going on?"

"He's getting so much money out of here with all his smart boogies, he's changed the rules," said Hector.

"Of course," said Henry. "It has to be. That's why the per is so low."

"He's going to starve you out, Tim," said Hector. "He's having such a good time and he's making so much money, he's going to keep dropping that per until you come across."

"That bastard," said Henry.

"You've got to pay him off," said Hector.

"No! No!" shouted Henry angrily. "He does not!"

"You've got to pay off Padgett, Tim," insisted Hector. "And part of the deal has to be he tells you what they're pulling, so you and Henry can put some protection into the computer."

"He doesn't have to pay anybody off," said Henry derisively. "We'll find it ourselves."

"I'm afraid he does, Henry," insisted Hector. "It's just one last thing you're missing, Tim. You've got to figure how to handle cheating in big groups."

"Just tell me one thing, Hector," demanded Henry, his eyes bulging behind his oversized glasses and looking even more intense than usual. "Why should he get dirty like everyone else in this business. Just because you are? That's the reason, isn't it? People in this business can't stand to let anybody stay clean, can they?"

Tim had to keep himself from smiling. Henry's unremitting devotion to honesty was so single-minded it was funny.

"You have to pay Padgett," said Hector. "It's a simple fact of casino life. You order dice. You buy politicians. You count the money in the morning. You buy politicians. Unless Henry is the mayor of your town."

He grinned mischievously at the unhappy Henry.

"Eat shit, you old bastard," said Henry.

"Don't think I haven't thought about paying off Padgett, Hector," said Tim softly, putting his hand on Henry's arm to quiet his animosity. "I think about it all the time, but I can't do it."

"Sure you can," said Hector. "What the hell do you care about giving some dumb nigger a few bucks to save your joint?"

"The books, Hector," said Tim. "Remember how tight I've made the controls. I've painted myself into a corner. I couldn't get money out to pay him even if I wanted to."

Hector looked quietly at Tim, pondering something. His mouth opened and closed, making the quiet spitting sound which signified his thoughts were deep.

"If that money were suddenly to appear—" started Tim, but he stopped, recognizing with repugnance an inane player's fantasy coming out of his own mouth.

"Shit!" cursed Henry. "How the hell are they doing it?"

Henry hit on an idea for testing the optical scanning system. They were all in the video room watching Wayne Brady, a roulette dealer. Brady was one of the originals Tim had hired at Padgett's bar. In imitation of his hero, Brady had grown a beard. It was an ugly, stubbly goatee. He had a skinny face with a dagger-like chin, so that his scruffy goatee made him look like a piece of upside-down black spruce.

Brady was disgusted with being a dealer at the Ondine. He was disgusted with the cheap tips. Where was his slice of the big money? The Ondine made all the big money while he did all the work. If Seagurt wasn't willing to give him his share, he was going to take it. He wasn't afraid of the computer and the cameras, and he said so nightly in the dealers' locker room.

Henry and Hector were watching the computer screen, while Jimmy and Tim were watching Brady on the regular monitors. If the computer system worked, they would all see him make his move at the same time.

As Jimmy and Tim watched Brady on the monitors, the large computer screen kept switching from table to table. When it hopped about like that, the computer was saying nothing was happening. The probability of cheating was leapfrogging about the casino without any clear-cut candidate. Usually a table would dominate the large computer screen for several minutes before cheating occurred.

Tim studied the players at Brady's table trying to find an agent. The Vietnamese with the high forehead and mongoloid appearance had been playing for some time. He had the quickest hands of anyone in the casino, including bosses and dealers. He was the only customer Tim had ever seen light a pit boss's cigarette.

Pit bosses, who were usually bored to the point of falling over from watching the mechanical repetition of their games, enjoyed the momentary distraction of lighting up player's smokes. They were especially quick at lighting their own cigarettes. They hated being in social debt to a player, no matter how insignificant the favor.

Tommy Van could beat them at their own little game. If a pit boss standing near him put a cigarette in his mouth, a little orange flame would appear at its end before the boss even realized the little Oriental was in the vicinity. He was so deferential about it, and flashed such a disarming smile across his mongoloid face, they actually enjoyed it.

Tommy had been a fixture around the Ondine since the night Tim had seen him sitting next to Robles. He had lost something near a medium five. Where would a Vietnamese, whose best job would be a deck hand on one of the hotel boats, get enough money to play the way Tommy did?

From being an agent.

Brady slid a small stack of yellow chips across the table to a man sitting with his wife. The man slapped the vest pockets of his camel blazer with delight. Brady made a flourish with his little finger as he delivered the chips. Tim ground his teeth. Everything Brady did seemed to get down in him somewhere and piss him off. Brady, perhaps because he resembled Padgett, or maybe because he worshipped him, had become a focal point for Tim's frustrations. Stealing, once only a business problem, had become a personal insult. Brady's arrogance made it even worse. Tim had listened to Hector's recording of Brady bragging in the locker room. Brady wasn't afraid of Seagurt. Brady had been beating Seagurt's ass all along, and these guys who were so afraid of the computer were pure chicken shit. Quickness could outwit the computer. The hand was faster than the eye, and Brady was faster than the computer. Just because the Toms see a couple of niggers get fired, they think Seagurt is some kind of wizard who knows their every move. Brady didn't think Seagurt was such a wizard. *Wizard.* For some reason Brady's insulting intonation of the word kept echoing inside Tim's head like a very large clapper ringing an acutely sensitive bell.

"This one I'm going to teach a lesson," said Tim under his breath. "I'm going to change the rules in this little game."

"Something might be coming up here, boss," said Hector.

Tim looked over to the computer screen. It had Brady on.

"He's been on for the past minute," said Henry.

Tim turned quickly back to the monitors.

"There it is!" said Hector. "There he goes!"

"It's not Tommy," said Jimmy in surprise. "It's the other guy."

"It works!" shouted Henry. "The computer works perfectly!"

Brady was on the computer screen when he made his move, and it was the first move he'd made since they'd started watching him.

But Tim wasn't there to hear Henry's shout of vindication; he was running through the casino. He lept over the roulette pit rope just as Brady finished sliding a large block of yellow chips to the man in the camel blazer. Brady was making a proud flourish with his little finger.

"WHAT IS THAT, BRADY?" Tim shouted into Brady's ear as loud as he could.

Brady jumped as if he'd been stuck in the ribs with a nightstick.

"What? What? What was what?" he asked, almost whining. "You scared the hell out of me, man."

The marker for the winning number was still on fifteen. Beneath it were four yellow chips. A dollar. Brady had just paid three hundred dollars for a bet that should have paid thirty-five. The man's wife was getting up and starting away.

"Are we paying three hundred to one now, Brady?" asked Tim.

The man in the camel blazer got up and ran after his wife.

"I've got you now, you bastard," Tim told Brady.

Brady stared at him with a smirk spread across his face.

"It's not so easy after all, is it?" asked Tim.

"Hey, come on, man," said Brady with disgust. "So you got me. Big fucking deal. You want to fire me, fire me. Don't stand there acting like you're some kind of hero."

"You don't get fired, Brady," said Tim. "I'm changing the rules of this little game. You're going to jail."

"Jail?" asked Brady in disbelief.

"That's right," said Tim.

Brady stomped his foot and spun around three hundred and sixty degrees. "You're putting me on, man!"

Tim felt a new wave of anger roll in on him. They all thought they had nothing to lose by stealing as much as they could.

"You're going to jail!" Tim shouted so they all could hear. He turned around to face the pit behind him. He saw a row of apprehensive faces. "That goes for all the rest of you! When I catch you, no matter who you think is protecting you, you're going to jail. Padgett can't keep you out of jail when I have you on tape!"

The faces all turned grim.

"I'm not going to jail," said Brady behind him.

"Hey, Tim, watchout!" shouted Teddy Long from a nearby blackjack pit.

"It's a knife!" called a woman in a frightened voice.

Tim turned quickly and saw Brady with a knife out.

"Nobody is putting Wayne-o in jail, man," said Brady.

It was a long ugly blade. Though old and pitted, it was quite sharp, and it pointed right at Tim like a long splotchy tongue. Tim suddenly felt exhausted. He hadn't been swimming in two months. His cardiovascular conditioning had completely reversed. He had used up every bit of his strength running through the casino. He could barely breathe. He stepped sluggishly back from the knife, looking for a security man. He saw one named Joel standing behind the roulette table, watching.

"Joel!"

"Don't look at me," said Joel quickly. "I'm not messing around with him. You hired all these niggers."

Brady laughed at Joel and began to advance on Tim. Tim's eye started blinking. Brady tossed his spotted knife from hand to hand, thoroughly enjoying himself.

"Wayne-o is *not* going to jail, man," he said.

Tim felt a strange loss of affect. He could detect no fear or panic.

He felt a mysterious calm. His mind wandered to one of his father's favorite complaints. Tim used to hear it all the time at the dinner table after they moved into Hartford. Black men love to stick knives into each other, his father liked to say. Every weekend ten or twenty blacks would end up in his emergency ward with stab wounds. There were never enough surgeons to operate on them all. Sometimes interns sawed them up like so much lumber for practise, but most of them were wheeled into a room at the end of the hall and left there to die.

"The fact is, Tim," said his father whenever Tim registered his outrage at the bastard's callousness, "once you get something screwing around in a vital organ, you have less than an even chance of surviving."

Tim knew he should feel very frightened, but he couldn't muster any of the vital emotions of self-preservation. He could see the knife, and he knew the significance of its entering his abdomen, but he couldn't make it register. He felt this unfathomable calm instead. The calm gave him a sense of seeing it happen to somebody else. It was happening to Tim, and he was Tim, but somehow the point of that knife was going to slice into somebody other than himself.

·21·

TIM SAW a flurry of movement on top of the roulette table behind Brady. It was the Vietnamese. He was scuttling across the top of it. Before Brady was halfway turned around to see what Tim was looking at, the little Asian was on him. An instant later, Tommy Van had the knife. Tim couldn't see how he'd done it, but Tommy had it and Brady didn't. Unlike Brady, Tommy made no sweeping gestures with the blade. He simply shot it forward and swept it across Brady's silk shirt. It left behind a trail of sheared silk and black skin. The black skin pooled up with tiny bubbles of red until there was a full red line all the way across Brady's chest.

"Hey!" yelled Brady.

"Back!" ordered Tommy, making a second perfectly straight line across Brady's chest.

"Ow!" shouted Brady, dancing backwards.

Tommy marched him backwards, making several new long wounds in Brady's chest.

"Ow! Ow! That hurts!"

"Just lines," said Tommy. "Not deep."

Brady turned and ran, trying to hurdle the velvet rope. It tripped him and he fell forward, sliding across the rug on his lacerated chest. He let out a penetrating mewl of pain, but was on his feet in an instant and running again.

Tommy turned back to the faces in the pit. "Anybody else want to kill boss?"

Tim had thought he didn't care whether he was going to get that knife in the stomach or not until Tommy took it away from Brady; then he felt a wave of relief so powerful it made him dizzy. His eye started blinking even faster than before. He took in one big breath after another, unable to shake the dizziness for several minutes.

He thanked Tommy several times, and then took him over to Neptune's Barge for a drink. It took him several scotches to get his eye to stop blinking. As they drank and talked, he liked Tommy more and more. He had the same kind of feeling that overcame him the few times he had been alone with Alfred Oakes. He felt as if he wanted to do anything to make friends. But Tommy was quite different than Oakes. Tommy was trying just as hard to make friends with Tim.

They drank and talked for hours. Tommy had a funny way of stringing three and four verbs together at a time which made him hard to understand, but Tim found him fascinating. He told Tim the story of his escape from Viet Nam after the war. He hadn't made it out of Saigon before the *bo doi* came.

"What's the *bo doi?*" asked Tim.

"*Bo doi* the army from the north," said Tommy. "*Bo doi* march in Saigon, make speeches, take over radio. Pose with big Minh."

Tommy escaped a few days later. He and some friends had a Navy launch hidden away. They took it to Thailand where they snuck on a freighter.

"We sleep, eat, hide below big freight boxes," he explained. "Freight boxes many high. As big as Atlantic City hotels, on top of each other up to the sky."

When he got to San Diego, he and his friends were caught. They ended up in Washington D.C. He called it "Washtun Dizzy." He went from one federal program to another around Virginia until he got a job running the Seven-Eleven store on Absecon Boulevard in Atlantic City.

"How did you learn to do that with a knife?" asked Tim.

"Red line?" asked Tommy. He unbuttoned his shirt in answer.

His citrine chest was lined from top to bottom with ridges of thin scar tissue. The scars were so neat and parallel that his skin looked like ruled paper.

"Chêt teach me for cowboy trick," said Tommy. "Old Chêt used to be in circus. He take me off the street and we sell porcelain in Cholon."

"Chêt?" asked Tim.

"English," said Tommy with some frustration. "Ten years here now and still think in Vietnamese. Chêt mean Chinamen. Small lines, Chinese circus trick."

"Nice trick," said Tim. "But weren't you afraid you might really slash him?"

"I hurt no one," said Tommy. "Everyone now think Tommy real dangerous, right?"

"Yes," agreed Tim. "Very dangerous."

"I know only to make red line," laughed Tommy. "I never hurt anyone with knife. Not even in ARVN. Tommy can only make show."

"You were in the ARVN?" asked Tim.

"Cerno Tam Van Tram," he said proudly. "Not bad for street cowboy?"

"Colonel?" asked Tim.

"Cerno," repeated Tommy, "yes."

"Not bad," granted Tim. "Is that why you had to leave?"

"No, no," said Tommy, as if Tim had implied some kind of disgrace. "I could stay in Saigon. My brother is high in *bo doi.*"

"Why didn't you stay then?" asked Tim.

"*Bo doi* now made things serious," said Tommy. "Life in Saigon now *thoung-thoung.*"

"What does that mean?"

"*Thoung-thoung. Thoung-thoung. Thoung-thoung,*" grinned Tommy with his weird winning smile. "Boring, boring, boring."

"What's exciting then?" laughed Tim. "War?"

"You think Tommy Van love war?" asked Tommy.

He was serious now, perhaps insulted. His serious face accentuated his Oriental character. He looked like a mentally-retarded child suddenly grown old.

"I'm sorry," apologized Tim.

"I don't like war," said Tommy. "But Tommy Van is not afraid when war comes. Not like *cahn-sat.* Not like him."

Tommy was pointing at Joel. Tim felt a surge of hatred for Joel and made a mental note to fire him as soon as he finished with Tommy.

"I have friends," said Tommy. "Many officers in ARVN like me. They live all places in States but know me. I can make them *cahn-sat* for casino."

"What's that?"

"*Cahn-sat,*" repeated Tommy. "Police. You police here afraid. Tommy call his friends."

"I'm sorry, Tommy," said Tim, feeling a wave of guilt the instant he said it. "I can't have armed Vietnamese walking around in here. You'd scare everybody to death."

"No arms!" said Tommy quickly. "No uniforms. We're waiters. Many Orientals in Atlantic City are waiters. No one notices until trouble. Then we are not afraid to fight for *Anh* Tim. Not like him."

He was pointing at Joel again.

"*Anh* Tim?" asked Tim.

"English," said Tommy, knocking on his head with frustration. "The boss. Like older brother. *Anh* Tim—Older brother Tim."

"Sorry, Tommy," said Tim, feeling an ugly wave of guilt again.

"Nobody help *Anh* Tim but Tommy," said Tommy, pointing at every uniformed security man he could see from the barge. "They all have chance to. Nobody help. Not even ones with guns. What good are guns to *Anh* Tim when *cahn-sat* afraid?"

Tim felt another intense wave of affection for Tommy. It was so strong it amazed him. Tommy had been nothing more than a suspicious face on the monitor an hour ago.

"How many people do you have in mind?" he asked.

"How many you want?" asked Tommy, a smile breaking again across the almost moronic-looking face. Tim was beginning to see considerable intelligence beneath that charming, imbecilic smile.

Tim and Margarite returned to making love alone. Friends and strangers and artificial excitement were no longer welcome. They were reaching for something, and it had to be done in private. Tim hit the core of what he was reaching for the afternoon after he hired Tommy Van.

Margarite had picked him up for lunch. He told her about Tommy, how he saved Tim, and the Vietnamese he'd brought in this morning to meet "*Anh* Tim." One was a chatterbox who called himself Willie Fudd. An older one named Thitch used to be in the ARVN like Tommy.

Tim was tender in his lovemaking, especially attentive to her breasts. Margarite responded with something far more genuine than anything she had reached with the aid of the pills. Maybe it wasn't as intense, but it was genuine.

When they were dressed and having a drink in her library, he explained in detail what had happened with the optical scanner and Wayne Brady. Margarite seemed to follow him point by point, fascinated with the mechanics of his creation. She looked surprised when he told her how perfectly it had worked catching Brady. She looked as if she had expected it not to.

"Don't look so shocked," he said. "It tested out perfectly."

"But it doesn't work, Tim," she said. "The results at the count say it doesn't work, so it doesn't work. You can't count money you think you *should* be earning. The only kind of money you can count is the kind you can put in and take out of banks."

"Of course," he sighed unhappily. It was annoying to have her repeat his own words as if she had created wisdom out of thin air. "I'm asking you if there is anything you can see in my system that I'm missing."

Margarite's business acumen, which he had first found such a welcome contrast to Caro's indifference, had suddenly become irritating. At first, he'd delighted in her ability to understand all the nuances of what optical scanning could accomplish. Caro not only couldn't understand, she didn't care. Margarite was fascinated. But Margarite, just like Caro, needed him to be a success. They were both all full of anxiety when the spectre of failure was hanging over him. The only difference between the two of them was Margarite's interest in the damning details.

"I see nothing beyond the dealers cheating all together in large groups." she said.

"Then you agree if I could figure that out, I'd have it," said Tim. "Yes."

"Can you loan me fifty thousand?" asked Tim.

"What?" asked Margarite with a sly laugh.

"Can you loan me fifty thousand?"

"Where did this come from?" she asked, her eyes all amused.

"I'll pay you back in three months," said Tim.

"You're breaking the rules, you know that, don't you?" she asked.

"What rules?"

"It's not fair to ask your friends for that kind of money," she said.

"If I pay off Padgett, I'll have the answer," he said.

"I never lend money to my friends," she said.

"Margarite, you give away thousands to your friends," he said.

"Your bill from Harris's is thirty thousand dollars a month. You're constantly sending jewelry all over the world. How can you not loan a friend some money he needs desperately?"

"Have you been going through my desk?" she asked, irritated. "Who told you about my bill from Harris's?"

"It's not important," he said. "That's not the issue."

"Yes, it is the issue," she said. "I won't have people talking all over town about my financial affairs. *Have* you been going through my desk?"

"Don't be an idiot," he said.

"Then tell me who told you."

"I'm not going to tell you," he said.

"I'll never do business there again," she declared.

He knew she meant it. He felt guilty for having repeated what the salesman there had told him. The poor guy had let it slip in small talk. Tim hadn't even asked him.

"I've been going through your desk," he said.

"You have not," she said. "You've been out researching my ability to lend you money."

"I don't have to do any research on your spending ability," he said. "We talk enough about your business life for me to know you can lend me fifty thousand dollars as easily as I can tip a waiter."

"Yes, you're right," she granted, softening. "But there's a principle involved."

"What is the principle?"

"You're asking me for a business loan," she said. "I never do business with my friends."

"I'm asking you," he said, "because I need a chance to come out of this thing with something—"

"I'm not in favor of throwing good money after bad," she interrupted. Her irritation was mounting again. He had angered her, and when she was angry, she was pompous and superior.

"Margarite, you just said it should work," he said.

"I also said it wasn't working," she said. "It's not my style of investing to keep throwing money at a problem until its solved. I find that when I do that, I tend to throw much more money at the problem than solving it will produce."

He was ready to argue. He was a step ahead of her, with his points all lined up, but he stopped. This was not a business problem they could take pleasure in worrying through together. She simply did not want to give him the money. The trouble was, he wanted it for his own purposes. It wasn't a surprise or a gift she could give him. If there was one thing Margarite didn't like, it was somebody asking something from her for selfish reasons. The gifts, all the gifts he had received, were advance payments for not asking for anything; and now that he had asked, he'd ruined it, and she was furious.

"What about all that money you had in the stock market?" she asked him.

Tim looked at her surprised.

"We talk about your business, too, don't we?" she mocked. "Why don't you use your money?"

"I'm not trying to take advantage of you," he said.

"Then why don't you use your own money," she retorted.

"Because it's not all mine," he said. "Half of it isn't enough, so I thought—"

"You won't ask her for it," she inserted, "but you'll ask me. Why is it everybody thinks that just because I have a lot of money, money means nothing to me? Tell me that! Why is it?"

There was something about this which enfuriated him. Her money did mean nothing to her. She passed it out like candy.

"Don't look at me like that!" she shouted. "I want an answer. I want to know why no one can get enough of me!"

"Goddammit, you fucking bitch!" he shouted. "You fucking bitch!"

He went out in the hallway and put on his coat. He expected her to come after him, but he was disappointed. He went downstairs and had the door open before she called to him.

"Just a minute, Tim."

She appeared on the landing. If she felt anything other than complete indifference over his staying or leaving, it was not discernible in her voice or on her face. She spoke, sounding as if she might be reading an article from that afternoon's paper. "I can't loan you any money. I care about you, but lending money isn't possible."

"Why not?"

She tossed her hair casually. "It's a rule I grew up with. Maybe it's wrong, but it has protected me from making many serious mistakes with men, so I live by it."

He looked at her, not knowing what to say.

"Can you love me as I am?" she asked him.

"No," he said.

Margarite had picked him up at the Ondine in her Mercedes, so he found himself outside without his own transportation back to the Ondine. Rather than go back inside and ask her for a ride, he decided to walk back. He turned down the street towards the beach.

He walked for a little while on the boardwalk, but he tired of saying hello to all the old women out walking their small dogs. The lower boardwalk had several tall apartment houses full of old ladies. Despite the fact that it was a nice day for December, they walked with their hands in fur muffs, their hats covering their ears, and their eyes circled with big astonished tortoise-shell frames. They all seemed to know him. He had become easily annoyed by such relentless familiarity, so he went out onto the beach and walked on the hard wet sand.

The seagulls were at work. They dug clams out of the sand, flew them fifty feet straight up, and dropped them. The shells fractured as if hit by a hammer, and the gulls were upon the wreckage in an instant, tearing out pink and nut-brown shreds of wet meat while shrieking angrily whether another gull challenged them or not, shrieking just for the pleasure of hearing themselves. It wasn't only their eating which excited them.

They did not scream at Tim. Without protest they opened a circle in their teeming flocks as he walked. They padded further up the beach or took to the air, gliding out to splash down in the small surf where they bobbed up and down like ducks. He could see them busy all the way up to Sinbad's where the island jutted out to show the Boardwalk Regency, the Monopoly, Controller Jacks, Viscaya, Fortunatas, and the Pier lined up like dominoes. As Tim moved up the wet sand towards the Ondine, the seagulls quietly moved out, leaving him alone in a wide circle of vacant sand.

He felt acutely lonely.

He reached into his pocket and took out the ruby. He had been to Harris's that morning to find out where it was. They knew exactly where Caro had pawned it and how to retrieve it for him. Rubies were their business, the salesman had said proudly. At first he had been angry when he found out she only got ten thousand for it, but then he told himself, what the hell, it was that much less to cover in the gift account. He still hadn't figured out whom he was going to claim he gave a ten thousand dollar ruby to. It would have to be a woman. Large gifts to players were common, but the Ondine didn't have a significant woman player in town at the moment. He shook his head and put the ruby back in his pocket. He didn't really care if they found out anyway.

He continued up the beach. The surf talked to him like monks moaning in Latin.

When he reached the Ondine and started back across the beach, he was surprised by the volume of clam shells all over the sand. Where the tide had been at its highest, there was a long, ragged mound of shells almost a foot high. The surf had piled the gulls' work up in a jagged wall, and retreated to leave the beach clean behind it.

He climbed onto the boardwalk, making his way towards the Ondine. He wished he could summon some kind of supernatural power and command the seagulls to grab the entire boardwalk population by the neck, fly them up fifty feet, and make the same wreckage of them they made of the clams so the sea could sweep the boardwalk clean.

He wished he could have a clean, safe circle to himself whenever he went among this ugly crowd.

·22·

HAAF DECIDED he had had enough of this particular party. The noise level was starting to hurt his ears and he felt horny. He picked out one of the girls Bewlay had sent up.

He had seen her in the coffee shop. She was a waitress. She looked much better in her cinnamon blouse than a waitress's uniform.

She had only the top button of the blouse fastened. The rest of the shirt was open down her chest. He could see into her small breasts whenever she turned. She had thick eyelashes and big hazel eyes.

She called him Mr. Haaf when he started talking to her.

"Why don't we go to my suite and talk," he suggested. "My ears are sensitive and the music is starting to bother me."

She was surprised he didn't live in the hospitality suite. He was getting notorious for all these parties, and everyone seemed to think he lived there.

"I don't give parties where I live," he told her.

She was a physical fitness buff. On the elevator she told him about her running regimen. Haaf listened eagerly. He had been feeling so good the past month, he had started running too. He had gotten in such good shape he could wrestle three minute periods without tiring. Maybe she would like to come watch him wrestle in the hotel gym some morning. There was a slot mechanic named Steve who wanted to take him on for a hundred bucks.

She said she'd love to watch. He opened the door to his suite and let her in.

"I see why you don't have any parties in here," she said.

Haaf laughed. His suite was a mess. He had been too lazy to put away his personal junk so the maids could come in and clean up.

He took her into the bedroom and started kissing her. He snuck his hand in through the opening of her blouse and rolled her breast around in his palm. She kissed him back with a busy tongue. She smelled of perfumed soap. Her nipple got hard quickly. When he finished the kiss, she was breathless.

"Take off your clothes," he told her. "I'm going to turn on the television."

"Television?"

"It's a special kind of television."

She was naked by the time he had the cassette in the recorder. She had a long, lithe body and her cute little tits looked perfect on her. He turned on the TV and started to get undressed.

"Oh! This kind of television!" she said, propping herself up against the headboard to watch. "I thought you were going to put on a soap opera."

He had selected the cassette of the woman from Pittsburgh. She and her partner came into their bedroom in tennis clothes. They were sweaty. Obviously they had just finished playing.

The boy was no more than eighteen. There were many such boys in Atlantic City waiting for women who could afford them.

The woman was thirty-eight or nine. She looked opulent even in a tennis outfit.

"I've seen her in the coffee shop," said the girl. "She's staying in the hotel, isn't she?"

"She's been here over a month," said Haaf. "Her name is Seybold."

The kid was taking Mrs. Seybold's dress off. She had a good pair of breasts. Her nipples were round wafers, as big as roulette chips.

"Her husband owns a string of foundries in Pittsburgh," said Haaf. "She lives in Swickley."

"Really?" asked the girl in surprise. "How did you get her to do this?"

"She doesn't know she's doing it," said Haaf. "The cameras are hidden."

"No kidding," said the girl. "Wow. This is fun."

The kid was fucking Mrs. Seybold doggy style. She was looking right at the mirror which concealed one of the cameras. The kid's hand was down there with his cock and he was rubbing her clit as he fucked her. She had an expression of pain on her face, but Haaf knew it was more pleasure than pain. Her breasts were hanging straight down, and her whole body was shivering as if she were cold.

"Look at her tits wiggle," said the girl.

The woman's mouth opened and she shouted.

"Too bad you don't have sound," said the girl.

"She's coming," said Haaf.

Mrs. Seybold frowned from the intensity of her orgasm. Her mouth opened again, but Haaf, who had watched this film many times, was sure there was no noise to this shout. It was a silent scream. Tears, nothing more than a thin line of moisture at first, started down her cheeks. They grew quickly to a vigorous salty rill. The water curled every which way down her cheeks. Her face suddenly turned blank. It was as if all her emotions had been extinguished. Her body was frozen rigidly stiff. On all fours she looked like an iron sculpture of a bitch dog with a single pair of cold metal teats. She looked as dead as a statue, except for the liquid whips of tears snapping back and forth across her cheeks.

Everytime he watched this film, Haaf got the idea he was going to make a deal for her husband's foundries; as if by doing so, he could buy her.

He unlocked the outer door and stepped into the quiet casino. The only noise was the hum of the slot machines shooting their spears of colored light up into the darkened dome. He walked swiftly to the innermost reaches of the casino.

He opened the door to the casino offices. It was a matter of routine for him to have the office keys. He passed through the casino manager's office, and the video room. He pushed the code numbers for the elevator to the vault, and descended to the vault room. The elevator doors opened and the dank smell came rushing at him. The smell was especially powerful in the early mornings. He disengaged all the alarms, and a few moments later was inside the vault.

He took off his sport coat, unbuttoned his shirt and laid his canvas money belt on a shelf. He picked up the first box and opened the left lock with Perez's key, then opened the right with the inspector's key. He pulled the box's door open and dumped the money out on the shelf.

It was late August when Perez had come into his office to put the keys away and discovered he had the inspector's keys. In an instant, Haaf knew what he was going to do. The inspector's keys were the missing link to a plan that had crossed his mind a thousand times. The inspector had picked up Perez's keys by mistake. He would be back for his own after lunch, because he had to go to the count at Fortunatas. Haaf told Perez to have lunch, that he would return the keys to the inspector himself. He had done so, but not before hurrying over to Atlantic Avenue to have the keys duplicated at a hardware store. Within a week, Haaf was in New York with evidence of Laboy's stealing. He had to get rid of Laboy to get control of the vault.

Haaf picked his way through the money from *BJ 1*, taking out nearly equal amounts of bills of all the larger denominations. When he had finished packing them in the money belt, he put the fill slips and the remaining bills back in the box and went on to the next one.

Haaf had thought he would be the next casino manager after Laboy, but Oakes had surprised him by giving it to Seagurt. Haaf had been forced to race back to Atlantic City ahead of Seagurt, call the safe company, and get them over to the Ondine in a hurry. Ostensibly he had done it because Laboy had been fired and still knew the combination. In reality he had done it to get through the last significant barrier to getting into the boxes. Getting Perez's keys copied was easy. They were kept in the hotel safe in Haaf's office.

The next box had a lot of money in it. Tim's incredible success in controlling the casino had been an unexpected bonus. He looked at his watch. Five-thirty. He had to speed up a little.

Haaf had been very surprised that first morning after Seagurt had hired all the black dealers. When he'd opened that first box, it had scared the hell out of him. He couldn't get the money out fast enough. He had watched the count before then, but he had never realized there was a skill involved in counting money until that night. After that night he came to appreciate that there were ten thousand hundred dollar bills in a million dollars, and ten thousand bills took a lot of counting.

At first his own lack of manual dexterity in counting the bills had prevented him from dragging the per down. The sheer volume of money was so large, he couldn't count out enough to make a dent in the total. But by repetition of the chore night after night, he had gained the skill he needed.

It was ironic, but Tim Seagurt's success had doomed him. It had proved him to be too smart not to figure out what was happening sooner or later, so Haaf had kept taking out more and more money, making the per and profits move gently downward. From his frequent talks with Henry, who was so in love with his computer he was only too happy to explain everything, Haaf knew how to create the illusion in Tim's mind that all the dealers were stealing. He needed that illusion to keep Tim busy until his own maneuvers were complete.

There actually had been some black stealing, all right. Seagurt was right about that. They did get corrupted, but it was never anything like what Haaf had made it appear. And now Tim and Henry were catching all of them with this optical scanning system. Tim actually had stopped every little bit of stealing in the casino, and the money in the boxes showed it.

Out of respect for Tim, Haaf had been forced to hurry up his scheme to buy the Ondine. His lawyers in Amsterdam had instructions to move the negotiations with Alfred Oakes along very quickly. Oakes believed a cash-rich Dutch ballbearing company wanted to buy the Ondine. Cash-rich was correct, but it was Dean Haaf and some partners doing the buying, not a ballbearing firm. Haaf was pleased to be in the unique situation of controlling the seller's anxiety. The lower he made the Ondine's profits, the more anxious Alfred Oakes became to sell.

They were so close now the rumors had started. It was only the beginning, but they had started. His partners were not the kind of men who knew how to keep a business confidence. For all their claims about their oaths and secrecy, they liked nothing better than to blab on about their business and everyone else's for hours. Thank God he had been able to fool them over how he was getting the money out. He didn't want it getting around to anyone that he had the keys to the Ondine's boxes.

As he went from box to box, sorting money with mechanical precision, Haaf reviewed the acquisitions he would make after he captured the Ondine. This time he could take all the time he wanted. This time he was going to do it right. This time he was going to build his empire with cash.

He was finished by six, plenty of time to get out ahead of the casino cleaning crews. He had become expert at his chore.

He made a mental note as he returned to his suite with the money. He had to get the details from Henry Moore about how the optical scanner worked. Moore might not want to work for him after Tim left. His devotion to Tim was strong. Besides, he might wonder why his system would suddenly begin to operate more efficiently after Tim left. It would be hard to sell him on the idea Haaf had found so readily marketable elsewhere. Elsewhere everyone was happy to believe that Tim was simply a clever thief, who, just like them, talked a clean house in order to disguise his stealing.

PART V

December, 198–

·23·

CARO LAY in bed savoring her dream. It was pink and yellow and had something that looked like a woman leaping through it like a dolphin. Suddenly the woman was up close. She was a lithe and beautiful ondine. It was the last of the morning's staccato of dreams. She knew it was the last because she was fighting to hang on to it and not wake up. As always, as soon as she realized she was trying to stay asleep, she woke up.

Her whole body twitched with a small jolt of electricity, as if she'd suffered a whisper of shock therapy. She sat quickly up in bed. She wasted no time beginning work on the blank sheet she had set up on her easel the night before. She did the big mermaid of the Ondine's neon sign in pink and yellow. A radiating ondine came up in swift and sharp strokes. It was hard to believe she was still getting better, that it was still getting easier and more in control, but she was and it was.

When it was right, it was better than fucking. When it was right, it was better than dope. Nothing could touch this feeling. She felt like Thomas Cole.

It had been right off and on from the first morning after she'd returned from Atlantic City. She had called Twomey the afternoon she got home. They told her to come in the next morning. She'd fallen asleep as soon as she hung up and didn't wake until five A.M. Without even thinking about it, she had begun drawing to pass the time until eight. She never made it to Twomey. Once started, she kept on going.

Now time passed as if she were falling down a funnel of days. The focus of her work became narrower and narrower, constricting and constricting as she dropped toward a small circle of beauty and ugliness. She was falling towards it, not knowing exactly what it was, knowing only she was falling and falling and enjoying the incredible feeling of speed as the bottom of the funnel drew closer and closer.

Once in awhile she thought of Tim. Unconsciously, she knew a lot of time had passed, and the thought of calling him had crossed her mind several times. But she hadn't. Now he intruded more and more on her work. She did some work on him. It was odd. He came out very realistically. She had never been very good at drawing him before.

Roskoe looked shaken. His puffy throat was pursing in and out with his anxious breathing. There were two neat six-inch rips in his overstuffed shirt. The fabric was stained with blood so that the wounds looked like obscenely red lips. Hector had just brought him into Tim's office.

"He didn't have to do that," Roskoe told Tim. "Why did he have to do that?"

"Where's Tommy?" Tim asked Hector. "What's going on?"

"Tommy's outside," said Hector. "I asked him to help me with Roskoe. That's why he's cut. He's been blubbering all the way over from the Pier."

"What happened?"

"He didn't want to come," said Hector.

"The Vietnamese pulled a knife on me and forced me out of the casino," said Roskoe. "That's what happened."

"He pulled knife on you after you left the casino because you refused to come along to the Ondine," corrected Hector. "It was out on the boardwalk, Tim."

"Why should I come to the Ondine?" asked Roskoe weakly. "Tim told me never to come in here again."

"I invited Mr. Roskoe back to the Ondine," Hector explained to Tim, "to pay us some of the money he owes us."

"You said I didn't have to pay off those markers," said Roskoe, suddenly regaining his loud mouth. "Isn't that right, Tim?"

"No, he didn't," answered Hector. "He said he wasn't going to drive you into bankruptcy to collect those markers. But you have just won eighty thousand dollars in cash, Mr. Roskoe."

"You pricks," said Roskoe. "You're going back on your word."

"We still have you on video tape, Mr. Roskoe," said Hector.

"All right, all right," said Roskoe.

He reached into his coat pocket and started taking out packets of money.

"How much do you want? I don't have to give you everything, do I?"

He was asking Tim.

"Here's thirty thousand," he said, counting the packets out on Tim's desk. "I've got to have the other fifty to meet the payroll on Monday. You can't take that or you'll put me out of business."

"You're bullshitting us again, Mr. Roskoe," said Hector.

"No, I'm not!" shouted Roskoe. "Honestly! I give you my word!"

"Mr. Roskoe, you've been having a very lucky week," said Hector. "You've paid all your old markers off except ours and you're a couple of hundred grand to the good."

"What?" asked Roskoe, shocked. "Who told you that?"

Hector had shown Tim a report on Roskoe from World Casino Credit earlier. Roskoe had won over a million dollars in the last week.

"All right, all right," said Roskoe. "Me and my big mouth. I'll pay you the whole sixty I owe you, and I'm clean here, right?"

"Okay," said Tim.

"Good," said Roskoe. "And I get my old credit line back?"

"Hector, you shouldn't have used Tommy for that," said Tim after Roskoe left.

"The nerve of that guy," said Hector. "Did we really hear him ask for his old credit line back?"

"Why did you do this?" asked Tim.

"You said you didn't have any way to pay off Padgett, didn't you?" said Hector, grinning conspiratorially. "This money's an ancient marker. It's already been taken off the books as uncollectible. It's perfect. You can find out what's going on out there in the pits."

Tim, who had been irritated with Hector, was suddenly no longer irritated. He felt a flash of affection for him. It took him a moment to realize the wolf sometimes did without a fleece coat and came on instead as a whinning, spitting old man as harmless as a guppy.

"Will sixty thousand be enough?" asked Tim.

Hector shrugged.

"Padgett is awful greedy," said Tim. "This won't make much of an impression on him considering what he must be getting out of here every night."

"Let's get enough to make sure then," said Hector. "What the shit. It's only money."

Hector came in with a list a few minutes later.

"Did Henry see you making this up?" asked Tim.

"He's too busy giving computer lessons to Haaf," said Hector.

"We're going to write some of these off as uncollectible," said Tim.

"Right, boss."

Tim looked down the list. He checked off the names of people who lived along the Jersey shore.

"I figured it out from the beginning," he said, feeling a need to justify himself. "I saw right to the heart of this business the first day I was here."

"Yes, you did," agreed Hector.

"The thing I missed was me," he said "I thought I could make gambling honest. I thought I was going to change the whole business."

He laughed at himself.

"You don't change this business," he said. "It changes you."

"Look, Tim, you've worked your ass off here," said Hector. "Why should you have nothing to show for it?"

"It's not a matter of getting something to show for it," said Tim. "It's not that at all, Hector."

"What is it then?" asked Hector, genuinely puzzled.

"I have to get it right," he sighed. "I have to make it work. Even if I end up selling it to Oakes for nickels and dimes, I have to make it work."

"Whatever it is you want, Tim, you've worked hard to get it," said Hector. "So you deserve to have it."

"Thanks, Hector," said Tim. "You keep ten percent of what you collect, okay?"

"Sure."

"Don't say anything to Henry," said Tim.

"I know," said Hector. "He wouldn't understand."

Tim pushed himself away from his polished aluminum desk and walked over to the small window. It was the only window in the office and it looked out beyond a courtyard where the truckers loaded all the freight. Past the courtyard was the ramp up the boardwalk from New Jersey Avenue and its parade of tourists. He felt sad and angry with himself at the same time.

"What's wrong, Tim?" asked Hector.

"I feel like I'm screwing Henry," he said.

"Oh, shit," said Hector. "He made his own bed. Let him lie in it."

Tim didn't answer. He enjoyed Henry and his fulminating honesty, and he hated the idea of letting him down.

"I've got to tell him," he said.

"He won't listen," said Hector.

"He'll listen when we have the answer," said Tim.

Hector laughed, spitting a minor storm of glee. "You're right. Once he has the answer to the riddle, he won't care how you got it, will he?"

Tim sighed again. "I still feel like I'm screwing him."

Hector left, and Tim started to call Caro. When he picked up the phone, he noticed Hector had left the door open. He could hear Henry in the outer offices explaining the optical scanner to Haaf. Dean Haaf hadn't been around the casino offices for awhile. He had been too busy getting drunk and fucking. Tim wasn't sure whether Haaf was having a last fling before it all ended, or whether he was deliberately ignoring reality.

When Tim got to the door, instead of slamming it closed, he strode through it and into the outer offices.

"It doesn't work, Henry," he interrupted, letting his annoyance flare. "Can't you get it through your head, it doesn't work."

Henry stared at him in surprise. "It caught Brady. That proved it works."

"It doesn't work, Dean," said Tim, as angry at him as Henry. "There's an enormous swindle going on out there that's driven the *per* down to eight, and Henry is so in love with his system, he's still pretending it's great. I don't know who's dumber—him for saying it still works, or you for listening to him."

Henry was turning red with embarrassment. Haaf was staring at the computer as if he hadn't heard a word Tim had said.

"We're going through a period of bad luck," said Henry. "Every casino has them. Back in Vegas the Flamingo lost ten million in one month a few years ago. We haven't even had any losses. This system is what's saving us from a really bad month."

"It doesn't work, Henry," repeated Tim.

"It has to," said Henry, staring at Tim with wounded cow eyes behind his oversized glasses. "There has to be a premium for honesty in this business."

"Honesty?" laughed Tim. "What the hell does honesty have to do with anything?"

STUPID, STUPID, STUPID, Haaf screamed silently at himself.

He stared at the computer in shock. He hardly even noticed the sudden appearance of Seagurt. He was so shocked, he was afraid to move in case he somehow betrayed himself.

How could he have been so lazy and so *stupid* that he waited two weeks to find out what the optical scanner was doing?

Luckily they hadn't programmed the small computing packs at each table to record the table's drop. No. They had been so busy making the packs and the mainframe dance together, they hadn't thought they had an easy way to check the results of the count against the night before.

They hadn't done that because they didn't yet suspect that the theft might be taking place when the casino was closed and their precious computer was asleep.

But there was still an easy way for them to find out what was happening. All they had to do was ask the mainframe for the night's per for the whole casino. It had to have that number, or it wouldn't have been functioning and catching all the stealing. All they had to do was figure out how to ask it for that number, and they could extrapolate the drop. The right question would show them how fabulously successful they had made the Ondine. If they asked that question, he would have no hope of ever buying the Ondine from Alfred Oakes. The computer had indirectly counted every single dollar he'd stolen out of the boxes.

· 24 ·

THE DOORS were locked and the vast planetarium casino was as dark as the most distant rim of space. Except for one soft star: *BJ 8*.

Kedar Padgett sat alone at the blackjack table. Behind him, like a crowd of kibitzers, was his collection of fops and mannequins. He wore a dirty shirt with an assinine picture of Atlantic City ironed across it. He retained his leather Hogan hat. He was smoking more expensive cigars, but still letting a generous amount of spit advance up the wrapper.

Tim spread thousand dollar bills out across the blackjack layout as if it were a counting table.

"That looks like serious money," grinned Padgett.

He was very much impressed by the litter of wriggling, live bills which were about to jump into his battered old briefcase.

"Two hundred thousand," said Tim, finishing his counting.

The money was fanned out across the layout for all the cameras to see. Jimmy was back in the video room with every camera in the dome pointed at *BJ 8*.

"It's a new record!" came a voice from Padgett's cheering section.

"Why so much?" asked Padgett, almost suspicious.

"I felt a sudden urge to get rid of some money," said Tim. "It's sort of like emptying a chamber pot out the window. Besides, your friend Powell tells me this is the only thing this kind of money is good for."

"It's good for more than that," said Padgett.

"Really?" asked Tim sarcastically, gesturing Padgett to go ahead and pick the money up.

"Hey, man!" came the voice from the entourage. "We're going to buy this city with your own money, and then we're going to send all you chucks on your way."

"Is that what you're going to do, Padgett?" asked Tim.

Padgett stopped gathering up the bills, smelling something in Tim's voice.

"What are you up to now, Seagurt?" he asked. "Is it time for your little trap?"

"Bring it over, Henry," Tim called down towards the dark end of the pit.

Henry came up out of the darkness and handed Tim a sheet of yellow paper.

"What's that?" asked Padgett.

"Something from World Casino Credit," answered Tim.

"Who is that?" asked Padgett.

"They are the people that Henry used to work for," said Tim. "They have their own little language. It's like talking by the numbers. They say that a gambler is a low four or a medium five. A low four is a guy good for one to three thousand dollars in credit. A high five would have seventy to ninety-nine thousand in credit."

"Oh, what I'd give to be a high five," came the voice from the crowd.

"You still wouldn't be quite the man your hero is," said Tim, waving the yellow sheet at all of them.

Padgett began collecting the bills again.

"Let me read you what they have to say," said Tim. "Kedar Padgett is an active medium six. Plays in the Caribbean. Lost low six at the Aruba Americana last month. Quick pay. Cash."

Padgett's crowd was silent.

"That was when you were supposed to be in New York for therapy on your back, wasn't it?" Tim asked Padgett.

Padgett ignored him, continuing with his work of packing away the money.

"A six, people," mocked Tim, "is over a hundred thousand."

"Hey, man," said the voice, suddenly stepping forward from the crowd. "Let's not put that shit out to the public."

It was Terdell Hurst, Padgett's favorite commissioner. He snatched the sheet of paper out of Tim's hand and stuffed it into his orange patent leather sport coat.

"I'm not running for office," said Tim. "It's your own nasty little secret. I just wanted you assholes to know I'm not taken in by all this bullshit about underpriviledged housing. This is extortion pure and simple."

No one argued.

"That Robin Hood stuff gets old in a hurry, doesn't it, Padgett?" asked Tim.

"We do buy houses," answered Padgett. "It doesn't say anything about the four hundred thousand I won in Antigua and bought half of Folsom Avenue with, does it?"

"Sure," said Tim. "Tell me all about it."

"Fuck you," said Padgett, a note of pleasure in his voice.

"You know something, Padgett?" said Tim. "Powell told me I'd feel better after I bought you—"

"You haven't bought me," snapped Padgett.

"Yes, I have," said Tim. "I can feel it. Powell was right about that. But he was wrong when he said I'd like it. I don't like it at all. I feel like I've taken a dive out the window, right into the shit I was trying to get rid of."

"Why do you always come off acting so saintly, Seagurt?" asked Padgett. "You done some business in this place. Quite a lot of business, from what I've heard."

"That's all rumor," interrupted Henry scornfully. "Everybody bad-mouths Tim because they're afraid of what he stands for."

Padgett put down his cigar and indulged himself in a long, boisterous laugh.

"Fool!" he said to Henry. "Where did all this money come from?"

Henry glanced quickly at Tim.

"Yeah, you ask him," said Padgett.

"It doesn't make any difference," said Henry. "The point is: now you have your money and now we would like to know exactly how you have been raiding our casino."

"Raiding your casino?" asked Padgett, puzzled.

"That's right," said Henry.

"I don't know what you're talking about," said Padgett.

"We want to know what Powell and you have worked out with our dealers and bosses," said Henry.

Padgett looked at Tim. His puzzled look turned to curiosity.

"I told you this one was a set up," said Terdell loudly. "Leave the money right there and you're all right."

"You can have the money and we won't do anything," said Henry quickly. "But if you don't tell us, we have everything down to the serial numbers of those bills recorded by telephoto lenses."

"I don't know what the fuck you're talking about, Moore," said Padgett. "If money is disappearing, you'd better look to your boss. I think he's pulled some wool down over those big glasses of yours."

"You can't sell me all those rumors about Tim," said Henry stubbornly.

"Believe what you want," invited Padgett. "People usually do."

"Why haven't you done anything about Tim after what you said to him at the Monopoly?" said Henry, now boiling with righteousness. "Why haven't you started your big campaign against gambling again? I'll tell you why. Because you're getting all the money you want out of this casino, that's why."

Padgett stared at Henry in astonishment. Tim was used to it, but Henry's outburst had taken Padgett by surprise. A smile began to creep up his jaw quickly giving way to boisterous laughter.

"You want the money you steal and this money too," shouted Henry, stung by Padgett's laughter. "Nothing is enough for you. You're like everyone else in this business. You just steal and steal and steal."

"Wait a minute, Moore," said Padgett, shaking his head and still laughing. "It's time somebody woke you up. I haven't stolen anything from this casino. And I don't believe your dealers are stealing very much either. You want to know why I haven't come after your boss? It's because I don't believe in beating a dead horse, fool. If he's going to be gone in a couple of weeks, why should I bother with him? They come and they go so fast I can't keep track of them."

"What do you mean, he'll be gone?" asked Henry.

"Didn't he tell you that either?" asked Padgett, his voice full of false innocence.

"What's he talking about?" Henry asked Tim.

"I don't know," said Tim.

"Horseshit, he doesn't know," said Padgett. "The Ondine is almost sold. It will be in new hands in a week. You think I didn't know why you invited me down here for this?"

Padgett laughed his raucous laugh again.

"You two don't have anything on me that's news to anyone in this town. Everybody has gambling habits in this town. That's why they all hate it so much," he said, then grinning up at the cameras in the dome and holding the money aloft as if it were a prize, "Hi, folks! It's me again! Your crooked mayor bringing you your legalized video-recorded crime! If it ain't money, honey, it ain't bribery!"

Terdell Hurst grabbed Padgett by the shoulder and shook him. "Kedar, what the hell are you doing? This one can do it to you. He doesn't care about the Ondine's license. He's leaving town."

Padgett shoved him away and looked at Tim. "Terdell thinks I'm suicidal. You know something? I think he's right."

"You're asking for it Kedar," said Terdell plaintively. "Why do you keep on asking for it?" He turned to Tim. "Hey, don't do anything with that film. He hasn't done anything with Powell or your dealers or anybody else. I'm not shitting you, Seagurt. Our people are not stealing from you. You have my word."

It was Tim's turn to laugh. "Thanks. I have your word."

Padgett was busy loading his briefcase with money again.

"What's he so worried about?" Tim asked Padgett. "How come you're grinning at the camera and he's scared to death."

"He's scared because before I heard you were leaving, I started the wheels turning again," said Padgett. He spoke matter of factly, but a sense of urgency came into the way he gathered up the bills, as if he wanted to get them packed away in a hurry now. "I didn't do much. I only started talking it up again. You know, gambling is the root of all evil and what are we getting out of it except a chance to lose our money to the short coats and all of that. I stopped as soon as I heard you were on your way out of town, but it didn't make any difference. You can't believe what a groundswell I started. Tim baby, they're all crazy for it again, and this time it's out of control".

"It's going to get you killed," said Terdell.

Padgett laughed again. "Don't I deserve it, turd?"

It was odd watching Padgett from a hundred different angles. Henry, Hector, Jimmy, and Tim studied the playback in silence, listening to the sound of the voices. Padgett's voice came through much clearer than anybody else's. His resonant timbre took well to the microphone. Tim and Henry sounded weak and far away in comparison.

As Tim listened and watched, he wondered exactly what he had accomplished. They had Padgett on tape, all right, but what the hell were they going to do with it?

"We'll have to edit you and Henry out of this stuff, Tim," said Jimmy. "Or we can just cut out a block of Padgett taking the money with no you and no Henry. Then we have a block of straight, uncut, damning tape."

"It doesn't say anything about the four hundred thousand I won," the hundred Padgetts were saying," . . . and bought half of Folsom Avenue with . . ."

Tim's scratchy voice answered, "Sure. Tell me all about it."

Padgett's magnified resonant voice, obviously enjoying the carriage of its message, responded, "Fuck you."

Tim turned to Hector. "Why is it that suddenly I like this bastard again?"

Hector spit with puzzlement. "He's a real enigma, all right."

"What are you going to do?" asked Henry.

"I'm not going to do anything with this," said Tim.

"Why not?" asked Henry.

Tim shrugged. Padgett had a talent for inspiring admiration and hatred in people at the same time. Now that Tim's hatred had dissolved, the admiration that had been there all along was taking over.

"I believe him," said Tim. "I don't think he's doing anything to us."

Henry turned away. Tim continued watching the monitors.

"Fool," Padgett was saying to Henry off camera. "Where did all this money come from?"

"I guess I could have found out he wasn't doing anything," Tim added over the recorded voice, "without giving him two hundred thousand fucking dollars."

"I was so glad we were going to find out what was going on," said Henry. "I never did stop to think where you got the money."

Tim looked at Hector, and Hector looked back at Tim.

"I sent Hector around to bag some stale markers," said Tim.

"Oh," said Henry, very disappointed. "It never even occurred to me it was dirty money. I wish you hadn't done that Tim. It ruins the whole thing—"

"Oh, come on Henry, grow up," interrupted Tim, suddenly impatient with him.

"There really is no such thing as an honest casino manager, is there?" asked Henry bitterly.

"No," said Tim.

"That's why you say honesty has nothing to do with it," said Henry. "That's why you say the system doesn't work."

"I say the system doesn't work because it doesn't, Henry," said Tim. "If the money is not in the boxes in the morning, the system doesn't work."

"You're doing it," said Henry. He had a disturbed look. It wasn't his emotional look he got when he was mad. It was something even more intense.

"Me?" said Tim.

"Yes," said Henry. "You."

Hector laughed.

"You sound paranoid, Henry," said Tim. "You think I've been stealing from the casino?"

"You're fiddling the system," said Henry. "I don't know how you're doing it, but you're doing it."

Tim had to stop himself from laughing. There was something funny about the accusation, but there was nothing funny about the way Henry said it. Henry was looking at him through his big glasses, his eyes tortured and angry, and Tim began to wish Padgett had known something, because now Tim had nothing to say to Henry.

"Henry, I'm weak," he said. "I'm not a hero. I couldn't find the answer so I tried to bribe it out of Padgett. I was wrong. He didn't have it. I'm sorry. But I haven't been fiddling anything. I've been as desperate to make it work as you."

"Is that why you've been sneaking money out of the gift account?" asked Henry.

"I haven't snuck any money out of the gift account," said Tim.

"You forget I'm in charge of credit too," said Henry. "You forget I know who is in town and who is not in town, and I know damn well Susan Hill hasn't been in this hotel for weeks. You didn't buy any ten thousand dollar ruby from Harris's for Susan Hill. You cashed it in. And how many markers did you write off? Did you take in a half a million and give two hundred to Padgett? Did you save a slice of cash for you and Hector? You've been pulling all kinds of shit all along, admit it."

Tim was astonished. He had forgotten about the ruby in the gift account. He hadn't even understood what Henry was talking about until he mentioned Susan Hill.

"That's Caro's ruby," said Tim. "I'll pay the gift account for it."

"Yeah, yeah," said Henry. "You thought I'd never see it."

Tim was silent. He didn't feel like arguing with Henry about honesty.

"You can't sell me those rumors about Tim . . ." said Henry's recorded voice from the monitors.

Henry turned and looked at the electronic Argus with hostility. "Shut up!" he shouted at his own voice.

"How did you know about that ruby, Henry?" asked Hector.

"That's none of your business," snapped Henry.

How did he find out? Suddenly Tim *did* feel like arguing with Henry. "How did you know about it? You don't have access to the gift account."

"Why don't I have access?" said Henry. "I asked Perez for it, and he gave it to me. I'm the head of credit."

"Why did you ask him for it?" asked Tim, beginning to understand. "It doesn't have anything to do with credit. You were checking on me. You have been checking on me all along. You have been tracking me just like I was another Laboy or McGray."

"And it turns out I was right to," said Henry, a distinct note of triumph in his voice."

"Henry, Henry," said Tim mournfully, trying not to get angry. "It's me. Tim. I didn't do anything."

"There has to be a reason why it isn't working," said Henry defensively, already doubting his own accusation. "And you're the only one left."

"You stupid asshole," exploded Tim. "It just doesn't work!"

"Because you cheat!" screamed Henry.

Tim was silent for several moments. He felt sad and tired. "Give it up, Henry," he said gently. "I promise you it doesn't work. I'm not doing anything to the computer. I'm not hiding anything from you you haven't found out about tonight. Please believe me. I'm promising you on my word."

"You're promising me on your word?" he asked. He had the same sarcasm in his voice Tim had used on Terdell, but there was something more underneath it, an almost hysterical grief. "You can trot out that 'on your word' with me?"

"I don't know what else to say," said Tim wearily. "I want you to understand it doesn't work."

"Okay, it doesn't work," he said dully. "What do we do now?"

"Does anybody give a shit?" asked Tim.

"Does anybody give a shit?" repeated Henry nodding his head abruptly up and down.

"Let's go to bed," said Tim. "I've had enough of this for one night."

Jimmy turned off the monitors and got up out of his chair.

"I give a shit," said Henry.

He picked up Jimmy's chair and threw it at the bank of fading monitors.

"I give a shit!" he shouted.

The chair broke several tubes with a loud popping noise followed by the sound of splintering glass. Henry retrieved the chair before any of them even understood what he was doing. He bashed at the ghostly cathode eyes again and again, *POP! POP! POP!* smashing fifteen of them before Jimmy wrenched the chair away from him. Getting the chair didn't stop him. He went to work on them with his fists, cracking them with one loud *POP!* after another.

"Let him go!" Tim told Jimmy who was trying to get a grip on Henry and stop him. Jimmy let him go, and they all stood there and watched him. He cracked another six screens before he stopped.

"Are you happy now?" asked Tim.

"I guess so," he said breathlessly.

"What the hell did you do that for?"

"I got pissed off," said Henry, studying his right hand. It was crisscrossed with deep red scratches. His knuckles were all puffed up like he had the gout. There was a bad gash above his wrist. It was weeping dark blood in almost purple drops.

"You really hurt that," said Tim. "Come on, we'd better get you to the hospital."

He took him by the arm and led him towards the door.

"Wait a minute," said Henry, gingerly removing his arm from Tim's grasp.

He picked up the chair again. "I forgot one."

He threw the chair through the single large computer screen.

"See?" he said. "I believe you. It doesn't work."

Dean Haaf had been intensely anxious ever since his conversation about the optical scanner with Henry Moore that morning. As he waited for the closing of the casino, his anxiety grew more and more acute.

He had to wait while Tim had some kind of private bribing party with Kedar Padgett and his cronies. Then Tim came out an hour later with Moore who had blood all over his arm.

Hector Knute was the last one out, but he didn't lock the door.

Haaf stood in the hallway outside the men's room and stared at the open door. There was no way he could go in now. The first thing anyone would do when they found the door open would be to search the casino. He couldn't risk being found inside.

He went back into the men's room. He paced up and back in front of the urinals. The smell of the lye cakes disgusted him.

All day long he had been planning what he was going to do. He was going to get in there and rape those boxes. He was going to give the Ondine a loss. He was going to give the Ondine such a ruinous loss, Alfred Oakes would want to sell the casino in a hurry at any price.

It was almost seven when Hector finally showed up with the keys and locked the casino door.

Haaf hurried inside to his work. The cleaning crews came in at eight-thirty. There was no question of sorting out the bills now. He had time only to grab and stuff.

·25·

THE APARTMENT felt incredibly empty. She went into the bedroom to get away from the feeling. She stood staring at the thing she had been working on all morning. It was a study of Roskoe. She had made his fingers a sickening yellow from nicotine. She had put all her revulsion into that yellow, the same revulsion that had made her vomit all over the blackjack table.

She wasn't angry any more. She wasn't angry at all. She missed Tim. He had become much more important to her as a real and struggling foolish Tim than as the secretive ironic genius. A strange, compelling curiosity washed through her again. It had been bothering her for the past week as it had never bothered her before. She wanted to know what he had been like as a child.

Twilight was almost over. As Caro drove into Hartford, more and more cars had their headlights turned on. She was distracted from the highway by the Connecticut River flowing alongside it. Late twilight had turned it purple. She got so busy measuring its wide purple water she almost forgot Mrs. Seagurt's directions. She looked up for the signs overhead just in time to make her first turn off the highway.

Caro had called Hartford to see if the Seagurts still lived there. Mrs. Seagurt had been delighted to hear from her. She had heard Tim was married from Tim's brother Martin. She didn't say she had been disappointed not to have been invited to the wedding. She didn't say she was surprised to finally hear from Tim's wife. She made no inquiry into Caro's motive for calling her. She only urged Caro to visit them sometime. There was no mention of Tim, only something so compelling and urgent in her request that it was easy for Caro to make up a lie about a trip to Vermont and how convenient it would be to stop by Hartford on her way up tonight. They agreed to it quickly, with still no mention of Tim. Without asking, Mrs. Seagurt seemed to know Caro was coming alone.

"It was a nightmare," she told Caro. "A fifteen-year nightmare. It was the kind that was so real you don't even know it's a nightmare until its all over, and then you go through something like waking up, only it takes years to get over it instead of minutes. It's only when it's over that you begin to see how unreal it was. When it's happening, you normalize it. You have to. We thought we did, anyway. Tim, don't you know, he didn't want to normalize it."

She was sitting with Mrs. Seagurt in her kitchen having coffee. Dr. Seagurt was out in the living room with the newspaper. The kitchen was exquisite. There were polished copper pans hanging over an island of gas burners in the center. The tile counter was decorated with curls of rich delft blue. Two beautiful Royal Copenhagen plates were set out on top of the tile, waiting for the work of what the kitchen suggested was a very accomplished cook. The coffee, smooth and aromatic, confirmed the suggestion.

Unlike Tim's father, Mrs. Seagurt had nothing in her face that looked like Tim. She had his height—she was tall with small bones—but her face was slender and narrow, nothing like the big square of Tim and his father. She wore her hair done up in a braid and reached back to check its pins when Caro asked her what the fighting was all about. It occurred to Caro that Tim never talked about his mother. Wisecracks about his father had been abundant, but he seldom referred to his mother.

"We thought he was wrong then," she said, referring to Tim. "The family got into the idea of thinking Tim was the trouble. Even when we had to move to Hartford, we still didn't see it."

Caro looked at her, puzzled. Mrs. Seagurt seemed to be talking around the point without getting close to it. She was taking some knowledge of Caro's for granted which Caro didn't have, but more than that, she was talking about something so painful she had to circle it and circle it, like an animal trying to get meat out of trap.

"Tim led the resistance," she said. "He performed a function for all of us that we were afraid to do alone."

She took a sip of her coffee and looked at Caro, as if she had explained something and she wanted Caro's reaction.

"Tim doesn't talk about his growing up, Mrs. Seagurt," said Caro gently.

Mrs. Seagurt looked away, hurt. When she looked back, she had collected herself for something. "I imagine he wouldn't," she said, more like she was making a resolution to herself than stating a fact.

Caro waited.

"Tim wasn't very good at school," she said abruptly. "He flunked third grade."

"Tim?"

"He was brilliant later," smiled Mrs. Seagurt, taking pleasure in

Tim's reversal, a pleasure she must have run through a thousand times, "but that was very much of a surprise. His father never could see it. Herb decided Tim was the slow mind of the family. His father is that way when it suits him. There is no change in his mind no matter how blind to reality he has to be. He was even very difficult over paying for Tim to go to college."

"But Tim must have graduated high in his high school class," said Caro.

"He did well from the beginning of high school," said Mrs. Seagurt. "But by then they hated each other so much it was unbearable. You would never think it possible for a father to hate his own son. Maybe in some poorer family, don't you know, where they must fight over everything all the time, but not a doctor and his son."

"Of course it's possible," said Caro.

Mrs. Seagurt looked up from her coffee and stared at Caro with new interest.

"They fought and fought and fought," she said. Caro's granting her premise seemed to release something inside her, "I'd sit there at the dinner table unable to eat. They'd taunt each other and keep on taunting until it exploded. He left Martin alone, but from the time Tim was eight, Herb wanted only to fight with him."

"You mean argue?" asked Caro.

"I mean fight, Caro," she said. "Herb would leap up out of his chair and get Tim by the hair. He'd drag him out into the living room and hit him. He was always trying to spank him but Tim wouldn't allow it. Tim never stopped fighting back, so his father couldn't get him down to spank him. They would hit at each other until Herb would get tired of it and put Tim in his room for hours on end."

Caro was shocked. She was astonished as much at Tim as she was by the beatings. There was no trap or cleverness in Tim's silence on this, but something much bigger. There was a measure of his hatred in this silence. For years he'd made thousands of ironic asides about his father the doctor, but never got down to why. Those wisecracks weren't the sum of his emotion as she had thought. They were only the steam hissing out of a pressure cooker.

"What happened when Tim got older and bigger?" asked Caro.

"It took longer for them to get where they'd fight, the bigger Tim got," she said. "They were both afraid of it, because he got to be almost as big as Herb by the time he was only fifteen."

Mrs. Seagurt paused. Caro could see she had gotten somewhere she didn't want to be and was going to begin circling again.

"Tim was getting very smart then," she said. "The smarter he got, the more Herb had to call him stupid. But he wasn't stupid, and he began to make a fool of Herb. Whenever Herb would make one of his sweeping pronouncements—Herb has a tendancy to make wrong generalizations—Tim would get on it. He would ask Herb one mocking question after another, and—"

Caro found herself laughing, and Mrs. Seagurt stopped for a moment, smiling herself.

"You know what I'm talking about, don't you?" she asked.

"You hardly know it's happening at first," said Caro, "but suddenly you're in a debate and you're sounding more and more like a fool."

"That's Tim," she said sadly. "One night, when Tim was nearly sixteen, Herb got so mad at him that he flung the serving dish across the table, getting the peas all over the rest of us. He got Tim by the hair and pulled him over backwards right there. He threw him to the floor before Tim could even get out of the chair. This one was different. We knew it right away. They had had a hundred fights, a thousand, but this, we knew, just from the way it started—"

She stopped, but only for an instant, wanting to go on to get it out, and her voice began to crack. "I feel so guilty about it. About all those years. I didn't realize it was going to affect him that way, that we wouldn't hear from him. I had gone from day to day wanting it to be over for years. I didn't stop to think."

She would have cried if it was a part of her to cry, but Caro could see it wasn't. She kept on going, suddenly closing her circle around what happened.

"Tim had been so obnoxious for months. He had been getting worse and worse the way he was baiting his father. I couldn't sort anything out except how much I wanted it to stop. Herb was Herb. He wasn't going to change. It was Tim that was changing. He was nothing like a child any more, but I still wanted him to be. I wanted him to stop transforming every supper into nuclear warfare. I was wrong. I was very wrong, don't you know. But I didn't see it then. All I saw was my husband's hands hurt from their fight, and Tim yelling like a criminal . . ."

She looked off with a detachment that reminded Caro of Tim. It was as if her mind had been called away on an urgent errand. When she looked back, she was sad, but the threat of emotion had completely passed. She looked at Caro as if she had told her all. There was more, but Caro couldn't bear to ask about it. Mrs. Seagurt wasn't going to give up her distance from it anymore than Tim was. She used the same detached posture to keep it away that Tim did. The only thing missing was the irony.

"Will you talk a little with Herb before you go?" she asked.

Caro moved uncomfortably in her chair.

"He's dying to know what I'm talking to you about back here," she said.

"Really, Mrs. Seagurt?"

She smiled. "No, I guess not. He'll be a little curious though. I really wish you would talk to him."

"I'd rather not," said Caro.

"Because of the things I told you," she sighed. "He wasn't a bad father to Martin. He's had his problems. Sometimes I think he didn't like Tim because—Well, Tim was—"

"Your favorite?"

"Yes," she said, surprised. "How did you know that?"

"Because Tim can't bear to talk about you," said Caro.

She looked away again, and Caro, regretting having hurt her, began to think about leaving as quickly as she could.

"Please talk to Herb," Mrs. Seagurt said urgently.

"I'd feel like I was betraying Tim," said Caro.

"Yes, I see that," she said, suddenly cold. "You would have to be very rude to him to satisfy Tim, wouldn't you?"

Caro felt like a fool. "I'm sorry," she apologized. "I'm being stupid. All right. I'll talk with him."

Her sharp, angular face collapsed into a brilliant smile. It was as if Caro had promised her her favorite son back. Any part of Tim talking to his father without hatred, even a part so far removed as his wife, his fighting and estranged wife, was enough to bring his mother incandescent relief. Caro wondered what part of that fight twenty years ago Mrs. Seagurt had withheld. What had she done which could promote such a happy smile on such tiny hope.

When she got back on 91, she drove in a daze. It had been disorienting talking with Tim's father. He looked too much like Tim. She had been stunned by it when he'd first answered the door on her arrival, and she was still unnerved by it, even after leaving. He had Tim's square face, and the same mouth, except she'd seen instantly that his mouth seldom smiled like Tim's. It was twisted down, and the wide brow he shared with Tim had his own dour downward curve to it. He wasn't a man who found much funny.

Despite Mrs. Seagurt's forceful hints, he didn't ask about Tim at all. He was more interested in flirting with her. He kept taking furtive looks at her bosom and talking to her with that doctor's authority which all doctors believe passes for charm. She kept trying to see the tyrant beneath his authoritative manner, but all she could see was this dour version of Tim, thirty-five years older and with all the humor drained out of his face.

He gave her a tour of his paintings when she said she was an artist. She would have said anything to get him off his flirting. He had Raphael Soyer, Hibel, and the like all over the walls, so she knew he'd be good for a lot of art talk.

He spoke the language, but the meaning of it, and the love of it, had escaped him. He bragged about his perspicacity. He had bought them all for bargain prices. She probed him, as Tim would have, asking him which one was his favorite. When he said the Soyer, which she knew had to be the most expensive, she asked him which was the most expensive. He stared at her cooly, instantly recognizing the gambit, saying with an ugly-looking silence: No wonder you married him. She'd felt a rush of hatred so strong it had made her tremble.

Robles was complaining, and it irritated Ernesto to have to listen to it. Joe DePre sat up front with Ernesto, his hands folded patiently in the lap of his corduroy jumpsuit. Ernesto was driving DePre's old Cadillac up and down First and Second Avenue while the three of them discussed their business. Unlike other prominent businessmen in New York, Joe DePre preferred old cars to new limousines. He changed them every two months or so. He liked them in ordinary colors and with over fifty thousand miles on them. No one paid any attention to people riding around in such cars.

Joe DePre had been writing soap operas when he saw the video-recording market begin to happen. He was a former hedge-fund manager who had quit money management to write. As a writer for "As The World Turns," Proctor and Gamble sought his opinion on a new project they were considering. They were thinking of marketing old tapes of "As The World Turns" in serial form. They would sell them the Monday and Friday tapes (nobody needed to watch the middle of the week; it was all wasted motion) edited together, releasing one tape a week. It would be very much like a magazine serial.

DePre was very enthusiatic about it. He saw it as a video Thackeray novel, and he predicted the soap-watching public would eat it up. He told Proctor and Gamble he wanted to distribute the tapes. They looked at him as if he were crazy. He didn't know anything about distribution; Proctor and Gamble knew everything about it. Marketing was their business. He wrote soap.

He quit writing. He saw the future of the entertainment, and it was video recordings. He turned out to be right.

The entertainment business began some serious changes after Joe DePre became a distributor for a tiny territory on the Lower West Side. Half the people in New York had a video-recording device of one kind or another. They used them to tape shows to watch whenever they wanted to and then swap back and forth among friends. The swapping process quickly disappeared when high quality, prerecorded tapes and discs began to appear in record stores. It was easier to buy a perfect recording than suffer through the low quality of home efforts filled with unnecessary commercials.

The market grew so fast that it cracked and fragmented. Record stores couldn't meet the demand for the product. Tapes and discs began appearing in drug stores and supermarkets. Bootlegging pirate tapes became widespread. The price structure collapsed. It was chaos.

Many people made money in this chaos. Joe DePre was one of them. But he saw his success eroded by pirate editions. Just as he had seen how fast the business could grow from the beginning, he saw how quickly bootlegging was undermining it, and he decided to fight it.

After he had expelled the bootleggers from his own territory, he moved up from the Lower West Side, buying one distributorship after another. He purchased all of them at good prices, because it appeared the bloom was off the rose. Each time he moved into a new section of Manhattan, he convinced retailers not to handle pirated tapes or discs, and he stopped persistant bootleggers from making trouble.

In three years he turned the chaos into an orderly market. Everyone in the business was eager to do deals with him. With DePre everyone got their fair share of the profit.

Ernesto had been with DePre for five years. He saw DePre, at only fifty years of age, as the most prominent leader in New York. His cases of cassettes and discs, distinguished by their handsome walnut cabinets, were in every kind of retail outlet in Manhattan. In one year, this French Canadian from Detroit made more money from video than all the men Ernesto had worked for in his entire life. Put their whole lifetime earnings together, DePre made more in a year.

He had become so successful that Edgar Robles had come to

DePre to ask to join. Robles had come for the same reason Ernesto had come before him. All the Italian powers were now too busy with other things to do real business. All the vitality in business was now in a new kind of company, a kind of company made up of men of all backgrounds who shared two things in common: They trusted each other, and they would not tolerate anything designed to prevent them from making money.

Joe DePre was a skillful leader of such men. He was adept at sensing when someone wanted to kill, and he knew how to kill first. That ability, coupled with his natural instinct to dominate whatever he entered, was what had made him so successful.

DePre's fortune grew so rapidly that he had to find large investments to contain his ever-expanding supply of capital. He settled on Atlantic City. There he built the most expensive hotel in the world, the Pier. Because DePre refused to go to Atlantic City himself, Ernesto was very closely involved with the Pier. Ernesto didn't understand why DePre wouldn't go, especially to see the hotel after it was built. DePre told Ernesto that he knew enough about Atlantic City without going. He had gone there several times with his parents as a kid. He told Ernesto he didn't want to run into any of the wrong people down there. He let Ernesto believe he was afraid of jeopardizing his investment by letting the Casino Control Commission see him in Atlantic City. But the real people DePre was afraid to run into were the French Canadians. They still came to Atlantic City in hordes, and there were signs out at all the hotels and motels welcoming them in French. One could even buy the Montreal newspapers at the newstands. DePre was pathologically afraid of running into anyone who knew he had spent the first ten years of his life on a milk farm.

Ernesto may not have seen why DePre refused to visit Atlantic City, but it was easy for him to see how it consumed DePre with interest. It was his hobby and his toy. He had a detailed model of the boardwalk in his apartment, and he would tap here and there with a pointer as he talked about who controlled which hotels.

Robles was railing on about killing Tim Seagurt, but DePre was against it. Harold Powell had sold him well on keeping things quiet in Atlantic City. DePre had agreed to refrain from the strategies which had made him so powerful in New York, in exchange for Powell's getting him the right to be the first to build a hotel on a pier.

"Joe, he sent a pong into our hotel with a knife," repeated Robles for the third time. "The pong cut our customer until he agreed to go to the Ondine and give them his money."

"You'll have to wait until Seagurt leaves town," said DePre. "You have to respect Atlantic City neutrality."

"Chinga!" said Robles. "Why is everyone so worried about this neutrality?"

"It would be fatal to tourism if shooting were to break out," said DePre. "Once it got started, too many bodies would fall. There are too many people in Atlantic City that like to fight every bit as much as we do."

"Let's do some killing and find out who in Atlantic City really likes to fight," argued Robles angrily. "We will find nothing but cowards, just like in New York."

Robles was the only person in DePre's organization who ever got angry in his presence. Ernesto hoped Robles would get mad enough to call DePre a Canuck to his face, the very same way he did behind his back. DePre was very sensitive about not being born an American citizen.

"No," said DePre cooly.

"Joe, this isn't the right way," said Robles. "This is New York all over again. You work for somebody? So, *maricon,* you work for somebody. So what, everybody says. They used to know when they walked around with their mouths open like that it would be pain. They knew it! It wasn't going to be a fire or the telephone, or anything they could live with. It was going to hurt. They thought twice about doing or saying a thing. Now all the somebodies get old and they want to join clubs and have their daughters marry bankers. They forget all about pain. Suddenly its no, no, no, nothing but fires and phone calls, and everybody knows it. Nobody is going to get up out of a barber chair and give it to you because they know you work for someone. No! They enjoy their shave. You're *nada.* No wonder they stop paying interest on their money. No wonder they deal their horse with anyone they choose. A lot of people still think it's that way, Joe."

DePre sighed. It was boring to listen to Robles making up reasons for the need to kill someone. He doubted that Robles had ever let anyone enjoy a shave while he waited. He doubted that Robles had ever let anyone he worked for stop him from passing out "pain" whenever he wanted to.

"We don't handle things like that," said DePre. "We move in different circles, Edgar. I am well understood where I want to be understood."

"They don't understand you in Atlantic City," said Robles. "They think you're content to let Seagurt send his pong into your hotel with a knife."

Ernesto understood that DePre tolerated Robles' talk because Robles was the current symbol and instrument of DePre's power. DePre knew he needed him for that. Robles, on the other hand, thought he was an irresistible power unto himself. He didn't understand, as Ernesto did, that anyone could do his work, including Ernesto. What was rare in business was a man like Joe DePre. The judgment and timing of the killing were far more important than the killing itself.

"What about the pong?" persisted Robles. "Nobody will care if we kill him. We will have our revenge and it will mean nothing to the newspapers. He will be a storekeeper killed in his Seven-Eleven by robbers. No one will even notice."

DePre consented.

Ernesto stopped at Thirty-fourth and let Robles out. He was silent all the way back to the apartment. Was DePre now letting Robles decide who and when to kill?

DePre could see the anger and jealousy on Ernesto's face. Ernesto hated to see Robles get his way in anything. It made him imagine that DePre favored Robles. In truth, DePre felt much closer to Ernesto. Robles was a constant threat to everything and everyone around him. Ernesto was affectionate and obedient. Violent and rapacious, but affectionate and obedient.

"THIS GUY Sheffing just lost six hundred thousand at baccarat to the Jewish kid, Gurstein," Hector said, coming into Tim's office from the cage. "We've got his check, but the only money in the cage is the morning money and the emergency bankroll."

"So?" asked Tim. He had a hangover and he didn't feel like trying to figure out what was on Hector's mind.

"It's Sunday," said Hector. "Gurstein wants cash. We don't have enough money until we count."

It was Sunday? He didn't know it was Sunday. He had lost track of the days of the week after his first month in Atlantic City. There was nothing in the mood or the rhythm of days to distinguish one from the other. His schedule was always the same, and there was no point in wondering which day of the week it was, especially since it was going to feel exactly like Saturday. The only thing that distinguished the real Saturday from all its imitators was the size of the drop. The real Saturday was always the biggest night of the week. The nights might look all the same to watch, but there was more money in the boxes Sunday morning than other days. The people who came into the joint knew when it was the real Saturday night, even if Tim didn't.

"Tim?"

"What?"

"What do you want to do about paying off Gurstein?" asked Hector softly.

"He can wait until after the count," said Tim.

"Maybe you ought to think about that," said Hector. "You know what a big shot this kid thinks he is."

"He's a real wise little prick, right?" asked Tim. "So fuck him."

"Yeah, but if he doesn't get his money right away, he'll get it in every newspaper across the country how the Ondine welched," said Hector. "You know how the newspapers love to print anything to do with Atlantic City. He's already making noise to Andy Map about calling the *Daily News.*"

"So?"

"Some of these hostile bastards who own hotels on the boardwalk would be pissed, Tim," said Hector. "It's kind of agreed in the business that you don't screw up a gambling town's reputation over a beef with a customer."

"So what do we do?" asked Tim.

"We've got to borrow some cash from the other hotels," said Hector. "I've already talked to Sinbad's, and I think they'll give us three hundred of it."

"Sinbad's is a hornets' nest of mafia people," said Tim. "I don't want to get involved with owing them money."

"Tim, the hotels are all hornets' nests, one kind or another," said Hector. "We've got to get it from someone."

The door opened and Teddy came in. He was early for the count, which wouldn't start for another half-hour. He had heard about Gurstein and he urged Tim to borrow the necessary money and pay him off.

"It's an old gambling hall tradition, Tim," he said. "We won't have any problems. We used to do it three or four times a month when Laboy was here. We were always having bankroll problems with that dude. Come Monday, we'd settle up and everybody'd be happy."

"Okay," said Tim. "Hector, you and Teddy go out and borrow it."

"They won't give it to us," said Hector. "It's a personal thing and the head guy has to sign for it."

"There's plenty of money in the boxes, Tim," said Teddy. "You don't have any risk. Last night was Saturday night, the biggest night of the week. We can pay the six hundred back right after the count."

To Hector's chagrin, it took Tim much longer to coax the six hundred thousand out of Sinbad's and the Pier than he had boasted. Both cashiers had to hear the whole story themselves and then wire World Casino Credit for Sheffing's credit rating.

When they returned with the money, Gurstein, the happy winner, packed it up and walked out with an obnoxious smile all over his face.

The count had already started when they finished with Gurstein and went back. The inspector was making a speech when they came in. Tim knew something was wrong immediately, because this inspector never said a word during the count. He usually unlocked the boxes and wrote down the numbers without comment.

"I can't say how serious the commission will say this is," he was lecturing Teddy. "Every single box we've opened has fill slips missing—"

"What's going on?" asked Tim.

"They really went crazy out there last night, Tim," said Henry. "The drop is way below what we make on a Tuesday, never mind Saturday, and a lot of the slips are missing. They deliberately screwed up, Tim. They weren't satisfied with just the money. They really wanted to screw us. I guess bribing Padgett last night was one night too late."

"Padgett?" asked Tim astonished. "There are slips missing?"

"We've lost over two hundred grand, Tim," said Perez, "and we're only half done."

"Teddy?" asked Tim in disbelief. "What happened out there last night? Christ, I wasn't even looking."

"I can't figure it out, Tim," said Teddy, unhappily. "Maybe they did go wild. They must have. But I didn't see it."

"Slips are missing, Teddy," said Tim. "Did you screw me?"

"No!"

Tim didn't believe it was Padgett, and with slips missing it had to be Teddy. But he couldn't believe it was Teddy either. Teddy was looking at Tim in utter despair. He seemed ready to hand Tim a gun and invite him to blow him apart with it.

"I give up, Tim," he said. "Fuck me. Let's close the place. I blew it."

Tim felt himself become convinced of Teddy's innocence. It occurred to him that he was also convinced of everybody else's innocence because he had run out of suspects. It also occurred to him Atlantic City was the catch basin for the most compelling liars in the world.

"Hector, go on out and tell them to start closing down the games," said Tim.

"We can't close now, Tim," said Hector.

"Why not?" demanded Tim angrily.

"You can't take three hundred thousand from Sinbad's and then close ten minutes later," said Hector. "They see that money as a personal debt signed for by you."

"And Gurstein has now disappeared with it," said Tim. "Hector, what the fuck is going on?"

"It will work out all right," said Hector, his lips wiggling up and down twice as fast as usual. "They know Sheffing's check is good. We only have to wait until we can get the money from his bank tomorrow morning. They'll understand we have to wait for the banks to open. We just have to keep the joint open until we can pay them back."

"It's my fault, Tim," said Teddy. "I'll go tell them at Sinbad's it was my fault. They know me, and—"

"No, no, don't do that," said Tim quickly. "Let's not spread the story that we might be in trouble. Let's just make sure that whoever goes to Chicago knows their way around credit and banks. Send your best runner, Henry. I want this thing cleared up tomorrow morning at nine."

"I'll go," said Henry. "I've been to that bank before. I'll have them wire the six hundred thousand directly to Guarantee as soon as they open."

He had forgiven Tim. This trouble had undermined his passionate disrespect for the dishonest.

"Good," said Tim gratefully. "Thanks, Henry."

They went out making up their quarrel. Henry said he was sorry, and Tim said he understood.

"It was my fault," said Teddy after they left. "He's really pissed at me, isn't he?"

"No, he isn't," said Hector. "Nobody is blaming you, Teddy."

Teddy stared unhappily at the door Tim had just closed. The inspector squirmed in his seat. He had something more to say that had been making him nervous.

"Gentlemen, I feel I must warn you," he began in his official tone. "You have spoken openly of bribes and organized crime. It is my duty to report these conversations to the Casino Control Commission."

Teddy and Hector looked at the bureaucrat in astonishment.

"The State of New Jersey will not tolerate organized crime infiltrating the casino business in the Atlantic City resort area," he said. "If you have dealings with, or know of anyone who can testify to dealings with—"

"Shut up, you fucking moron!" shouted Teddy.

The inspector winced from the noise of Teddy's shout.

"You can't talk about things like that in front of me," the inspector whined plaintively at Teddy. "Don't you know what kind of a position that puts me in?"

"Who gives a shit?" asked Teddy, still shouting. "You take that stupid fucking 'State of New Jersey ain't going to tolerate organized crime' and sell it to the newspaper! They're hungry for that shit. Around here, you shut your fucking mouth and fill in the numbers on your sheet."

The inspector picked up his pencil. He carefully averted his eyes from Teddy's glare.

"And if I tell you six is nine," added Teddy, "you write down nine."

The inspector's pencil wiggled between his thumb and forefinger like the tail of an anxious dog.

Teddy slammed the next box down on the counting table. *"BJ 41!"*

"BJ 41," said Perez.

"BJ 41," echoed the inspector quietly.

Edgar Robles was proud of his vitality, so he fucked her twice. It was easy to keep it hard because the pong's wife was a pretty one. She had beautiful brown skin and nipples as black as two lumps of coal. She was probably part Thai. She didn't act like she was being raped. She enjoyed it. He imagined she used to be a whore. When he finished, he yanked her up off the floor behind the counter and dialed the Ondine. He asked for Tommy Van in the casino.

He watched her while she told her husband. She talked in Vietnamese. It was a whining nasal language. After she hung up, Robles tied her up and stood off in one of the dark aisles to wait.

Thitch was tired from standing around in the casino and anxious to get to bed, but he noticed something was wrong the minute he turned onto Absecon Boulevard from Virginia Avenue. The lights in the store were out. Hanh would not turn out the lights or close the store at eleven. She liked to stand at the counter waiting for stray gamblers and watching television until past midnight. He drove past the store without stopping.

When he was a half-mile past, he stopped and got his night-scope out of the trunk. Through his precious scope he could see through night as if it were day. He easily spotted the gigantic man standing in the darkness of the soda aisle.

Thitch drove down to the gas station and called Tam. Tam already knew. Thitch was to continue watching the store through his nightscope.

As he watched, Thitch talked to the gigantic man. He told him he was a fool to set such a simple trap for Colonel Tam. He told him of Tam's cleverness. It was a cleverness beyond Americans. He told him in Vietnamese. Thitch had not learned English and had no desire to. He didn't even want to learn as much as Tam had. Tam, who had learned only what he had to, spoke English like it tasted bad. Thitch liked him very much for that. The others were all in a hurry to be Americans. They jabbered in English and wouldn't hold hands walking down the street. They gave them-selves names. Idiotic names. Buu called himself Willie Fudd, after the radar plane, because he said it was "cool." It made Buu angry that Thitch insisted on calling him by his real name. Tam wanted to be called by his Vietnamese name. "Tommy Van" was only for the Americans.

The giant came out from behind the sodas. He untied Hanh and picked up the phone. Thitch was struck by how large and hand-some he was.

"Your husband is a coward," Robles told the woman. "You will have to call him again."

The bitch pong looked at him with her blank Asian face.

"We will have to teach him how to be angry," said Robles. "Anger makes men strong."

He wondered if she could speak English. She hadn't said a word to him since he'd come in. He had used sign language to get her to turn out the lights and lock the door. How the hell did she sell milk?

"Anger gives men the courage to kill," said Robles. "Your hus-band will want to kill me."

Maybe she couldn't understand him because of his accent.

"Habla Español?" he joked.

She looked at him as if he weren't there.

He didn't give her the phone when he got the pong. First he told

Van he was going to make a noise that would sicken him. The noise would be his wife. He handed her the phone, and took a hold of her free arm.

"Tell him I'm going to break it," he said.

Her eyes flooded with fear. She did speak English after all. She spoke into the phone in rapid Vietnamese. Robles twisted her forearm in his massive hands as if it were a wash cloth needing wringing. It broke with a loud pop. She added her screams to the snapping sound. Splinters of bone punctured through the cocoa skin as he kept on twisting her slight arm. It nauseated him but it also pleased him. She stopped her screaming. She had fainted. He let her drop and picked up the phone.

"I'm not leaving until you come to talk to me," he told Tam.

"You want to kill me?"

"Are you angry?" mocked Robles. "Did she tell you I fucked her? She's a good fuck."

The pong didn't answer.

"She liked it," said Robles. "I had to do it twice. I'll bet she's a whore. Is your wife a whore?"

The pong had hung up. Now he had to be angry.

Robles waited half the night, but the pong didn't show up. He didn't even send any scouts. Finally Robles couldn't stand listening to the *puta* groan any more, so he went over to the Pier, got a room, and went to sleep.

The phone rang and he thought it was his wake up call, but it was Powell. It was still dark out. Powell apologized for waking him up, but he had to call the moment he found out Robles had returned to Atlantic City. He had left instructions at the Pier's desk to notify him.

"It's important I talk to you about Seagurt," said Powell. "I don't want someone to get the wrong idea about what he's done."

"What's he done?" asked Robles, delighted to hear Seagurt might be getting in even deeper trouble.

"He borrowed some money from your casino and Sinbad's," said Powell. "Now he has bankroll problems. I want it explained to someone. I don't want him hearing it from the wrong people."

"I'll be right over," said Robles.

The someone Powell was talking about was DePre. Robles couldn't wait to find out exactly how wrong Seagurt had gone. He would explain it to DePre so well that he wouldn't have to wait for Seagurt to leave Atlantic City after all.

The lights were on in Powell's office when Robles parked on a dark Pacific Avenue. He heard a scream from inside as he got out of his car. It was a shrill sound, higher than human shriek. It was like a cat in pain. He raced down the steps to Powell's office.

He had almost reached the bottom when he felt a blinding pain in his shin. He fell forward into the cement wall, stopping his fall with his huge hands. He landed on the bottom cement landing. He sat for a moment trying to recover himself from the pain in his shin. He realized he was sitting on a wet drain. When he tried to get up, his wounded leg wouldn't hold his weight. He had to pull his way up and into Powell's office by the door knob.

The lights were on but the office was empty. Robles fell down into a chair to examine his leg. His shin was cut in two. Something incredibly sharp had passed all the way through the bone. He hopped back to the door and turned on the stairway light. A broken wire gleamed around an achoring cement nail.

"Conyo!"

He hobbled out to look at it. It was piano wire, filed and sharpened like a knife. It had been anchored with eight inch cement nails so that it wouldn't break. He had broken it anyway, but at the cost of his shin bone. He would get the pong for that. He started jumping up the stairs on one foot. He wasn't far from the Atlantic City Medical Center.

A small form appeared at the top of the stairs.

"Mr. Robles," it said.

It was the pong.

"Here is Tam now," he said.

Robles stared up at the pong and thought about the pain in his leg. He focused in on it until it occupied his entire mind. His anger rushed into him in an instant, obliterating his pain. He climbed the stairs on two feet. The pong retreated a few steps as he approached the top. Robles needed only to get a hold of him. One hand on him would be enough. Once he got his hand on the little pong it would be as simple as killing a ten-year-old boy.

When he reached the top of the stairs, Robles almost crowed with delight at what he saw. The Vietnamese wasn't even armed. He had only a short sword with some kind of long ceremonial handle. Robles had thought it was a forty-five automatic when the pong was standing at the top of the stairs. Was this one so stupid he wrote Edgar Robles off after only one wound to the leg?

Then Robles saw what he was doing. Three more pongs stood on the sidewalk watching. Van was showing off. He wondered what the other three would do when he killed Van. He reached out for Tommy. Once he got hold of him with one hand, just one hand, he could fling him up against the wall like a stray cat, and then they could watch and see if their hero landed on his feet.

Tommy cut Robles' hand off.

Robles drew his arm back and watched in astonishment as his hand fell to the sidewalk. There was no pain to the wound. He held up his stump and looked at it, as if to make sure the hand was gone. Blood spurted out of the end of his wrist in rhythmic gushes.

It drove Robles mad. He lunged at Tommy. He meant to get him in his grasp no matter what now. He reached out with the wounded arm and grabbed again at Tommy. He still didn't understand the hand was gone.

Tommy stepped inside the long arm and took Robles' head off with a short violent stroke of the blade.

The gigantic trunk of flesh kept coming forward, and, as Tommy turned to dodge away, slammed up against his shoulder and crushed him down to the sidewalk. He found himself pinned beneath the suffocating dying weight. He struggled to wriggle out, but it was too heavy. Blood, as warm and disgusting as urine, poured all over him. It was only an instant before they rolled Robles off him and pulled him back up, but it was long enough to make him angry at last.

He jumped to his feet and looked for Robles head. He found it lying on its ear on the sidewalk not five feet away. It wasn't dead yet. Its eyes turned in its sockets and watched Tommy as he approached. The mouth was moving. Robles was talking. He was trying to say something but there was no voice-box to make the noise.

"Didi mau!" shrieked Tam.

He kicked it into the street towards the truck. The handsome head skidded across the pavement, bouncing and turning like a die before it stopped at Buu's feet.

Buu picked it up and threw it into the back of the truck. It took all four of them to lift the rest of the enormous body.

·27·

TIM WAS getting worried. Ten-thirty in Atlantic City was nine-thirty in Chicago. The banks had been open there a half-hour. Henry should have called and told him the funds had been transferred to the Ondine's account in the Guarantee Bank. Tim called the bank in Chicago. Henry had not arrived. The bank had no account in the name of Scheffing.

"You know what he did," said Hector.

"Check his room," said Tim.

Hector returned five minutes later. "He's gone, Tim. There's nothing left in his room."

In the five minutes of Hector's absence, Tim had tried to convince himself it was possible for Henry to cheat him out of six hundred thousand dollars, but he couldn't believe it. He and Henry were too close. They had worked too hard towards the same thing for one of them to smile in the name of friendship and disappear with a bogus check.

"I don't get it, Hector," he said, numbly.

"Yes, you do," said Hector.

"Maybe I'll get it tomorrow," he said. "It's not sinking in now."

"He had it ready, Tim," said Hector. "He had it ready all along."

Tim nodded his head in amazement.

Henry had programmed World Casino Credit with a credit rating for a nonexistent Scheffing. He had then stood by and watched while Tim okayed the check and his two accomplices took the money from the Ondine. The man playing as Scheffing lost to Gurstein on purpose so Gurstein could demand cash immediately. They had chosen baccarat because it was the only game in the casino which pitted players against each other instead of the house. In such a game, they were able to make sure who was the winner and who was the loser. It had been carefully calculated down to the last detail. The last detail had been Henry's volunteering to take Scheffing's check to Chicago.

"Anybody that talks that way about honesty all the time," said Hector, "anyone that is always on top of it like that, you know they're fighting something inside themselves. He had it ready from the moment he came here. He had that Sheffing stuff in the World Casino Credit Computer for months. You know he did. He was just waiting for the chance to use it."

"I'm beginning to get the message," flushed Tim angrily. "This business has been trying to tell me something from the start, and I'm beginning to get it."

"You know he did it," repeated Hector thoughtfully. "For Christ sake, he grew up in Las Vegas."

"You can't trust anyone in this business," said Tim, "Not *anyone!*"

"That's right," said Hector, nodding up and down. "That's right."

As quickly as it came, the anger evaporated. "What kind of business is this?" he asked Hector. "What kind of business is this, Hector?"

"This is the gambling business," nodded Hector.

"Look where he's put me," said Tim quietly. "I still owe Sinbad's that money."

"He figures you can go to the bank for the money now," said Hector. "Today's Monday."

"Go to the bank," repeated Tim ironically.

"Can't you?" asked Hector.

"You and Henry don't know Oakes," said Tim. "We have to get that money back."

Failing at every other way of finding Henry, Tim called Gurstein at the Gurstein family brokerage firm on Broad Street. A secretary put him on hold.

"Gurstein," came a voice after five minutes of waiting.

"I'm surprised you even talk to me," said Tim. "What you pulled on this casino was fraud. We can put you in jail for that."

"I haven't done anything," replied Gurstein in a happy voice.

"You pulled a cheat on us," said Tim. "A transparent cheat."

"You might have something on some guy named Scheffing, if you ever find him, because he did stick you with a rather large check," admitted Gurstein, "but all I did was make a bet at your baccarat table. Wasn't I lucky to win?"

Gurstein was quite proud of himself.

"How long ago did Henry recruit you for this?" asked Tim.

"Why should I tell you?" asked Gurstein, toying with Tim.

"Don't tell me," said Tim. "Just let me know where I can reach Henry."

"You think he'll talk to you?"

"I've got to have that money back," said Tim.

"It won't do you any good to talk to Henry," said Gurstein. "Besides, he didn't recruit me. I recruited him. We were poker-playing buddies at UCLA. I had the idea, not Henry. He didn't want any part of it at first. It took me three years to convince him."

"Really?" asked Tim with mock interest.

"He had just put it in the computer, and we were getting ready to work it in Vegas when you gave him a job," said Gurstein. "You really gave him religion for awhile, I have to admit that. Henry's pretty smart about most things, smart enough for me to get him into Mensa, but he's always been a little dense about wanting to believe in truth and honesty. I imagine you've straightened him out for good on that score, however."

"Gurstein, you're worth millions of dollars," said Tim. "Why are you wasting time ripping us off?"

"Now you're upset that you're getting ripped off for a little," laughed Gurstein. "You didn't think it might happen to you while you were so busy screwing everybody else."

"I don't know what you're talking about," said Tim impatiently.

"We all come to Atlantic City to have a good time," said Gurstein. "You people know that. We sit down to play cards and have some fun and what happens? You ding us. You take all our money and leave us with nothing. Well, now it's my turn. How do you like it?"

Tim listened helplessly. He had heard this complaint from a thousand different players. When they lost, it was as if Tim had sprung the law of averages on them from some nefarious hiding place, pointed it at them like a gun, and ordered them to empty their pockets. They gambled because they believed they were exempt from those averages; and when it didn't work out that way, it was the casino's fault. Once they came to that conclusion, they'd try anything to get their money back. Here was Gurstein, worth millions, now telling Tim that the Ondine had taken all his money and left him with nothing. There was no point in telling Gurstein the Ondine was not at fault for what he had lost. Casino's were mirrors. Gurstein had looked into this one, seen his own image, and found something predatory and greedy indeed.

"We need that money back, Gurstein," said Tim. "You were very clever, but now we need the money back."

"We're not giving you a penny of it back," said Gurstein.

"I'll put this around the boardwalk," said Tim, "and around the world. You won't gamble in any casino ever again."

Gurstein laughed. "I play for cash. I'll be welcome anywhere I want to go."

"You're putting yourself in an ugly position," said Tim, his patience exhausted.

"Fuck you, Mr. Seagurt," said Gurstein. "You can forget about Henry's number, too, because he doesn't want to talk to you. Face it. You've been had. What's a few hundred thousand to the Ondine anyway?"

"A few hundred thousand?" asked Tim. "I love the way all you clever sons of bitches are so sure a casino makes so much money. Do you know how much the Ondine lost Saturday night?"

"Lost?" said Gurstein disdainfully. "I've seen how big those boxes under the table are. I know how much money they can hold. I can tell *you* how much money you make."

"The boxes?" asked Tim in amazement. "You think you can judge how much money a casino makes by the size of the boxes?"

"You're damn right I can," boasted Gurstein. "It's a simple matter of finding the volume of the box—"

"You idiot!" shouted Tim. "Those boxes are never full! Never! Not even on the busiest night of the year!"

"Right," said Gurstein sarcastically. "And I have to give the money back to save the Ondine from going out of business. After all, you're a business like every other business, blah, blah, blah. Sorry, Seagurt. It's your turn to be the sucker, and I'm not—"

Tim hung up on him.

"What'd he say?" asked Hector.

"He said he could tell how much money a casino makes from the size of the boxes," said Tim.

Hector bit his wiggling lip.

"I've got to think, Hector," said Tim.

"Sorry, boss," said Hector. He turned and hurried out to the cage.

All the things Tim had meant to say to Henry wouldn't go out of his head. He wanted to tell Henry it wasn't worth it. He wanted to tell him to come back with the money, and they would resume their friendship on an equal basis. Caro's ruby to Henry's swindle. He wanted to tell Henry he was actually more likeable for having finally cracked. "And please, Henry," he said to the empty office, "don't leave me standing between Alfred Oakes and Sinbad's."

But Henry, he realized, was gone. Henry would take his share of the six hundred thousand and disappear. He would be gone long enough for the story of his swindle to turn into a myth. By the time he surfaced again, after the money was gone, he would be able to get a job as a cashier in a joint in Paramaribo or even Nice. He would tell his new employers of his scheme and how it worked, and they would tell him he was clever as hell.

Tim thought about Gurstein. He could see him making calculations to find the volume of the boxes.

It occured to Tim that he hadn't seen to the heart of the gambling business at all. He had only seen one side of this one-eyed jack. It wasn't simply that everyone was dishonest. The other side was that you couldn't trust anyone. Not anyone. It was a very lonely feeling. It was so lonely that it wasn't worth it. No matter how much money they made, even if they made as much as everyone was trying so hard to imagine they did, it still wasn't worth it. The laugh was that the money wasn't nearly that much anyway. Only the desire to believe was great. The money itself could never measure up to the size of the dreams.

He felt himself getting angry again. His eye was blinking.

Something strange was happening to him. His emotions were coming and going in weird, uncontrollable swarms. He went over to his window and opened it. Forty yards away was the ramp from New Jersey Avenue to the boardwalk and its perpetual parade of fantastic and demented tourists.

"You idiots!" he shouted at a group going up the ramp.

He felt like Henry venting one of his little speeches about honesty.

"It's never as much as you think it is!" he shouted.

There was something out of control about himself and he knew it. He had caught some sort of emotional syphilis from Henry. One couple stopped on the ramp and looked curiously around. The rest rushed mindlessly by.

"The money!" he called to them. "It's never as much as you think it is!"

The quizzical couple kept looking about trying to see where the mad shouts were coming from, but the origin of the voice was as mysterious as its meaning.

The count was over and the result was as dismal as Sunday's. Tim's hope of being rescued by a big count disappeared beneath a torrent of red fill slips. Curiously, none of the slips were missing this time. In fact, they seemed to outnumber the bills two to one.

"Phone for you, Tim," called Hector from his office.

"Must be the Pier," said Tim. "Sinbad's has already had their ugly word with me."

But it wasn't the Pier. It was Alfred Oakes. This would be his second conversation of the day with Oakes. Oakes had called earlier because someone had told him about Saturday night's loss. He had told Tim he didn't understand why the casino hadn't been closed after the loss. Tim had tried to explain, and then promised to call Oakes back after the count.

"Are you finished counting, yet?" asked Oakes.

"We lost close to three hundred thousand for Sunday night," reported Tim. "Not quite as bad as Saturday."

"That's two serious losses in a row, Tim," said Oakes. "We must close it now."

"I'm trying to close it as soon as possible, Alfred," said Tim.

"Trying?"

"I have to get six hundred thousand down here from Chemical Bank in New York first," said Tim.

"I've ordered the Chemical Bank to hold that money," said

Oakes. "I'm not paying six hundred thousand dollars out to any-one until I understand this situation better."

"Alfred, the casinos I borrowed the money from consider it a personal loan," said Tim.

"To be honest," said Oakes, all traces of understanding gone from his voice, "I haven't quite made up my mind that you're innocent in this, Tim. Dean insists that you are innocent, but I have some questions about six hundred thousand dollars disap-pearing in the hands of someone who was working so closely with you."

"Alfred, the people I borrowed the money from made some very ugly threats against me this morning," said Tim.

"They're being melodramatic," said Oakes.

"No, they're not," said Tim. "They're dangerous."

"You should have thought of that before you borrowed from them," said Oakes. "To be honest, Tim, I wonder if you haven't turned into another Oscar Laboy."

"Whatever I've turned into, it makes no sense to leave me in this kind of jeopardy over money," said Tim. "Money is numbers on a balance sheet. It's just ink, Alfred."

"I don't dismiss six hundred thousand dollars quite so easily," said Oakes.

"I don't care if it's ten million," said Tim angrily. "You can't put me in this kind of position."

"I'll be down there tomorrow," said Oakes curtly. "Meanwhile you and Dean see to closing that casino immediately."

Oakes hung up.

"The hell I will," said Tim, his eye starting to blink.

"He stopped the six hundred?" guessed Hector.

"Yes," said Tim. "And he wants me to close down until he gets here tomorrow."

"You can't do that," said Hector.

"I'm not going to," said Tim.

"Good," said Hector, "But these losses are eating the bankroll down to nothing. We've got to get some more money to stay open."

There was a knock on the door and Dean Haaf came in. Two men in baggy navy-blue suits came in behind him.

"I'm sorry I have to preside over this," Haaf said to Tim. "It wasn't my idea."

"Preside over what?" asked Tim.

"These are federal marshalls," said Haaf. "Oakes got mad when you didn't close after the first loss. He's had the Coloney lawyers get an injunction against you."

"An injunction?" asked Tim stupidly.

"To seize the bankroll," said Haaf. "He told me he would call you first."

"He didn't say anything about this," said Tim.

Tim sat down helplessly at his desk while Hector took the marshalls into the counting room where Andy was sorting the day's bankroll.

"This is the last straw for Oakes," said Haaf. "Colony is going to sell the Ondine to some Dutch firm."

"Thanks for standing up for me with him," said Tim gratefully.

"Tim, you know you're in trouble in this town," he said solicitously.

"Yes, I know," said Tim.

"I wish there were something I could do," he said. "I hate to see this happening to you. I'll do anything I can to help."

Haaf knew he was lying like a junky, but he couldn't stop himself. He felt incredibly guilty about having put Tim in this position, but he had to continue raping the boxes to keep the pressure on Oakes and to prevent Tim from seeing what was happening. Unfortunately the people at Sinbad's, believing Tim had been taking money out of the Ondine with regularity, were infuriated not to be paid back their bankroll money immediately. As far as they were concerned, Tim was now stealing from them. Haaf wished his lawyers could get the deal signed with Oakes so he could rescue Tim. To that end he had called Oakes and told him about the first loss when Tim had failed to. But the meetings went on and on while Oakes bargained. The man had an inexhaustible appetite for negotiating.

"You can do something for me," said Tim. "Does the hotel have much cash on hand?"

"Not six hundred thousand," said Haaf.

"I only need enough to keep the casino open," said Tim.

"You'd keep it open?" asked Haaf in surprise. "How would you do that?"

"The marshalls are only taking the bankroll," said Tim. "I'm still licensed to operate the casino, and I have to keep it open anyway I can."

"I see," said Haaf.

"Does the hotel have any cash?" asked Tim.

"No."

After Haaf left, while the marshalls were still loading the money into the armored truck in the courtyard, Tim called Konnie. Then he called Caro. At least this thing solved one problem

for him. No matter how much danger he was in, he had no desire
whatever to call Margarite and ask her for money again. In fact,
the more dangerous the situation got, the more he thought about
Caro.

"Be there," he said into the mouthpiece as the bell started to
ring at the other end.

·28·

TIM FELT strange fitting the key to his apartment in the front door.
He hadn't been home in four months.

He found the apartment quiet.

"Caro?" he called.

No answer.

There were sketch sheets and canvases everywhere. They were
piled up on the coffee table and stacked against the walls five and
ten deep. He walked about looking at the piles. There were many
efforts, but they were all of the same six or seven scenes. There
were fourteen different versions of a body builder with lucite
muscles and red jewel dust in his veins for blood. Another large
set of canvases stacked up against the television were views of the
Atlantic City beach. He could see a progression in them, and
found the last effort laying up against an arm of the easy chair.

He remembered going to the beach with Caro a couple of times
during the early September heat wave. It had been full of old
ladies complaining in shrill voices about the temperature and the
flies. They all stayed in the old hotels which had no air conditioning, and the heat had driven them outside against their wills.
They sat in fabric chairs and put their feet out to the very edge
of the water's reach. The sun glittered in the wet sand like a lost
dime. They worried about a sudden advance of the tide. They
didn't want too much cold water rushing up their legs and giving
their hearts a shock. Timidly, they reached out with their feet
towards the last small frothing tongues of the Atlantic, hoping to
absorb some of the famous chill through their toes. But it was
hopeless. Defeated by their fear of death, they wiggled in frustration as the soapy wavelets, baked tepid on the long approach of
the hot sand, lapped at their discolored feet like puppies.

He found another group of works on the Atlantic City night. In
them the nighttime beach reflected a diffused glow of color from

the neon signs of the boardwalk. It was all beautiful work, and it filled him with euphoria. She had taken the intense, assaulting colors of Atlantic City and made them beautiful. It was intense and vibrant, and somehow beautiful.

He found some heads of himself over by the window. They looked like very recent work. They were better than anything she had ever done of him before. The anxiety which had been preying on him for the entire drive up disappeared. He knew he had to explain this right or lose her, and that was a very anxious thought, but seeing his portraits dispelled it. She had missed him as much as he had missed her.

It irritated him that she wasn't there. How could she be scatter-brained at a time like this?

"Caro?"

Maybe she was back in the bedroom and hadn't heard him come in. She had let the damn phone ring forever when he'd called in the morning.

The bedroom looked like an exploding galaxy of paint. There were acrylic and oil colors spiraling all over the bed and around the room. They dotted the walls and even the ceiling. They were densest right in the middle of the bed where the sheets and blankets were thick with pied blots of color. He could see twenty shades of blue alone: ultramarine, Prussian, cobalt, French, azulene; coral, cerise, and Tyrian reds; yellow spun about in buff, tawny, xanthin. The blots grew more and more dispersed ranging outward from the bed. They were ground into the rug, spotted on the dresser, and dotted across the wallpaper.

He heard the front door open. "Tim! Tim!" called Caro.

She came rushing into the bedroom, ran to him, and gave him a very wet kiss.

"I've missed you," she whispered.

"I've missed you too."

"I'm sorry I'm late," she said, breathless. "I saw this exhibit at the Museum of Modern Art before I got to the travel agent, and then I had to hurry, and when Manny said you were here already—"

Out of breath, she stopped. He laughed at her. She looked uncommonly pretty with the panels of her smooth cheeks turned coral by the brisk December air.

"I'm glad you're home," she said.

"These new paintings," he said, "they're wonderful, Caro. They're the best things you've ever done."

"I know," she said happily. "It amazes me. I've been going and going and I can't stop. It's been getting a little messy in here because I sort of jump around the mattress while I work, and—"

"A little messy?" interrupted Tim, impressed with her understatement. "It looks like some kind of pavonine star went supernova in our bed."

Caro laughed. "Speaking of going supernova in bed—you know what's happened? All this work has made me horny as hell. All the painting and jumping around in bed all day without you has been driving me crazy."

She kissed him again, her tongue enthusiastic and sexy. She began unbuttoning his shirt.

He took her hand gently away from his shirt. "Caro, I don't have time."

"We have plenty of time," said Caro. "Our plane doesn't leave until nine tonight. We were lucky. They have a direct flight to Quito from Miami on Monday nights, so—"

"What is Quito?" asked Tim. "What are you talking about?"

"It's the capital of Ecuador," said Caro enthusiastically. "It's this incredibly beautiful city. I saw pictures of it at the travel agent's. It lies way up in the lap of the Andes, over nine thousand feet high, and all round it are these mountain peaks. It's nine thousand feet high, but it's still in a valley! You can even see Cotapaxi from Quito—"

"It sounds great, Caro, but, I have—" interrupted Tim.

"It *is* great," interrupted Caro right back. "The travel agent said that absolutely no Americans go there, so you won't have to worry about anyone finding you there. He told me about this incredible train we can take up and down over the Andes. It's filled with cattle and Indians with felt hats, and it only goes twenty miles an hour but it climbs peaks fifteen and sixteen thousand feet high. Can you imagine a ride like that?"

"Caro, I have to go back to Atlantic City," said Tim.

"I don't understand," said Caro, her enthusiasm smothered by her surprise.

"I have to get back to Atlantic City with the money so that the casino stays open," said Tim. "Hector and Teddy can keep it open only so long."

"You said you were in all kinds of trouble and you'd have to get out of the country for awhile," she said dully. "I thought you meant—"

"I am in trouble," said Tim. "But I have to go back to Atlantic City first."

"But you said it would be best to get out of the country for awhile," she said.

"Afterwards," he said.

"Then what did you come here for?" she asked suspiciously. "Why didn't you just tell me to bring the money to you?"

"I was afraid you wouldn't bring it," said Tim.

Caro was silent while it all sunk in.

"I'm sorry," said Tim. "I didn't explain it all to you on the phone because I wanted to explain it to you face to face."

"Oh, shit," said Caro in disappointment.

"See," he said lightly. "You wouldn't have brought it."

"You're damn right I wouldn't have brought it," she said.

"Where is it?" he asked. "I have to get right back there."

"I can't believe this," she said. "You sent me down to Konnie to get our seventy thousand turned into cash so you could put it in the casino? You want to keep the casino open with our money?"

"Okay, I'm sorry," he said. "But, yes. That's what I have to do."

She sighed. "Tim, you don't have to go back. We can disappear with this money and nobody will ever find us. It will be fun."

"It won't be fun," said Tim. "What would I do in Ecuador for the next ten years?"

"You can go into some kind of business down there," she said. "You'll get rich on your yankee know-how. That's what I thought the money was for. You said you wanted to go into some small business and be with me."

"I do," said Tim. "That's exactly what I want."

"Then let's go," said Caro. "Tim, you have to get out of Atlantic City."

"I know that," said Tim.

"No, you don't," argued Caro. "You don't know at all. Do you know what was wrong with me in Atlantic City?"

"No," he said impatiently. "What?"

"I kept thinking I had to paint the greatest painting in the history of colors," said Caro. "But I couldn't even get close because I couldn't give any one idea more than half an hour. You see, you have to learn a painting like a song. You have to stick with it, like you always said, and play it over and over again. It always comes out different but somehow the same, and then one time you get the music that's in it, and you have it. You can stroke it out like you're in a trance. It's so elusive. It looks so beautiful when it comes out right that you can't know all the shit that went on before I got there, especially since the whole idea is to bring something up that looks effortless and beautiful—"

"Yes, they're beautiful, Caro," interrupted Tim, 'but I have—"

"Gamblers, they swallow this little deception whole," Caro continued, "They love that effortless quality. They love it in everything. But because you hear a song and like it, that doesn't mean you can play it. Gamblers think they can. They think they can appropriate the singer's emotion for themselves; and as long as they feel the emotion, they imagine they're singing real swell. But it all comes out like shrieking."

"Caro . . .

"I'm still not sure this is fun," persisted Caro. "I still feel like something's got a hook in my neck, but now I like what comes out, and I end up so horny, God am I horny for you, and I don't give a shit about what a talent I am. All I worry about is what's happening on the canvas in front of me. The whole thing in Atlantic City is that they're all looking at themselves to see if they can get it for nothing. They don't have the energy left over to work at it. That's why they believe in magic. They have to. Once I got away from there, I could see it. You have to get away from there too, Tim."

She tightened her arms around his neck and rubbed her breasts hard up against his chest. "Come on. Let's fuck all afternoon and then fly to Quito."

"I know I have to get out," said Tim quietly, "but, I—"

"No, you don't," repeated Caro. "You can't know until you're out to stay and you know you're out. That's why we have to leave tonight. If you go back, Tim, you'll never make it out. Believe me, please. I know the difference. I've been in and out. You can't see it when you're still in it. You think you do, but you don't. You just keep plugging away while things get worse and worse."

"They'll kill me if the casino closes," said Tim. "I have to go back to survive."

"No," said Caro. "You don't have to go back to survive. You have to go back because you're a gambler."

"I'm on the other side of the table," said Tim sharply.

"So what," said Caro. "There's no fucking difference."

Tim was silent.

"You tell me the difference," she challenged.

"You don't want to hear it," he said.

"What are your plans?" she asked him. "Tell me, what are your plans?"

For the first time since they'd been together, Tim had the eerie sensation that Caro was ahead of *him* this time, that she was waiting ahead with her own answers to everything he said.

"Hector has put up fifty thousand, and Teddy twenty," said Tim. "Another seventy and we can make it to closing time. I'll be safe, and my share of the casino's profits for the night should be enough to buy some kind of business."

"Profits?" asked Caro.

"We're putting up the money, not Alfred Oakes or Colony," said Tim. "We're entitled to the win."

"Will there be a win?"

"We're only keeping a few pits open," said Tim. "We've got it small enough so we can control the games ourselves."

"So we're going to finance our future with money you win in the casino," said Caro.

"Yes."

"And you're not gambling?"

"The odds are in favor of the house," said Tim. "You're not gambling when you have the advantage."

"But you haven't made it pay for two straight nights." Caro said urgently. "Come on, Tim. What would your heroes do? They wouldn't do what you're doing."

"My heroes?" asked Tim, puzzled.

"All those legends you're quoting all the time," said Caro. "Bernard Baruch and Warren Buffet and all the rest. What was it that was so hot about Buffet? He got out of the stock market at the top because he said there were 'no more fat pitches.' "

"So?"

"This gambling thing didn't turn out to be the fat pitch you thought it was," said Caro. "It's time to get out. Warren Buffet would have left long ago."

"You've got to stick in and stay and make it pay," said Tim sarcastically.

"Don't give me that," said Caro, getting angry again. "Don't quote Alfred Oakes to me like he's another one of your heroes, because I know he isn't."

"How do you know he isn't?" asked Tim.

"Because you don't have any heroes," said Caro, springing her trap. It was her turn and she intended to make it sting. "You never did have any heroes. All you've got is a lot of fake humility. You don't really admire anybody."

"Why don't I have any heroes?" he asked, responding almost involuntarily.

"Because you think you're better than all of them," she snapped. "You study them and quote them, but the only reason you do is to convince yourself you're smarter. And you still want to prove it, don't you? You're going to 'stick in and stay' and revolutionize the gambling business because you can do what no other man can do, can't you?"

Tim was quiet.

"Bernard Baruch couldn't revolutionize the gambling business, could he?"

Tim looked at her, hatred beginning to flare in his light eyes as the left lid fluttered.

"How about Warren Buffet?" she persisted. "He wouldn't have a chance, right?"

"All right, godammit!" exploded Tim. "Yes! I am better! I am better than all of them! I don't have any fucking heroes and I never did. I never read anybody I couldn't take two steps farther. I never met anyone I wasn't smarter than. So fucking what? That's the way it is! Yes, I pretend I'm just as dumb as they are, and I don't tell everyone how fucking smart I am because I don't want to be mistaken for the rest of these idiots, but I know I am smarter. All right? I'm a fucking genius. Are you happy? Is that what you want to hear? I'm the smartest cocksucker who ever looked at a fucking dollar."

"You can say that?" demanded Caro. "You can still believe that? Look at where you are."

He stared at her, still furious, his eye blinking madly. Now he knew where she was going.

"You're up here getting money just to stay alive," she said, "and you still haven't figured it out."

He turned away in frustration.

"Don't you see what you're doing?" she asked. "You want it all. You have to be smarter than all of them and you'll risk everything to prove it. Even your own life. It's a gambler's syndrome and you're caught in it just like I was."

"Okay," said Tim defiantly. "So I'm caught in it. Give me the money, and I'll do my best to get out."

"I won't give you the money to do this," said Caro. "I won't."

Tim was silent.

"We can make it in Quito," she said. "You can have a business down there. I understand. You love businesses and all the formulas that make them work. But it's not the money that matters, or who you're smarter than, or even where you do it. It's the work itself that counts. The doing is the pleasure. Not the narcissism of saying how great you are because you can beat everyone else at it. That's the unfillable well. If you'd get out of Atlantic City, you could see that."

Tim walked away from her out into the living room. She had stuck him somewhere. He didn't want to believe it, but he knew she had because it hurt. She followed him right out.

"You know I'm right," she said.

"All the little insights you just trotted out, they're probably true," he granted. "Not probably. They are. But I still can't let it go."

"Why not?" asked Caro.

"Because I still feel like I can make it work," said Tim.

"What?"

"The system," he said. "There's just one thing missing. I know it. I know I'm close, Caro."

"I don't believe you," she said.

"I'm going to make it work," he said.

"Let me understand this," she said bitterly, her anger welling up in her again. "You want the money because you have a mystical awareness in the back of your head. You just need a break. It's almost a magical power you have to sense things."

"Get off of this damn gambler stuff," snapped Tim. He couldn't listen to it anymore.

"All right," she said. "I'll get off the whole case. Why should I care what you do? You didn't care about me."

Tim felt a wave of panic wash through him. "That's not true."

"Oh, bull," she said. "You came up here because you wanted the money, that's all. The rest of it was all saleswork."

"Don't say that, Caro," said Tim urgently. "I have to have something to come back to or it doesn't mean anything. I want to be with you, I need you. Can't you see that?"

"I thought we were on our own," she said. "You couldn't possibly need me. You don't need anybody and neither do I. Let's take ourselves at each other's word."

Tim sighed. "I was wrong when I said that," he said. "You were right. I was wrong."

"This is too fucking much," she said. "So now I'm right because it suits you. You've led me down the path again. I don't believe it."

She disappeared into the bedroom. An instant later she came out with the striped green tennis tote she always took to go swimming.

"You have mousetrapped me for the last time, you son of a bitch," she said. She flung the tote across the room at him. "Take the fucking money. I won't have your getting killed by a bunch of goons on my conscience. You take the money and get out of here!"

He unzipped the tote to make sure the money was in it. It was filled to the top. All small bills ready for the expedition to Quito. The bundles still had the bank wrappers on them. He zipped it back up.

"I'll call you," he said.

"I won't fucking answer!"

Hector, in a long speech about Atlantic City as neutral ground, had argued against Tim's leaving the island; but Tim had responded that there wasn't much choice. Tim had forgotten all about his conversation with Hector when he pulled out of the garage in the BMW. He was preoccupied by his fight with Caro. He was convinced they were finished together. He thought he should probably blame himself, but he didn't. He blamed her, and as he reviewed the reasons why again and again he didn't notice a tan Camaro follow him down Lexington Avenue.

He had just passed Eighty-fifth when the Camaro pulled up alongside him. He looked over and saw the black hole of a machine gun pistol. Instinctively he slammed on the powerful brakes of the BMW. The shriek of his tires was interrupted by a deafening string of explosions. He saw a line of tracer bullets speed across the purple BMW hood like phosphorous flies.

The Camaro stopped a few yards in front of him.

The gunman hung out the window and turned the gun back towards Tim. Tim ducked and hit the accelerator. The gun didn't go off again until he made Eighty-fourth and turned left. The BMW bucked as if he had driven into a large pot hole. The car lurched right and left and back again. He realized the right rear tire was flat.

He raced wildly up and down the cross-streets of Yorktown on three tires, twisting the wheel frantically to keep the BMW balanced. They shot at him again and again but the erratic path of the BMW made it a difficult target. He didn't look back. He kept the gas down. All his attention was commanded by making the three-wheeled car go fast. When he had heard no shots for what seemed like minutes, he granted himself the luxury of looking in the rear view mirror. They weren't there.

He spun into a garage beneath an apartment building and stopped between two aisles of cars. He jumped out to change the tire. He already had the BMW on the jack when a lady in an ultrasuede skirt got off the elevator and told him he was blocking her car.

"I'll be gone in a second," Tim assured her.

She hissed with disgust.

When he had the flat off and was juggling the spare on, he heard the elevator door open again. It was the woman getting back on. She was probably going for her doorman. Perhaps even the police. The shooting must have already attracted plenty of them.

He spun three nuts on the tire without tightening them and pulled out of the building heading for the Holland Tunnel. The

Camaro would certainly be waiting for him at the Outerbridge Crossing or the Garden State Parkway.

He reached the turnpike without seeing the Camaro. He hurried south with one thought in mind. He had to get to Atlantic City where they wouldn't dare harm him.

He settled down as he drove down the turnpike. His panic retreated. He became convinced they had chosen the Outerbridge Crossing and would wait for him along the parkway. It was the obvious route to Atlantic City.

His calm was disturbed when a spider appeared on his windshield. It had a small black body and several white crooked legs. Then he heard the noise. It was a gun shot. A bullet had thumped into the seat beside him. They were shooting at him again. More spiders spread across his windshield. He didn't even know where they were coming from. He pressed the gas pedal to the floor and kept it there, peering out between the holes, trying to see who was shooting at him. He saw nothing but other cars driving innocently down the turnpike.

He got the BMW up to a hundred and eighty miles an hour; so the speedometer said, but the digits went no higher than one-eighty. His fright grew more and more intense, but he held on without letting up on the throttle. He had to dart carefully in and out of all the cars backing up to him. He kept looking frantically for the Camaro. He drove looking in the rear mirrors as much as ahead between the holes in the windshield. The wind came whistling in through the holes making his eyes tear, and he knew he was going to hit someone, but he couldn't stop.

He reached Exit 7 in less than twenty minutes. He got off the turnpike to take 295. He had driven right by the police building at Exit 9 and he was certain they were after him by now. The toll-taker, however, said nothing, and barely even looked at the holes in the windshield. He stuck to the speed limit on 295. His mind kept flashing to how he'd felt when Wayne Brady had pulled the knife on him. This was a lot different. This time he didn't feel stoned or disembodied at all. This time he was really frightened. He was breathing frantically, and even though he couldn't seem to get enough air, he felt like the air he was breathing was suffocating him. Every brownish car he saw made his body spasm with fear. He couldn't stand doing only the speed limit, but he was too afraid to speed anymore. He was frightened the police would stop him and then ask him what he was doing with bullet holes in his car and seventy thousand dollars in cash. He didn't like the idea of ending up in a New Jersey jail while on the mafia's shit list.

The fear hadn't lessened when he reached the Atlantic City Expressway. It wasn't going to go away until he was safe at the Ondine. At Hammonton, a tan Camaro crept on to the expressway behind him. He took the BMW right up to a hundred and eighty again. The Camaro disappeared behind him. A Camaro might be great from a standing start, but high speed and turns were the BMW's meat.

Just before he reached Exit 17, the BMW started to shimmy and buck like a wild horse. The wheel was coming loose. The bolts were coming off the spare. He cursed himself for not stopping to tighten them earlier. He got off on Route 50 and then turned down into the pine barrens. He drove down a highway between a long avenue of pines looking for a place to stop, but he soon found himself running parallel to the expressway, easily visible to the Camaro if it should come speeding along the faster expressway. He took a turn on one of the unmarked paved roads. He had to get somewhere where they couldn't find him so he could have time to fix the wheel.

He almost shouted when he finally stopped and got out to look at the wheel. There was only one bolt left on it. The wheel could have come off any time and sent him tumbling down the expressway at one-eighty.

He had to take bolts from the two front wheels to get the tire securely on. He decided to stay in the pine barrens and drive in the general direction of Atlantic City. Even if they had seen him get off at Exit 17, they couldn't find him in the pine barrens. All he had to do was keep his progress easterly, and he could get to Atlantic City without getting shot at again.

But the easterly choices thinned out and soon he was driving aimlessly about on sandy roads taking random turns as he tried to find a route with a number on it. He was running low on gas. He hadn't stopped to think how much fuel an engine could use going a hundred and eighty miles an hour. The sun was getting low. He had promised Hector and Teddy he'd get the money to the Ondine before six. It was already seven-thirty at least.

His feeling of panicky paranoia worsened. He hadn't seen a gas station or even a house since he had turned into the pines. He had no idea where he was. He kept trying to head away from the setting sun, since the coast had to be to the east, but every road he turned onto seemed to wind him back towards the west.

His mind felt paralyzed. All those months in Atlantic City suspecting that everyone was out to cheat and rob him had made him super-sensitive to menace. Now he was so afraid he couldn't think.

He took yet another hopeless turn trying to get away from the setting sun. The road came to a dusty dead-end, and he had to back up and drive into the sun again.

The sun was down and it was starting to get dark when he saw something like a black beetle flying way off above the pines. It was leaving a pink vapor trail across the rose colored horizon. He watched it as he crept along the bumpy trail. The BMW's bottom bumped against the rise between the ruts of the tiny road. This beetle was coming right at him. He stopped the car and got out to look at it. It was an enormous black insect-like monster, not really a beetle, too unreal to be a beetle. It had swollen, puffy wings which looked like waxy black plastic. It was coming right in on top of him. He was certain it was a part of his paranoid madness. It had come out of the roseate sky discharging a pink fluid behind it. In the logic of his madness, the pink fluid was digested blood. The thing made a noise like the whirring of thousands of low flying swans.

He began to run.

It closed on him even faster.

It was immense. It was nearly three hundred yards from end to end. He waited to hear himself start screaming. He knew the thing wasn't real, but he also knew that it didn't matter. What mattered was that it was driving him mad and he would have to smash his head up against the trunk of a tree to make it go away.

It passed right over him and he saw eight sets of huge wheels come folding out of its rubbery belly. It was an airplane. He ran after it to the top of a nearby ridge.

It whirred straight ahead driven by pairs of huge turbine engines which were squirting air out the back of its massive wings. It was going in for a landing.

He watched it touch down on a very long landing strip.

This enormous black beetle was nothing more than an aeronautical experiment. He had stumbled on NAFEC, the National Aviation Facilities Experimental Center. He was ten minutes from Atlantic City.

29

POLLY MARCINEK read the story of Edgar Robles' killing in the newspaper. The headless Robles had been found on a bed in one of the suites at the Pier, his corpse covering the king-size bed, the blunt end of his arm hanging all the way to the floor. His head and hand had been found in a bureau drawer. The killers were trying to double the horror with a clever little trick. It struck him as Vietnamese. An hour after he read the story, Joe DePre called him. He was right. It was Vietnamese.

Polly was delighted to get the call from DePre, even though it meant working with DePre's chief ignoramus, Ernesto Polo. Polly had waited a year to hear from DePre. His wife Penny was DePre's first cousin, but for all her bragging about how close her mother was to DePre back on some milk farm in Canada, Polly had seen DePre only twice. The first time was at his wedding. DePre had come in a jumpsuit. He found out later that DePre wore jumpsuits everywhere because he found them comfortable. It raised a certain question, but Polly didn't ask it. The second time he saw DePre was at his apartment in New York a year ago.

He had explained to DePre that he didn't make much money as an assistant professor of media at Stockton State College. In three years of marriage, he and Penny had acquired two sons. Penny wanted them to go to prep school when they grew up and so did Polly, but there was no way he would make enough money teaching media for his two kids to go to prep school.

DePre said he understood.

Ernesto Polo asked Polly what DePre was supposed to do about it.

Polly said he wasn't looking for charity. Polly had spent six years in Nam. He was an intelligence and propaganda officer specializing in oil spots. Oil spots were pacified villages. Some killing was necessary to keep Charlie at bay.

DePre was very interested. Polly told him war stories and he seemed to lap them up. He looked Polly over again and again as if memorizing him. Polly was easy to remember. He stood six-two and weighed two-thirty. He was bald and older now, but he still had the agility which had made him an all-conference tackle at Purdue. His stories demonstrated again and again his proficiency at exercising authority. He mentioned he had risen to captain in the army. He had some brains to go along with his Polish muscle.

"Of course," DePre had agreed. "You're a professor."

Polly returned to his home in Absecon. When he heard nothing, he assumed Ernesto Polo had blackballed him. He gave up on DePre and started roofing houses in his spare time. At least one kid was going to go to prep school. And until DePre had called him that afternoon and told him to meet Polo at Harold Powell's house, he had thought it would be only one.

Now he sat in Powell's basement office with Polo and eight other men. Powell was trying to explain the situation to Polo. Polly, who had understood what Tram was up to in the first three minutes of Powell's long explanation, was looking over the men from New York. They had been introduced to him as DePre's élite. Polly marvelled at them. He couldn't believe DePre had kept him waiting for a year in favor of stones like these.

"From what you tell us, Harold," said Polly, interrupting the discursive and pointless dialogue between Powell and Polo, "we have to take care of Tam Van Tram first. There is no way we can take Seagurt out of town without going through the Vietnamese, and I imagine you don't want a pitched battle right in the middle of the Ondine casino."

"We had him out of town, *capo*," said Polo, deriding Polly's army rank.

"And someone blew the chance," snapped Polly. "Twice."

Silence fell across the office. Polly was only supposed to be an adviser, but he felt himself slipping into the role of command. He knew Ernesto was vulnerable. Ernesto had failed to catch a car with only three good wheels on it. Polly would take as much authority from Polo as he could over that mistake.

"So we understand we have to take care of Tram first," reasserted Polly.

Ernesto didn't argue.

"This time we have to make him fight on our terms instead of his," said Polly. "We don't want to get into the same kind of mess Edgar Robles got into."

"This gook is clever," volunteered Vince, a cab driver in Brooklyn when he wasn't busy for DePre. "That was a fine Sicilian trap he sprung."

Powell shifted nervously behind his desk. He had explained to DePre on the phone that Tommy had lured Robles to his office with a threat against Powell's life. Powell hadn't explained that he had actually invited Robles over for a phony conference. Powell was glad the ex-army captain was turning the conversation into a lecture about Vietnamese culture. The less talk about Robles, the better.

"You make a good point, Vince," said Polly. The cab driver had touched on his favorite theory. "These Vietnamese have a lot in common with the Sicilians who came to this country at the turn of the century and made up the Mafia."

"These pongs have something in common with Mafia?" asked Ernesto scornfully.

"Their country has been a battleground for centuries," explained Polly patiently. "They have been forced to live under hostile authority time and time again, so they've developed codes of their own that function beneath and against established authority. They have their own code of silence. They can't be terrorized and they can't be infiltrated."

"We'll see about the 'terrorized,' " said Ernesto.

"They aren't afraid of death," Polly warned Ernesto. "They know sudden death, giving and taking both. They've known it for hundreds of years. When it comes to surviving, these people are every bit as cunning as the Sicilians and probably a lot more vicious."

Polly looked about the office for appreciative faces. As Assistant Professor of Media at Stockton State, he had given this same lecture to thousands of college students. It didn't have anything to do with media, but he liked to talk to his classes about the Vietnamese, and his students loved to listen. How things had changed from when he'd first come back from Nam. Everyone had made him feel uncomfortable when he'd tried to talk about it then. Now they all loved to hear about the Vietnamese, and he had gotten used to seeing faces glow with pleasure at his insight whenever he mentioned his little thesis about them and the Mafia. But here in Powell's office his audience stared at him like so many wooden spoons.

"Do you have any ideas on how to get this guy?" asked Ernesto impatiently.

"If we're going to avoid all the publicity that Harold is so afraid of," said Polly, "we'll have to get him alone somewhere. Maybe set up a meeting between him and Harold."

"Good," said Ernesto. "That's Joe's idea, too. Harold, you'll have to be a decoy."

"Me?" asked Powell in surprise. "I never get involved in this kind of thing."

"Joe wants you to," said Ernesto.

Powell felt the symptoms of his dysphoria begin to stir. He wondered if DePre was suspicious that he was more involved with Robles' death than he had admitted. He wondered if DePre knew how glad he was that Robles was dead. Perhaps DePre had smelled it in his voice when they talked on the phone. Maybe DePre was hoping something would happen to him, just as it had to Robles.

"No thanks," said Powell.

"What do you mean, no thanks?" demanded Ernesto.

"I don't even want him killed," said Powell. "This is all your idea, I'm only talking to you about it so that I can explain it to anyone who might get upset about it. People are going to get upset, Ernesto. It's a clear violation of Atlantic City neutrality."

"Oh, fuck that," said Ernesto.

"Harold, it will be easy," said Polly, trying to calm things down. "You get Tam on the phone and tell him you want to talk. Tell him you're frightened by what he did to Robles. Make sure he understands that you're old and pose no threat."

"I'm supposed to say I'm old?" asked Powell. "What good will that do?"

"The Vietnamese revere age," said Polly. "You've got to lay it on him about how old and wise you are and how you want to help him. Tell him you are afraid of his men and want to meet alone. And then tell him you want his help, too."

"What if he wants to come here?" asked Powell.

"That's too much to hope for," laughed Polly. "He'll want to meet outside somewhere. He'll insist on being away from buildings or anything else that somebody could snipe at him from. We have to figure out a place that will look good to him."

"I'm not walking into anything like that," said Powell.

"Don't worry," said Ernesto. "We'll scout the place and make sure it's all right."

"But why would Van even agree to meet me?" asked Powell. "He knows he might get killed."

"He'll meet you," declared Polly.

"Why are you so sure?"

"Don't you see what this one is after?" asked Polly impatiently.

"No," said Powell. "What is he after?"

"He wants to run this town," said Polly. "He knows you're the key."

Powell fell silent with shock. Of course. Just like all the rest.

"You talk to him right," said Polly. "Don't be too obvious. Just talk to him, and he'll be there."

"I don't like it," said Powell.

"It has nothing to do with your liking it," said Ernesto. "You're the don of Atlantic City, aren't you?"

"Of course many people think that," said Powell. "It suits all our purposes for people to believe that."

"You strut up and down the boardwalk and invite magazine reporters into your office for pictures," complained Ernesto. "Everyone pretends here is Harold Powell, the powerful and lovable old criminal. They all hint that here is the man who rules Atlantic

City, and you love it. You love playing the part of the big gangster while others do the dirty work. Now you have to pay for all that bullshit, Powell,"

"All right, I'll make the phone call," said Powell. "But I'm not going to get close to Tommy Van again."

"What's the matter, Mr. Gangster?" mocked Ernesto.

"You read what he did to Robles," said Powell. "I'm not letting myself in for that."

"Any asshole can mutilate corpses, Powell," said Ernesto, disgusted with Powell's squeamishness and cowardice. "That's just part of the game."

"I think I'll call Joe," insisted Powell.

"Joe has gone into hiding as he always does in situations like these," said Ernesto in a voice which closed debate. "He has given me all his authority."

After he gave the money to Hector to put in the cage, Tim got a phone call from Margarite. She had broken a resolution calling him, she said. She had been waiting for him to call. He said he'd been busy and told her he'd left the BMW out in the pine barrens.

She wasn't upset. Her voice was warm. She seemed refreshed by the news of his problems. As he recited them to her, he began to sense that she had been looking forward to his failure.

She said she had been dreaming about him. Her dreams woke her up in the middle of the night. She hadn't had bad dreams since she'd fallen from her horse as a child. Now she often dreamed of Tim as horselike, which was terrifying to her.

After Tim hung up, Teddy Long came in to show him the newspaper article about Robles. Without any help from Teddy, he knew it was Tommy and he knew why he had been shot at that afternoon. He told Teddy to send Tommy back to the office right away.

He vented his anger on Tommy. He had almost been killed because of it, and he shouted at Tommy for several minutes before he even asked how it happened. When he finally asked, and Tommy tonelessly explained what Robles had done to his wife, Tim felt stupid. He apologized several times, which Tommy uncomfortably acknowledged.

"Hanh good in hospital now," he said, obviously wanting Tim to drop it.

"Good."

"Tim okay?" he asked.

"Okay,"

"Good," he parroted.

"Why did you take Robles' body to the Pier?" asked Tim.

"To tell them to leave us alone," said Tommy.

"It probably will make them mad, Tommy," said Tim.

"No, no," said Tommy quickly. "Banana cat called me today. He's afraid of you."

"Me?" asked Tim. "What for?"

"I told him last night when I make him make call to giant," said Tommy proudly. "He think giant dead from your order."

"No, Tommy," said Tom angrily. "You shouldn't have done that, goddammit!"

Tommy was very surprised and upset that Tim was angry again. "What I wrong?"

"The next time I drive out of Atlantic City, they'll kill me," said Tim.

He wondered if he would ever be able to convince Powell he hadn't given Tommy any instructions. Perhaps if he got rid of Tommy now and called Powell to explain. After all, he'd paid Padgett. No, that would be like calling the axman to announce that his neck was ready.

"What are you thinking?" asked Tommy.

"I don't know what to do with you, Tommy," said Tim.

"You want Tommy fired?" Dismay tinged his mongoloid features.

"No," said Tim, still angry. "Not yet. Let's say you work for the casino. I want you to stay and help me until I can leave, but I don't want you to get me killed as soon as I get out on the parkway. So you're not my bodyguard, and you're not killing people on my orders. Do you understand?"

Tommy made no sign of acknowledgment. He could see Tim for what he was. It puzzled him that Tim couldn't and was talking about leaving. Tommy had seen it the first few nights in the casino after the banana cat came with the giant. It was so powerful and easy to see. After watching Tim come striding out into the casino night after night to fire dealers, Tommy had abandoned his idea of trying to arrange something with the banana cat and thought only of Tim.

"Why is Tim angry?" asked Tommy in frustration.

"I'm angry because I'm afraid they're going to kill me," snapped Tim.

"No," declared Tommy. "Tim is not afraid."

Tommy had never contradicted Tim before. Everything Tim

asked, Tommy was quick to execute. Everything Tim said,
Tommy accepted as natural law. This contradiction, though issued in his friendly, street-cowboy voice made a loud new noise
between them.

"The banana cat called me," said Tommy, taking a new tack.
"Banana cat wants to talk about Atlantic City."

Tim disagreed. "He doesn't want to talk about anything. Don't
meet with him outside Atlantic City. He wants to kill you."

"Meeting to be in Atlantic City," said Tommy. "He tried to kill
me. But can't. So now he wants me to take giant's place, banana
cat will ask me to kill you, I think. Everybody in Atlantic City is
afraid of you and Tommy now."

"Maybe it doesn't make any difference that the meeting is in
town," said Tim, worried about Tommy. "They already tried to
kill you in town once. Shit, maybe we're all in danger here."

"I tell banana cat three take charge of Atlantic City," said
Tommy, his English beginning to break up as it always did when
he got enthusiastic about something. *"Anh* Tim. *Cerno* Tram.
Powoe."

"What?" asked Tim, amazed.

"It is easy," laughed Tommy. "We have Powoe's fear. We have
Atlantic City."

Suddenly the eye was blinking and Tim was angry again. "No,"
he told Tommy. "They're not getting me into this. As soon as this
money thing is over—"

"Yes! Yes!" interrupted Tommy. "Tim—" he stopped, unable to
find what he wanted to say, and the effort of reaching for it made
him look distressingly retarded. *"Da tam!"* he burst out. "Tim *cao
tay . . ."*

He went on in passionate Vietnamese. Then, in frustration, he
called Willie Fudd into the office to translate. The words he had
been trying to find for Tim were: "Clever, savagely ambitious,
angry, boastful, violent, and greedy."

"Tim is already like Powoe and Tommy," concluded Willie for
Tommy. "To pretend other is now to get killed."

"LISTEN TO this, Abe," said Powell. He was an avid reader and
loved to recite things aloud to Abe. Abe enjoyed listening to him.
Powell had a nose for the interesting.

"Pastfall," read Powell. "Experiencing time as moving backwards."

"What?"

"Pastfalls are caused by the sudden evaporation of the future," continued Powell. "A pastfall comes on subtly. One often has the illusion that time is moving forward right up to the precipice of the pastfall. The sensation of falling is at hand when the sufferer begins to perceive the future as predictable because nothing new is going to happen ahead. Therefore, the *past* must lie ahead. In the moment that he sees the future and the past join, the sufferer begins his pastfall. A pastfall can last an instant (do not confuse with *deja vu,* no matter how brief) or years. Pastfalls are very unpleasant because one has the sensation of falling into events which are immutable. Hope perishes as the glorified past and the rosy future become saturated with the unpleasant odor of the present, which is another name we give to reality."

Powell looked up at Abe, waiting for his reaction.

"Who is that man?" asked Abe, confusion twisting his scarred face as he reached for the book.

"R.L. Krim," said Powell, handing it to him. "He's a science fiction writer."

Abe studied the page.

"Mr. Powell, this is drivel," marvelled Abe. "It goes around in circles."

"Yes," agreed Powell. "I think that's what he's trying to tell me."

Abe wanted Powell to get some sleep before he went to meet Tommy Van at four. The doctor had prescribed rest. At Abe's insistence, Powell had finally gone to the doctor. That was over a month ago. The doctor had said Powell was suffering from dysphoria. Its symptoms were headaches, a throbbing stomach, and nausea. Tonight Powell's dysphoria was acute, and he wasn't going to get any sleep because King Cerkez had insisted on coming to visit.

King, though nearly Powell's age, still had a baby face. He wore expensive Western leisure suits whose pockets smiled with gold braid. He had a cuddly look to him and a charm that went along with it. They all had charm, reflected Powell. There wasn't one of them, whether from crime or the corporate world or of the self-made industrialist ilk, who didn't have this same vigorous egotistical charm. They were all going to do for Atlantic City (as Cerkez put it) what Guy MacAfee had done for Las Vegas. Cerkez boasted he had known him when MacAfee was operating in Los Angeles. When they could talk about Guy MacAfee in Los Angeles, they were old. After they had closed everyone down in L.A., MacAfee had built the original Golden Nugget across from the post office in Vegas. Cerkez had once owned the Sal Sagev, which had been two blocks down Fremont from the Nugget.

"MacAfee had a partner in the Nugget who invented the big neon sign," said Cerkez.

Cerkez had insisted on coming over to visit, despite Powell's plans to nap, because he had made up his mind what he was going to do and he wanted to run his thoughts by Powell. Powell had spent months with Cerkez, trying to guide him, but he had the sudden feeling it had all been wasted. His dysphoria was getting worse.

"It was Laddy Odo who invented it," continued Cerkez. "He got this idea that the sign meant more than the joint; and, of course, he was right. Everybody copied the big sign he put up over the Nugget. All you have to do is walk down your boardwalk to see that they're still copying him. But I've got an idea that will put Laddy's to shame—"

"How about a hotel with no sign," interrupted Powell, trying to postpone the inevitable. In his old age, falling into the past with dysphoria, he was becoming a talker instead of a listener.

"How do you have a hotel with no sign?" asked Cerkez stupidly.

"An architect came to me with a great idea yesterday," said Powell. "It's just right for you and for Atlantic City. You make the hotel with all kinds of angles and edges, then the shadows from the sun makes designs across the face. You'd get a bright bleached section of stone and right next to it a section where the shade pools up like black water. Think how beautiful that could be. I'll introduce you to this guy. He'll sell you on it."

"No sign is going the wrong direction, Harold," explained Cerkez patiently, as if Powell were dense and didn't have the slightest clue about hotels, signs, and gamblers. "I'm going to put up a hotel that runs neon tubes right through the glass of the hotel. The hotel is all glass, and we run the neon right up the whole eighty stories. The whole hotel is the sign."

"King, that's the same old monster sign idea carried to a ridiculous extreme," said Powell.

"In the gambling business, nothing is extreme," replied Cerkez. "My hotel will be the only thing they see when they start across that swamp to town."

"We have enough glass," said Powell. "If you have to use glass, can't you do something beautiful like the Pier or the Terrarium?"

"The Terrarium," said Cerkez disdainfully. "You want me to imitate that dumb stunt? How are you going to make any money in a hotel where it takes five minutes just to get through the door. You got to have traffic in this business, Powell. No wonder that place is going busted."

Powell wondered how Cerkez knew the Terrarium was doing poorly. It was supposed to be a secret. He wondered if Cerkez knew how many millions Powell himself had funneled into the Terrarium to keep it looking prosperous.

"King," said Powell, taking a new direction, "you were a pioneer in Las Vegas. How about being a pioneer here. Let's start building up the Inlet. I've got everybody behind me on this now that the anti-gambling talk has come up again, and I'd like to see you start this thing."

"What thing?" asked Cerkez. "What about the Inlet?"

"We'll make it elegant again," said Powell. "Let's build something really impressive, something really fine up past the Ondine. The elegance will work its way all the way up the beach and all the way back to Gardner's Basin. We don't need any more tacky hotels. We need hotels we can be proud of."

"What kind of hotels are you talking about?" asked Cerkez, without any genuine interest.

"Hotels like the Traymore when it was new. Or the Dennis," said Powell. "They weren't beautiful because they were loaded with flashing lights. All this Vegas stuff scares people out of town after a couple of days. We need a section of this city where people can come and stay and be comfortable for as long as they like."

"Yeah," agreed Cerkez unenthusiastically. "But that Inlet is such a mess. Besides, Harold, for most people gambling is like jerking off. They can't keep doing it indefinitely. They need some time away from it to recover before it feels good to do it again. That's why gambling towns are always going to be three-day towns."

"King, have you ever heard of the Needlecraft shop?" asked Powell.

"No?"

"Garfields?"

"No."

"Garfields was a handkerchief store," explained Powell. "It sold nothing but handkerchiefs. Everything from pure white cotton to Spanish lace. Wouldn't you like to see the boardwalk full of shops like that?"

"What do I care?" asked Cerkez. "Besides, nobody buys handkerchiefs anymore."

"They would if there were a Garfields on the boardwalk again," said Powell. "Some people used to buy a year's supply of handkerchiefs from them. They'd come to the shore for the summer, and they'd shop for the entire winter. Not just handkerchiefs, but everything. It was a whole different kind of atmosphere—"

"That's a lot of sentimental shit, Powell," interrupted Cerkez. "Let me tell you something about handkerchiefs: Kleenex is better because you can throw the snot away when you're finished with it. The same thing goes for hotels. The Vegas-type of operation is far superior to those old dinosaurs. You put up a joint with a lot of rooms to keep the casino busy, and when it gets old, you knock it over and build another one."

"But why do that when you can have something beautiful and lasting," said Powell. "It's a waste of money."

"The casino pays for it."

"But we can have something better—" Powell began again.

"I don't want anything better. If you and DePre and the rest of them want me to build a hotel like the Traymore up in the Inlet, I'm out of it. You assholes aren't going to use any of my money for urban renewal in the nigger section. If you guys want to buy the boogies out, use your own dough."

Powell could feel all three partners in his dysphoria hard at work. He had a headache, his stomach hurt, and he felt nauseous. He gave up. There was no point in talking to Cerkez anymore.

Abe came back in after Cerkez left. "You're going to be all right up at Hackney's."

"Why do you say that?" asked Powell.

"It's overcast," said Abe. "The first clouds from that storm have come in. You can't see a star."

Powell went upstairs to his bedroom to lie down, but he couldn't sleep. He called to Abe. Abe came up and they talked. Actually, Powell did all the talking because Abe was Powell's listener. Even Harold Powell, the man who understood everyone, had to have a listener.

Powell was taken with R.L. Krim and the pastfall. The best time in Atlantic City, Powell explained to Abe, had *not* been the grand days of the twenties and thirties when the island was in its heyday. The best time had been the fifties and sixties. It was in its decline that Atlantic City was nicest. It was an intimate small town then. Everyone had moaned and complained about the sickening of the island, but they dreamed and planned to revive it together. They all shared an affection for each other because they cherished something they remembered as genuinely grand.

Then the gambling issue came up. They all thought, especially

Powell, that they had found a way to recapture the glory. They sold themselves on it because they were so hungry for it. It was a fantasy they had nourished together for years. Suddenly they could see the 500 Club and the Bath and Turf Club coming back in beautiful new forms. They could see new Traymores and new Claridges. Atlantic City would be grand again.

But it hadn't turned out grand. And now it was becoming obvious it never would. What there was left of that grand vision, The Terrarium and the Ondine, was going to die. And nobody was going to create the old Atlantic City in the Inlet. Nobody was going to build a refuge from the Las Vegas infection on top of the ruin. He had lied to Cerkez. Neither DePre nor anyone else had the slightest interest in the Inlet. They weren't going to try to buy Padgett again. They were all ready to give him the same thing Tommy Van was about to get. He imagined Padgett's killing would come swiftly on the heels of this one; as swiftly as this one was coming after Robles'.

"So we let DePre spear the little yellow canker, and the puss squirts all over Atlantic City?" Powell asked Abe. "So what? There's nothing worth saving anymore."

Powell could be disgusting when he wanted to be, thought Abe.

"It's been coming on for years, and we're all about to fall over the precipice," added Powell "It's one of these damn past falls."

"How is that, Mr. Powell?"

Powell explained it to Abe. The passage of gambling had ruined not only Atlantic City's future (which Padgett had seen), but also its past, which no one had seen. No one ever would see that except Powell. The new Atlantic City had forced before his old man's eyes the visions of what the old Atlantic City had really been. What he had celebrated in his mind as so grand and beautiful was nothing more than the distortions of his youthful ambition and enthusiasm. For sixty years he had savored these select visions without calling to mind the realities beneath them. But now the realities of the past had cooked to the surface, heated up to the top by the exploding corruptions of the present, where they gave off the disgusting smell of truth. Cheap and blatant dice games on the boardwalk had been every bit as noisome when he was twenty-one as they were now. The only difference was that they'd used barkers then instead of neon. One walk down the boardwalk would find them shouting out in front of twenty stores or more, calling the crowd inside to card and dice games in the backrooms.

There was little exclusivity or style to these joints. Many of them didn't even bother with a door to the backroom. Any jerkwater John Bates with three-days' beard could walk in and take his chances. And his chances were none too good, since more than half of these parlors were flat shops which would separate John from his money in short order. Did legal odds make any difference now? Not really. As far as John Bates was concerned, the result was still the same. Nucky had always known it was a phony distinction. Nucky wanted the same from straight joints as from flat shops when he sent Powell around on his bagging errands.

"The truth, Abe," said Powell, "is that Atlantic City has always been a noisy tourist town with no interest as big as figuring out new ways to sell a nickel cigar for a dollar."

"I see what you mean, Mr. Powell," said Abe softly.

"So where is the difference between then and now?" Powell asked Abe.

"Nowhere, I guess, Mr. Powell," said Abe.

"And how is it ever going to be any different?"

"It isn't."

"Doesn't that make you feel like you're falling?"

Abe didn't know what to say.

"You ready, Harold?" shouted Ernesto up the stairs.

The combination of his dysphoria and the past fall had given Powell the urge to talk. As Polly's station wagon cruised slowly with its lights off up Atlantic Avenue, he couldn't stop himself from rambling on about the old boardwalk.

Polly said he had heard the stories of backroom games from his parents. He even had a couple of stories to tell about Nucky. Powell was amazed to find out Polly was from Absecon. He took a liking to him. Polly confessed he'd never done this kind of work before. Powell found himself wanting to explain something very personal.

He wanted the young army captain to understand that the whole idea of organized crime was ridiculous. There was nothing organized about it at all. These people might be ruthless and bloodthirsty, but they were far from clever and efficient. They were mostly clucks who couldn't control themselves or the people that worked for them. They were criminals because they couldn't be anything else. They didn't have the ability to be anything else. All they had was a brutalizing pride. The crux of "organized crime" was sneaking out onto a deserted Inlet boardwalk because some vicious bastard had to blow apart an ambitious immigrant. Wasn't that what the criminal rivalries always came down to?

Who was the most vicious? It wasn't the smartness that was at issue; it was the viciousness. That's where their pride was.

Polly looked across the front seat at him as he drove. Powell could tell he might as well chant to him in pig Latin, but he couldn't give it up. He went on to talking about Nucky and Torrio and Gatsby and all the others.

"They were so glamorous when I was twenty-three," he said. "These were the people that controlled every big city in the country. These were people that had no use for the rules because they had money enough and courage enough to have their own way. But that was only my own dream I saw in them. That was what I wanted for myself. They weren't really powerful at all. They were too afraid of each other to exercise any real power. Each one thought the next more vicious and powerful than he, and wanted to kill him because of it. They were the same paranoid vicious bastards that are teeming all over Atlantic City now. I thought Nucky had all the power in the world because he handled Joey Adonis, but Nucky kissed Anastasia's ass as eagerly as a dog wags his tail."

The marine was still glancing at him funny, unable to understand.

"Old age rolls back a lot of lies," Powell explained. "Nucky was one of my biggest to myself. Nucky's pretty clothes, his good looks and his charm were all armor against the dirt of being a crook. I was a smart kid. I knew how to reason things out. I should have seen it. Nucky was a thief and a prick who would use anybody and do anything to get what he wanted. I guess I did see it. I saw it all along. The only trouble is, when you want something badly enough, like the way I wanted to be like Nucky, you'll eat shit and say it's chocolate cake."

Polly laughed raucously at the joke, but Powell knew he hadn't made a convert. He gave up. Old age and Atlantic City's second coming had turned his sea island and his hero into something ugly, something as ugly as himself, and he didn't care anymore. All he knew was he had a throbbing headache, an agonizing stomach, and he had to stop talking because he felt like he was going to throw up at any moment.

A few seconds later they stopped on Maine Avenue. Ernesto came over and quietly opened his door. Powell got out, surprised at how dark it was in the Inlet.

Polly felt as if Powell had adopted him. The old criminal had been barking at him incessantly from the moment he'd mentioned he'd grown up in Absecon. Polly writhed in his seat as

Powell went on and on. When he finally said something funny, Polly's laughter quieted him.

As he followed Ernesto's car, Polly thought about the rest of the men who had gone on ahead hours before. DePre's élite. He marvelled at them. Powell was right; they were all morons. Polly failed to see, however, how this was to be considered a drawback. It operated to his distinct advantage. It would be even easier to succeed here than in the army.

Ernesto turned left on Maine Avenue and came to a stop. Polly pulled in behind him. They had reached the Inlet. He was startled at how dark it was.

·31·

THE NIGHT was incredibly black. The only visible light was a string of bulbs stretched out over Hackney's dock two hundred yards away. The bulbs were powerless against the darkness.

"It's perfect," Ernesto told Powell. "The pong won't see a thing until it's too late."

The lights on Hackney's dock went out. Polly crossed the street at the signal, dissolving into now unequivocal darkness. The only sign that light had ever existed in this secluded corner of the ruined Inlet was a tiny gray glow in one of the upstairs rooms at Hackney's. Powell stepped down onto Maine Avenue.

"Here's your flashlight," said Ernesto.

Powell groped until he felt its cool barrel against his palm. He was supposed to train it on Tommy's face.

"We've got three minutes," said Ernesto, his quartz watch lighting up like a tiny red meteor storm.

They crossed the street to the cement stairs for the old boardwalk. Ernesto was on one side of him, and Vince joined him on the other.

Their plan was simple. It was so dark, Tommy Van would never see his killers. Powell would shine his flashlight in Van's eyes to blind him. Ernesto and Vince would bring him down with their machine-gun pistols.

If Tommy was quick enough or lucky enough to escape only wounded, there were many more men waiting under the bathhouse, on the beach, and along the street, all with their own flashlights and guns.

The boardwalk creaked as they stepped onto it. Powell's heart began to speed.

"I hate this," he whispered.

"This is the best part, old man," said Ernesto.

Finished with his work, Tommy climbed up onto the Inlet boardwalk. Several minutes later he caught the sound of boards creaking through the darkness. It sounded like more than one man, but the small surf of the Inlet made it hard to tell. He could see nothing.

"Van?" came a voice. "Are you here?"

It was the banana cat and he had killing in his voice.

"Powoe to come alone," said Tommy angrily.

A powerful flashlight came on, and almost simultaneously two machine-gun pistols began firing.

But the flashlight found nothing, and the bullets raced down the empty boardwalk and slammed into Hackney's innocent plaster flanks.

Tommy had jumped over the railing and disappeared into the sand like a crab crawling down its hole.

A rifle stuttered from a distance. Vince fell over backwards, screaming. Powell took three rounds in his midsection. They climbed diagonally across him, from his kidney to his heart, knocking the wind out of him and throwing him back over the railing of the boardwalk. He fell to the beach dead. Ernesto was turning to run when a bullet sliced through his neck and made him gag on his own blood. He stumbled down onto the boardwalk, immobile with shock.

Across Maine Avenue, a hundred yards below Hackney's in an abandoned three-storey house, Thitch released the trigger of his M-14. He quickly reset the rifle for semi-automatic fire.

His first sweep of automatic fire had been very successful. He had started low on the man to the left, and the rifle had bucked steadily upwards as he crossed, but he had hit all three. He pressed his cheek to the stock and peered through the starlight scope again.

The man with no knees was motionless. He could wait. The banana cat was over the rail and probably dead. The one he had hit in the neck was beginning to struggle away. Thitch squeezed a round into the back of his head.

He felt himself getting excited. He was shooting well despite the long wait.

He had been waiting for hours. He had seen the men who came early search the buildings up and down the street. They had not searched near him. He had placed himself well outside what they had guessed was the perimeter of danger in such darkness.

When the string of lights on the dock had gone out, Thitch had felt a moment of anxiety. Quickly, he had turned his starlight scope up to full power. His fears were empty. The light from the dull bulb in the restaurant window was more than enough for his scope. He had viewed with ease the last of the ambushers as they took their positions.

He began killing them one by one.

They were stupid, waving their flashlights about looking for him. It was obvious they didn't know what was happening. He killed several with the lights quickly, losing count he was shooting so fast. Then they got smarter and turned off their flashlights.

He picked them off where they stood. They still hadn't realized he could see in the dark. They shouted wildly to each other. Finally, they started to run.

But there were only two of them left to run and he brought them down easily.

He watched and waited. He felt very satisfied. He had done some very fine shooting.

He remembered the one on the boardwalk he had hit in the knees. He found him in the scope again. He was a glowing shadow on the beautiful starlight screen. He was crawling like a spider with half of its legs torn off.

He sent Tam the all-clear signal, four quick rounds followed by two long, through the beautiful shadowy spider's back.

Tommy took one last deep breath through the flavored straw he had picked up from the counter of his Seven-Eleven and dug himself out of his vertical bunker. Once out of his sandy hole, he found the banana cat easily.

His flashlight lay beside him, still on. Tommy propped Powell up in the sand, and then took his head off with his blade. He slit Powell's pants so he could reach his flabby penis. He pared it off and stuffed it into the banana cat's severed windpipe.

He fixed the flashlight in the sand so that it shone directly on the mutilated body.

The white penis looked like an old broken finger beckoning everyone close to see what Tam Van Tram's enemies had to fear.

Polly lay on the beach trying not to shiver. The frigid waters of the December north Atlantic had soaked through his coat and shirt and were icing his abdomen all the way up to his chin. His legs, wet from the instant he went down, were already numb from the washings of the Inlet's miniature surf. He tried to guess how long he'd been waiting. Twenty seconds? The water was no more than thirty-one or -two degrees. It could kill him. It could wash over him again and again until it sucked the heat of life right out of him. The tide was coming in, and, when it came in, it rose in the Inlet much faster than on the oceanside beach. A wave crawled all the way up the sand to his mouth, and he slowly shifted his head to breathe. But breathing wasn't the problem, with this climbing water he'd be dead from hypothermia long before he ran out of breath.

It had taken him several moments after first hearing the voice of the M-14 to realize he had made a fatal mistake. He easily recognized its voice and his first reaction was that it was friendly fire, and he had nothing to worry about. But then he had quickly relocated himself. He wasn't in the Nam. He was in the World and it was the enemy who was firing the fourteen.

He had jerked quickly onto the downside of the beach, hoping the boardwalk would put him out of the sniper's view. He had to remain motionless to find out if the shooter had a starlight scope or a heat scope. If it was a heat scope, he was dead. Against the dark background of the frigid waters of the Atlantic, the sniper would see the heat rising from the red coal of his body like crimson steam.

He waited in agony as DePre's morons flashed their lights wildly up and down the beach looking for prey. One by one the lights went down. Then they finally wised up and turned off their bulls-eyes.

But, of course, the sniper kept killing them.

Two finally ran. A few more shots and they were groaning with death like all the others.

More shots. Four short, two long.

A minute's silence told him it was a starlight scope. He would be dead if it weren't.

Now he had to keep his own agonizing desire to get out of the incredibly cold water from killing him. He had known snipers who waited hours to make sure everyone was dead. This one would surely wait ten minutes. He had to stay motionless until the police arrived.

It seemed like an hour before he heard the sound of sirens. The cop cars made a lot of noise as they inched up Maine Avenue. The flashing lights and loud sirens went on for a long time before he finally heard a car door open. At last he dared raise his head.

The cops were still three hundred yards up Maine Avenue. They were approaching the beach as if a battalion of Charlies was waiting for them.

"Fucking chickenshits," he whispered at them.

He got to his feet. His whole body was numb. He felt dizzy and kept seeing red bursts as he tried to walk. He saw the flashlight on the headless Powell with his cock in the stump of his neck as he stumbled down the beach.

"Wait till they see you," he said to Powell. "They'll run back to their cars and take another trip around the block with their sirens on."

He hurried away down past Hackney's. It started to rain. Some of the drops were frozen and pelted him like little BBs.

DePre would be in a rage when he learned that all his enforcers had been killed. Polly would have to blame his mistake on Ernesto. He would say Ernesto had insisted on walking into an ambush against his expert advice. He would ask for full authority in the future.

Polly felt a little thrill in his blood. This thing had suddenly become far more than a simple revenge killing over Robles. He shivered with pleasure. This was war.

·32·

HE WAS sitting in his suite drinking when the door opened. He wondered why Willie Fudd would let anyone in. It was Caro. She looked very worried about something.

"Tim, how can the casino be closed?" she asked. "It's just four o'clock now."

"We had to close at three," said Tim, trying to think why Caro would be coming in now.

"What are you doing here?" he asked.

"Is that all you have to say?" she returned. "I've been driving all night through this damn storm, and that's all you say?"

"Storm?" he asked. "What storm?"

"It's moving south and I didn't get out in front of it until I got past Beach Haven," she said. "By that time I was a block of ice on wheels. I couldn't see a thing. The whole car was covered with ice. I don't know how I kept it on the road. I kept leaning up close to the windshield to see through all the ice, and my breath would freeze on the inside of the glass."

Tim struggled up out of the big sofa and went to the window. It was black out. Freezing rain was pinging up against the glass.

"Why is the hall full of Vietnamese?" asked Caro. "And I thought you were going to get killed if you closed the casino. Why would you close the casino?"

Tim kept staring out the window.

"Which one is Tommy Van?" asked Caro. "The one by the door?"

"Tommy went up to the Inlet to meet with Powell," said Tim, weaving his way back to the sofa.

"You're drunk," said Caro.

"It's my eye," said Tim. "This is the only way to stop the thing from blinking. It's still blinking, see? It's been going since midnight."

He watched Caro staring at him. He was glad she was here, but he couldn't figure out why she was here. Had she come for her money?

"Our money is all gone," he said. "I forgot about something when I took it."

"What did you forget?" she asked, worried.

"Bad luck," he said. "I forgot all about bad luck."

"You had bad luck?" she asked. "The casino had bad luck?"

"That's right, you know all about bad luck, don't you?" said Tim.

"Is it all gone?" she asked.

"You should have seen the joint tonight," said Tim. "Here I was thinking we had everything under control because Hector and Teddy and I, we each had our own pit, and no one would put anything over on us, especially since we had our best dealers working. We went with our élite. We assumed the best. But we got the worst. Everytime someone hit twenty, they made twenty-one. Everytime somebody got ten for a point, they made it coming right back. Then the word got around the boardwalk. It was the Ondine's night to give away money. They swarmed all over us. There were lines six and eight deep behind every blackjack chair."

"How did you pay everybody?" asked Caro.

"We didn't," said Tim. "We got down to one blackjack pit and we still had to write most of them checks. Wait until they come back with those checks in the morning and find those doors locked. Forget about the doors. They'll crush right through them. We've got the bad luck now. They all want a piece of us. They'll tear the place down."

Tim filled his glass back up with Scotch. Caro was walking up and back the living room. She didn't seem angry about her money.

"Oakes isn't coming until tomorrow afternoon," said Tim. "People will be lined up outside the casino screaming to get in, screaming to cash their checks. Did I say that? We promised them we'd cash their checks tomorrow morning after the banks opened. Wait until Sinbad's hears I went broke on their money. Did I tell you what they said to me yesterday? That's why I came to get your money. They—What did they—"

He had lost his train of thought. His mind was a vortex of voices, images, and plans.

"You've got to get the casino open in the morning," said Caro.

What was she doing here? Hadn't they had a fight? She would be furious when she found out he'd lost all her money. He'd already told her he'd lost all her money. She wasn't worried about it. What was she doing here?

"What are you doing here?"

"What am I doing here?" she asked, puzzled. "We're trying to figure out how to get the casino open."

"Our money's all gone," he said.

"I've gathered that much," said Caro.

"You're supposed to be furious," said Tim.

"I'm furious."

"No, you're not."

"No," she said, "I'm not."

"Oh, yeah, I forgot," he said. "You're a gambler."

"Yes, I am," she said. "And so are you."

"Yes, me too," said Tim. "I've learned the thrill of watching hundred dollar bills sprout wings and buzz around the casino looking for an open door."

She laughed.

"I'm sorry, Caro," he said.

"You don't have to apologize," she said.

"I do," he said. "I put you through hell. I was so busy with my stupid—"

"All right, you're sorry," interrupted Caro. "I'm sorry too, because it was me that made the mess."

"Oh, shit," he said. "Come on. Tell me I'm as asshole."

She sat down on the sofa next to him, "You're an asshole."

"That's right."

"You're nice when you're drunk," she said tenderly.

She put her hand up to his wide forhead and smoothed back his curly auburn hair.

"Want a drink?" he asked her.

"No."

"Why are you looking at me like that?" he asked.

"I went up to see your parents," she said.

"Herb and Ilene?" he asked, surprised. "You went to see the doctor?"

"Tim, I think I know what this is all about," she said.

"What what is all about?" he asked.

"This thing between you and your father," she said.

He leaned over and snatched up his scotch. "You went to see the doctor. Amazing."

"Your mother told me you and your father used to fight alot," she said.

Tim laughed explosively. The drink was at his mouth and he sprayed it all over himself.

"What's so funny?" She was mad. "Why do you always think it's so funny."

"It's not funny," he said.

"You're damn right it's not funny," she said. "And it never was funny."

"It never was funny," he repeated mechanically, dusting the drops of his drink off his trousers.

"Your mother told me about a fight you had with him when you were almost sixteen," she said. "A really bad one. He threw you over in your chair at dinner."

Tim took a quiet sip of his drink. "You had a lot of fucking nerve going up there."

"She didn't tell me the whole story," said Caro.

"What the fuck were you doing up there?" he demanded.

"What happened after he got you down on the floor?" she asked.

"My mother told you about that fight?"

"Tim, she was so happy to have someone to talk to about you, she was ready to answer every question I could think to ask," said Caro.

He took a deep breath. "Jesus."

"What happened?" she repeated.

"Nothing happened," he said. "The same thing that always happened happened. Except for her getting into it."

"What happened?"

Tim shrugged. "He beat the shit out of me again."

"Is that all?"

"No."

"What else?"

"Jesus," he repeated.

"Tell me, Tim," she insisted.

"For the first time I was afraid of him," he said, shaking his head morosely. "I was actually afraid of him. He'd been kicking me around from the day I was eight and suddenly I was afraid of him. I let him hit me. I couldn't do anything. He beat the living shit out of me. He kept hitting away at me, banging me in the head with his fists. He got one right in on my eye. I thought he'd squashed my fucking eye. It isn't easy to get a knuckle between the brow and cheekbone, but the doctor managed it. My eye got so swollen I couldn't see out of it. It wasn't just a shiner, don't you know. It was the eye itself. It got as swollen and purple as one of Harry and David's grapes and I couldn't see out of it for two weeks after that."

He stopped.

"What happened then?" asked Caro.

"It would take a surgeon to get his knuckle in there all the way to the eye," he cracked.

"Why do you make it ironic?" asked Caro. "It's not funny."

"Okay," he agreed, "it's not funny."

"How did your mother get into it?" she asked.

Tim laughed. "The things this man could say, you'd wonder how he got through enough school to become a doctor."

"I asked about your mother," said Caro.

"It wasn't her fault," he said. "It was the way she was."

"What did she do?"

"He stopped when he saw what he'd done to my eye," said Tim. "It was puffing up fast and he was afraid he'd done something serious—"

"What did she do?" insisted Caro.

"Caro, all I remember is stumbling around that dining room trying to get away from her," he said. "It had always been him but suddenly it was her. She was shrieking to me about his hands, how I'd hurt his hands. The doctor, you see, was sitting down in pain. He'd banged his knuckles up beating them against my skull and she was shrieking to me about how it was all my fault and didn't I stop to think I might have ruined his hands forever."

"She was blaming you for what he'd done?" asked Caro. It didn't fit with the woman she had talked to eight hours earlier.

"Yes," he said. "And after that she never stopped. Once she got hold of the idea it was all my fault, she never let it go. After that night, it was like everything I got from them, either of them, was a big favor. Even college was like that, a dispensation to the criminal from the holy."

"I find that hard to believe," said Caro. It couldn't be the same woman who had said Tim was her favorite son.

"You know what it was," said Tim philosophically. "They were the surgeon's hands. They were the money-makers of the family. Without those hands, Herb and Ilene would go broke, especially since he couldn't write prescriptions any more. She couldn't let anything get between her and her money. If there was one thing my mother and father had in common, it was a great fondness for money."

"Oh, Tim, I'm sorry," she said. "I'm sorry."

He looked up at her, puzzled. "What are you sorry for?"

"It sounds so awful," she said.

He blushed and got a half-smile on his face.

"I'm glad you came back," he said. His face was glowing red.

"So am I," she said.

"Maybe you won't be when you get the rest of the bad news," he said carefully.

"What bad news?"

"I'm going to be stuck here for quite awhile," he said.

"That's why the halls are full of Vietnamese?" she asked.

"Somebody tried to kill me when I was coming back here with the money," he said. "Twice. I still don't know how they missed."

He told her the story of his escape and getting lost in the pine barrens.

"How did you get into the Ondine from NAFEC?" she asked.

"One of the engineers in there recognized me," he said. "He gave me a ride."

"But now that you're back in Atlantic City, you should be all right."

"Maybe," said Tim. "But what's to stop them from kidnapping me and taking me somewhere else to kill me."

"Tommy Van," said Caro, beginning to understand.

"That's right," said Tim. "And I'm afraid that makes me one of them."

"One of what?"

"Carlo Gambino," said Tim, "Jeff Crolich. Harold Powell. Take your pick."

"Why?" she asked. "Why does that make you one of them?"

"Because I'm caught, Caro," said Tim. "No matter what Tommy works out with Powell tonight, I'm still caught. The casino won't open in the morning, and to these guys that's like declaring war."

"But what if we *do* open the casino?" said Caro.

"We can't."

"But what if we do?" persisted Caro.

"There's no chance."

"There has to be a chance," said Caro. "There's always a chance. We have to keep working at it until we find it. Come on, think."

"I'm too drunk," he said.

"Then I'll think," she said.

"And I had the idea I was going to make a fine gangster," he said. "I can't focus on anything. I'm another drunk with a big mouth."

"What about the hotel funds?" asked Caro. "Dean will open the casino for you no matter what Oakes says, won't he?"

"I already asked him," he said. "The hotel doesn't have much money in the bank."

"Can we borrow money from the bank?" asked Caro.

"Oakes has stopped our credit," said Tim.

"What if we gave them some collateral," she said.

"We don't have any," said Tim.

"You could pledge all the casino equipment," she said. "It's worth millions."

"The equipment is Colony's, not the casino manager's," said Tim. "I can't sign for it. Besides, there's no market for the stuff. There's more equipment in town than anybody needs."

"Slots have a big resale value," she said. "We can sell them right out from under Oakes' nose. We can get on the phone and get people over here with their money in the morning."

"Slots aren't in demand any more either, Caro," said Tim. "Maybe in Florida where they're still opening new joints, but not here. I get mail on local slots for sale every day of the week."

"The slots!" screamed Caro. "What about the slots?"

"Didn't we just cover them?" asked Tim dully.

"We can empty the money out of them," said Caro. "We can take the silver dollars to the bank when it opens at nine and be back in time to open the casino at ten."

"The slots!" said Tim, struggling to his feet. "Oakes forgot all about the slots. He only took the paper."

"The silver dollars will be enough, won't they?" asked Caro.

"Everybody forgot about the money in the slots," he said. "How did everybody forget about the money in the slots?"

"Maybe it takes a couple of weeks putting money in them for six and seven hours a day to remember," said Caro.

"We've got to do it now," said Tim, weaving towards the door. "We've got to do it ourselves now so that nobody can tell Oakes and he gets the idea the silver is part of the bankroll. The slots! There's a hundred thousand in the dollar machines alone! What a great idea!"

They had only the colored lights of the slots to work under. Tim's drunkenness and blinking eye made it difficult to get the buckets of silver dollars into the bags without spilling them. Caro was nervous and she was spilling coins, too.

Tim stopped to look back down the aisle of machines. The floor looked as if a snowstorm had passed through the Ondine and dumped silver wafers all over the carpet.

He turned back to Caro and began to talk to her about his father. The long silence was broken and he talked on compulsively as they worked.

"Did you know he didn't believe in the theory of evolution?" asked Tim, his ironic smile made a ghostly circuit of his mouth and disappeared.

"Yes."

"A surgeon," he said sarcastically. "A man who must have studied the bodies of everything from grasshoppers to primates, and he used to tell us at dinner how the theory of evolution was all bullshit. It was one of his favorites. Men were a million miles ahead of monkeys, he'd say. He started in on that with Gary, my roommate, right after commencement when I was getting the last of my stuff out of our room. Gary laughed at him and the doctor went berserk. He got him by the shirt and slammed him up against the wall, screaming at him."

Tim stopped, gazing off into his memory.

"That was you he wanted to slam up against the wall, not Gary," said Caro.

"I know," said Tim. "Gary was scared shitless. He looked at me all bug-eyed and I didn't know what to do. I couldn't do anything. I was scared of him. I was still scared. By that time I was bigger and stronger and I could have murdered him in a fight. I never would have a better reason. He was behaving like a maniac. But I didn't do anything. I couldn't do anything."

"And you have gone on trying to pick this same fight again and again," she said. "Trying to find these wild and stupid authority figures and goad them into a fight so that maybe, somehow, you'll be able to overcome the fear that paralyzed you as a fifteen-year-old when he nearly put out your eye."

"It's not that—"

"That blinking eye of yours," she said. "It blinks because it's afraid it's going to get hit with that knuckle again."

His eye did blink everytime he got into a confrontation with someone. His eye had started to blink when he'd wanted to attack Robles. As stupid as that urge had been, it had almost taken him over. He got an image of himself, eight years old, kicking furiously at his father's shins.

"What does the money have to do with it?" asked Caro.

"What do you mean?" he asked thoughtfully.

"Why did you choose business?" she asked. "You were smart enough to do anything."

"I guess you're right," he said, looking at the scattered silver dollars on the carpet. "When we moved into Hartford, my mother was panic-stricken. She thought we were going to go broke."

"How come?"

"Because the doctor had just been sentenced to five years probation," said Tim. "He had been writing speed prescriptions for all comers, and the district attorney had nailed him for it."

"A thoracic surgeon writing speed prescriptions?" asked Caro.

"Transparently stupid?" mocked Tim. "That's the doctor. Besides, it brought in sixty thousand a year. It also got him five years running an emergency ward in a ghetto. It was 'volunteer' work."

"I see," said Caro.

"It kept him so busy he didn't have as much time to operate as before," said Tim. "And the sixty thousand a year from the funny prescriptions was gone, so we all had to make do on about eighty thousand a year."

"Which wasn't enough for your mother?" asked Caro.

"No."

"Which is why you hate to give me presents," said Caro.

"I guess so," said Tim, grinning sheepishly.

"Which is why you went into business," said Caro.

Tim laughed.

"What's funny?"

"I don't know exactly," said Tim. He was fishing around in his pocket for something. "I just remembered I've got something I want you to have, no matter what."

His hand came out of his pocket with the ruby.

"I've been saving it for you," he said. "But I kept forgetting to give it back to you."

"Tim," she said, surprised and suddenly sad. "I'm sorry. I didn't even know you knew it was gone."

"I knew," he said, sliding it carefully on her finger.

"I love you," she said.

"Now, no matter what happens," he said, "we know we need each other and we're always going to stay together, right?"

"Oh, God, Tim," she circled her arms around his neck and hugged his curly head to her cheek. "I'm so happy."

"Even though I've fucked everything up?" he asked, amazed. "You're really happy?"

"Oh, yes," she said, letting him go to look up into his eyes. "One moment like this, when everything bitter between us is gone—it's so sweet, Tim, it's so sweet, it's worth anything."

She was quiet as he hugged her back.

Their embrace was interrupted by the sound of a door closing. It was a very familiar door.

"Holy Jesus," Tim whispered to Caro. "What the hell is he doing in his office at five in the morning?"

"Who?"

"Haaf."

"Oh, shit," whispered Caro, panic-stricken. "He's going to catch us."

"Sssssh," warned Tim.

He dragged her back around behind the row of slots. Haaf was already coming down the casino towards them. He would have to see the money all over the carpet down the aisle.

He was in a hell of a hurry.

Suddenly Tim knew what he was watching. He was drunk, but he hadn't spent four months in a casino without learning how to recognize a thief when he saw one. Haaf was stealing something. Money. From the safe? He had the combination.

"Jesus," he whispered.

He raced down between the slots and turned the corner after Haaf. Haaf heard him coming only seconds before Tim tackled him. Tim landed on top and felt something bulky beneath Haaf's sport coat. He tore the buttons off Haaf's shirt reaching to see what it was. It was canvas. It was a money belt.

Tim was so surprised he scrambled to his feet and backed away.

"Holy shit," he said, staring at Haaf with stupid astonishment. "You've been doing it all long. You've been doing it at night."

"What the hell are you doing, Tim?" demanded Haaf as he stood up and brushed himself off.

"Where did you get the keys to the boxes?" asked Tim. "How could you get the keys to the boxes?"

Haaf straightened his shirt, not paying attention.

"You must have bribed the inspector," said Tim. "Is that it?"

"Where did you come from?" asked Haaf.

"What do you have in there, Dean?"

"In where?"

Tim reached for the money belt. Haaf pulled away.

"What's inside that belt?" repeated Tim.

"Nothing," said Haaf, buttoning his coat.

"You've got money in there," said Tim, reaching out to stop him.

Haaf grabbed Tim's arm and Tim found himself quickly on the carpet with Haaf on top of him. Haaf had a hold on one of his arms and the opposite leg. Tim felt sharp pains in both of them. He thought of the picture Haaf showed off so proudly on his desk. Utah State Wrestling Champion. He struggled violently to get loose, but the struggling made the pain worse and he found himself twisting hopelessly across the carpet. Even with a fifty-pound weight advantage, Tim was easy work for Haaf.

At least there was nothing Haaf could do other than keep him pinned to the floor. It was a stalemate. Tim stopped struggling. As he lay there, taking an instant's rest, he saw the whole sequence. The slips had been missing from Saturday night because Haaf hadn't had enough time to take money out of the boxes. No wonder Haaf had been in such a good mood for the past week. He was going to buy the Ondine from Oakes. He had been planning to all along. He had been guiding the profits down to make Oakes sell. No wonder he had been so interested in the computer. The fucking thing worked and Haaf knew it. He was following him and Henry so he could create the illusion of the *per* moving down. How could he have been so DUMB. He should have seen it. It was all happening when the computer was turned off. Haaf had done everything when Argus was asleep.

His astonishment was replaced by an incredible wave of hatred. Dean Haaf, his pet father, had been tormenting him for months. He had even refused to give him enough money to keep the casino open.

"Come on, Haaf," he said angrily. "Let me go, this is stupid."

"No, it isn't," said Haaf, reviving the pressure on Tim's leg.

Haaf had been resting for a moment too, and now he was starting in on Tim again.

"Go ahead," said Tim, resisting the pain. "Play wrestler. But when you get tired of this, you're going to jail."

"Move you bastard," commanded Haaf.

Haaf doubled the pressure on his shoulder, and Tim spidered forward to escape the stinging pain. Haaf was moving Tim towards something. Tim saw a row of slots ahead. Haaf was planning to slam Tim's head up against the sharp corner of a slot stand.

Where was Caro? Tim twisted his head around and saw her gaping at them.

"Do something!" he called to her. "Hit him with a roulette stool!"

Haaf saw Caro, too, and the pains in Tim's leg and shoulder grew even sharper. He was moving him faster. Tim could feel Haaf's breath speeding against his neck. He was getting ready to switch to some new hold. He was going for the hold he would use to slam Tim's head against the slot stand. The pain in Tim's leg was great, and he was drunk and tired. The drunkenness magnified his fatigue. He dwelt on the feeling, cultivating it, as if it were welcome. In a way, it was. This was the feeling he was always trying to get when he trained and when he swam in meets. In fact, this pain wasn't much against the last twenty-five yards of the two-hundred butterfly. Flyers pray the night before championships to make the last turn ahead, because no one can close on them when blinding fatigue leaves them barely enough pull in their arms to get out of the water for their breaths. Flyers have nightmares in which they make the last turn, find someone beside them and have to sprint the last twenty-five yards. Not Tim. Tim *wanted* to see someone dead even with him when he made that turn for the last lap. He trained and trained and trained for it, fantasizing finding someone red-faced and looking right at him after that last turn, which was exactly where Haaf was now; because if Tim was going to get his head split open, so was Haaf.

Tim threw his head back as hard as he could. He hit Haaf somewhere in the forehead. Tim felt like someone had hit him in the skull with a hammer. "Ow!" He heard Haaf's shout of pain through his own. He kept slamming his head backwards aiming it right and left, getting some glancing blows against Haaf, and some direct. His head was pulsating. The pain wasn't the orange-white blindness of swimming. It was a sickening purple with red bursts. Haaf was dodging him. He kept throwing his head back, trying to find the pain, because it was Haaf's pain too, and he would be happy to destroy them both. But Haaf was riding him, trying to get his head square in the middle of Tim's neck to stop him. Tim jerked violently. He felt his shoulder muscle tear like paper and he screamed from the pain. Haaf tilted to one side and Tim threw his head back again. Haaf had his head turned and this time Tim felt no pain. He had hit something soft.

"My ear!" screamed Haaf. "My ear!"

Haaf was off Tim and rolling on the floor. He was holding his ear with both hands and grimacing. Tim scrambled to his feet.

He saw the picture on Haaf's desk again. He saw the big red ear-protectors Haaf was wearing in that picture. He kicked Haaf in the other ear. The point of his shoe got right up behind Haaf's jaw, and Haaf screamed like a wild tropical bird.

"Tim!" cried Caro.

Haaf was holding onto both ears and writhing about the carpet in agony. He twisted and turned like paper going up in flames. Tim's foot was trembling with the urge to kick him again. It was intoxicating to have Haaf, who had been secretly tormenting him for so long, helpless and guilty on the carpet before him. He would be justified in kicking him again. He could kick him and kick him and kick him, like Hercules throwing Antaeus to the ground, and no amount of it would be enough.

"Tim!" shrieked Caro, and suddenly she was all over him. She was screaming and pushing and clawing, and his face felt like he was being attacked by bees. *"STOP IT! STOP IT!"*

He fell to the floor with her on top of him. She landed on his shoulder and he almost passed out from the pain. He lay still for a moment, paralyzed by her attack and the agony in his shoulder.

"Jesus, Caro, get off," he whispered. "He separated my shoulder!"

She scrambled to her feet, and he struggled to get up with one hand.

"My ears! My ears!"

Haaf was shouting very loud as if he were trying to hear himself. Suddenly he stopped shouting and let go of his ears with both hands, as if they had given his hands an electric shock. He looked frantically at his palms.

"They're bleeding! Look! They're bleeding!"

He rushed to show his hands to Tim and Caro. His palms were spotted with liquid red freckles.

They found, among the plenteous junk of Haaf's suite, money everywhere. Tim found some in drawers and shoes; Caro in the back of a radio. Money was taped to the lid of the toilet and stuffed into a bandaid can in the medicine chest.

Tim's face in the mirror caught his attention. It was a red version of Tommy's scarred yellow chest.

"You were pretty hard on me, Caro," he called out to her. "Look what you did to my face."

"I'm sorry," she said, her face appearing over his shoulder. "I was desperate to stop you."

"I wasn't going to kick him again," he said.

"It sure looked like you might," she said, putting her arms around his waist.

"How come you wouldn't hit him with a stool, but you climbed all over me?" he asked, turning around inside her embrace.

"I don't care about him," she said, a smile pinching her cheeks.

"I wasn't going to kick him," he repeated.

"I don't believe you," she smirked. "You were going to murder him if I didn't stop you."

"No, Caro," he said seriously. "I wasn't going to touch him again."

She stopped smiling, "I know."

"You do?"

"It turned out you're not as vicious as we thought you were," she said.

"I'd been waiting for a chance to do something like that since I can't remember when, and then when I did it, I wished I hadn't. He looked so pathetic, showing us his hands and wailing about his ears. Jesus, I almost did kill him."

"But you didn't," she said. "Of course, there was a little wild persuasion thrown in by me."

He laughed, brought her close to him, and kissed her. He had forgotten how much fun it was to kiss her. She finally broke away, struggling for breath, giggling, and happy.

They let go of each other and began looking for money again. They found it between the pages of magazines, behind mirrors, and in lamp shades. They had been piling it up on the bed as they found it.

"That pile is almost two feet high," said Caro. "How much is two feet of money?"

"Not as much as it looks like," said Tim.

He pulled open the drawer to Haaf's night table. It was full of little red, yellow and green envelopes, stiff cardboard envelopes that keys are kept in. On the outside of each of them was scrawled a name in Haaf's handwriting. Peter Gray, Karl Windman, Jim Jesse . . . There were nearly thirty of them.

"I think I've found the money," said Tim.

"Found the money?" laughed Caro. "God, you can't lift anything up in this place without finding money."

"No," said Tim. "I mean I've found the real money."

He picked up a handful of the small cardboard envelopes and showed her.

"What are they?"

"Safety deposit box keys," he said. "They're for banks in Pennsylvania, Maryland, and Delaware."

"Is there money in them?"

"Caro, the reason we've found this money here so easily is that it's the loose change," said Tim.

"This is the stuff he leaves lying around?" she asked in shock. "There's more?"

"Much more," said Tim. "It's all in these safety deposit boxes."

"This is really just the *loose change?*" she shouted, getting very excited.

"Yes."

"Let's steal it!" she cried.

"What?"

"Let's steal the money in the safety deposit boxes," she said. "We'll take it to Quito and live like Augustus and Livia. It will be fantastic. Haaf can't stop us and who is he going to tell after we're gone? It must be millions. We've got a million here at least. We can pay off the other hotels now and take off with the keys."

"It won't work," said Tim. "Haaf will know we have the money."

"What's he going to say?" demanded Caro. "Is he going to tell Oakes that he stole millions and then you stole it from him?"

"He'll find someone to tell," said Tim. "And they'll come looking for us."

"Shit." Caro's face fell. "You're right."

"Besides, I have plans for this money," said Tim.

"Yeah," said Caro glumly.

"What do you mean 'yeah'?" asked Tim.

"You want to pay off Sinbad's and the Pier," said Caro.

"No."

"What do you mean?" she asked. "Why not?"

"I want to open the casino again," said Tim. "I can't do that if I use this money to pay them off."

"What?" asked Caro, dumbfounded.

"I have to find out something before Oakes gets here this afternoon," said Tim.

"Find out what?" asked Caro.

"Oakes wants to get rid of the casino," said Tim. "He wants it closed. He won't give me a chance to see if the system really works or not."

"You still want to revolutionize the casino business," said Caro. She felt herself getting giddy and lightheaded. The fight had come back so quickly it took her breath away.

"The computer was catching the crooked dealers all along," said Tim. "It was working the whole time but we didn't know it because Haaf had the keys to the boxes. Now I've got them and nobody can screw up the totals. Caro, maybe we had a per of forty all along."

"But what if you open the casino and you have bad luck again," said Caro.

"We won't," said Tim. "That's over. It was over the instant we caught Haaf. I can feel it. We were lucky to catch him, and we're going to stay lucky."

"We can leave this town with all our money," said Caro, "but you still want to open the casino to prove how smart you are. You want to prove you can take any business, even one as weird as gambling, get to the heart of how it works and make it pump money."

"Caro, you said you learned you had to stay with one idea until you found out what was beneath it," said Tim. "This damn casino, it's my painting. I know I made a poor choice to start with, but I've been sticking with it all along, and I have to keep on sticking with it until I find out what's beneath it."

"It's not the same thing," she said.

"I'll never see another chance like this, Caro," he said. "Some men wait their entire lives for a chance like this. Think of the clarity of it. I can prove in one afternoon what I've been working for ever since I left business school."

"Are you asking me if you can open the casino again?" asked Caro. "Or are you telling me that's what you're going to do?"

"Of course I'm asking you," said Tim. "If you don't want to do it, we'll pay off Sinbad's and the Pier and head for Quito right now."

Caro was silent, looking at him. His light eyes were ablaze.

"But we'd be risking our lives," she finally said.

"It's not that much of a risk," he said. "We open the casino, win lots of bucks, pay back the six hundred thousand, sell the system to Oakes, and leave town."

Caro laughed. "You make it sound so simple,"

"It seems pretty straightforward to me," grinned Tim.

"It sounds like a gambler's fantasy to me," said Caro.

"It isn't," said Tim. "And it's not the money. And it's not beating up the doctor. I put all of that behind me when I stopped myself from kicking Haaf again. Look at the eye. It's not blinking."

Caro laughed, despite herself. "Let's open a few tables like you did before," she suggested. "Then we can take the rest of the money to pay off Sinbad's and the Pier."

"The system won't work with just a few tables," said Tim. "It needs a whole universe of numbers."

"What about all the monitors?" she asked. "You said Henry broke most of them."

"That's no problem," responded Tim quickly. "I can hook the

computer up to any television. We can take one out of a hotel room. That's the beauty of this system. You only need one screen to see it all."

THE ICE storm had ended only an hour before. Alfred Oakes was anxious to get to the Ondine. He and Tony Martirano had taken a private charter to Bader Field to save time, but now they sat on Albany Avenue waiting for traffic to begin moving again.

Like many prominent Wall Street figures, Oakes was a tall man. He was six-four; and sitting in passenger seats, both in airplanes and cars, gave him leg cramps. The cab had now been motionless for more than ten minutes. The lack of progress made his legs hurt more.

"It's spilling over onto Albany from the expressway," remarked the cab driver.

"It took us fifteen minutes just to get out of the airport onto this street," complained Oakes. "Why has everyone on the East Coast decided to come to Atlantic City in the middle of an ice storm?"

"The same reason you're here, ain't it?" said the cabby.

Oakes stared at the cabby. Oakes had large blue-green eyes with long black lashes. They could have been the eyes of a very good-looking woman. They looked out of place in a fifty-five-year-old man's head.

"What reason is that?" he asked.

"The killings," said the cabby.

"The killings?"

"I have my own theory," said the driver. "I got a cousin in Ducktown and he knows what everyone is thinking, and he agrees with me."

"What is Ducktown?" asked Tony Martirano.

"That's the Italian section of the island," said the driver. "Where the White House sub-shop is. That's where all the gangsters hang out. Ducktown."

"They know in Ducktown why everyone has come to Atlantic City today, do they?" asked Oakes.

"They know that everywhere, mister," snapped the cabby. "Everywhere but in the back seat of this cab. Don't you guys own a television or a radio?"

"We've been in meetings," said Tony.

They had been negotiating the sale of the Ondine. Oakes was at war with a battery of Dutch lawyers. Even though he was desperate to sell the hotel, he kept arguing over every point. Tim's six-hundred-thousand-dollar loss had given him fresh ammunition. Most people would have concealed it and made a quick sale. Not Oakes. He had made it a negotiating point. He wanted the sale of the hotel predated so that the Dutch company would have to take the loss. It had become the point on which the deal would be made or broken. It was also the reason Oakes was coming to Atlantic City. He had negotiated himself into a corner.

"Harold Powell and eight other guys were killed up on the Inlet Beach last night," said the cabby. "It's a gang war. That's what I've been trying to tell you about the traffic. They've been pouring into town ever since the news hit the TVs and radios."

"Pouring into town?" asked Tony. "What for?"

"I think they all want to see somebody get killed," said the driver. "It's because it's football season."

"What does football season have to do with it?" asked Tony.

"They follow the mob in the papers just like the football teams, don't they?" said the driver. "This is like coming to the stadium to watch the Eagles. They have a chance to catch some live action and they don't want to miss it. There hasn't been a mobster super bowl since Chicago during prohibition."

The cabby looked at them patiently in the rear view mirror, waiting for them to agree.

"We have been here twenty minutes without moving," said Oakes.

"The funny thing about it," continued the cabby sharply, "is that all the stuff about keeping Atlantic City neutral was complete malarkey. You know how the mobsters all said there would be no killings and no trouble in Atlantic City because it would be bad for business? That wasn't the reason they wanted the island neutral. They wanted to save their own hides, that's all. Bad for business? Look at this crowd."

"Is there any other way we can get to the Ondine?" asked Oakes.

"You can walk," said the driver. "It's up to you. It's only a few degrees above zero out there."

Oakes sighed and leaned back in his seat, trying to stretch out his legs.

Tony didn't like sitting in a cab alone with an impatient Alfred Oakes. He wanted to get to the Ondine and get it over with. He didn't relish taking part in Tim's cross-examination. He and Tim had been friends for years. Tony had been shocked to hear Oakes tell him Tim was a thief. He still didn't believe it. Unfortunately, Tony was the only executive at Colony who knew enough about the Ondine to accompany Oakes. Tony had been Dean Haaf's rubber stamp when Haaf had originally brought the idea to Oakes.

Tony could still remember being called into Oakes's office to meet Haaf over a year ago. It was his first visit to Oakes's office. He'd never been in an office like that before. Not that it was big; what was impressive was the way it was decorated. It was done in Early American furniture. Not the kind that looks like it has been knocked around for two hundred years. It was two hundred years old, but it looked like it had been made yesterday. His mahogany desk looked like it had been carved from a clean block of wood the same way Michelangelo worked marble into bodies. The stuff had been in his family for years. They had bought it from the original cabinet makers. Oakes still had the bills, and had shown one to him once. It was dated 1755 and signed in a handsome script by someone named John Townsend.

His office was full of pieces like the desk. Oakes treated them all casually, and they were every bit as comfortable as the junk in the rest of the executive suites at Colony. It was all so gracefully carved, so clean and neat, it was beautiful. You could say you didn't like it because it wasn't your taste, but you could no more say it was ugly than you could say Greta Garbo was a dog because she didn't have big tits. It was far more elegant than any other office on Wall Street; and, if you knew the numbers on American furniture, as Tony had taken an afternoon off at Israel Sack to research, you knew there was a half million in chairs alone in there.

"Powell was killed by some Vietnamese guy," the driver was saying. "He didn't care too much about keeping Atlantic City neutral. All the home team goons make rules about no killing in Atlantic City to protect themselves, but what has the zip got to lose by breaking the rules? You know what I think? I think he's scared them all. He's really vicious. He sliced off Powell's head and stuffed his dick down his neck. Can you see that?"

"Let's get out and walk," Oakes said to Tony. "I'm not going to sit here any more."

They started out on foot. The bright winter sun and the sea air made it pleasant to walk at first, but the bitter cold quickly diminished their enjoyment.

"We can walk up the boardwalk," said Oakes when they crossed Pacific Avenue.

The boardwalk turned out to be worse than sitting in the cab on Albany Avenue. A crush of pedestrians swarmed up and down, making the boardwalk look like a gigantic moving sidewalk. It was so cold and damp that people's breaths billowed out of them in great mists. The crowd looked like steam-driven robots pressing aggressively into one another, urgently trying to reach some preprogrammed destination.

Oakes beckoned Tony to follow him down onto the beach. Oakes stared at the ocean as they walked. He watched the surf rolling up ramps of ice left by the storm's high tide. The Atlantic must have come rushing up the beach during the storm the night before and left its high seas frozen on the sand in these great icy banks. Thousands of clams were fixed in the dull green ice like bleached studs. The tide had gone out once since the storm, but now it was coming back in, eagerly climbing the levees of ice again. Like curling tongues, the gray-green waves lapped up the ramps of ice and left some boiling spittle to freeze there before they quickly withdrew.

Oakes looked away from the sea and back to the hotels above the boardwalk. He saw all the hotels as one bizarre structure. He imagined it an ice palace commissioned by a four-year-old Tsar with a fabulous treasury. But not even the ice looked real. It looked like model airplane glue. The infantile Tsar had ordered it swabbed on everything in sight. To everyone's disappointment, instead of coming up wet and gleaming, the glue had dried in ugly, fibrous lumps.

Caro came in at the end of it. Tommy wasn't comprehending what Tim was saying. For the first time since Tim had met him, his sad head looked genuinely dull and vacant.

"So *Anh* Tim run away?"

"It's not running away so much as getting out, Tommy," said Tim.

"Tim is *not* afraid?" he asked again. It was clear he believed Tim was not afraid, but he kept repeating the question, as if somewhere in Tim's answer was the clue to what was wrong.

"It's the whole scheme of this thing," said Tim, repeating what he had said before in different words. "I don't think it works. I don't think it's worth it."

"What does Tam do with money?" he asked.

"Whatever you want."

"And Tim is leaving?"

"Today or tomorrow."

Tommy shook his head again. "Everything is perfect now. You can't leave."

"It doesn't work, Tommy," repeated Tim a fourth time. "You're either going to get killed, go to jail, or end up so paranoid that you might as well be dead anyway."

"You know what he's been doing all morning?" Tim asked Caro after Tommy left. "You know why he didn't come in until now?"

Caro looked upset. She had stood nervously by while he said goodbye to Tommy. He assumed it was because Tommy made her frightened because of what he had done to Powell and the rest of them.

"No," she responded to his question nervously. "Why?"

"He's been out visiting the hotels on the boardwalk."

Caro looked puzzled. Hector came into the office from the video room. "What for?" she asked.

"He went around with Willie and Thitch to every hotel on the boardwalk and told them he wanted ten thousand a day," said Tim.

Hector laughed. "That's what they all deserve," he said.

"What did they say to him?" asked Caro.

"Most of them gave him the money on the spot," said Tim. "The rest promised they would."

"I'll bet they did," said Hector. "And they will, too."

"He says he already has over two hundred thousand in the safe in the floor of his Seven-Eleven," said Tim. "It's a good thing I made some phone calls as soon as we found out about Powell."

He had called Sinbad's when he heard about the killings. The cashier there had sounded very frightened. Tommy had already been there. Even after Tim told him Tommy wasn't working for him anymore, the cashier remained skeptical. He said Tommy seemed to think he was working for Tim. Tim had finally been forced to talk to McGray, who was working as a pit boss at Sinbad's. He and McGray had worked out a payment on the loan, plus interest, which had calmed the cashier down. McGray had then called someone he knew at the Pier and they were amenable to the same terms. Tommy had come in, proud of his work, offering Tim control of Atlantic City, just after Tim had hung up with the Pier. While he had been making his frantic phone calls, Caro had been in the video room watching the casino with Hector, Teddy and Jimmy.

"You know, I'm not so sure," said Caro, her voice nervously loud, "that we should let Tommy walk out of here right now."

"Caro, we can't have Tommy around anymore," said Tim. "He's only going to get us in deeper and deeper."

"You want to let them kill you?" asked Caro.

"I want to pay them back," said Tim, "plus their exorbitant interest, and get out."

"You made a deal with them already?" asked Hector.

"Over the phone," said Tim. "I told them I had fired Tommy, and—"

"Tim!" complained Caro. "Why did you tell them that?"

"And I'd pay them before the day was over," concluded Tim, ignoring Caro.

"How much do they want?" asked Hector.

"Only twenty percent a day," said Tim.

"Twenty percent!" said Caro, getting louder and louder. "How much is that?"

"For three days, it comes out to three hundred and sixty thousand in interest," said Hector.

"For a six hundred thousand dollar loan?" said Caro. "You know what a miser Oakes is!"

"It's my only hope of convincing all of them I'm not in with Tommy and I'm not trying to take over Atlantic City," said Tim.

"But Oakes will never agree to pay them that kind of interest!" said Caro, still shouting.

"What are you shouting about?" asked Tim. "Why are you so upset. We'll make that money in one day."

"You haven't seen what's been happening out there while you were on the phone," she said.

Tim looked quickly at Hector.

"What's happening?"

"The money is going out awfully fast, boss," said Hector.

Tim jumped up and hurried into the video room. The old Admiral TV they had wired to the computer sat in the corner on its wooden haunches like a toad that was all one big colored eye. It was dizzy. It revolved from table to table with a wild kind of confusion. It wasn't the random sampling of images which signified a controlled casino. It was flitting about from table to table in a panic to make up its mind which one to watch. Tim turned quickly to the large bank of monitors.

Teddy and Jim were watching the wounded Argus. Crippled from Henry's wild attack (over a third of its eyes were vacant sockets tangled with a useless red and blue spaghetti of optic fibers), it helplessly scanned a casino crowding to the bursting point.

"The joint is really filling up, Tim," said Teddy, pleased with the idea.

"How long has this been going on?" asked Tim.

"Ever since we opened," said Jimmy.

"And they're still coming in," added Caro quickly.

The five of them watched silently as the casino got more and more crowded. They had heard how busy the other hotels were, especially Sinbad's, since it was supposed to be the home of the mob, but it was doubtful even Sinbad's was as crowded as the Ondine. Word of the Ondine's losing streak had turned it into a gigantic play pen.

"They look like maggots," said Caro.

The crowd had snapped the ropes and swarmed into the pits. They were teeming about the blackjack tables demanding the dealers deal nine and ten hands a table. It was illegal to deal more than seven hands a table, but the dealers were scared to death. The crowd wanted their money and they were going to have it.

The crap tables were worse. They were dense with howling white faces. The layout was so thick with chips, the dice careened wildly off the stacks without getting halfway down the layout. With each roll there was a surge of arms and shoulders pressing over the rim of the table to collect bets and put down new ones. The pit bosses were using four dealers per table instead of the usual two, with the boxman and stickman also handling chips, but it was impossible to keep pace. Half the bets weren't paid, and another half were paid to fictional claims. The crap table figures gyrated wildly, making them dominate the Admiral. It made the computer useless. Not that it mattered. No one could get out through that crowd to stop anything anyway. They were at the dealers' mercy.

"You'll be all right, Tim," said Teddy. "There are a lot of straight guys out there doing a straight job for you."

Teddy had been ecstatic from the moment he'd heard it was Haaf and not his men who had been running the *per* down. "We did it!" he'd marvelled. "We started out to prove something and we proved it. You're a hero, man. I mean it. You're a real hero. If we had closed this place today, they would have said the black squad stole themselves right out of their jobs, but they didn't, and you proved it. You're a hero, Tim."

Teddy kept on beaming at Tim, undaunted by the Ondine's declining bankroll. He did make Tim feel a little like a hero, except the dice and cards didn't know what Tim and Teddy had proven, and the Ondine's losing streak from the night before continued unabated.

Jimmy and Hector cursed their luck. Caro got more and more anxious and Tim felt more and more like confessing how stupid he'd been. It hadn't been business to him after all. It had been a gamble. Caro was right. Like a stupid loudmouth player on a losing jag, he'd pretended that bad luck was an inconvenient state of mind which could be brushed away with a show of mania. But it was too late for a *mea culpa*. There was only the waiting and watching while Hector ran back and forth between the video room and the cage posting them on the declining bankroll.

"Tim, please," said Caro. "You have to get Tommy back. You never should have let him leave."

"We have to wait for Oakes," insisted Tim.

"At least call him up and see if you can borrow some of his money," she said.

"I'm afraid we don't get Tommy's money without getting Tommy," said Tim.

"But they're going to come in here and kill us for what happened to Powell," she said. "Nobody will stop them. There's so much noise out there, nobody will even notice."

"We'll be all right," said Tim hopefully. "Here he is."

Up on monitor twenty-four, Alfred Oakes, with Tony Martirano behind him, was shouldering his way angrily through the punishing crowd.

·34·

"I DON'T know whether to believe you about Dean Haaf either," said Oakes, still irritated. "He's in the hospital deaf, where I can't talk to him, and you have all these safety deposit keys. What does it prove? After all, it was your assistant who ran away with over half a million dollars in the first place."

"Alfred, if I had been stealing all that money, would I have used Caro's and my savings to keep the casino open?" asked Tim.

"I don't know that you did," said Oakes. "As far as I can see, you and your friends saw a chance to make some money on your own, to have your own private casino—"

There was an urgent pounding on the door from Tim's office to the cage, and Tony went to answer it. Hector came in looking very anxious.

"I know you want to be alone with Tim," he said to Oakes, his mouth wiggling frantically. "But the money is all gone. As soon as they find out, this joint will go berserk. They'll tear the casino down, and they'll beat the hell out of all of us while they're at it."

"What the hell have I walked into?" asked Oakes. "Isn't there some way we can keep the crowd under control for awhile?"

"We could try getting some money from a couple of blackjack tables," suggested Hector. "Tim has Haaf's keys to the boxes. We could get some money from the boxes."

"Good," said Oakes. "Do that. And then don't reopen the table. We'll close this place down table by table."

"I don't think you'll be able to get away with that, sir," said Hector.

"Why not?" asked Tony.

"These people came to gamble," said Hector. "If they smell what's going on, they'll get mad."

"Then how do we get this place closed?" asked Oakes.

"I don't see any way of doing that until the crowd thins out," said Hector. "And that won't start to happen until four in the morning with a crowd like this."

"This is impossible," said Oakes. "You mean we have to keep it open all night?"

"I'd better go, sir," said Hector. "They're waiting in line to get their money, and I still have to get those boxes open."

"All right, go ahead," said Oakes. "Tony go with him."

"Tim, can I have the keys?" asked Hector.

Tim threw him Haaf's keys, and he hurried out with Tony right behind him.

This newest threat made Oakes mad again, and he went off on a long reprimand about how Tim had risked Colony's investment in the casino equipment. Tim explained the murders in the Inlet. Oakes was amazed to find out Tommy Van had been an employee of the Ondine until an hour ago. He began to understand that Tim was in genuine danger, but he didn't like the idea of paying loan-sharking interest to anyone.

Tim was insisting that paying the exorbitant interest was the only way he could leave town safely, when Tony came bursting back into the office from the cage.

"Come out here, Tim," Tony shouted to him excitedly "You've got to see this!"

Tim got up cautiously. He was in no hurry to see the crowd destroying the casino.

Hector had joined Tony at the doorway. "This is amazing," he shouted over the din coming into the office from behind him. "I saw it once in the Hilton in Havana and I thought I'd never get to see it again. Not like this, anyway."

"Like what?" asked Tim.

"You don't know what I'm talking about, do you?" Hector said, rushing to Tim's desk. "I was the credit manager at the Havana Hilton back in the fifties. This one night it was so crowded with Cubans you couldn't breathe. We were certain we were going to run out of money. Boy, if you've ever owed money to a Cuban on a gambling debt, you know what hot water can be; and there we were with a whole fucking casino of them, and at least half of them had guns because this was Havana. We thought we were all dead."

Hector took Tim by the arm and led him from his desk into the cage. The roar of human voices was deafening. Everyone was shouting into each other's ears to make themselves heard. Caro was leaping up and down like she was on a pogo stick. She was shrieking something, but Tim couldn't hear her.

"We didn't have keys to these boxes," Hector shouted in Tim's ear, "so we had to jump on them and hit them with hammers until they finally came open, but we found the same thing. Here, look at this!"

There was a box on the cage counting desk. It was *BJ 2* and Andy Map was opening its little door.

"It's just like *BJ 1*!" he shouted and showed it to Tim.

Tim was astonished at how much money was inside it. The whole box was full. Not only was it full, the bills looked like they had been packed in with a trash compacter.

"See!" shouted Hector, ecstatically. "It was the same thing in Cuba. We found enough money in the first box to pay off every Cuban in Havana. We thought we had been playing unlucky, just like you, because the bankroll was going down so fast. But it wasn't bad luck. We were having a fantastic volume of action. We were doing an enormous business, that's why we had to pay out so much money. That's what's happening now, Tim. Every box in the casino is like that one. They can't get the plungers down a quarter inch. We've got to start taking down all the boxes and count the money so they'll have room for more. Tim, you haven't been on a losing streak. This is going to be the biggest night any casino anywhere has ever had. It already is!"

"Lord, look at all that cash!" shouted a voice behind them. "How much is that?"

Tim turned around in surprise. It was Alfred Oakes. He was staring intensely at Andy digging the bills out of the box onto the cage's counting desk.

"They're mostly hundreds!" Oakes shouted into Tim's ear.

Tim watched as Oakes looked at the money. Oakes's big eyes were on fire. Tim was amazed that Oakes, with his background and his personal wealth, could get that look in his eyes. Oakes came from a family whose money went back as far as American history. His brother was the vice chairman of The Morgan Guaranty. But there it was: He was mesmerized by the cash. A dollar sign in a financial report next to the largest number in the world didn't have half the magic of real, live money jumping and twisting out of a metal box.

He began to feel a glow himself, but not over the money. What he felt was the warm aura of vindication. He had turned the Ondine into a cash factory after all. He began to wonder how much cash there was in Haaf's safety deposit boxes. He was very curious to know exactly how successful he had been.

Whatever it was, it would give the true drop and the true per. He wondered how high the per had actually gotten. Had he really revolutionized the casino business? Maybe he could figure it out by asking the computer to average the pers of all the tables according to the optical scanner totals, since the count results were obviously way wrong. Maybe he could extrapolate the drop from the scanning figures, because the computer had to use the drop to—

"*THAT'S IT!*" he shouted.

Everyone in the cage, as noisy as it was, jumped at the sound of his shout and turned to look at him. He ran by them, out of the cage, and through his office to the computer. He sat down and began working frantically at the keyboard.

"The real drop is in the computing packs," he told Caro and Oakes, who had followed him. "I can figure out how much Haaf stole."

"Seventy-four million," said Tim.

"Seventy-four million?" asked Oakes eagerly.

"That's a rough estimate of what he's taken in the four months I've been here," said Tim.

"Incredible," said Oakes, openly astonished. "You mean your net profit was actually seventy-four million higher."

"That's right," said Tim.

"And I wanted to sell this company," marvelled Oakes. "Tim, I have to congratulate you."

"Thank you, Alfred," beamed Tim.

"You stuck in and stayed," he said. "And now it's really paid."

Caro looked at Tim and they both laughed at Oakes' revision of his favorite little homily. "Now let's pay off this debt of yours. We have to make sure that you can stay in Atlantic City without any problems."

Tim swiveled around in his chair and looked at Oakes. The fire all that cash had lit in Oakes' eyes was burning very bright.

"I don't want to stay in Atlantic City, Alfred," said Tim.

"Really?" asked Oakes, thinking for a moment. "Then we'll have to make some sort of arrangement so that Colony can use this computer and your optical scanner idea."

"I'd be happy to sell the system and all rights to Colony," said Tim, his light eyes burning bright as Oakes'.

"This casino business is an amazing business," said Oakes, savoring the idea as he paced away from the computer. "It has no fluctuating raw material costs. Inflation helps it more than it hurts it. The labor costs are insignificant because its sales per square foot are staggering." He stopped and turned back towards Tim and Caro. "It draws buyers in as if everything were on sale for free; but, in fact, the exact reverse is the case. The customers pay all the money they have to purchase nothing. It's almost the ultimate pure business."

"At first glance, maybe." Tim grinned.

"The firm that can operate casinos successfully," said Oakes, not even hearing Tim, "can use that expertise all over the world. The way gambling has gotten so popular, that firm would be on to something that can be as big as automobiles or steel or even oil."

"It's never as much as it looks like, Alfred," said Tim.

"What are you talking about?" asked Oakes.

"The money."

"I'll tell you what, Tim," said Oakes. "Colony would like very much to buy this invention of yours."

The crux of Oakes's offer was that he would pay off the debts plus interest to Sinbad's and The Pier, and prevent Tim from being injured or killed if Tim would sign over all rights in the casino surveillance system to Colony.

Caro had heard Oakes was a miser, but this offer shocked her. Tim, however, almost seemed to expect it.

"You're not even going to give me a profit?" he asked Oakes. He wasn't upset. His tone suggested nothing more than curiosity about Oakes's incredible greed.

"Tim, I'd like to see you stay here in Atlantic City," said Oakes.

"That, of course, is what your offer is intended to accomplish," said Tim.

"Exactly," said Oakes, smiling. An affectionate manner had

crept into his voice. It was something he was famous for. Executives at Colony were known to work three years for a few drops of Alfred Oakes' affection.

"I can't stay here, Alfred," said Tim. "This business has already twisted me too far out of shape."

"Then you must seriously consider my offer," said Oakes. Now his voice had a familiar and much less affectionate ring to it. Tim recognized the new tone easily. It was the same voice he used on company presidents when he wanted to buy them out. It was his negotiating voice.

"I'd like more than enough to simply settle the debts, Alfred," said Tim. "Caro and I have seventy thousand in the bankroll which we are entitled to, and I'd like another hundred thousand so Caro and I can take a vacation out of the country for a few years. I've made some enemies here that I really have to avoid."

Caro was dumbstruck at how little Tim was asking for.

"You may have your own seventy thousand of course," said Oakes.

"What about the extra hundred thousand?" inquired Tim.

"My offer stands," said Oakes. "Will you sell?"

"Mr. Oakes," interrupted Caro, "you're going to make millions on Tim's invention. Tens of millions. Hundreds of millions."

Oakes looked at Caro curiously. He didn't like women interfering in their husband's business affairs.

"Caro, please don't interfere in this," said Tim impatiently.

She sighed and kept quiet. Tim's light eyes were still on fire. She was sure he had something waiting for Oakes.

"Alfred, on the point seven percent we agreed to in my contract," said Tim. "You owe me five hundred and eighteen thousand, assuming my estimate of what Haaf stole is right."

"Let me tell you something about that, Seagurt," said Oakes. Tim had touched him in a sore spot. "I still have a very bad taste in my mouth over that contract. You rushed me into something that afternoon. You knew something I didn't, and I don't like being taken advantage of that way."

Tim sighed. The light in his eyes seemed to go out. "So you're going to use the fact that my life is in danger to take this invention from me for nothing?"

"My offer stands," said Oakes. "You can still remain in Atlantic City."

"No, I can't."

"My offer stands," said Oakes.

When Oakes began to repeat himself, it was a dependable sign he had made his last offer.

"Who will you get to work it?" asked Tim, trying a new tack. "You have no one who understands it but me."

"You said Haaf had manipulated the figures so the results would come out the way he wanted them to," said Oakes. "He must understand the system very well."

"You'd ask Haaf?" asked Tim.

"Why not?" asked Oakes. "I have all the keys to his safety deposit boxes, and I'll certainly make sure he can't get into the casino vault again."

"But how can you hire a guy who is so obviously a thief?" asked Tim.

"It's a necessary evil," said Oakes. "Thieves seem to be as common in this business as men with two eyes. Will you sell?"

"Of course."

Oakes smiled. "I'll have them pay your debts and count out your seventy thousand."

Caro watched Oakes walk out victoriously. She couldn't believe it. She stood there stupidly, still waiting for Tim to snap his head off.

But Tim had absolutely no interest in Oakes anymore. He was busy with the keyboard of the computer again. He had deliberately surrendered to Oakes. She imagined she was supposed to feel grateful that it was all over. She felt something far removed from gratitude, however.

Tim watched patiently while the computer printed out the answer. The real per from the day the optical scanners had been installed was 18.03591%.

"Eighteen?" Tim asked it aloud. "What the fuck happened to forty?"

He asked the computer several more questions. Nothing changed. The final answer kept coming out the same no matter how many ways he made the computer compute it.

18.035981%.

The per had never dropped below fifteen nor had it gotten above twenty-two. There was seventy four million in extra profit, but it had not come from a higher per. It had come from a higher volume of business. The per, in fact, had declined. For some reason, quite beyond Tim, the increased efficiency of the casino against a higher volume of business led to a lower per.

That paradox, he noted happily to himself, laid to rest his fantasy of personal genius. To his amazement, he didn't feel the smallest urge to call himself dumb. He felt a tremendous weight lift off him. It made him giddy. There was no such thing as being right. What was right had a way of turning quickly wrong and leaving its supporters with the exhausting job of making it look right again. Perhaps it varied from business to business, but he nominated the casino business as the worst offender. For four months he had been Sisyphus rolling the stone up to the top of the hill. The night he'd hired the black dealers he had rolled it up all the way to the top. But once there, it had promptly flattened him on its way back down to the bottom. Now he had rolled it to the top again, but this time he wasn't going to be the idiot who tried to push it over and down the other side. He would leave that to Oakes. He got up from the keyboard.

"What are you looking so smug about?" Caro asked him.

"I've just found out I don't care that I'm no smarter than all the rest of them," he said.

"Congratulations," she said, irritated.

"What's wrong?" he asked.

"How could you let Oakes walk all over you like that?" she demanded.

Tim laughed.

"Why am I angry and you're not angry?" she asked. "Where's the big thunderstorm of righteous pride, goddammit. I don't believe that the guy who is better than Bernard Baruch, and Warren Buffet, and all the rest of those idiots can let Alfred Oakes outsmart him and grin like a guy who wants to be taken."

"That's me," laughed Tim. "I've found victory in defeat."

"Bullshit," said Caro. "What the hell is wrong with you?"

"Nothing is wrong with *me,*" he said, getting serious.

"I'm going to go in there and have it out with Oakes then," she said.

"No, you aren't," he snapped.

"I will if you don't," she said.

"Come on," he said. "Let's get the fuck out of this town."

She sighed and gave up. His voice had taken on a tone she wasn't about to argue with.

It was dusk when they started out across the causeway. Before the lights came on above the boardwalk, for that last instant before all the hotel electricians raced each other to their switch boxes, the glass towers of the playground of the world were transparent.

"Look!" said Caro.

She turned over the top of the seat, and Tim watched it in the rear view mirror. The boardwalk looked like a row of diphanite jewels.

"Look how blue it is," she marveled.

They could see the inside of the city. It was a rare and beautiful sight. The towers all seemed to be filled with vitreous blue liquid. She got an idea for the painting of the city showing this blue liquid. It filled the buildings like spent blood.

"It's all blue," she repeated.

"It amazes me that I didn't figure Haaf out sooner," said Tim. "It was relatively simple what he was doing. I think the problem was that I got so paranoid and upset and wired, the way this town makes everyone, I couldn't think. If you'd have come up to me and asked me how much one and one were, I probably would have said thirty-eight. It gets crippling. This town makes you stupid no matter how smart you think you are. It strips your intelligence from you, like an electric sander taking off varnish."

Slowly, reluctantly, Caro gave up looking back at the blue city, and turned to sit beside Tim again. They were almost to the toll booths before she spoke again.

"Why did Haaf keep on taking and taking?" she asked. "You'd think he would get enough after awhile and just leave town. Why would he risk getting caught?"

"He had a big empire to rebuild," said Tim. "And like everyone else in Atlantic City, he wanted more, no matter how much he got."

"There's something about gambling that brings that out in people," said Caro.

"The gambling business's problem is that it has no product," said Tim. "It's not really selling anything to its customers. It's just taking. So all the customers and employees get the idea they have as much right to take as you do, and I'm not sure they're wrong. At any rate, you need goons, spies, and bribes to stop them, and it gets to be a big fucking mess."

Tim thought about Oakes for a moment and laughed.

"Oakes thinks he's got my system now and that's going to stop them," he said. "But it doesn't work that way. They'll figure out ways to beat it. I know two guys already working on it. Soon that *per* will start going down, and Oakes will have to hire an army to take care of all the people who aren't playing fair."

"I guess we were lucky to get out," said Caro bitterly.

"All business is a contest between greed and self-respect," continued Tim philosophically. "The trouble with the gambling business is that it's more war than contest. The competition gets too bald and serious because there is money everywhere. As soon as Oakes saw all that cash, he went crazy with greed. Okay, so I'm leaving town, but it was really stupid of him to fuck with Teddy and Hector."

"Why didn't he give them their profits for keeping the casino open with their own money?" asked Caro, still outraged with Oakes's greed.

"He saw all that money coming out of the boxes and he couldn't bear to do it, Caro," said Tim. "Just like he couldn't give me my point seven percent."

"They don't have to leave town," said Caro. "They should sue him."

"They won't have to."

"Why not?"

"From the looks I saw on their faces," said Tim, "I'd say they were going to get their money out of that casino one way or another."

Caro laughed gleefully.

"And more, right?" she said.

"And more."

"It will serve the bastard right," said Caro. "Now I don't feel so bad."

"What's to feel bad about?" asked Tim.

"We got screwed," said Caro. "That's what to feel bad about."

"We didn't come out of it with nothing," said Tim.

"No?"

"We have our talents," he said.

"Yes, I guess we do," she said, getting a little less morose.

"And we are back together, so we can resume fucking each other's brains out," he said.

"There's always that to look forward to," she said, cheering up.

"See?" he said lightly. "We don't have to have it all. We don't have to be like Alfred Oakes and all the rest of them."

"I still wish we had a fair return for all we put into it," she said.

"You'll feel better about it when you get to Quito," he said.

"I doubt it."

"Of course, we have to take a little drive to Wilmington before we go to Quito," said Tim.

"What are you talking about?" asked Caro, annoyed again.

Tim reached into his coat pocket and produced a small red cardboard envelope. It had *Peter Gray* scrawled out in Haaf's handwriting.

"And we'll have to stop along the way to practice my penmanship—"

"Tim!" shrieked Caro with delight. "You didn't!"

"I did," said Tim.

"Holy shit!"

"And there's no trace that I did," he beamed proudly.

He had snapped his little trap after all. "But what about Haaf?" she asked anxiously.

"What about him?"

"Won't he come after us when he gets out of the hospital?" asked Caro.

"You think he's even going to know one key is missing?" asked Tim laughing. "The way he's organized? Besides, he'll be too busy robbing Oakes blind to worry about us."

"I wonder how much is in this one," she giggled happily as she studied the red envelope.

"We'll soon find out," said Tim.

She took the key out and turned it in an imaginary lock. She laughed a loud, happy laugh. "I can't believe it. I can't believe it."

"Why not?" asked Tim, laughing too. "It's a fair return for our labor, isn't it?"

"Yes, but you're just taking it," she said, nuzzling fondly up against his neck. "That makes you a little like Oakes, and McGray, and Laboy, and Henry and all the rest of them."

"Guilty," said Tim happily. He turned to give her a kiss on the top of her head. "But look, I said business was a *contest* between greed and self-respect. I never said we had to let self-respect turn it into a rout."

Tim pulled over after they drove through the causeway toll booth. They got out to give Atlantic City one last look. The electricians had reached their switches and the comet had exploded with light. But from so far across the wetlands, the wild nighttime neon was reduced to the brilliance of a few colored bulbs, the kind hung out by used car lots to burn some excitement into their tired old trade.